WINDY CITY SERIES
BOOK TWO

LIZ TOMFORDE

Scan QR code for Content Warnings

Visit my website at www.liztomforde.com

THE RIGHT MOVE

Editing: Erica Russikoff

Cover Design: Ever After Cover Design

*To Marc, Allyson, Paige, and Camille-*

*One of the themes in this book is finding friendships that fill your cup instead of draining it.*

*Thank you for being the people who fill mine.*

# Playlist

| | |
| --- | --- |
| **trust** - thuy feat. RINI | 3:17 |
| **Be Alone** - Blxst | 2:34 |
| **Every Good Girl** - Blxst | 2:56 |
| **First Time Thing** - Calabasas | 2:11 |
| **nirvana** - Dylan Reese feat. Phabo | 2:33 |
| **Concentrate** - Lucky Daye | 3:36 |
| **Morning** - Marc E. Bassy | 3:26 |
| **slower** - Tate McRae | 3:07 |
| **Let Me Love You** - Mario | 4:09 |
| **Overrated** - Blxst | 2:26 |
| **Naked** - Ella Mai | 3:17 |
| **Better** - Khalid | 3:49 |
| **Still** - Lecrae feat. DaniLeigh | 2:55 |
| **ALL MINE** - Brent Faiyaz | 3:36 |
| **Keep Comin' Back** - Blxst | 2:25 |
| **All Me** - Kehlani feat. Keyshia Cole | 2:58 |
| **Try Me** - Jason Derulo feat. Jennifer Lopez | 3:20 |
| **Easy** - Camila Cabello | 3:14 |
| **Change Your Life** - Kehlani feat. Jhené Aiko | 3:11 |
| **Butterflies** - ASTN | 2:55 |

I'm not a dreamer. Not in the traditional sense, at least. My dreams are within reach, attainable moments in time, not romanticized notions of the impossible.

Grown men fall to their knees and pray to their gods over these forty-eight minutes of basketball. Me? I don't glamorize fate or leave things to chance. I believe in hard work and dedication. My life has a plan. Opportunities are in my path because I've willed myself in their direction.

The rest of my teammates, however, have certainly romanticized the idea of a championship if they think they can walk into the first week of practice as out of shape as they are.

"Dom, you need to roll off that screen twice as fast. You're slow as fuck right now. What the hell were you doing all summer?"

"Living my life, Shay. You should try it sometime."

Dom Jackson, our big man, slumps over, his palms on his knees, trying to catch his breath along with every other guy I call my teammate.

I use my practice jersey to swipe sweat from my brow as one of the rookies passes me the ball at the top of the key.

"Let's run it again."

"Ryan, practice was over an hour ago. Some of us have wives and kids we need to go see." Ethan Jeong, our veteran shooting guard, stands with his hands on his hips in the corner of the court.

"Yeah, and some of us have dates with…" Dom looks over to one of the young guys on the sideline. *"What was her name?"* he silently mouths. "Raquel! Some of us have dates with beautiful women named Raquel."

My eyes wander around my teammates, everyone exhausted but me. "Fine," I resign. "We'll call it."

"Thank God!" Dom turns around, throwing his hands up and slipping his sweat-soaked jersey over his head. The rest of the team quickly follows to the locker room.

"It's still pre-season, Ryan." Ethan puts a comforting hand on my shoulder. "They'll get it together."

"I'm tired of losing. We can't even win a wildcard game to make the playoffs. I spent my entire summer running two-a-days to get in shape for this season. Everyone else needs to get on my level."

"They'll never be on your level. That's why you'll be one of the greats, but as a new captain, you need them to respect you, and I'm not referring to the way you play." He backs away, following the rest of the team. "Besides, I don't want you tiring yourself out too much. I need you to carry me on your back and get me a ring so I can retire."

Ethan's lips slide up in a smile before he ducks into the locker room.

He's a good guy. Family man. Father of three children and long-time NBA vet. He was the team captain for the last seven years until he asked to step down this season, wanting to have a better work-life balance.

And as of last week, I earned the title and am now the newest captain of the Devils, Chicago's NBA team.

I knew it'd happen one day. I just didn't know it'd be when I was twenty-seven and before my fifth season in the league. I still have a lot to learn at this level, and now I have the weight of being the team leader, on and off the court.

The General Manager of the Devils was against the promotion, but that's not how it works around here. Our captain is determined by a team vote, and after unanimous support by my teammates, I was given the title.

I want to be good for my guys, but I want respect for more than the way I play. I get plenty of it for my talent throughout the league. I've dedicated my life to my craft, sacrificed relationships and most of my twenties for this game and it shows.

Year after year, I've beat my own records on my path to greatness, not letting distractions get in the way of what I want—to be one of the best to ever play the game.

Though, I have quite the shoes to fill, seeing as my home court is the same as the GOAT himself. The championship banners that hang from the United Center remind me of the greatness that came before me and the gaps in years since we've had one, taunt me to earn my own.

I need my guys to take this game as seriously as I do. I need them to live, eat, and breathe it the way I do if we're going to have a shot this season, but how do I voice that without sounding like the controlling point guard they've come to know me as? Now, as the team leader, I need to figure out how to communicate with them in a way I haven't been able to before because *"listen to me, I'm the best player you've ever shared a court with,"* doesn't exactly work when you're the team captain.

I'm not particularly close with any of my teammates besides Ethan, so the vote was a bit surprising. My game has always spoken for me, and I got away with being domineering on the court, but now I have another title to wear and I'm not sure how to adjust.

"Casey!" I call out to one of the interns as he quickly scurries my way. "That's your name, right? Casey?"

"Yes, Mr. Shay."

I roll my eyes. "Call me Ryan or Shay or literally anything other than Mr. Shay. You got plans? I need someone to rebound for me."

"I uh…I…well, my mom…"

"You got plans or what?"

"Nope." He quickly shakes his head. "I can rebound for you, Mr. Shay." His eyes go wide. "Ryan! I can rebound for you, Ryan."

His nervous strides take him to the net where he stands underneath it, wearing a pair of khaki cargo shorts and a polo shirt with our team logo. He can't be older than eighteen or nineteen, but the staff has him dressing like he's in his mid-forties.

I take my spot at the free-throw line where I plan to stay until I get at least a hundred shots up, but by shot number seventy-six, the doors to our private practice get thrown open.

"Ry!" my sister calls out. "Practice was over two hours ago. I went by the apartment looking for you."

"Hey, Vee!"

Shot number seventy-seven barely touches the net as it floats through the hoop. Casey cleans up the rebound and passes it back.

"You already worked out this morning. What are you doing?"

"Getting my free throws in."

My twin sister stands a few feet away from me with a hand on her hip. I don't look her way, but in my periphery, I can see her shaking her head at me, her curly hair bouncing with the movement.

"What's your name?" She directs her attention to the intern.

"I'm Casey."

"I'll take over for you, Casey." Stevie intercepts his pass to me and steals his spot under the net.

The intern's nervous gaze bounces between my sister and me.

"Do you have a ride home? It's late." My twin is as sweet as can be, and unlike me, I didn't even realize the kid might not have a ride home.

"Yeah. My mom is parked out back waiting for me."

"Ryan!" Stevie scolds. "His mom has been waiting for him."

"I didn't know!" I throw my hands up. "Sorry, man."

Casey quickly shakes his head. "It was an honor, Mr. Shay."

My eyes narrow at him.

"Ryan, I mean. It was an honor, Ryan Shay. Anytime." Casey awkwardly waves before scurrying out the main doors.

Stevie turns back to me, standing under the net. "His mother was waiting for him," she laughs. "How fucking adorable is that?"

"Adorable," I deadpan, clapping my hands together and asking for the basketball that's resting on her hip.

"How many do you have left?" She passes the ball, perfectly nailing it in my shooter's pocket.

After twenty-seven years together and her rebounding for me more times than I could count, my twin sister has it down.

Sinking another shot, I tell her, "Twenty-two."

She passes it back.

"What's up? Tired of Zanders already? You ready to move back in?"

"Ha-ha," my sister says dryly. "Not a chance. I'm obsessed with that guy."

My lips quirk in a proud smile. Evan Zanders, who I thought was going to be an absolute piece of shit, has turned out to be anything but. He plays professional hockey for Chicago, and my sister met him last year when she was a flight attendant on their team's plane. Their relationship was under wraps until early this summer, and the past four months have been a nonstop public love fest between the two of them.

Stevie moved in with him, which is thankfully just across the street from my place, and as much as I like to be right, when it comes to Zanders, I'm happy I was completely wrong about the guy. He lights my sister up like I've never seen before, allowing her to own who she is with confidence. Hard to hate the guy when he's the best thing to happen to your favorite person.

And I'm not going to lie, he's become a good friend of mine as well.

"Well, I'd say he's equally obsessed with you, if not more so."

My sister rests the ball on her hip. "I know. Isn't it great?"

Lightly laughing, I shake my head and clap my hands together, needing the ball back.

There's no denying I'm a different guy around my sister. I'm the man I was before the fame and fortune. Money has never gone to my head in the way you'd expect it to for a young first-round draft pick, but it has made me more wary and paranoid than most people realize. Stevie is the only person I unequivocally trust with my life and having that freedom, not watching my every turn, allows me a moment to relax. To be myself.

"So, what's up?" The ball slips through the net with another made shot. "What's so urgent you had to come down here and rebound for me?"

Stevie doesn't pass the ball back. Instead, she holds it in front of her with her arms across her chest. "I have a favor to ask."

I hold my hands out for her pass, but she refuses.

"What is it?"

"Well, you remember how I moved out?"

"Yes, Vee. I'm pretty sure I remember I live alone now."

"In your huge, beautiful, empty-when-you're-on-the-road apartment." Her eyes sparkle.

"And?"

"You know my friend, Indy, right? My old coworker."

"The chick who showed up at our apartment and sobbed all night, then puked on my shoes in a bar the only other time I met her? Hard to forget."

"Because she caught her long-term boyfriend with someone else," she reminds me. "You see, her parents moved to Florida—"

"No."

"Ryan," Stevie protests. "I haven't asked anything yet."

"I know. And I'm stopping you before you do. You know I'm terrible at saying no to you, so I'm not going to let you even ask the question. She's not moving in with me."

"Ry, she has nowhere to go. She got promoted at work, and she's going to have to give it up if she can't find a place to live in the city. You know how little we make."

"You make enough to pay for a place to live."

"She's…" My sister hesitates. "She's going through some financial stuff and can't afford to live alone here. Chicago is expensive."

"Then she can find a friend to mooch off. I don't even know her other than she got cheated on and can't hold her liquor."

"Ryan, don't be like that. You have a huge apartment and you're on the road for work half the time. Indy travels for work as much as you do. Hockey is the same season as basketball. You'll barely see each other."

"No."

"Why not?"

"Because it was one thing when you lived with me. You're my sister and my best friend, but I don't want a roommate. You know how sacred my time at home is. End of discussion." I clap my hands together, needing to get the ball back from my twin so I can finish my daily shots.

Instead, Stevie's shoulders drop in disappointment before she turns on her heel and heads to the exit, taking my basketball with her.

"Vee, what the hell? I need to finish shooting."

"You can rebound for yourself then." She continues towards the exit, not bothering to turn around.

"You can't be mad at me for saying no."

"Not mad. Just disappointed. Would it kill you to care about someone or something other than this orange ball?"

"I care about *you*," I remind her, but she charges through the double doors leading towards the hallway, dropping the basketball in the corner before she goes.

Fuck.

I try not to give a shit if I disappoint people. Their standards are never as high as the ones I hold for myself. However, my twin sister? Her opinion is the only one I care about besides my own.

I jog after her.

"Vee," I call out as I open the doors to the hallway. She's almost to the exit but turns on her heel to face me. "Tell me why I have to do this. Are you really that upset? Why does this matter so much to you?"

"You don't have to do anything, but she's my friend. She was my *first* friend in this city. You know how hard it's been for me to make friends that weren't just looking for a way to get closer to you. Well, Indy has been that friend, and if she can't find a place she can afford, then she's going to move to Florida so she can stay with her parents. I don't want her to leave Chicago, and I don't know how else to help her. The guy she was planning to marry cheated on her and she was the one who had to move out. She needs a win."

Why does my sister have to pull at my goddamn heartstrings all the time? Someone else could give me this same exact speech and I wouldn't blink an eye, but with Stevie saying it, my resolve is crumbling, wanting to give her anything she asks for. I'm the reason my sister has had a hard time making real friends, and now she's giving me an opportunity to make it up to her, even just a little bit.

"I trust her," she continues. "You can too."

I care about Stevie's happiness far more than my own. In fact, I've given up on that idea for myself, which causes the next thing to slip out of my mouth.

"To make it clear, I don't want to do this."

"I know."

"There needs to be a move-out date."

Stevie's lip twitches as her eyes begin to sparkle.

"I want some sort of makeshift leasing agreement, and she's paying rent. This is not a free ride."

"Of course, she will. But could you make it affordable? It's not like you need the money."

Here I am doing her a favor and she's making special requests. "This is temporary. She's not staying with me forever."

"Got it." Stevie's smile is unable to hide. "Have I told you that you're my favorite person in the entire world?"

"Yeah, yeah." I turn back to the gym. "Come rebound for me. I have fifty free throws left."

"You said you had twenty-something."

I continue to the free-throw line, not bothering to turn around. "Looks like I lost count while I was letting my sister talk me into having a random chick move into my apartment."

Stevie's beaming smile radiates in her tone. "Fifty it is."

# 2

# Indy

"No."

"What do you mean 'no.'"

"I mean no. I'm not moving in with your brother."

Stevie's eyes narrow in confusion. "Why not?"

"Hmm, let me think. Because it's a terrible idea." Yes, moving in with my best friend's brother sounds like a plot pulled straight from one of my favorite romance novels. Not to mention, said brother is Ryan Shay —basketball superstar who looks like he just walked out of one of my wet dreams. But more important than all that is… "Because he hates me."

"He hates most people." She pops her shoulders, and the casual-ness of her tone is a bit alarming.

"Really selling him, babe."

Stevie takes a seat on the hotel room's couch as I finish cooking my breakfast on the single burner stove. My vegetarian sausage looks like dog shit thanks to this god-awful cooking pan the hotel provided.

*Extra-flavor*, I tell myself, hoping I can put up with living in this hotel for a bit longer.

"I know Ryan is my brother, so I'm probably biased here, but he's great. Sure, he may come off cold because he doesn't exactly wear his emotions on his sleeve, but he's a good guy. I love you and you're my best friend. Ryan and I share the same DNA which means he's going to love you too. Eventually."

"Nice logic, Vee."

"It's science."

I don't honor that with a response, so she continues. "You both travel for work so much that you'll barely cross paths. Plus, he doesn't date, so you don't have to worry about random girls coming in and out of the apartment."

A single brow raises. "Just because he doesn't date doesn't mean he doesn't sleep around. Have you seen the man?"

"I don't want to think about that, thank you." Her face scowls with a bit of disgust. "All I'm saying is he never had anyone over, and I lived there for almost a year."

Probably saves his hookups for the road. Smart. And it would be nice not to worry about finding random girls in my home for once.

"I've offered our place, but you don't want to move in there either. Zee has two extra bedrooms," she continues.

"Vee," I sigh. "The last thing I want to do is play third wheel and I sure as shit don't want to hear the two of you going at it like a couple of rabbits every time we come home from a road trip. Really, I'm fine." I take a seat on the ottoman next to the coffee table with my breakfast in hand. "Look at these places." I toss the stack of printouts across the table, hoping my future home is in that mix, seeing as they're the only places I can afford in this city.

The more papers Stevie flips through, the harder it is for her to hide her disbelief. "Indy, no. You can't live in any of these places. Some of these are sketchy as hell and look at this." She begins reading one of the descriptions. "Fifty-something-year-old male looking for a twenty-something year old female roommate."

"I'm a twenty-something year old female and that place is only five-hundred bucks a month!" I take a bite of my veggie sausage, but it's burnt to shit so I spit it back on my plate.

"Yeah, probably because you'd have to pay the remainder of rent in a different way."

"Okay, gross." Pulling that page from the stack, I crinkle it up, adding it to my plate of inedible garbage.

"Indy," Stevie sighs, dropping the papers on her lap. "Please move in with Ryan. If not for you then for me. I wouldn't be able to sleep at night knowing you're staying in one of these places. You can text me daily updates of how it's going, and I can keep Ryan in check if I need to."

Pulling out my phone, I decide to send her one now.

**Me:** *Daily update—if you make me move in with your brother, I will sexualize him every chance I get. I will text you every single day and remind you that he is the hottest man I've ever laid eyes on. Daily, you will hear just how badly I want him to do dirty, dirty things to me.*

She pulls her phone out, a grimace forming on her lips.

Stevie blinks rapidly as if she were clearing the image from her mind. "I'm going to gamble here and hope you're bluffing."

"Well, this is going to be fun."

"If you move in with Ryan, we'd be neighbors!"

I can't help but allow the smile to pull at my lips, thinking of living across the street from my old coworker and her boyfriend. I love them together, and I got a front-row seat to watch their relationship unfold last hockey season. As much as I'm going to miss having her on the road this year, I'm glad she and Zanders don't have to hide their relationship any longer. Love like that shouldn't be hidden away.

"That would be fun," I agree.

"See! Plus, your favorite coffee shop is two blocks away and Ryan's doorman is an absolute gem. You're going to love him."

While the idea of living in a luxury apartment in downtown Chicago stacked with every imaginable amenity sounds like a dream come true, I can't help but hold back from saying yes.

I guess in part, I'm still convincing myself that being back in Chicago is a good idea. Every corner, every building, every street reminds me of him. That's what happens when you spend your entire life loving one person. Every memory includes them.

And now I'm left grieving a version of my life that no longer exists.

It took everything in me to finish out the hockey season last year after I walked into our apartment and found Alex with someone else, but as soon as the Raptors won the Stanley Cup, I threw my shit in storage, packed a bag, and followed my parents to their new beach-front retirement home in Florida. Spending my summer there was a nice reprieve from the heartbreak, but being back in this city, where my entire life fell apart, it's like I'm starting the healing process all over again, regardless that the initial shock occurred six months ago.

And after living in this hotel for a few weeks and training two new flight attendants to work under me, I can't say for sure that I made the right choice by coming back here.

As if she could read my mind, Stevie shifts the subject. "First road trip of the season starts in a few days. Are you ready?"

"Ready as I'll ever be with a completely green crew. Watching hockey boys strip down every flight won't be the same without you."

She tilts her head, shooting me that sweet Stevie smile. "Part of me will miss flying, but mostly I'll just be missing you and Zee while you're on the road. Though, I am excited to catch all of Ryan's home games this year. How does it feel to be the new lead flight attendant and boss everyone around?"

"Weird. I never thought I'd be in charge of the Raptors' plane in my second year, but I'm excited. And unquestionably stoked that Tara is gone for good."

"Fired for fraternization," Stevie laughs. "The irony."

There's a strict no fraternization rule as far as flight attendants spending time with our passengers—the Raptors, Chicago's NHL team. And last year, Tara, the previous lead flight attendant, made sure to rub that in Stevie's face as much as possible, but part of accepting my promotion was getting those rules to bend a bit. There's still a strict no dating, no sleeping, no fucking around with the team, but we are allowed to be friends now. Kind of had to change the rules when my best friend's boyfriend is the alternate captain, and we see each other around too much to pretend as if we're not friends.

"It'll be good to get away from Chicago for a few days too," I add.

"What are you talking about? You were in Florida all summer. You've only been back here for a couple of weeks."

A long stretch of silence lingers between us as I keep my eyes down on my lap.

"Oh, Ind. I'm an idiot. This has nothing to do with living with Ryan, does it? If you don't want to be in Chicago, I get it. Trust me, I get it. I was trying to help you stay in town by finding you a place to live, but I didn't even think about the fact you might not want to be here."

"You're not an idiot. You're a good friend. It's just kind of hitting me, you know? Being back here, knowing I could run into Alex at any moment has me sick to my stomach, but at the same time I'm tired of his decision ruling my life."

I was days away from taking a job in Florida and making the move a permanent one before I got the call about the promotion. Alex took everything from me that night—my future, my apartment, my friend group. I wasn't going to let him take this too.

"Indy, I get it," she says gently. "Sometimes leaving is easier. Are you sure you want to be here? In Chicago."

"I want to feel better." I hold my head up high. "Maybe being back in Chicago, where everything went down, will force me to face the situation and heal quicker."

"Well, if you change your mind and decide Florida is a better fit for you right now, I'll help you pack your bags, but I hope you take Ryan's offer. He won't charge you more rent than you can afford. You can save this way. Things will be different for you, but I think they can be better."

"You didn't tell him anything—"

"Of course not," Stevie interjects.

Looking around, I take a quick inventory of my hotel room. A mini-fridge so mini that I have to go grocery shopping every three days because full-sized items won't fit inside. The suitcase I'm living out of because there aren't enough hangers in the closet for my exorbitant wardrobe. Towels so tiny they barely wrap around my hair.

I miss having a home base, even if said home base is shared with one of the most attractive men I've ever laid eyes on. I've only met Ryan Shay twice in all these months, but you don't forget a face or body like that. However, if I could have one wish right now, it'd be that we could both forget our previous encounters.

"If I knew I was going to live with the guy one day, I would've made a better first and second impression."

Stevie's blue-green eyes shine as she mashes her lips together, holding in her laugh. I was waiting for her to ease those worries and tell me her smoking hot brother doesn't remember me at all.

"He hasn't forgotten, has he?"

"Not even close."

It took all but ten minutes to move out of my hotel room and another twenty to empty my storage unit. The U-Haul was embarrassingly bare. It's sad, that twenty-seven years of life can't even fill half a U-Haul.

Every piece of furniture or kitchen appliance that was bought during our six years together is still at our apartment. *His* apartment, and I've succumbed to starting over and trying to be okay with that. I didn't notice the absence of my things when I moved in with my parents for the summer but having next to nothing is becoming blatantly obvious as I sit in Ryan's apartment.

*My* apartment.

Though, this apartment is so bare it feels like I'm sitting in the middle of a museum more than anything and maybe that's why my lack of things is evident. He doesn't have much either.

His place is spotless and minimalistic. Black and white with no pops of color in sight—besides my wardrobe currently skewed across his living room as I attempt to organize. *Attempt* being the key word here.

I've been to this apartment a handful of times since I met Stevie, but it never looked this empty and…lonely. Stevie is as bright as I am. I guess all the color left when she did.

However, the view is breathtaking, the city skylights and the sunset over the Navy Pier distracted me for the first hour I was here.

My self-guided tour takes me to the kitchen. A single-cup coffee maker with one mug nestled underneath, ready for tomorrow morning, I guess. Dishes—four big plates, four small plates, and four bowls—all in black, like they came in a set, as if he'll never have more people in his home. Not so surprising, when I open the first drawer—four spoons, four knives, four forks, most likely purchased in a small set.

I get that he travels for work as much as I do, but what if he wants to have friends over? Or what if he brings a woman home one night and she's hungry, but he hasn't done his dishes from the previous day yet?

Seems impractical to me, but something tells me that Ryan Shay thinks having just enough to get by is completely practical.

Back in the living room, my finger trails over his bookshelf, praying, hoping it picks up a layer of dirt or dust. Something to tell me this guy is human and not a robot as the rest of his apartment suggests.

There's not a single photo in his home, but countless books. Every kind of motivational or self-help book you could imagine lines the shelves and they're organized by…Are you kidding me? Alphabetical order of the author's last name. This guy is a monster who probably runs marathons for fun and passes out nutrition bars on Halloween.

Lifting my finger from the shelf, it comes up clean. Not one speck of dust.

I hate it here already.

The click of the front door halts my movements.

He was supposed to be gone all night at some fancy event for the city. I was supposed to have time to clean my mess, get my clothes hung in the closet and my books picked up and piled neatly before he came home. This place is a disaster, and I was hoping to make a better third impression on Ryan Shay.

Kicking my piles of clothes into one, I try to take up as little space as possible, hoping he might not notice the bomb that went off in his home since I moved in two hours ago.

"What. The. Fuck?" His tone is dry and even.

Attempting to get myself together, I brush the stray, wispy hairs away from my face and plaster on my most charming smile. It works every time.

"Hi—" I turn around with a wave, but it dies in the air when I see the owner of this apartment standing inside the doorway.

I've met Ryan twice. Once he was shirtless and the other time, he was in casual clothes at a bar. But right now? In a fitted suit? Jesus Christ, I can't live here.

It's black with a subtle pinstripe throughout, and the dark color somehow makes his blue-green eyes that much more vibrant. His light brown skin and freckles match his twin sister, but I can guarantee I've never looked at Stevie the way I'm staring at her brother right now. Licking my lips, my eyes wander over his hair—chestnut and freshly faded on the sides with a bit of the Shay signature curls on top.

Ryan and Stevie's mom is a white woman with freckled skin, blue eyes, and copper hair. Their dad is a black man, tall with a head of dark curls. The Shay twins are a combination of both their parents, but Ryan and Stevie seem to have inherited all the same attributes.

I've blurted it out both times we've met, but Ryan Shay is hot. He might be a robot, but he's the sexiest robot I've ever seen.

"Indy." He snaps me out of my trance.

Closing my mouth and crossing one leg over the other, I meet his eye. "Hmm?"

"I asked what the hell happened to my apartment?"

"Oh." I awkwardly laugh. "You see, I'm organizing."

"Organizing?"

"Yep." Motioning to the chaotic mess I made on his living room floor. "My clothes."

"If that's your version of organizing, I don't know if this arrangement is going to work out."

I laugh at his joke before realizing, unfortunately, there's no teasing in Ryan's tone. He's serious.

He hangs his keys on the small rack by the front door like the organized monster he is before quickly taking off to his bedroom without giving me a second glance.

This third impression is going to shit just like the last two.

"I was thinking maybe we could have breakfast tomorrow," I quickly interject before he hides himself in his room for the night.

He doesn't spare me a look as he reaches his door. "No."

"It'd be nice to get to know each other, you know, since we're living together now."

"No."

"Okay, no breakfast. You're a busy man. Maybe lunch? Or maybe you don't eat. Robots don't eat."

"What?"

That finally earns his attention as his head snaps in my direction, his aggressively ocean eyes locked on mine.

I swallow. "Kidding. It was a joke." Another awkward laugh. "Coffee? It'd be nice to get to know the person I'm living with. Who knows, maybe we'll even be friends?"

His eyes narrow.

"Okay, no friends." I hold my hands out in defense. "No friends. No food. No fun. Got it."

A soft chuckle vibrates in his chest and at first, I enjoy the sound, thinking he might find me funny, but then I realize the laugh is condescending.

"Let's get one thing straight. I don't want you here. I didn't ask for you to move in, and the only reason you're here is because you're my sister's friend and I'm the reason she doesn't have very many. I like my space, and if it were my choice, I'd be living alone. So, no, Indiana, we're not going to be friends. We're going to coexist in the same apartment until you can find yourself a different situation while I fulfill my brotherly duty."

He closes the door behind him a little harder than necessary.

Fucking *ouch*.

The third impression was worse than the first two.

Fuck.

Sinking my forehead to the back of my door, I close my eyes with regret.

That was mean and I didn't intend to be. In fact, the entire walk up here I kept reminding myself to be nice, trying to come up with some stupid greeting to say to her for the first time.

*Welcome home*. No, that makes it sound like *our* home.

*Happy you're here*. That's a lie. I'm not.

*Anything you need, let me know*. Don't let me know. Get it yourself.

Every phrase I rehearsed sounded exactly like that…rehearsed.

The plan I came up with was a simple, "I'll get a spare key made for you," before walking to my room where I could have a moment alone.

But then I saw her standing there barefoot in the middle of my living room, wearing a sweatshirt so oversized I'm still not convinced she's got anything on underneath. Her blonde hair was in a braid flowing over her shoulder, but most of the pieces were pulled out in a frazzled mess. Her brown eyes were softer than I remember and that just pissed me off.

All night long, my teammates gave me shit about her moving in. They've met her once, about five months ago and I thought the lasting impression she left on them was because she threw up all over my shoes that night. But unfortunately, the only memory they have of her is that she was an absolute smoke show.

I knew she was pretty. I'm not blind, but there's no way she was as beautiful as they recalled. I was certain they played it up in their minds.

They didn't.

I walked into my apartment and realized my mistake. They were right—she's stunning, and I hate it.

I'm not easily distracted, but if I could manifest my perfect distraction, it'd look a lot like her.

I can't have someone like that living here. I don't want *anyone* living here. I need my space. This apartment is my one reprieve from the outside pressures. I need to concentrate on my first season as Captain, and I don't know how I'm going to be able to do that when my roommate looks like she just stepped off the beach with her sunkissed legs, golden hair, and her colorful clothes strewn around my apartment floor.

Fuck this. I need to go to the gym.

Maybe I'd be a little calmer if I had a moment to relax and prepare to come home to a new roommate, but I didn't have a single calm minute tonight. I was being watched and therefore on edge every moment of the evening.

Typically, the stares are from fans and reporters, observing my every move, but ever since my promotion, Ron Morgan, the team's General Manager has been watching me with more disdain than normal.

Ron liked me for the first three years I played for him, or at least he liked me as much as an employer can like an employee whose salary takes a large chunk of their yearly budget and has yet to lead the team to a championship, let alone the playoffs.

But Ron's evident distaste for me really began last winter after I escorted his niece to a movie premiere as a favor to him. His niece, who is practically his daughter, had gotten in some trouble with the law and what better way to clean up someone's image than to call in good guy Ryan Shay?

It was one night, one event, but the real problem began when more than one night was asked of me. It's been constant, and I've turned down his request to take his niece out every time since, using my sister as some kind of Morgan family shield.

*"You should take Lesley to that charity gala."* Can't. I already invited my sister.

*"End of the year weekend on the lake. Everyone is bringing someone. You'll bring my niece."* Can't. Stevie already snagged my plus-one.

*"Lesley is really smitten with you. You should invite her to team dinner on Friday as your plus-one."* Ah. Damn. Wish I could, but my sister is really excited to go, and I can't bail on her.

It's worked well all year, using Stevie as my pseudo-date, but then she had to go ahead and fall in love. And with not just anyone, but someone who is at ninety percent of the same functions as me because he's an equally big name in Chicago sports. Without her help, my motive became clear that the real reason I couldn't continue seeing Ron's family member was simply because I didn't want to, and that's when his indifference turned to blatant dislike.

That aversion was aggravated at the end of the season when Ethan stepped down and the team named me Captain despite Ron's vocal disagreement. But I don't date, haven't done it since college, and I'm not going to change simply to appease the man who signs my paychecks, especially when it's regarding a woman who I'm genuinely not interested in.

You'd think Ron would appreciate my ambition. My mind is on a single track and that's winning Chicago their first championship in decades and topping it off with an MVP trophy for myself. That means no women, barely any friends, and keeping my eyes on the prize. Not letting anyone take advantage of my name or who I'm going to become in the sport of basketball.

It's happened before and I'll never make that mistake again.

I need a fucking workout. Clear my mind from the mess my night was and the disaster my apartment turned into while I was gone.

Slipping off my suit jacket, I hang it in the closet where it belongs—between my black jacket and the dark gray one. Unclasping my watch, I carefully lay it in my nightstand drawer, back in its velvet box, exactly where it goes every time I remove it.

Getting some shots in will calm me down now that my apartment seems to have the opposite effect on me. But before I can slip out of my suit and into gym shorts, a soft whimper from the living room stops me.

This must be a joke.

Why the hell did I agree to let this girl live here? Oh, that's right—Stevie. I need to learn to start saying no to my sister, because not being able to just earned me a crying blonde in my living room.

I'll ignore it. It'd be more embarrassing for her than anything if I went to check on her. Was what I said really all that mean that she's *crying* over it? I've only seen this girl cry or drink herself into oblivion, so I guess it's not so surprising she's emotional once again.

Another whimper and another muffled weep punch through my closed door and invade my chest.

*You don't owe her anything.*

Ignore. Ignore. Ignore.

I can't. As much as I'd love to be that guy, I'm not.

Taking a deep breath, I open my bedroom door to check on my new roommate.

Little miss blondie has her knees tucked into her chest as she sits on my couch, hiding her face in her crossed arms, and I don't know what the fuck to say to get her to chill out. How am I supposed to get her to stop? I don't even know the girl.

*Say something nice, something comforting.*

"You're emotional."

Her head snaps up from her arms, brown eyes bloodshot and swollen. "Thanks for the observation, Ryan. You're real perceptive."

Okay, clearly that was the wrong thing to say.

"Why?"

Her brows furrow. "Why what?"

"Why are you so emotional?"

"Why are you so cold?"

I switch gears because she's not getting that answer so easily. "What's wrong?"

"What's wrong?" She laughs condescendingly. "What's wrong?!" Her voice rises with her as she stands from the couch. I let my wandering eye trail down those mile-long legs, and I can't help but wonder how they might feel wrapped around my waist.

*Not the fucking time, Ryan.*

She's tall for a girl. And at this moment, she's a little scary too.

"What's wrong is my life has gone to absolute shit, okay? Sorry, I can't control my emotions because my shitty boyfriend of six years cheated on me with some chick from his office! And I was the one to lose my apartment because of it. I can't afford to live on my own in this city, and now I'm sitting in my best friend's brother's apartment who doesn't want me here either! Do you think I want this? I don't! I want my old life back."

I stay casually leaning on my bedroom doorframe, watching her mini meltdown.

*Mini* might not be the right word.

"What the hell am I doing here?" she quietly asks herself.

She stares at me, expecting me to respond, but I have no clue how to act around someone so sensitive. She's quite frightening.

"You're right," she says. "I am emotional. But at least I'm not a fucking robot!" She motions towards me. "At least I feel things. When's the last time you felt something?"

"Well, currently I'm feeling amused."

"What the hell is wrong with you?" she spits. "You're a monster. And reorganize your goddamn bookshelf. Author's last name? You're sick."

I try to bite back my smile, I really do, but it lifts on one side of my lip.

"Do not laugh at me!"

I shake my head. "Not laughing."

She inhales a deep, centering breath as she runs her hands down her sweatshirt that looks about five sizes too big on her. "I'm going to move out. We don't know each other, and you're right. You didn't ask for me to be here and that's not fair to you. I leave on a work trip tomorrow night, but I'll be back in a few days, and I'll get my stuff out. I'm leaving Chicago."

"No, you're not."

"Excuse me?"

"You're not moving out. I'll have a spare key made for you, Indiana."

I close my bedroom door behind me, finally saying the line I rehearsed all night.

She's right, I don't really want her here. But she is wrong about one thing—I'm not a monster. She's clearly going through shit—shit I find myself having a weak spot for and I can't toss her out on the street. I'm not that kind of guy as much as I'd love to be at this moment.

A loud thud hits the back of my door. A shoe perhaps. "My name is *not* Indiana!"

Yeah, I'd *really* love to be that guy right about now.

I wake before my alarm, and as I reach my doorway wearing only my boxers, it dawns on me that I can't exactly walk around my place naked anymore.

After slipping on a pair of basketball shorts and an old tee, I step into the living room. Indy's mess is cleared out, but the apartment feels different than it did a couple of days ago.

I've been alone for a long time. Having Stevie live here for the nine months she did was a nice reprieve from the quiet, but the silence returned when she moved out. I like my alone time, thrive on it really. But the difference in the air this morning, having someone else here, doesn't feel like the worst thing to happen to me. It's not as alarming as I assumed it would be.

The door on the opposite side of the living room is cracked slightly. The sliver of pale-yellow paint burns my eyes as the morning Chicago sun bounces off the walls. There are no drapes or blinds in there anymore. Stevie used her own funky curtains for the time she was here, but before and since her living here, I've kept that room shut.

But Indy's new bedroom won't close completely because of the books and clothes thrown about her floor, keeping the door from shutting.

I learned another thing about the girl during our third meeting. Not only is she emotional and can't hold her liquor, but she's messy. Real messy.

*She's colorful too,* I remind myself. It's glaringly obvious around my black and white apartment. The dresses shoved in her doorway are shades of light purple and floral prints, but I think the biggest culprit of the doorjamb is the strappy pink heel sticking out from under the vibrant fabrics.

Maybe that's the shoe that left a scuff mark on my bedroom door last night.

# 4

## Indy

"Are you kidding me?" I bury my face in my pillow, trying to shield my eyes from the blaring morning sun pouring into my bedroom windows. "Why are there no blinds?"

The sun beats off the yellow walls of my new room. I need to ask Stevie why the hell she painted this room such an obnoxiously morning color because I know there's no way in hell Mr Doesn't Like Color did.

I don't know what time it is. I didn't set up anything in my new room, including my alarm clock and only God knows where my phone could be, but I can tell by the obscenely bright sunrise filtering into my room, it's too goddamn early to be awake.

I have an overnight flight to work tonight, our first of the season, and I need my sleep. I'm not a morning person regardless, but especially not on days I have to fly all night.

I slept like shit. On the floor with a single pillow and two throw blankets. I don't have a bed or mattress yet and my stubborn ass refused to crash on Ryan's couch after last night's debacle.

I need to go shopping for some things. It feels weird starting over, but no part of me wants the mattress or bedding from where I found Alex with someone else.

Thinking of his name alone reawakens the ache in my chest that likes to hide for periods of time until a simple reminder brings a tsunami of pain along with it.

Finding my phone digging into my back, I squint my eyes, careful not to blind myself with its bright screen.

**Me:** *Daily update—why the hell is this room the color of a baby duckling?! I wish your bed was still here. Zanders is rich enough to buy a different one for your guest bedroom. Oh, and your brother is a dick.*

**Stevie:** *Well, at least that'll keep you from wanting to sleep with him!*

**Me:** *When did I say that? I'm a romance reader. I have a thing for assholes.*

She doesn't respond and I wonder just how many daily updates it'll take for her to block my number.

Burying my head, I use my pillow to blind my eyes, hoping to get a few more hours of precious sleep, but as soon as the waft of fresh coffee filters into my room, I'm on high alert. The smell is enticing as it is, but couple that with some crackling bacon and I'm out of bed and stumbling over my clutter to get to the kitchen. I don't eat the stuff, but God does it smell amazing.

"Morning," Ryan says, not bothering to turn around as he faces the stove top.

"Yes, it is," I mumble, taking a seat at the kitchen island.

A cutoff T-shirt and basketball shorts grace his body, but his outfit doesn't give off the frat boy vibes you'd expect. His shirt seems so old and worn that he had to cut the sleeves off simply because the fabric was garnering too many holes—surprising for someone as clean as him. Regardless, I'm not complaining because his sleek, curving oblique muscles peek out perfectly from the deep cut sides and his bulging quads make my imagination dance with all the things those powerful legs could do.

God, he's cut.

Ryan finally turns to face me, catching my admiring stare before his eyes flicker to my chest. I probably should've thrown a bra on. Thanks to this thin, smiley-faced tank top, I'm not the only one greeting my new roommate this morning.

"We aren't into bras?"

"We? I personally don't love wearing one with my pajamas, but you do you." I hold my hands up in surrender. "Judgment free zone."

He shoots me an unimpressed glare before placing a piping hot mug of black coffee on the counter in front of me, followed by a plate of scrambled eggs, bacon, and wheat toast.

I pull my gaze up to meet his. Blue-green eyes bore into mine, waiting for me to say something, but I can't. The edge of frustration he wore last night has washed away slightly and he looks softer, kinder.

"You wanted to have breakfast together," he reminds me, nodding towards my plate.

He remembered, although I forgot all about that after my little meltdown. I figured I would be greeted with an eviction notice after last night, not with a homemade breakfast.

This meal is an olive branch. And even though he was a royal jackass, I did throw a shoe at his door, so I don't know that he's the one who should be apologizing.

"Was it the bright pink ones?" he asks, pulling my stare away from his bedroom.

"Hmm?"

"The shoe you threw at my door. Was it your pink heels?" He motions to the mess in my doorway.

I guess I should be embarrassed, but I'm not. "Probably. Those are my I-don't-take-shit shoes."

A slight smile tugs at the corner of his lip, but I don't get my hopes up for a genuine grin. I've quickly learned that Ryan Shay finds me neither funny nor charming.

He holds a fork out for me as he stands opposite the island, but before he begins to eat his breakfast, he cleans the two pans he used, dries them, and replaces them to their rightful home.

"Sorry about last night," I finally apologize with my mouth full. "I'll scrub that scuff off your door."

He doesn't respond, shifting his attention to his plate as he begins to eat his breakfast.

"You don't like bacon?" He points his fork at my plate.

"I'm a vegetarian."

His eyes bounce to mine with horror before he swoops up my bacon and slips it between his deliciously full lips. "And you don't drink coffee?"

"I love coffee. But I don't drink hot coffee. I'm waiting for it to cool down, then I'll add some ice. And creamer. Lots of creamer."

His brows furrow, probably wondering how he landed the world's most difficult roommate. "You only drink iced coffee? What about in the winter?"

"It could be negative twenty, and I'll hold an iced coffee in my hand while I wear my winter gloves."

"Are you a Starbucks girl? A bit basic don't you think, Indiana?"

My eyes narrow at the name. "Ever hear the phrase 'she's not like other girls'?"

He gives a small nod of his head.

"Yeah, that's not me. I'm just like every other chick. As basic as they come. I had an Uggs phase. I had a skinny jeans phase. I like my books with romance, my coffee with more creamer than caffeine, and I even take aesthetic pictures of my food anytime I'm at a restaurant."

His chest moves slightly, and I give myself an internal pat on the back for pulling the smallest silent laugh from Ryan Shay.

We finish our breakfasts in silence. Ryan doesn't look up at me, but I can't stop my wandering eye from falling over him as he eats. He really is a beautiful man. Square jaw with a light dusting of scruff. Lips a bit full that I can't help but wonder how soft they feel. Eyes that are light and bright, alluring even if he doesn't mean to be. He's not the nicest, not the most outgoing, but attractive, nonetheless. The oddest thing about him might be that he doesn't realize this.

"What?" he asks without looking up at me.

I'm not embarrassed being caught red-handed, so I keep my attention locked on him. "Do you have any friends?"

"Yes."

"You don't have much in your kitchen. What if your friends come over for dinner and there are no extra plates or silverware?"

"I don't spend time with my friends here."

"Where do you spend time with them?"

"At practice or at our games."

"Your teammates, you mean."

"I work too much to not consider my teammates my friends. Stevie's my friend, too."

"Your twin sister."

"And Zanders."

"Your probable future brother-in-law."

"What's your point, Indy?" His tone is laced with exasperation.

I casually pop my shoulders. "No point. Just trying to get to know you. What's your favorite color?"

"Black."

"I kind of thought robots would be more into silver."

He offers me a fake smile. "Cute."

"Why don't you have a dog or a pet to keep you company? It'd be lonely living here by yourself."

"I'm allergic to dogs. And I'm not lonely."

"Ah, that's right. I forgot about your allergy. Really pissed off the big guy upstairs to earn that allergy, huh? What about a cat then? Something to take care of."

"I don't need anything or anyone to take care of, and I don't need added company. I like being alone."

"I love flowers. I could get you some. Or a plant. Maybe you'll feel more masculine with a plant. Something that will thrive in the bitter coldness of your personality."

"You're pretty…*bold* for someone who just got here yesterday and still hasn't signed a lease. And you ask a lot of questions."

"You think I'm pretty?"

"You heard the first two words and tuned out the rest, huh?" He raises an eyebrow, unimpressed.

"Just trying to get to know you."

He eyes me for a moment, studying. "Fine. My turn."

I sit up straighter. "Oh, this is fun! Roommate bonding. Shoot."

"Tell me about your ex and why you don't have a place to live."

Well, fuck. Starting off real strong, I guess.

"My favorite color? So glad you asked. Lavender."

"That wasn't my question."

Exhaling a deep, resigning sigh I ask, "You already think I'm a mess. Are you sure you want the details?"

"I do."

He holds my stare, unwavering. Realizing this honesty might be a non-negotiable to living here, I tell him. "My ex and I lived together for a long time. We dated for a long time, and that all ended about six months ago when I came home early from a work trip and found him in our bed with someone else."

Ryan's jaw tics as if he's grinding his molars together. "I know most of that. How long is a long time?"

"Six years."

Blue-green eyes widen. "You were together for six years?"

"Yep, but we've known each other our entire lives."

"Six years and you weren't married or engaged yet?"

"We were getting there. He had the ring. I was waiting for him to be ready for the next step."

I keep looking down at my plate because this is humiliating. I used to love our love story. It made us unique, connected. Childhood friends getting married. I was excited to display our kindergarten pictures at our wedding one day.

But now? Now, it's mortifying. We've known each other twenty-two years, dated for six of them, and I still couldn't get the guy to marry me. I couldn't even get him to remain faithful.

"You should never have to beg someone to be ready for a future," he says, and the words come out more tender than I think he anticipated.

"Regardless of your apartment décor, life isn't always black and white, Ryan."

"It is when it comes to love. Either you want each other, or you don't. Six years and a lifetime of memories is more than enough time to figure it out. He was stalling. You need to move on."

"Jesus. A little harsh there. I'm trying."

"No, you're not. Not really. You were crying last night because of him. You can say it was because I'm an ass and what I said was mean, but it was because of him. You're living here because of him and that hurts your feelings. He didn't want you. He proved that by waiting six years to propose, and he practically screamed that from the rooftops when he decided to fuck someone else in your bed. So, yes, Indiana, it is black and white. You need to move on. He doesn't deserve shit from you, including your tears."

Ignoring the nickname, anger bubbles inside of me. "Maybe work on a softer approach there, Roomie. You have no idea what it feels like to have your entire future ripped out from under you, forcing you to start over."

He swallows, eyes staying locked on mine. "Trust me, I know better than anyone."

Shit. The vulnerability covering his annoyingly beautiful face tells me I struck a nerve.

I soften my tone. "My name isn't Indiana, you know. So the nickname makes absolutely no sense. Not to mention it's longer than Indy."

"Your real name is Indy?"

"Indigo, actually. But I prefer Indy."

"Indigo? Like the color?"

"Yes, like the color. My parents had an interesting phase when I was born. They had one kid and went with 'Indigo.'"

"So, your name is Blue?" He genuinely laughs and it's the first time I've heard it. Regardless that he's laughing at me and not with me, I like the sound.

"My name is Indy," I remind him. "So, can we stop with the Indiana nickname that makes no goddamn sense?"

He smiles. Wide and perfect, not holding back. He's even got dimples, lucky son of a bitch. "Sure thing. I'll stop with the nickname, Blue."

"No. Absolutely not. It's Indy, just Indy."

He takes my now room temperature coffee and pours a bit in the sink before turning back to the fridge and filling my mug with ice. Pulling a small carton of milk from the refrigerator, he sets them both down in front of me.

"I don't have any creamer, so hopefully milk will do. You're not lactose intolerant too, are you?"

There's a nervous bounce in his eyes as he looks at me, as if he can't handle another thing I won't eat or drink. "Milk is great. Thank you."

"Let's talk about your lease."

"You still want to let me live here after I threw a shoe at your door and told you what a colossal clusterfuck my life is?"

"I don't know if I'd use the term *want*, but it's only temporary. Until you're back on your feet."

*Temporary*. I'm over my entire life being temporary. I want stability and a future, but I'm one hundred percent fine with this living situation being temporary. Ryan won't be able to handle me for long anyway. I can tell.

"Okay, let's talk about the lease."

He takes my now empty plate along with his own and begins washing them in the sink. "How much can you afford in rent?"

I don't get embarrassed often, but two of my more embarrassing moments have occurred with Ryan Shay so let's add this to the list. How am I supposed to tell one of the most attractive men I've ever met how much money I make? Looking around his apartment, it's clear he's never felt financially strapped, at least since he was drafted by Chicago.

His place is phenomenal, and I don't make enough money to even rent the linen closet.

Keeping my eyes down, I ask, "My max budget, or how much I can afford while still eating and putting gas in my car?"

"How much could you pay a month that you could still save money for your own place and feel comfortable with all your other expenses?" Ryan puts our plates and forks on the drying rack next to the sink.

"A thousand?" It's a question, not a statement. That's stretching it while having only seven months to save, but I could eat ramen packets and survive.

He raises a questioning brow. "My sister said you were having financial issues. You could find somewhere else to live for a thousand. That's the whole point to you being here, to save money."

Fourteen thousand. I have seven months to save fourteen thousand dollars and that's if everything goes smoothly.

I knew fertility treatments were expensive, and I was aware that they were most likely in my future. What I hadn't planned was that I would be paying out of pocket to get my eggs frozen at age twenty-seven after my life-long love and who I thought was going to be the father of my children decided to sleep with someone else.

My doctor warned me we should've started trying years ago, but Alex wasn't ready. I don't blame him because I wasn't ready either, but he continually made it a point to dangle the whole "I want to start trying soon" thing in front of me. Which is why I didn't seek out egg freezing sooner while I was still on my parents' insurance. No, he had to wait until I was a year too old to be covered by them to put his dick in someone else.

Diminished Ovarian Reserve—such a formal phrase to say my ovaries are aging more rapidly than the rest of my body.

Even though my body is in its late twenties, my eggs are on the brink of retirement thanks to my mother's genetic line. If I want to keep the option of biological children someday, I need to do something about it yesterday, and seeing as I can't afford to take time off work, my plan is to save, save, save until next summer—hockey's off-season.

Ryan grabs a notepad and pen from a drawer. I'd assume this is his "junk drawer" but the guy has pens lined in a row and every little thing has its specific place. Psychopath.

He writes *Blue's temporary leasing agreement* on the top of the pad of paper.

He underlines *temporary* twice.

I don't know what's more annoying—the blatant reminder he doesn't want me here or the nickname I earned over breakfast.

He writes his first line item—*Rent.*

"How do you feel about five hundred bucks a month?" He hovers the pen over the page as he leans on his forearms.

I try my very best not to stare at the bulging veins running down his muscular arms as I go over his offer, but he sure is distracting.

Five-hundred bucks a month? That's nowhere near enough to charge me. That might not even cover the extra utilities I'll be charging to his bills.

Maybe he really does want me here and this is his way to get me to stay? I can afford five-hundred bucks a month.

"Only..." he continues while my mind is still reeling over the possible hidden meaning behind his words. "If you take another five-hundred dollars a month and put it in a savings account for your own place."

And never mind. He's going to charge me next to nothing in order for me to leave as soon as possible. It's generous nonetheless and I'm no martyr. If he wants to pay my way, I'll gladly let him. He clearly has the money. Little does he know that though my savings account will be filled, it'll be allocated in a different way.

"Deal."

His eyes lighten, the skin slightly creasing around the corners, but he doesn't fully smile. "You're not going to fight me on it? You're not going to offer to pay me more?"

"Nope." I pop my shoulders. "I think you can afford to house me just fine, Ryan Shay."

His attention falls back to the pad of paper and the corner of his lips lift as he writes *$500 + $500 in savings* next to *Rent.*

Next line item—*Rules.*

Here we go. "Let me guess. Quiet hours start at 8:30 PM, and you conduct a small human sacrifice before every home game that no one can find out about."

"Cute."

I lean my cheek on my palm with a smile. "You keep saying that, Shay, and I might get a big head over here."

"No guests," he says as he writes the same thing.

"I can't have friends over?"

"Stevie can come over."

I lightly laugh in disbelief.

"And Zanders," he offers as if he's giving me more options. "A couple of my teammates too."

My brows lift excitedly. "An apartment full of NBA boys? Sign me up."

"Not for you."

"You're no fun."

"I don't want strangers here," he continues. "So, no overnight guests."

"You're *really* no fun. Are you jealous already, Ryan? We've only lived together for twelve hours, and you can't stand to see another man with me. Is that it?"

He motions with his index finger, circling in my general direction. "This thing works for you? You get through life this way?"

"The charming thing, you mean? Twenty-seven years, baby."

Another light lift of his lips. Well, if that's not the most addicting thing I've ever seen.

"I'm not cockblocking you. Do what you want," he says, and the words don't sit well with me. I liked the idea of him being my over-possessive roommate who couldn't stand another man to be near me because he wanted me for himself.

"Just don't do it here," he continues. "I don't want strangers here. Not to sound like that guy, but I can't go anywhere without being recognized. My apartment is my safe place, my only true moment of privacy, and I'm not willing to lose that. So no guests. This is non-negotiable."

"I get it," I brush him off. "I work with a professional hockey team, remember? I understand the spotlight thing."

"No, you don't get it. This is different. More extreme than anything the guys on the Raptors have experienced."

A moment of silence lingers between us as he holds my stare, unyielding. I hadn't done my typical internet stalking session on Ryan Shay, but maybe I should've. There seems to be more that he's trying to say without coming off like a cocky pro-athlete and now I wish I understood the unspoken words.

When I met Stevie's brother six months ago, I had to keep myself from searching his name on the internet. He was unquestionably the most attractive man I'd laid eyes on, but more than that, he didn't like me. And that bugged me more than I'm willing to admit. I didn't want to know about him because he didn't want to know about me.

"No guests," I agree.

"Promise?"

Apparently, it's a big deal for him to allow a total stranger into his home. I didn't realize. I'd taken this living situation lightly, but clearly, he hadn't.

I sit up straight, hoping he can see how serious I'm taking it now. "I promise."

His chest deflates as he writes *No guests* next to *Rules*.

He follows that up with *No friends. No food. No fun*, referencing a line from my terrible third impression.

Well, I'll be damned. Ryan Shay has a sense of humor.

"What about *your* guests?" I ask before we can veer too far off that subject. "Where do you…*entertain* your guests?"

His eyes lift to me before they trail down my face, glide along my neck, and linger a little longer on my chest. He takes his bottom lip between his teeth, and my nipples harden from the attention, straining against the thin tank top.

He smirks at that, and fuck, is it gorgeous.

"What are you asking?"

Jesus, his voice got husky.

I swallow, crossing one leg over the other to dull the sudden throb from his panty-melting grin. "I'm asking…" I hesitate, as if the thought of knowing where Ryan Shay has sex isn't making the spot between my legs painfully ache. Clearing my throat, I begin again. "I was wondering—"

He leans in closer across the island as he keeps his eyes locked on mine. "Are you asking where I fuck, Blue?"

No. We aren't doing this. He's not the one that gets to be in control here. I get to make him uncomfortable with my outgoing personality. He doesn't get to slide in here with his weird, control-freak thing and that sultry voice and ask if I'm curious about his sex life. I am, God, I am, but no.

"Actually, no." I straighten. "That doesn't seem like something I want to know."

"You sure about that?" He nods towards my breasts.

My nipples sure as shit want to know where Ryan Shay fucks. They're practically ripping through my tank top, wanting to find out. Two smiley faces on the fabric are perfectly lined up, and they're puckered so far out from the rest of the shirt, they're practically screaming at my roommate to find out where he has sex if it's not here.

Huffing, I rub my palms over them, trying to get them to stand down. "What the hell, Ryan? You're supposed to be shy when it comes to talking about girls."

"I'm not *shy*. You just surprised me with how goddamn blunt you were the first couple of times we met." He straightens. "But I don't have overnight guests here. I think that's all you need to know."

Well, okay then. Clear line drawn.

He adds the third line item which seems like the final one—*Signature*. Sliding the notepad across the island to me, he holds out the pen.

"That's it?" I ask with skepticism. "Pay you five-hundred dollars a month and don't have guests over?"

"Plus make sure you're quiet when you come home late from road trips, and I'll do the same. Be nice to my doorman, and maybe we can work on the messy thing."

I raise a brow. "Now you're asking for too much."

Shifting my attention to the pad in front of me, I decide to sign before he adds more rules that I won't be able to get on board with. So far, these are tame, and I'd like to keep it that way.

He peels off the top paper and uses a magnet to stick our lease agreement on the fridge for both of us to see. Every day. For as long as I live here.

"I'll see you when you're back from your road trip." He takes a fresh coffee with him to his room.

"Wait, that's it? That was only thirty minutes. You don't have to hide in your room."

"I'm good."

"I could…I could make us lunch!" I quickly suggest, and the desperation for quality time is seeping from my voice. I sound pathetic.

"I have practice."

"Oh, okay."

Stopping in his doorway, he turns on his heel to face me again, looking me up and down as I sit on the stool, desperate for some attention. Can he sense how reliant I am on someone else's company, or does he assume it's his time in particular I want? Because it's not about him. I just don't want to be alone.

His lips tilt again, but this time there's no amusement in his slight smile. He pities me.

And for the third time since I've met Ryan Shay, he hides in his room, away from me.

# 5

# Indy

"Indy, I'm just saying, if you need a place to crash, my bed is available." Rio, a third-year defenseman for the Chicago Raptors sits in the barstool next to mine, facing me and ignoring his two teammates across the table. "You don't have to pay rent. I'd be happy, *thrilled*, to have you."

"Jesus, Rio," Zanders laughs. "Let it go. She's got a spot. Indy isn't moving in."

Rio's face falls as the rest of us laugh at his disappointment, but he's known my answer since he offered his bachelor pad to me last June.

"Thanks, Rio." I sling an arm over his shoulders as I sit next to him at a local bar in downtown Edmonton. "But being roommates is tricky business and I don't want to ruin our friendship."

I emphasize the word *friendship*.

His green eyes begin to sparkle. "You know what they say about friends. Some of the best relationships start as—"

Curling my hand around his neck, I silence him with a palm over his mouth. "Not gonna happen, buddy."

I feel his cheeky smile stretch against my palm. "A man can dream, Indigo."

Regardless that nothing would ever happen between me and Rio, I wouldn't risk our friendship. Rio is too young, too sweet, and too naïve to be anything more than my friend, but even if he were my age and his house wasn't filled with parties and late nights on the Xbox, I truly love having him as a friend.

Besides, I have nothing left to give someone else. Alex took it all. The only thing I could possibly offer is a physical relationship, something to add that last piece of separation between my ex and me, but there's no way I'm letting Rio know that's where my head is.

He'll offer and I'll say no…again.

He checked in on me all summer after he went home to Boston. And even though last year I wrote him off as childish, goofy, and overexcitable, I didn't realize over the four months of off-season that he would become such a great friend. Rio genuinely cares about me, regardless that he's joking around 99% of the time.

"I'm kidding." Rio's shoulder nudges into mine. "I'm happy that you're getting settled."

"How do you like the building so far?" Maddison, Captain of the Raptors, asks me as he sits across the table with Zanders.

"It's extravagant and beautiful and I'm trying not to get too used to the luxury lifestyle, but I've only slept there for one night and I have an attachment growing."

Maddison smiles. "It's cool you're close by. Ryan is a good dude."

Maddison and his family live on the penthouse floor of Ryan's building, and Zanders and Stevie are in the building across the street. Rio's house is about twenty minutes away, but Maddison is right; it is nice to be surrounded by friends, and takes the edge off the idea of being alone, even if I did just move in with a stranger.

"Are you doing okay over there, Zanders?" I ask the defenseman across from me as he nurses the warm beer in his hand, pouting.

"I miss Stevie."

We try to hold it in, we really do, but a small laugh settles among the table.

The boys played last night in Vancouver and tomorrow night in Edmonton. This is the first night off while on the road, and it looks a whole lot different than it did last season for Zanders. A year ago, he was on the prowl. Tonight, he's moping at a bar about missing his girlfriend who he hasn't seen in forty-eight hours.

"But she got to go to Ryan's home opener tonight which is awesome." Zanders holds out his phone to show me a picture of number five on the basketball court, but I make sure not to linger my stare too long. "How was your first night in the apartment with him?"

"I cannot believe you live with Ryan Shay," Rio whines, his forehead lightly banging on the tabletop in front of him. "How am I supposed to compete with that?"

I roll my eyes at his dramatics.

"To be honest, Ind, I don't know who I'm more jealous of. If this were any other guy, I'd hate them, but this is Ryan Shay we're talking about. I wish I were you."

I turn back to Zanders. "To answer your question, he made me cry."

"I'll kill him," Rio decides.

"Settle down there, tiger. I don't know that it was necessarily Ryan's fault. I think I'm just having a tough time in general."

All three guys know why, and they shoot me with pity smiles in apology. I hate it.

"What did he do?" Zanders asks.

"He said something to the effect of 'I don't want you here, and I'm only doing this to fulfill my brotherly duty' or something like that."

"Ouch." Maddison winces.

Zanders cuts in. "Ryan is a good guy, but he's not like you. He's not the most welcoming to new people and he thrives on doing his own thing. He pretty much only cares about basketball and Stevie. Give him a chance. He'll come around…hopefully."

"He likes *you*." I motion towards him. "You guys are close. How'd you get him to like you?"

"He hated me, remember? It wasn't until he realized that I was in love with his sister that he was cool with me, but even then, it took some time to get to know him. He's admittedly guarded."

"I get that he's doing this for Stevie, and it has nothing to do with me, but I'm living with a guy who wishes he were living alone. It's awkward and uncomfortable."

"You know what," Zanders continues. "I thought this was going to be a disaster, the two of you under the same roof, but you might be good for Ryan. Force him out of his shell. Make him spend time with someone who isn't a teammate or his sister. Maybe having someone normal around will give him a little hope in humanity."

"Aw, Zee. You think I'm normal?"

"You teeter the line." He smiles into his glass as he finishes off his beer.

"He told me I couldn't have people over. That's weird, isn't it?"

"Ind," Rio cuts in, eyeing me suspiciously. "How much do you know about your new roommate?"

Clearly, not enough judging by the three pairs of eyes cautiously watching me as if I'm missing a huge piece to the puzzle.

Over the last few nights, I've attempted to do some internet sleuthing on Ryan, but every time his handsome face filled my screen, I got too nervous to know more. I'm not sure what I was looking for or what I expected to find, but part of me wants to learn about Ryan organically and not through the headlines that litter the internet.

"What do you mean?" I look around for the answer. "Because he's a professional athlete? I get it. I'm friends with you three, aren't I? I know there's a lot of attention on you."

Zanders shakes his head. "This is a little different."

"A little?" Rio scoffs. "Ryan Shay was the number one draft pick out of North Carolina—a team who won back-to-back national championships under him. He's…what do you think?" Rio shifts his attention to Maddison and Zanders. "Top five, maybe top three players in the league? And he doesn't even have a ring or an MVP yet. It's impossible for him to leave his house without being recognized, I'm sure. These guys are big in the NHL, and they're known throughout the city"—he motions across the table towards his teammates—"but it's nothing in comparison to what Ryan Shay experiences."

"You remember my little media debacle with Stevie last spring when everyone found out I had a girlfriend?" Zanders asks me. "Well, when Ryan makes headlines, we're not talking national news. It goes worldwide. He keeps his image squeaky-clean for a reason. All eyes are on him."

Swallowing down the thickness in my throat, I ask, "He's really that well-known?"

"I feel for the guy." Maddison shakes his head. "We're both captains of our respective teams and we're in the same city, but I'll never have to experience the kind of pressure and attention he lives with."

"Zanders, how much money do you make?"

"Really, Rio?"

"I can look it up online. I'm trying to prove a point."

"Eleven and a half."

"Twelve," Maddison smugly cuts in, sharing his own salary.

Zanders flips him off as he tries to hold back his smile.

"See." Rio turns to me. "Two of the biggest names in the NHL make almost twenty-four million dollars a year combined. Ryan Shay makes double that. Hell, he's got shoe deals and endorsements that are probably worth more than that."

"Rio, you really are in love with my future brother-in-law, aren't you?"

"Undoubtedly." He shifts his attention to Maddison. "How does it feel knowing he lives under you?"

"Like a joke," Maddison laughs. "Guy makes so much money he could own the entire building."

"Why does he live there then?" I finally cut in. "The apartment is gorgeous, but if he makes that much—"

"Because he's practical," Zanders reminds me. "He doesn't indulge in anything."

Four plates, four sets of silverware, four bowls. Organized to the point of insanity. Is it self-control to live as precisely as Ryan does or is it a form of self-punishment?

Remembering how rude he was the night he came home and found the mess I created, it's all starting to make sense. I upended his structure, his routine. His control was taken away in the one space he finds solace.

And I'm the crazy new roommate who threw a shoe at his door.

I can't imagine going through life the way he does, never being able to let his guard down with all eyes on him, but if his apartment is the one place he can do it, then the black and white minimalistic prison he's living in isn't going to cut it.

It's decided. I'm going to bring some color into Ryan Shay's life if it's the last thing I do.

The sun was already rising by the time I left the airport. Between the overtime win in Edmonton and clearing customs, I made it home hours after I had planned. Coffee seemed like a good idea. Hell, it's always a good idea, but especially when it's my first full day in the apartment and I have a mess to unpack. Not to mention, I'm hoping to spend time with my new roommate today, so I want to be as perky as possible because I'm going to make sure Ryan Shay enjoys living with me if it's the last thing I do.

"Would you like a carrying tray?" the barista asks.

"Please. That'd be great. Thank you."

"Indy?" I hear from behind me as I stack my coffees. "Oh my God, Indy, is that you?"

Turning, I find a group of girls—my friends. My childhood life-long friends.

"Maggie? Hi!" I burst, quickly engulfing her in a hug. "I missed you. Hi, you guys." I look over her shoulder before hugging three more of my long-time girlfriends. "I missed you all! What are you doing downtown so early?"

Hesitating, Maggie's face drops. "We're…uh…we're going shopping for the bridesmaid dresses."

"Oh."

"I'm sorry. I would've invited you. I honestly didn't know you were back in Chicago. I thought you might still be in Florida."

"I texted you when I got back. I texted all of you."

"Well, come with us! This is perfect that we ran into you today."

I look down at my uniform, needing to change, needing to sleep. Wishing she would've told me, so I could've planned.

"Mags," Angie cuts it. "We only booked for four."

"That's okay," I offer with a forced smile. "I just landed from a work trip and haven't slept yet. I need to change. I have a really full day," I lie. "Just…let me know which dress you guys pick so I know what to order."

"I miss you, Ind." Maggie runs a palm down my arm. "Can we all get together soon? It's been way too long."

"Yes, please," I sigh in relief. "I miss you all so much. Is everyone still doing Wednesday night trivia at Scouts? I'm in town this week. I can come!"

The girls exchange nervous glances. "We are…" Angie hesitates.

Maggie's head tilts with sympathy. "But Alex still goes, and you know how close the guys are."

"Right. Of course, they are." There's a lump in my throat that I'd like to blame on exhaustion or being an emotional person as it is, but that hurt.

There was a big group of us kids who were glued to each other from a young age. The numbers never dwindled, and we formed what I thought was an unbreakable bond and a lifelong friendship. Maggie and Kevin started dated shortly after Alex and me, and the other couples formed years later. I thought these were my people. I thought I was going to raise my future children with these women, and now it feels as if I'm the one left out. As if I was the one who was unfaithful to my partner of six years.

"Let's have a girls' night soon, yeah?" Maggie suggests. "When the boys are busy."

Another forced smile because that's what I do. "Definitely. You and Kevin, you're good?"

"So good! I mean, the wedding planning isn't really Kevin's thing, but we're great." She leans in closer to whisper in my ear. "He said we can start trying on the honeymoon."

She pulls away with wide and excited eyes, and by "try" she clearly means for a baby. Maggie doesn't know about my fertility concerns, none of these friends do, but her words unknowingly twist the knife in my chest.

"That's…that's amazing, Mags."

"Oh! I'm so glad I ran into you." She reaches into her bag. "I didn't know where to send this. I'm not sure where you're living, but here's a save the date. You're in the wedding, so you already know all the details, but I wanted you to have one."

I take the ivory envelope from her. "Thanks. I'm so excited for you both." My smile is far from genuine, and I feel terrible for it.

"Where are you living anyway?" Angie asks.

*With my friend's brother who happens to make more money than God, is hotter than sin, and plays basketball for a team my ex-boyfriend idolizes.*

"I'm crashing with a friend I know through work."

Pity smiles flash back at me.

"You'll help with the bridal shower, right? And the bachelorette if you're in town? I'll need you to help with the theme and décor. Food." Maggie laughs. "All of it. You're the best party planner we've got."

It's my self-assigned role. Host. Event coordinator. The one who always makes a huge deal of birthdays and promotions. The friend who wants to celebrate every exciting moment of my people's lives, to give them a moment of recognition so they know how special they are. The one who ensures those around her feel good about themselves.

I truly do love it, but it hurts a bit to remember that not a single one of my friends, outside of Stevie, congratulated me on my own promotion.

Plastering on a smile, I tell Maggie, "Of course, I will. Anything you need."

"Are you doing okay?" she quietly asks.

Is she kidding? No, I'm not okay. My entire life was upended because of a decision someone else made. I had no place to live, no bed to sleep in because of someone else's decision. The life I envisioned for myself, the family I imagined, have all disappeared thanks to Alex's decision.

But before I can answer, Maggie adds, "Alex is still in the wedding, so I totally understand if you have any hesitation. You both have a plus-one though, so I'm hoping that'll help the situation."

What does that mean? Is Alex using his? Would he do that? Clearly, I know nothing about the man I thought I would marry, so I can't answer those questions.

She lightly squeezes my arm. "Can't you forgive him? I want everything to go back to how it used to be. All of us spending time together."

"What?" I force out a laugh. "Maggie, he slept with someone else in our bed."

*And he's never once asked for forgiveness, let alone apologized.*

"He made a mistake."

Sharp pricks of unwanted tears sting my eyes because I want to try on bridesmaid dresses, I want to go to trivia on Wednesday night, and I want my friends to have my back over Alex's in this situation. Does that make me a terrible person? I don't think so. That feels like the bare minimum.

I quickly grab my tray of coffees, tucking the save the date under my arm. "I'm so happy I saw you guys. Send me dress pictures later, okay? Have fun." My tight-lipped smile carries me to the door where I'm able to hold the tears until I'm outside.

God, that hurts. Why am I being punished? Why do I feel like I'm losing my friends? They should hate him. He did this to us. Just because their boyfriends are still buddy-buddy with him? What about me?

Am I being irrational? Maybe Ryan is right. Maybe I am overly emotional, but that really hurt my feelings.

I have two blocks. Two blocks to be upset before I have to get my shit together. Two blocks until I'm at Ryan's apartment where I need to be happy and fun Indy because I'm in his place and his life outside those four walls is stressful enough as it is. He needs his home to be a safe space. He needs a friend.

And right now, more than anything, so do I.

"Miss Ivers, welcome back." Ryan's doorman opens the lobby door for me.

Stopping in front of him, I set my suitcase aside. "Dave. Can I call you Dave?" His name tag says David.

"Sure, you can."

"Do you like lattes? Because I got you a latte from my favorite coffee shop around the corner." I take his off the tray and hand it to him.

"I love a good latte. Thank you so much." He wraps his hands around the paper cup.

"I think you and I are going to be friends, Dave." Grabbing the handle of my suitcase, I enter through the open door.

"I think you're right about that, Miss Ivers. You had a package delivered. It's upstairs for you."

Ryan said he'd leave the key he made for me under the mat, but when I step off the elevator and turn the corner, I find him opening our apartment door.

"Hey!" I call out in an excited whisper from down the hall, not wanting to be too loud at this early hour.

Ryan turns to face me, looking ridiculously fuckable without trying. He's dressed casually wearing a backwards cap as he pulls his own suitcase out into the hallway.

On the contrary, I look awful. Up all night, still in my uniform, with smudged makeup that needs to be removed. Typically, I don't let strangers see under the perfect mask, but screw it. The guy is about to live with me. He's going to see worse.

"Hey." He swallows, shifting a backpack over his shoulder. "I was wondering where you were."

*He was?*

"The team had a late game and clearing customs was a nightmare." I gesture to the tray in my hand. "I got you a coffee." Smiling brightly, I hand him his caffeine. "Where are you off to?"

"Practice. Then catching a flight to Milwaukee for a game." He starts down the hallway.

"Oh." Today's disappointments are becoming exceedingly harder to hide. "Well, good luck with that!"

"I'm back in two days. Key is under the mat for you," he calls out without turning around.

Tears are burning and for no good reason. I'm just exhausted, and admittedly, really lonely.

I'd call Stevie to see if she'd want to hang out, but Zanders essentially sprinted off the plane once we landed, so I know she's preoccupied.

"Blue," Ryan calls out from down the hall. I'm not sure why I acknowledge the nickname, but I find myself turning to face him as he pops his head out of the elevator. "Thanks for the coffee."

I offer him a slight smile as I enter the empty apartment.

The ivory envelope feels like a heavy weight under my arm. The burden of knowing I'm going to see Alex soon sits heavy on my chest. Is he going to bring her? Are they seeing each other or was it a one-night thing? Have my so-called friends met her?

I have. Multiple times. She was an intern at Alex's financial firm. I saw her at the office Christmas party last year and I complimented her sage-green chiffon dress. I don't regret it. It really was a stunning dress. Were they sleeping together then?

Maggie looks beautiful in her save the date photo. Kevin and she are so happy, and I'm happy for them. I am. But there's an envious part that wishes it were me. We were supposed to plan our big days together, but instead I wasn't even invited to try on bridesmaid dresses. And it's not the wedding I'm jealous of. It's the future—what comes after that day. I want the rest of my life more than anything.

God, I'm terrible for feeling this way. I pride myself on being a good friend, but not today. It's no wonder they left me out.

Using a magnet, I secure the save the date to the fridge as a blatant reminder that by February 2$^{nd}$, I need to be ready to see him.

The bright part of my morning is the Amazon package waiting for me on the kitchen island. Sure, an air mattress isn't quite as great as an actual bed, but I'm on a budget and it's better than the floor.

I have a lot to do today, but the spark to stay awake and get my life together has burnt out, so I put my iced latte in the fridge for later. I need to sleep. I'll deal with the reality of my messy room and being alone in this apartment later.

The sun is already spilling through the crack of my bedroom door, reminding me that my first task after a nap is to buy some drapes. My clothes and shoes are still on the floor, but they're pushed to the side, creating a walkway I didn't have before.

Immediately, my attention is drawn upward.

Right there, on the wall opposite me is the most beautiful bed I've ever seen. Cloud-like pillows and a white comforter create a vortex I want to fall into and never get out. Luxurious and expensive with a bit of texture on the duvet. It's stunning and it's new with no taint of my previous life or relationship.

It's mine.

And it's from Ryan.

For someone who doesn't care about anyone or anything, this sure is thoughtful.

My eyes burn from fresh tears wanting to surface because I'm a crier and I can't help it. Sue me. But this is one of the most kind and attentive things someone has done for me in a long time, and it means more than I know how to express. Especially after a rough morning.

Running a hand over the soft fabric, I pull out my phone. I'm not one of those people who is going to fake complain about this being too expensive and extravagant or act shocked when a multi-millionaire spends some money on me. But I am grateful, that's for sure.

**Me:** *Did you buy me a bed?*

A few moments pass before three gray dots dance along my screen.

**Roomie:** *You needed one.*

Practical answer.

**Me:** *Thank you so much, Ryan.*

A pop of lavender peeks out from under the pile of pillows. New sheets in my favorite color, and I don't know how to process how I feel about him remembering that.

He doesn't respond, so I double text because fuck it, I want to talk to him.

**Me:** *How much did it hurt to buy something that wasn't black or white?*

**Roomie:** *Almost killed me.*

**Me:** *Is this your love language? Gift-giving?*

**Roomie:** *Nothing about this situation has to do with love, Blue. You needed a bed. Don't think too much into it.*

**Me:** *Mm-hmm. Watch out, Ryan. You keep doing nice things for me like cooking me breakfast and buying me bedding and I'm going to think you want me to stay or something.*

**Roomie:** *Gotta get to practice.*

Nice avoidance, big guy.

**Roomie:** *Clean your room, it's a safety hazard.*

My cheeks hurt from the splitting grin on my face.

Ryan Shay doesn't totally hate having me here.

# 6

# Ryan

"Plane leaves at ten. Be there by nine thirty at the latest." Phil, our team coordinator, keeps his pointed gaze at Dom.

"Why are you looking at me?" he innocently asks from his spot on the gym floor, sweaty from an early-morning practice.

"If you're late again, I'm fining your ass."

"Phil. Philip. My guy. You love me and you know it."

"You're the biggest pain in my ass and the reason I'm balding. My wife is pissed at you for pulling me out of bed last night."

"Suzanne loves me too. And hey, at least I didn't drink and drive. I was responsible and called you for a ride."

Phil turns my way. "Get him to the airport on time, will you, Shay?"

"On it."

Phil shakes his head as he walks away.

"Love that guy," Dom sighs.

"Where'd y'all go last night?"

"Sway," Ethan answers for him.

"You went too?"

"No way. Annie would've served me divorce papers if I went out partying the night before a road trip, but Dom was persistent in trying."

"Oh."

"Did you want to go?" Dom questions. "You almost never go out with us, so I didn't think to ask. Sorry, man."

I shake my head. "Nah, it's cool. I wanted to be home."

Ethan and I are the two homebodies on the team. Ethan because he has a wife and three children and me because leaving my house and risking negative headlines is almost never worth it. The last time was almost a disaster. I punched an old teammate for treating Stevie poorly, and thankfully, my sister's boyfriend took the blame to keep the heat off me. But I didn't realize I had declined my teammates so much already I was no longer getting invited.

Dom could've called me for a ride at least. Sure, he didn't realize that I was wide awake most of the night wondering why my new roommate wasn't home yet, but I was.

I have ten more minutes to ice my shoulder before I can hit the showers and head to the airport, so I stand around shooting the shit with a handful of my teammates. Dom recounts the hookup he had in the back of the club last night, and Ethan fills us in on how his oldest daughter's dance recital went.

The two spectrums of our team. Sleezy hookups in a club and dance recitals with children. I don't know where I fall between these guys. It's hard to relate to anyone when the only thing I care about is getting this team to the playoffs.

"Ethan," our GM projects from across the gym. "Caroline is looking forward to dinner on Monday."

Ron Morgan wears the happiest motherfucking grin as he looks at the previous team captain at my side.

"Annie is stoked too," Ethan replies. "Can we bring anything this time?"

"We've got it! Caroline is making that rhubarb pie you love so much."

"Oh man!" Ethan's head falls back. "I can't wait." He smiles, holding his hand up in a quick wave.

"What the hell was that?" I ask.

"What was what?"

"That. *Caroline is looking forward to dinner on Monday.*"

"It's exactly what it sounds like. His wife is looking forward to having dinner on Monday."

"How did you get so chummy with him? He hates me." Looking back, I find Ron speaking to the head coach. His creased forehead and disappointed features are back, quickly replacing the relaxed smile he wore while he spoke with Ethan.

"Exactly that. Caroline. The man goes completely soft when it comes to his wife, and she loves Annie. We've been doing date nights together for years now. You get in with Caroline, you've got Ron too."

I nod my head. "Caroline is great. That should be easy."

He laughs condescendingly. "Not a chance, man. She doesn't give a shit about basketball. The topic never comes up at the dinner table and you don't know how to talk about anything else. She's big on family, they both are, and the only reason Ron invited us out the first time is because Caroline wanted to get to know Annie. She was and still is the only consistent woman around the team, so I should really be thanking my wife that Ron likes me as much as he does."

"Holy mama," Dom says loudly enough to pull my attention, his eyes glued behind me. The rest of the team follows suit, turning back towards the practice gym's entrance.

"Hot damn."

"Good God," they echo.

Turning around, I'm not so pleasantly surprised to find Indy strutting into the building like she owns the place, wearing a soft purple sundress on this unseasonably warm October day. Her high-top white Converse are embroidered with colorful shapes, and her hair and makeup are re-done, looking like a completely different woman than I left at the apartment a few hours ago.

"Shay, you are the luckiest man alive. Please tell me you're hitting that."

My head whips around to my teammate. "Watch your fucking mouth."

"Well, if you don't try, I will."

"Dom," Ethan warns, trying to hold back his laughter. "Ryan is about to combust, so I'd tone it back there, buddy."

Shifting my attention back to Indy, her eyes wander the practice facility. Even though she's clearly out of her element, nothing about her stance seems nervous. And her being comfortable in a place where she has no business being is something else I've quickly learned about her. I don't think the girl knows how to be embarrassed.

Multiple pairs of eyes stick to the blonde beauty as Ethan watches me with amusement.

"Stop looking at her," I warn. "Go hit the showers or get to the airport or just about anything other than look at her. She's not available."

"So, you *are* hitting that." Dom nods in approval.

"No, I'm not *hitting that*. And neither are any of you. Stop looking at her or she'll be the last thing you ever fucking see."

"Ooooh. Protective Shay is here, and his sister is nowhere to be found. Someone write this date down. History is being made, people. Ryan Shay gives a fuck about someone other than Stevie and something other than basketball."

"Dom, you're about to get your ass kicked. If not by Ryan then by me." Ethan shakes his head at our big man.

I ignore the retort Dom comes up with as I quickly make my way to Indy while she wanders into our practice space.

"What the hell are you doing here?" I ask, taking her arm to pull her into the corner of the gym.

"Well, hello to you too."

"How'd you get in here? This is a closed practice."

She circles an index finger around her face. "Charming. Remember?"

Of course, my overconfident roommate could talk her way past security and into our closed practice while the gates outside are lined with eager fans, hopeful for a photo or autograph.

Her eyes fix to the ice bag strapped to my shoulder. "What happened?"

"Nothing. Indy, you can't be here." I want to add *especially not looking like that* but she could be wearing a potato sack and all my teammates' eyes would still be on her.

She holds out a key. "The key you made me didn't work. I went to buy curtains and when I got back, I couldn't get inside."

"You're sure?" I take the key from her.

"Positive."

"Okay. I'll get you mine, but we need to get you out of here."

"Shay!" I hear my name coming from the offices that line the top half of the court. "Come here for a moment. I'd like a word."

Ron Morgan stands in the doorway of his office, hands tucked in his suit pant pockets.

"Fuck," I exhale, turning back to Indy. "Stay here. Don't move, and don't talk to anyone either."

"Cranky this morning," she mutters under her breath as I jog away from her.

I hold my hand out when I reach the office. "Mr. Morgan."

"Shay, I've known you for four years. Call me Ron." He puts his hand in mine.

"With all due respect, sir. I'd prefer to call you Mr. Morgan."

"Of course, you do. With your sirs and ma'ams. You've always had those Southern manners."

He stares up at me, eyes narrowing, and I'd be lying if I said this man didn't intimidate me. He might be smaller than me, but he holds my future in his hands. I'm here as long as he wants me, and the moment he doesn't, I'll be traded. That's how this business works. I'm worth a pretty penny and my salary takes up a good amount of his budget. I'm acutely aware that I haven't delivered him a championship or even a playoff berth in return for his investment.

"We have a press conference booked before the game tomorrow night. It'll be you and me fielding questions about your captaincy and what we expect to see from the team this season, so be prepared for questions."

"Yes, sir."

"And Shay, try to have a personality while you do it. Yes, we're going to talk basketball, but you're the face of this team now and they want to know about the real Ryan Shay."

"What kind of questions should I expect?"

"I don't know. Things about your family. How much you enjoy your city. How you feel about your promotion. How *I* feel about your promotion."

Time freezes with the unspoken innuendo in his voice.

Fuck it, the moment is here. May as well ask.

"How *do* you feel about my promotion, sir?"

He exhales a deep, resigned sigh. "I'm sure you know how I feel about your promotion."

I shake my head. "What did I do to make you dislike me so much? Is this all because I didn't want to continue seeing your niece? It truly had nothing to do with her—"

"No. God no. How petty do you think I am? I don't *dislike* you, Shay, but I also don't think you're cut out to lead this team. Being the captain is about more than being the most talented on the court. It's about family, camaraderie. You're a lone wolf, which is fine, but that's not the type of leadership I'm looking for in my organization. I wasn't upset that you didn't want to continue seeing my niece. She's a handful, even for me, but I know firsthand the effects a woman can have on a man. I was hoping maybe you'd meet someone along the way, and you'd change. That you'd be ready for this role when the time came. Take Ethan for example. The guy is a hell of a shooter, but his real talent is being approachable to his guys, and I know a lot of that came when he met Annie. I don't think you're ready for this, Shay."

*Well, shit. Tell me how you really feel.*

As if he didn't just make me feel two feet tall, he smiles and waves as Ethan leaves the gym.

Honestly, fuck this. I work harder than any other guy on this team. I'm *better* than any other guy on this team, but Ron has an issue with me because I don't have a *girlfriend*? Or that I'm not soft enough because I don't have a woman in my life.

The smallest part of me wants a trade. If that's how he really feels about me, then trade me. Then there's the reminder that Stevie lives here now and she's not going anywhere since Zanders signed a seven-year deal with the Raptors, so I need to make this work. I need to make this right.

"Actually, sir. I *did* meet someone."

*What the actual fuck just came out of my mouth?*

Ron laughs. "What?"

Instead of responding because I can't find it in me to repeat the lie, I quickly nod.

"Shay, you've played for me for four years. I think I'd know if you were seeing someone."

"It's new."

"Well, is it serious?"

*Is it serious?* It's seriously delusional just like me because I'm a fucking idiot thinking I could pull this lie off.

"Mm-hmm. Yep."

"I'm looking forward to meeting her," he continues, eyes narrowed. "Next week. At the fall banquet. Where your attendance is mandatory, and you'll bring your *girlfriend*. I know Caroline will want to meet her too."

I'm fucked. Utterly and completely fucked. How was having a fake girlfriend my solution to this? Why couldn't I have just offered to work on my leadership and that be it?

I can't even use the excuse of taking my sister instead of my nonexistent girlfriend because the fall banquet is a fundraiser hosted by the four major sports teams in Chicago where Stevie will be in attendance with Zanders.

A flash of blonde hair and lavender fabric catches my attention as Indy stands where I left her, lightly swaying her hips and bobbing her head as she scrolls on her phone.

My face screws up with regret. This is a terrible idea, but fuck it, I'm in it already. "Or you could meet her right now?" I motion to Indy as she entertains herself, completely oblivious to the colossal lie I'm creating about her.

"That's her? Well, introduce me, Shay."

I clear my throat. "Indy," I call out, waving her over. "Will you come here for a second?"

She heads towards us with a bit of a skip in her step and I hope she can see the apology in my forced smile.

"Indy, this is the General Manager of the Devils, Ron Morgan."

"Nice to meet you," she says with a bright beaming smile because of course she has no problem meeting strangers.

I place my hand on her lower back. It's the first time I've really touched her, and she instantly stiffens from the contact. "Mr. Morgan, this is Indy…my girlfriend."

My roommate's smile instantly drops.

"So wonderful to meet the woman who finally caught the attention of our Ryan Shay." He studies her and though Indy might not be able to tell through his tone, I know he's trying to figure this out. He's trying to catch me.

*Please go with it, Blue,* I beg through my eyes.

She stays silent in shock.

"I'm sure she's happy to meet you too," I quickly interrupt the stretched silence. "But she's heading out right now." Using my hand on her lower back, I turn her towards the exit.

"Oh, already?" Ron asks. "What a shame."

"Yep. She's got to go." I push against Indy's back, needing her to get a pep in her step and get the fuck out of here.

"Not so fast, honey bun." She snaps out of her trance, stopping me as she wraps both arms around my waist. "How am I supposed to be without you for two days? We've never been apart, cupcake. I'm going to miss you so much."

She nuzzles her head on my un-iced shoulder, looking up at me with a wink.

I'm going to kill her.

"Well, aren't you two the sweetest," Ron laughs.

"Oh, it's all him. Sweetest man I've ever met. And emotional! Did you know he was so emotional?"

"I had no idea. Shay is always so composed around here."

"Oh, he's emotional all right! Huge crier too. He sobbed the first time we made lo—"

I slap a palm over her mouth. "We've got to go. See you on the plane, Mr. Morgan."

I don't let go of Indy as I turn us around and march towards the exit.

"I look forward to seeing you again at the fall banquet next week, Indy!"

Indy waves at Ron over her shoulder like a woman gone mad, but she can't respond because I refuse to uncover her mouth until we are away from my colleagues.

"What the hell are you doing?" I snap once we're alone in the empty hall outside of the gym. "And what the fuck is with the food nicknames?"

"What am *I* doing? What the hell are *you* doing? Your *girlfriend*?"

"Fuck," I exhale, pacing the small hallway. "I panicked."

"Well, go un-panic and correct him."

"I can't."

"You can't?" She laughs condescendingly. "What do you mean you can't?"

"Look, Indy. That man in there holds my future in his hands. I can't exactly go tell him I lied to his face. He just told me he doesn't think I'm cut out to lead this team. That I'm not approachable and that I spend too much time alone."

"Sounds like he knows you *too* well."

"I need his support. I can't spend the rest of my career playing for a GM who doesn't think I'm the right man for the job. I just need you to go to this event with me, get his wife to fall in love with you, and Ron will change his mind about me. Caroline is his weak spot. If she's a fan, then he will be too."

Indy laughs. "And you call me emotional and dramatic."

"I've never once called you dramatic."

"I know." She pops her shoulder. "I added that in because I wanted a reason to call *you* dramatic. Which you are. Go take that robotic personality of yours and set him straight."

I take a deep breath. "Indy. It's one night. One event. Help me out here."

"No. That's so weird! I can't pretend to be your girlfriend."

Okay, I lied. She is dramatic. This isn't a big deal. "Do you want me to get on my knees and beg or something?"

"Now that you say it." She cocks her head to the side, eyes roaming my length. "I wouldn't mind knowing what you look like on your knees, Shay."

"Indy, please."

"This is ridiculous. We can talk about it when you get home."

"Perfect. Great. All I'm asking for is one night."

"Go get me your key so I can go crash in my new expensive bed."

"What an amazing guy to buy you a bed. Probably makes you want to return a favor. He seems like a wonderful person."

Indy rolls her eyes. "He's on my shit list at the moment."

# 7

# Ryan

Our first game on the road was a success. I had a triple-double which doesn't happen all that often. I have no problem with scoring or assists, I lead my team in both those categories, but rebounding is a different game. At 6′3″ I'm tall in the real world, but when it comes to the NBA, I'm one of the smaller guys in the league. My body takes a pounding anytime I drive the lane, but the aches are worth it whenever I sneak past a big man or hit a three over a 6′8″ beast.

I'd be lying if I said I wasn't feeling last night's game though. My shoulder has been screaming at me all morning after too many missed calls. I don't know if it's because of my height or what, but some games I'm not given the respect of calls made on dangerous plays. Fouls that would be a flagrant for any other MVP nod aren't even called for me, and the resulting body pain catches up to me the next day.

But worse than my shoulder, my brain has been in overdrive since I left Chicago. I've never allowed someone to stay in my home who wasn't my sister, and I don't know if I can trust Indy yet. She doesn't seem malicious, and Stevie trusts her, but people can surprise you. Giving her unbridled access to my apartment is overwhelming to say the least. I had to keep myself from calling my twin and asking her to crash there while I was out of town, but I know Stevie would've been disappointed in my unearned distrust of her friend.

So, as I make my way home, the only thing bouncing around my brain is the hope that Indy didn't find something she could use against me later or information she could sell to make a quick buck. I'm aware of my paranoia, but it's not without reason and someone in my position always needs to watch their back. I can't let my guard down.

Grabbing the key from under the mat, I go inside. The apartment is quiet but fully lit. It's early, and the sun is starting to peek though the buildings of downtown Chicago, but it's not enough to illuminate the space. Apparently, Indy left every single light on last night before she went to bed, which is just wonderful. Not only did I earn a new roommate, but it's one that's going to hike up my electrical bill.

Something feels different inside. I don't know if it's because there's a woman sleeping in the other room, but the energy around me has changed. As my eyes slowly adjust, I find pops of color which I know don't belong to me.

A light purple knitted blanket thrown over the couch.

A pink reusable coffee cup with a straw sits by my mug.

So many goddamn throw pillows on my couch, there's no room left to sit.

There are yellow curtains with fucking pom-pom balls pushed to the edge of my panoramic window.

Green. So much greenery between the succulents on my bookshelf and the giant leafy tree in the corner by the window.

Speaking of my bookshelf, it's a fucking rainbow. My books are completely rearranged, and the amount seems to have doubled in size since I left. Indy has taken my well-thought-out and organized bookshelf and made it look like a unicorn threw up on it as it goes from red to purple, sorted by color. What god-awful reason should *Investing 101* be sandwiched between two books with shirtless men on the covers? Because they're all orange?

And why the fuck are there naked dudes on my bookshelf?

She's a romantic. Of course, she's a goddamn romantic. She waited six years for a proposal that never came. She likes flowers and girly clothes. I should've known.

I circle my apartment in a frenzy. This was a mistake, letting her move in. Forty-eight hours alone and she's taken over. Everywhere I look there's a piece of her. Something she touched or changed. Color decorates every nook and cranny, but overall, there's so much fucking *Blue*.

I hate it. I can physically feel the control slipping away. My usual even-keeled composure is crawling with anxious thoughts, and I need my space back. I need it to be mine.

"Indy!" I yell into the silence. I don't give a fuck that it's the ass crack of morning. I need to fix this. "Indigo, wake up!"

"What happened to being quiet when you come home from road trips? I'm sleeping!"

I pound on her door. "Indy, I swear to God if you don't get out here, I'm coming in your room."

"Please do! I sleep naked."

Oh.

Heavy breaths keep words from coming out. Hands rest on either side of her doorframe as the image invades my mind. Her, naked. In my house. In the bed *I* bought her. Heat mixes oddly with the frustration thrumming through my body and the arousal is so sudden and so heady I'm almost lightheaded from the blood rushing south. I'm not sure how long it's been since I've seen a woman's naked flesh, but my body angrily reminds me with a jolt of my cock that it's been far too fucking long.

Pushing those images away, I take a centering breath. Her most likely flawless naked body is the last thing I need to think about.

She opens the door, fully dressed in pajamas, startling me, and pulling me out of my daydream. "I knew that'd work. A naked woman in your house is practically your biggest fear." She ducks under my arm and heads to the kitchen. "I know you did not just wake me up without bringing me coffee."

"What the fuck happened to my apartment?"

"What are you talking about?" She keeps her back to me as she turns on the coffee maker.

"Why is all your shit all over the place?"

"Because I live here."

"You have a bedroom."

"So do you."

God, this is like talking to a child. "Keep your things in your room."

"You want me to keep my coffee cup in my bedroom?" She holds it up, trying not to laugh.

"Well…" I stumble. "Okay, that can stay, but everything else… I like my space a certain way, Indy."

"Boring, you mean. Ryan, your house was like a prison cell. It needed some life."

"There's a fucking tree in my living room!"

"Actually, it's a Fiddle-leaf fig plant and it's there because this window faces the east, and the perfect amount of sun comes through here. Bright but not too direct. I have a north facing window. It wouldn't thrive. So, maybe you could take a breather thanks to the oxygen it's providing, yeah?"

What the fuck?

"What?" she asks as she puts her hot coffee in the fridge to cool down. "I'm not some blonde Barbie without a brain."

"I didn't say that."

"You didn't have to. The dumbfounded look plastered on your face said it for you. Most people think so, and apparently you do too."

My expression softens. I don't think that at all, but she is a gorgeous human and I'd be lying if I said that wasn't the first thing I noticed.

"I thought you liked flowers over plants." My attempt to shift the tone of conversation is nowhere near smooth, but somehow, even though she's the one who has taken over my apartment, I'm the one who feels bad.

"I do, but flowers are typically more high-maintenance and with how much I travel for work, I can't always take care of them."

I scratch the back of my neck. "I could…maybe help you take care of them."

What am I doing? I pulled her out of bed so I could get my apartment back to normal and here I am asking her to make more of a mess by offering to water her fucking flowers?

But I need a favor from her, and I came in hot with my yelling this morning.

"You'd do that?" She stands up straighter as a bit of hope overtakes her.

Well, shit. I can't exactly take it back when she looks like that. "Sure." I shrug.

"Thank you, Ryan! I haven't been able to have fresh flowers at home for years. I'm so excited! There's an adorable flower stand a few blocks over. I'm going to go there today!"

I get it. I can read between the lines. The asshole she lived with before didn't offer to take care of them while she was traveling for work so she couldn't have any.

Fuck that guy. Unfaithfulness puts you in another category in my book. You're automatically unredeemable. Which is probably why I'm doing everything I said I never would by allowing this girl to live in my home while making her life as easy as possible.

What she's going through resonates with me, and if Indy having some flowers in my apartment will make her happy, well then, I guess I'm growing a green fucking thumb.

Jesus, how'd she get me to agree to this?

"You'll have to teach me what to do," I remind her.

"I will." She quickly nods with excitement, skipping around the kitchen island to meet me. Her arms swing around my neck in a hug, pressing her body to mine.

Stilling, I stand with my arms at my sides as she grips me tighter, not allowing me to get out of this. I'm not sure that I want to. Her hold is surprisingly calming and the nervousness I felt over the change in my surroundings is long gone. I haven't been touched in a long time, and I know this is platonic and only a hug, but I forgot how nice it feels to have a woman wrapped around me.

"Hug me back, Ryan," she mumbles into my shoulder.

Cautiously, I press my hands to her back and their size overtakes her. But apparently that's not enough reciprocation because she stays holding me, not letting this end just yet.

My cheek falls against hers, sliding against the column of her neck until blonde hair surrounds me like a curtain. A soft tropical scent, maybe coconut, invades me and as I inhale, my hands slide around her waist, pulling her body closer to mine.

Two peaks pucker between us, pressing into my upper stomach and her unexpected arousal stirs mine again.

Indy is tall for a girl, 5'9" if I had to guess, and the bulge in my pants is resting dangerously close to the apex of her legs. I know she can feel it, but she's not pulling away.

God, I'm pathetic. I'm so starved for human touch that I'm getting a hard-on from a fucking hug.

"How the hell did you get me to agree to that when I woke you up with the intention of clearing your shit out of my living room?" I whisper against her.

She pulls away and instantly, I miss the connection. "It's that charming thing I've got going."

I wish I could disagree.

"If you want me to take down the curtains, move the plants, and put my blanket in my room, I can. I was reading on the couch last night and left it there. Sorry."

She floats around my kitchen pulling out eggs and bacon from the fridge, including a mixture of fruit I put together the other night. Taking my mug out from under the coffee machine, she hands it to me, offering her brightest smile as if I didn't just wake her up by yelling at her. "Good morning, by the way."

"You're awfully cheery for someone who claims not to be a morning person."

"Well, if I let a bad mood take over every time you annoy me in the morning, I'm never going to be happy again." She turns back, cracking a few eggs into a pan while stretching bacon out onto another.

Taking a seat at the kitchen island, I adjust myself, trying to push the needy erection away as I watch her. "I thought you were a vegetarian."

"I am. But you're not, and I'm making you breakfast."

"You don't have to do that. I woke you up by yelling at you." I scrub a palm over my face. "I can take care of myself."

"I'm sure you can. But I like taking care of people. It's kind of my thing." She smiles at me over her shoulder.

Fuck, she's pretty.

I sit in silence, drinking my coffee while she cooks. Truthfully, I wanted to be the one to cook her breakfast again. It seemed to impress her last time, and I got off on seeing her happily eat my food.

"Your curtains can stay. And the plants and your pillows and blanket. But you've got to get your naked men off my bookshelf."

Her back vibrates with a laugh. "Deal. Although, you could learn a thing or two from my book boyfriends. You do have that broody, mysterious thing going for you already though."

"And that devastatingly handsome thing," I add for her.

She places my breakfast in front of me, a knowing smile pulling at her lips. "You're all right, I guess."

Indy takes the seat next to me, and I'm not going to lie, this is nice. Sharing a meal with her, spending a morning together. Of course, I'd probably feel this way if it were anyone, but I'll admit it's nice to come home to someone for once.

"Speaking of boyfriends…" I begin with caution.

"Please tell me you straightened that out with your GM."

"Not exactly."

"Ryan!" She cocks her head in disappointment and the eye roll she gives me is pretty fucking adorable.

"He brought you up three separate times while we were gone. It's like he was testing me to see if it's real."

"Because it's not!" Indy hides her face in her palms. "This is a terrible idea. It's going to be ten times worse when he finds out you were lying to him later."

"He's not going to find out."

"Oh, he's not?" She laughs condescendingly. "He's going to take one look at us together and know it's a lie."

"I'm good at putting on an act in public. Please, Blue. Help me out here."

She pops a strawberry in her mouth and my attention falls on those pink lips. "For someone who likes to have control, it does sound awfully nice when you beg."

I shoot her a pointed glance.

"Can't you find someone else to be your fake girlfriend or here's a thought, get a real one!"

"I don't trust anyone, and I don't date. And don't even suggest I fake it while letting some poor girl believe it's real. I can't lead anyone on like that. But I'm not leading you on because this"—I motion between us—"will never be like that."

"Well, that's one way to make it clear." She pulls her attention away from mine. "I can't. I'm working."

"You're home for the fall banquet. All of Chicago's teams are home."

"I got a second job. I need to work that night."

"A second job? Doing what?"

"Rideshare. It works perfectly with my flight schedule. I can work when I'm home."

"Indy, no…that's…that could be dangerous."

"It's fine." She rolls her eyes. "I need the extra cash and I get to talk to people in my car all night. That sounds like a dream come true to me."

I can't get into all the reasons I think this is a terrible idea right now, so instead I offer, "I'll pay you whatever you'd make that night."

She scoffs. "I'm not letting you *pay* me to be your date. I'm not an escort. Jesus." She stands from her stool, leaving me.

Shit. Clearly the wrong thing to offer.

Circling her wrist, I stop her, softening my tone. "What can I do?"

"Nothing. It's not that I don't want to help you, but I can't. Besides needing to work, you're famous, Ryan. Like really fucking famous."

"And you're worried about making headlines." Of course, she is. She saw what my sister went through last year.

"No. Not at all, actually. I think that'd be fun, but I just got out of a six-year relationship. If he finds out—"

"Good. Let him think we're together. Fuck that guy."

"That's not what I mean."

A moment of silence lingers before her eyes drop to my hand encasing her wrist. She doesn't move for a moment, and I find myself using all my restraint to keep from circling the pad of my thumb against the soft skin of the inside.

She pulls away, and regret instantly floods me. What the fuck am I doing?

"I'm in my friends' wedding coming up and so is he." She takes a save-the-date card off the refrigerator, sliding it across the island. "I need to focus on finding a real date to this thing, not being someone's pretend girlfriend. I can't exactly be pictured with you for one night then take a random guy to this wedding. Anyone else will be a downgrade from NBA superstar Ryan Shay."

I hold a hand over my chest. "Blue, you flatter me."

"I'm serious, Ryan. I already feel like the laughingstock of my friends right now."

"What do you mean by that?"

"Nothing." She shakes it off, replacing the card on the fridge. "Look, I'm so fucked up from Alex, that I can't even think about being in another relationship right now or maybe ever, and I don't know that I'd be able to fake that. I'm sorry, I can't help you."

I don't know what causes me to say it. Maybe it's the downturn of her lips or her sad brown eyes that I'm afraid will start watering soon. Or maybe it's the thought of her ex assuming he's come out victorious, but it slips out of my mouth before I have time to fully think this through. "When's the wedding?"

"Why?" Suspicion laces her tone.

"Just answer the question."

"February second."

Pulling out my phone, I check my schedule. No games, home or away. I have practice, but I can get out of it.

"I'll be your date for the wedding."

She pauses before breaking into laughter, and it's deep and uncontrollable, coming from her core.

"What's so funny?"

"You." She sucks in a deep breath. "That was hilarious."

I wait for her to calm the fuck down. "I'm not joking."

Her smile is giddy and wide, the kind you can't pull off your face after a genuine laugh attack. "Yes, you were."

"Take the night off work. Be my date to the fall banquet, and I'll be your date to the wedding. Try your best to fake it. That way this arrangement is mutually beneficial. If your little shithead ex is taking a date, there's no way in hell I'm letting you go alone."

Her smile drops as realization hits her. "You're being serious right now. Ryan, it's one thing to lie to your GM, but it's an entirely different thing to lie to my childhood friends. They know me too well. They'll know we're faking it."

"Well, then it looks like we're going to have to practice. If all goes well, Ron and Caroline Morgan will be inviting us over for family dinners."

In a state of disbelief, Indy plops back in her stool next to me. "You're serious about this."

"Deadly."

She sits there, pink lips parted, and eyes zoned out. I can practically see the wheels spinning in that head of blonde hair.

"Any chance whatever the hell his name is, is a basketball fan?"

"Alex, and yes. He and his friends are huge basketball fans. He about lost it when he found out I was friends with your sister."

Typically, I despise the thought of anyone thinking Stevie is an avenue to me. My career has made my sister's life and friendships exponentially harder until she met blondie sitting next to me who didn't give two fucks about what my job was. But knowing Indy's ex is a fan of mine is going to make this fake boyfriend thing all the more enjoyable.

"Wipe that mischievous grin off your face." She playfully pushes my head away.

"I can't. This is going to be fun."

She tries to hide her smile as she rolls her eyes, but I know I've got her.

"Indy, please. You scratch my back, I'll scratch—"

"Ew. Don't say it like that."

"Fine. You do me a solid, I'll do you one. I'll be the best fake boyfriend you've ever had."

"My one and only."

"So, is that a yes?"

"That's a maybe." She pauses, rolling her fingertips along her temple. "I'll go to this banquet with you as a test run. Then we'll see about the rest."

"Deal."

"But we need some ground rules."

"Like?"

"Like what we're going to do once you inevitably fall for me. Do I let you down easy or do I exploit all the newfound emotions you're going to feel once you realize you're in love with me?"

A laugh bubbles out from me. "You don't have to worry about that. The emotional part or the falling-in-love part."

She sighs dramatically. "That's what they all say."

"So it's settled then. You're my fake girlfriend."

"Not so fast. If I'm going to even consider taking you to this wedding, I'm going to need to turn you into one of my book boyfriends first."

That earns a raised brow.

"Oh, come on. If we're going to be acting, we may as well go all in. Do you know how to flare your nostrils in anger?"

My breakfast almost comes back up. "What?"

"If you see me across the room, talking to another man, I need you to stare intently then flare your nostrils. Or grind your molars together and tic your jaw."

"Blue—"

"Do you know how to growl?"

"What?"

"Yeah, I don't really know what that's supposed to sound like, but every one of my book boyfriends is big into growling. Oh! And can you darken your eyes?"

"Darken my eyes?"

"Yeah. When you pretend to get angry or act really turned on, can you darken your eyes?"

"No, I can't fucking darken my eyes. What the hell are you reading?"

"Don't hate on my books. You could learn a thing or two from them. And they're much more entertaining than your shelves of masochism."

I can't hold back my laughter. "You think my reading books as a way to better myself is a form of self-inflicted pain?"

She turns her stool towards me. "Absolutely. Does anyone truly enjoy reading about that kind of stuff?"

"Don't hate on my self-improvement books."

"My books could qualify as your self-improvement books." She earns another pointed glance. "Okay, okay." Her hands go up in surrender. "But if you ever want to learn how to make a woman come three times in one chapter, I've got you covered."

It's been a while, but making a woman come sure as hell was never an issue.

She rounds the island once again and pulls out a notepad and pen from the drawer.

"We're making a list. No, we're making a *bucket* list. For you. If you can knock out this list, I'll take you to the wedding." She speaks as she writes. "Book Boyfriend How-To."

"I won't be that bad that I need a fucking list to become a passable boyfriend."

She ignores me, continuing a column of numbers down the left side of the notepad.

"Fine. Then you're getting a bucket list too."

"Me?" She laughs in disbelief. "I've been in a relationship practically my entire life. I think I've got this handled."

"Yeah, but do you have any idea how to be alone?"

Her face drops. "What?"

"When was the last time you were alone with no one else to take care of?"

"Why does that matter?"

"I'm not judging. I'm simply asking. When was the last time you had to think of only yourself?"

"That has nothing to do with our arrangement."

Indy's typically confident demeanor has shifted, showcasing her vulnerability. She looks away from me, brown eyes bouncing along the wall as she avoids my question.

"Ind—"

"Never. Okay? I've never been alone."

I figured as much. Between her constantly wanting company and her long-term relationship that seems more like a life-long thing and not only the six years it was official.

I hold my hand out with impatience until she reluctantly places a piece of paper and a spare pen in my hand. "I'm making you a bucket list too."

I hand it over after titling it and finally, a soft smile spreads across my roommate's mouth.

"Indy-pendent Woman 101." She raises a questioning brow.

"You know how much I love my self-help books."

She relaxes a bit which eases the tension around us.

"You can teach me how to be with someone, as long as I get to teach you how to be alone. Or at least how to put yourself first."

"Okay," she finally agrees. "That seems fair."

Individually, we work on our list for the other.

Mine is fairly simple—do everyday tasks alone. Go out to dinner by yourself. Go to a movie you've been wanting to see by yourself. Grocery shop and only buy the things you want to eat. Sleep without stacking pillows on the other side of the mattress to trick yourself into thinking you're not sleeping alone.

The last one might throw her off when she realizes I noticed that this morning when she opened her bedroom door, but maybe some accountability will be good for her.

"All done." She looks over her list with pride.

I slide mine across the kitchen island, trading with hers.

Indy's list for me starts fairly tame and reasonable: *slow dance together, get comfortable with casual touching, plan a date* which is finished with *in public* between parentheses.

"Were the parentheses really necessary?"

"Yes. Knowing you, you'd plan a dinner date at this very kitchen island, so we don't leave the house."

Okay, so she knows me a bit better than I assumed. I get back to my list—*show some jealousy*.

I have a strong suspicion that showcasing jealousy won't be the issue —keeping it under wraps will be.

The last and final point on the list—*kiss me*.

"Indy, the last one—"

"Is a non-negotiable. I'm not showing up at this wedding and you never once touch or kiss me. It can be a peck on the lips for all I care, but this whole thing won't be believable without a little PDA."

I shake my head. "I don't feel comfortable faking intimacy."

"Ryan, it's just a kiss. It means nothing."

"It does to me. I won't fake that part."

This is fucking embarrassing, a twenty-seven-year-old man refusing a stunning woman the kiss she's asking for. But I can't do it for show. That's not me.

"Okay," she softly resigns. "No kissing."

I break eye contact, unable to look at her. "Thank you."

She clears her throat. "How did you know about the pillows?"

Glancing up, I find Indy staring at the list I made her.

Throwing a thumb over my shoulder in the direction of her room, I tell her, "I saw your bed."

"I haven't slept alone in six years. I have a hard time with an empty bed. I do it in hotels too."

"You can cross it off." I reach out, attempting to take my list back.

"No." She holds the paper out of my reach. "You're right. I need to figure it out. It's my life now, sleeping alone. I should get used to it without having to make a wall of pillows in order to trick myself."

She takes both our lists and hangs them on the refrigerator, next to our leasing agreement. The three hand-scribbled papers act as the strangest display of our bizarre relationship.

Cocking her head, she examines them. "Heads-up, Shay, I'm an expensive girlfriend. Fake or not. I can't help it."

"Then I guess it's a good thing I've got money."

She playfully smacks the counter. "That's what I like to hear!"

I grab her empty plate along with my own and begin washing them in the sink.

"Do you ever let your dishes sit for a minute? You don't have to do them the second you're done using them. It's okay to relax, Ryan."

"I like an organized space."

"No shit, Sherlock." She stays silent for a moment, and I can sense her watching me. "Why *don't* you date? You could have any girl you want. You've got that sexy protective thing going on. Plus, you cook and clean."

Stilling, I pause with a plate in my hand, the water rushing over it. Indy has had no problems telling me exactly how she feels about me but hearing that she thinks I'm sexy hits differently. Like because we're starting to know each other and we live together, the words hold more weight. But that could be me overanalyzing the girl opposite the kitchen island whose company I might enjoy more than I let on.

"I don't have time right now. I have more important things I need to get done first."

"So, eventually you will?"

"Maybe after I retire. I'm not sure. I haven't thought too much about it."

Lie. Bald-faced lie. I've contemplated this decision for years. If I ever open myself up in that way again, it'll be well after I'm retired. It'll be when I'm just a footnote in the history books. It'll be once I can leave my house and not feel like a zoo animal on display. It'll be once the only thing to gain from me, is me.

But that's *if* I open myself up again.

"I hope you do," she says softly. "You'd be good to someone. You'd make someone happy. I can tell."

The untrusting part of me is screaming with the hidden meaning of her words. *Because of how much money you make.* Or *you're so well-known any girl would love to be on your arm.* But there's something about the kind smile Indy is wearing as she watches me do the dishes that makes me want to believe my gut. That she means I, as a man, as a normal everyday person would make someone happy, and I haven't let that thought invade my mind in a long time.

# 8
# Indy

**Roomie:** *Do you have a dress for tomorrow night? These things are kind of fancy.*

Clearly Ryan doesn't know me very well yet because I have an outfit for every possible life event.

Wedding guest? Check.

Funeral? Check.

Formal fundraiser with Chicago's pro teams? Check.

An afternoon spent at a bookstore where I'm casually browsing the shelves, appearing effortless and academic. When all the sudden, a handsome man down the aisle makes eye contact, shyly smiles, then holds up the same book that's in my hands. Specific, but yes, I have an outfit for that too.

I'd love to buy a new dress, but I'm working with a budget these days.

**Me:** *I'm sure I have something in my closet.*

**Roomie:** *And here I was about to offer my expensive girlfriend the opportunity to take my credit card out for a spin.*

**Me:** *Now that you say it, I'm pretty sure my entire wardrobe got lost in the move.*

**Roomie:** *That's weird because your bedroom door still won't close thanks to all the clothes sitting on the floor.*

**Me:** *Oh, that's where it all went! Lucky you, I'm covered for this one.*

**Roomie:** *Great. And Blue, I've got to tell you something.*

Oh God. What's wrong now? My mind is racing with the endless possibilities. *Something happened to Stevie. You need to move out. I found someone else I would rather have as my fake girlfriend.*

That last one has crossed my mind more than a few times this week, that Ryan will change his mind and back out of our deal. Because if I'm being entirely honest with myself, I want this to work. I might even consider myself desperate for this to work thanks to the revolving thought of showing up stag to Maggie's wedding and running into Alex with *her* on his arm.

***Me:*** *???*

***Roomie:*** *I killed your flowers.*

My chest deflates with an odd sense of relief. He really is dramatic, but I'll play into it.

***Me:*** *Ryan!*

***Roomie:*** *I tried! I really tried to keep them alive, but I think I watered them too much and drowned them. Then when I went down to the flower stand today to buy the same ones in hopes you wouldn't notice, they didn't have them. So I bought you some called Black-eyed Susan? Which is the weirdest fucking thing to call a flower.*

My cheeks are sore from the splitting grin on my face. The idea of Ryan Shay, NBA superstar, leaving his apartment and facing the streets of Chicago to replace my flowers which he tried so hard to keep alive that he *over watered* them is beyond charming. As if I were a child whose parents wanted to protect my feelings and thought I wouldn't recognize a new goldfish in my fish tank every week.

***Roomie****: Sorry.*

***Me:*** *That's okay. I like Black-eyed Susans too. Thank you for trying.*

***Roomie:*** *Heading out for warm-ups. See you at home.*

I pull my book off the nightstand, needing a fictional boyfriend to distract me from how much I liked hearing *see you at home* from my very real roommate.

This is the third book I've read this week and I couldn't tell you what any of the heroes were supposed to look like because somewhere along the line, in my mind they all end up being 6'3", with light brown skin, ocean eyes, and a particular knack for home organization.

I don't know what's going on. Yes, I'm attracted to Ryan. I've always been attracted to Ryan, but he's infiltrated my mind this week more than he should.

Maybe it's the prospect of pretending to be together or living side by side that's causing these unrealistic fantasies to pop into my mind, but the likeliest culprit is that hug in the kitchen from last week when I felt what he's packing down below.

He was hard. I was wrapped around him, and he was hard.

I'm just pent-up and frustrated that Alex is the last man I've been with. The *only* man I've been with. I haven't gotten laid in almost seven months and that's all this is. I'm living with a stunning man, athletic, tall, and knows his way around the kitchen. It would be stranger if I *didn't* have these thoughts.

It'll pass. I just need to figure out how the hell to disassociate sex from love. I've never done it before, but I am so depleted, so damaged still that my heart has nothing left to offer. All the while my body is reminding me something is wrong. That I'm twenty-seven years old and haven't been able to orgasm in seven months. I feel broken, in more ways than one, and I'm almost desperate to prove to myself that I'm not.

A normal night game on the West Coast means a very late flight home for us tonight. Ryan is on the East Coast, so his game starts in fifteen minutes and suddenly the idea of watching sweat drip down his body on my television screen is the only possible solution to pass the time until I need to get off this bed and into my work uniform.

A quick search pulls it up on the TV in my room. Number five is in the corner of the court during warm-ups, two basketballs in his hold, each one bouncing against the hardwood with speed and accuracy. Slight flexes of his hands change their direction. Between his legs. Across one another. Behind his back. Long slender fingers rule every movement.

Precision. Power. Control.

The Ryan Shay wearing a Devils jersey is much like the one I live with. Governing of his space, not letting anyone close enough to affect him. But what if someone came along and swiped one of those balls out of his hand. It'd make no sense. He's simply warming up on his own, away from any other players. But I wonder if he'd get upset at the loss of control, kind of like how he wanted to yell at me for switching his apartment up on him.

He was so wound up and frustrated, but I was able to calm him down. A jolt of victory flooded my veins as we sat and ate breakfast together, when he hugged me, when he offered to water my flowers while I travel for work. And at the end of it all, he let me leave a bit of color in his stark apartment and I'm almost positive he didn't hate having me there.

Five minutes into his game and I can't keep my eyes off him. I knew he was good from the reputation he carries, but he's like a god to some of these fans. The Boston fans outweigh the Chicago ones, but the majority of those wearing red and black are sporting his last name.

He's amazing. Graceful. Composed. Even when plays don't go his way or calls aren't made properly, he keeps his emotions locked in. He looks small on the screen, but his talent and ability tower over the competition.

It's sexy as hell.

This is the type of control I like. Everyone on the court bends to him. He creates the plays. He makes the calls. He's in charge and I can't look away.

He's fouled on a breakaway, but he still makes the layup, putting him at the free-throw line for one.

Calm, cool, and collected he makes his way to the free-throw line and when he lifts his jersey to wipe the sweat off his brow, I'm anything but calm, cool, or collected. His chest heaves as he regains his breath. Sweat drips down, cascading in ripples until they fall prey to the crevices of his taut ab muscles. A spattering of dark hair dusting under his navel directs my daydreams to imagine where it leads.

The way his stomach muscles contract, quick and sharp, I can't help but picture the way they'd tighten, hovering over me. The way his arms might quiver as he held himself up. Would he be able to hold on to his precious control? Or would he let me take it from him, becoming wild and unruly?

My curtains are closed, my room is dark. The only light is the glow from the television. No one would know. Maybe one very much-needed release will get me to stop lusting over the man across the hall. Maybe the overwhelming attraction will go away as quickly as it came on.

Sliding my fingers down, I slip them under my cotton shorts. I'm hot already. My middle finger grazes my clit and it's swollen and needy and I'm wet. So goddamn wet because of my roommate. Circling, I imagine my fingers are his. The ones that flex and move and have so much control he runs an entire game with those fingers. With those hands, commanding and powerful. The way they overwhelmed my body when he hugged me. The way I wished he would've slid them lower, cupping my ass. The way it would've felt for him to lift me up, my legs wrapping around him as he carried me to his bed. How heavy his body would be on top of mine. How solid his legs would feel, pinning my own to the mattress.

*Oh God, this feels good.*

His body, shining with sweat. His blue-green eyes dilated and dark, crazed. My hands running the length of his back, my fingers digging into his skin and into his hair. His blonde hair falling over his eyes, sticking to his forehead.

*Wait. What?*

Ocean eyes are replaced with brown ones. Calloused fingertips are replaced with soft hands that have never worked a day outside of an office. Blonde hair replaces Ryan's chestnut fade, and my body is replaced with hers.

I'm no longer here. I'm standing in the doorway, reliving the worst day of my life. Him inside of her while on our bed. The way she cried his name—the name that belonged to me. His pace, his tempo, how lost he was in the moment that he didn't hear the front door open, didn't see me standing there watching him. How she fucking came and neither of them knew I was there. I was cemented in place, in shock and disbelief while I watched the only man I have ever loved make someone else come.

It's gone. The moment has passed. There's no possible way to get back in the right mindset to get myself off. He's ruined this, just like he ruined us, our future, our history, and just how he's ruined every orgasm I've chased over the last seven months.

Every time I'm close, that picture invades my imagination and I'm done. I can't do it. It leaves as quickly as the moment comes and I haven't gotten off in seven goddamn months because of him.

# 9

# Ryan

"What the fuck is a meet cute?" I take a seat on the couch in my living room, projecting my voice to be heard through Indy's bedroom wall and her blaring music.

"It's the way a couple meets. It's usually a charming story about an accidental run-in or how two dogs wound their leashes up around their owners' legs, forcing them to meet face-to-face."

I'm thankful Indy's in her room with the door closed so she can't see the slight tug on my lips. Custom-fitted suit, cuff links, and a Rolex look a bit out of place paired with the stupid smile I'm wearing over my twenty-seven-year-old roommate referencing *101 Dalmatians*.

"I guess if anyone asks how we met, we tell the truth," I decide. "You came to my apartment crying then drooled over how amazing I looked as I stood shirtless in my kitchen. Then you threw up all over my shoes. Is that cute enough for you?"

One tune shifts to another, but in the break between songs, Indy asks, "Have I reminded you of how much you suck today?"

"Only twice."

There's a subtle comfortability between us now, most likely because I have to trust her enough to fake our relationship and vice versa. Unluckily for us, we've only seen each other in passing this week between her travel schedule and mine, so we're left nailing down our relationship story five minutes before leaving for the fall banquet.

She projects her voice past the wall. "How about you saw your sister's best friend from afar and instantly knew she was the one. I continually rejected you, because of course I did. But you followed me around like a lost puppy until I caved and gave you a pity date."

"So much for a realistic storyline."

"I think most people would buy it." Her bedroom door opens. "What do you think?"

Lilac-painted toes and white strappy heels are the first thing I see as she steps into the living room. My admiring eye trails the never-ending path of her golden legs, though only one is fully on display tonight thanks to the slit falling dangerously high on her thigh. Shimmering satin paints her body in a bright pink, and I don't understand the mechanics of it all, but the dress stays perfectly in place by a single strap across one shoulder.

I wonder how quickly it'd pool at her feet, revealing what's underneath, if it slipped off that slope.

"Ryan."

"Hmm." I force my eyes up to meet hers.

"I asked, what do you think?" She holds her hands out, gesturing to herself.

*Jesus Christ, get it together.*

Nodding, I stand from the couch, smoothing out my suit. "You look lovely, Blue."

"You look lovely, too."

My chest heaves. "I was going for intimidating, regal, and suave."

She takes a step towards me, and between her natural height and the added inches from her heels she almost meets me eye to eye. "We'll work on that for next time."

It takes all my willpower to keep my hands at my side when all they want to do is rest on those hips. I can only imagine how cool the satin would feel against my palms, how small she would feel under my touch. She's utter perfection, feminine and beautiful, but we're roommates and she's my sister's best friend, and the only touching that should be done is while prying eyes are watching us. *Only* while prying eyes are watching us.

Her matching lilac fingernails find my tie as she straightens me out and I can't help but watch her work. Her eyelids are shimmering, her cheeks are painted rose, and her lashes are darker than usual. Maybe it's my angle, but they're the perfect frame for her whiskey brown eyes as she fixates on my tie.

"You did a good job on your makeup."

Her head snaps up, brows creased in confusion.

I motion towards my own face. "Your makeup. It looks pretty on you."

"That's a weird thing to say."

"Why?"

"Because you're supposed to say you like me natural or something to that extent. That's the typical opinion of the male species."

"Well, what can I say? I'm not like other guys."

She catches onto the mocking tone of the cliché phrase as she rolls her eyes and releases a subtle laugh. "You're funny sometimes, Shay."

"Do you like your makeup? Did you spend time on it?"

She keeps her stare on my tie and not on me. "Yes."

"Exactly. So, I think you should know you did a good job on it."

Those rose-painted cheeks flame. "Thank you."

"How tall are you?" I keep my words low because she's only inches from my lips.

"Five-nine, and no, I'm not going to change into shorter heels."

"Why would I ask you to do that?"

She's done straightening my tie, but her hands are lingering, fingers pretending to work. "Because I'm only a couple inches shorter than you right now."

"I don't mind."

Looking down, I watch those flaming cheeks ignite once again. At this rate, I should've warned her not to wear blush at all tonight.

"We should go." She takes off to the door, grabbing her tiny purse on the way.

"Your jacket," I remind her.

She turns with attitude, showing off that shiny pink dress. "I'm not taking one. Beauty is pain, and this outfit needs its moment."

It took the entire drive for Indy to stop shivering thanks to the short walk from my apartment to the town car. I offered her my jacket, but she refused, claiming if she's going to be photographed on my arm then it's going to be in this dress. I don't blame her because *goddamn, this dress,* but I'm going to come off like an asshole allowing my date to freeze in the Chicago evening temperatures.

"You ready?" I ask her as we pull up to the swanky hotel hosting the fall banquet. And though the question is directed at Indy, I'm internally asking myself the same thing.

Besides the favor-date last year, I haven't been photographed with a woman since I moved to Chicago, and now I'm regretting pulling Indy into this madness. My life is forever on display, and I hate it. Anonymity is rare and I'm about to take hers away.

"Yeah, I think so." Her words are breathy, fogging the back window as her eyes stay glued to the hoard of photographers right outside.

An image of Stevie flashes through my mind. I couldn't protect her from the scrutiny of the press last spring, and I vividly remember the mental toll it took on her. She was a normal girl and I kept her out of the limelight the best I could, but once word got out that Evan Zanders had a girlfriend, her life was upended for weeks.

And I'm intentionally about to do that to her closest friend.

Although, I doubt speculation over my dating life would be as big of a deal as it was for Zanders. I'm not a playboy. I'm not flashy. I've never flaunted my single life the way he used to, but it's still too risky.

"Harold, turn around," I project to my driver. "Back home, please."

Indy's head snaps to me. "What are you doing?"

"I can't let you go out there with me." Fidgeting, I run my palms down my thighs as I wait for Harold to pull out of the lineup and get us back home.

Indy's hand settles on mine in an easy move, unthinking. As if we've touched and comforted one another hundreds of times in the past. "What's wrong?"

I stare at where we're connected, her hand small in comparison to mine. And even though she's big and bold in spirit, she's soft. She has feelings. A lot of them.

"You're a normal person, Blue."

Her lip quirks. "Very observant tonight, Shay."

"Being normal is special. I won't be the reason you lose your privacy. Especially over something as trivial as a fake date."

My driver turns the wheel to get back on the main road.

"Don't you dare drive." Indy's words are harsh and commanding, causing Harold's nervous stare to meet mine in the rearview mirror.

He's been my driver for four years and I've never seen him so quickly shift loyalties than in this moment as the blonde at my side shoots him commands.

She turns to me, that sinful slit inching its way over and taunting those golden legs. "I get that you want to be left alone, and you're worried about me." She pats my chest. "Cute, by the way, but I like people. I'm excited about this. You're not forcing me. I *want* to go."

"Indy—"

"What are you worried about? Sure, there might be a few headlines and my name might get released, but who cares? It'll last a day, maybe two. When they deep dive into my life they'll find out I go to trivia, I cross-stitch in my free time, and I read dirty books. No one cares about me. I'm not you, Ryan. It's *you* they worship. So, please, let me go be a social butterfly because I'm starved for attention."

Her eager brown eyes lighten with humor.

"You cross-stitch?"

"Proudly."

"You grandma." She smiles at that, matching the now relaxed grin on my lips. "Are you sure?"

"I didn't shave and moisturize every inch of my body to go back home. Yes, I'm sure."

Making eye contact once again, I offer a small nod of approval to Harold.

Once we pull up, my door on the street side is opened. I step out, rebuttoning my suit as flashes illuminate the dark sky. My name is yelled, cameras are blinding, but I stay on task. Rounding the car to Indy's side, I stop the doorman when his hand finds the handle. "I've got it."

He gives a polite nod and steps back with his hands folded behind him.

I open Indy's door by only a fraction, giving myself a moment to check on her and make sure she's truly okay with this before subjecting her to the entire world. She's wearing an eager smile on those heart-shaped lips and her brown eyes are shining with excitement.

I dread these nights when I find them on my calendar, and she couldn't be more stoked.

The photographers and paparazzi behind me are relentlessly trying to get a shot, but I'm not worried about impressing or convincing them. We aren't doing this for them. I just need to make sure we're on our A-game by the time we inevitably run into Ron Morgan.

Indy puts her hand in mine, one white heel finding the ground as she glides out of the car with so much grace and polish, those previous notions and lack of concern go up in flames.

Because with how perfect she looks tonight, no one is going to believe she's mine.

Cameras explode with light as we step onto the carpet leading to the hotel. Indy's fingers link with mine in the most natural way, but I don't know how the fuck to do this. I didn't think this through. Typically, I find myself sprinting to get inside and away from the fanfare, but I can't exactly hurry Indy along when she's wearing those heels and commanding everyone's attention the way she is now.

She floats along as I follow, stiff as a board and uncomfortable beyond belief. Clearly, the girl is stunning, but the perfect show she's putting on tonight is different than the version I get at home.

I'm not sure how to take that.

"Ryan Shay, a photo!"

"Over here!"

"Ryan, over here!"

My date stops on the carpet, pulling me to a halt with her.

"What are you doing?" I ask.

She smiles at the crowd, speaking behind her teeth. "Loosen up and pose with me."

I turn towards the collection of photographers as she puts a hand on my chest. "I don't pose," I say quietly enough for no one else to hear.

"You want to sell this? Well, running inside doesn't exactly sell this."

She's right. Ron already thinks I'm lying. If I bring a date who I claim is my girlfriend and only show her off for a few moments in front of him, he'll know.

Standing stiffly, I smile, allowing Indy to lean into me.

"Put your arm around me."

"No."

"Ryan," she warns behind that sparkling smile. And how does she speak so clearly behind her teeth? She should be a damn ventriloquist.

"You're not going to burst into flames from touching a woman. Put your goddamn arm around me."

Inhaling deeply, I swing my arm behind her, placing my palm at a respectful height—on her shoulder blade.

"Lower."

Lower shoulder blade.

I can feel the annoyance flaring off her body as she reaches behind her, finding my hand and curving it around her waist. She presses her body into my chest and sells it.

How is she so fucking good at this?

"Kiss me," she quietly mutters. "Cheek. Forehead. I don't care."

"Absolutely not."

"Kiss—"

I hold my hand out to the crowd in a swift wave. "Thank you, guys. Have a great night."

Keeping her hand in mine, I pull Indy towards the hotel, needing to get the fuck out of here.

She sighs. "We have so much work to do."

*One more hour.*

*Put on the bullshit Ryan Shay smile for one more hour. Be basketball's shining golden boy for one more hour. All eyes are on me for one more hour, then I can go home and relax.*

I've internally repeated those sentences for the last twenty minutes as Indy and I worked the room, greeting season ticket holders, upper management, and saying hello to guys I know who play for the other major league teams in the city.

Another random man pats my back as he walks by. "Great game last night, son." I've seen him at events, he's a wealthy fan, and I'm sure he paid a pretty penny to be at this one tonight.

A small tip of my head. "Thank you, sir."

Indy turns to stand directly in front of me once he's out of earshot. "Why are you so tense? You're allowed to smile, you know." She puts her hands on both shoulders, pushing them down. "Chill out and let's have fun." Her eyes are sparkling with excitement as she takes in the room around us.

"I don't *chill out* when I'm at these kinds of things."

"Why not?"

*Because I don't trust anyone.*

But before I can answer, ironically, one of the few people I do trust catches my attention across the room, making his way to my date and me.

"Ryan Shay!" he says in excitement, putting his hand in mine and swinging his other over my shoulder. "I can't believe I caught you at one of these things before you slipped out."

"Good to see you, Kai."

Kai Rhodes is a good guy and one hell of a baseball player. Starting pitcher for the Windy City Warriors, Kai signed one of the biggest contracts in MLB history last season when his free agency brought him to Chicago. We share the same agent who got him set up with an apartment in my building, and I can't explain exactly why I like him so much, but I do.

There's not a bad bone in his body, and I think my soft spot for him is due to the massive shift his life has taken over the last couple months and how well he's stepped up and handled his responsibilities. The guy could be out partying every night, getting away with any and every thing, but instead, he's at home taking care of his son as a single dad.

"And who is this?" Kai's eyes linger on the woman at my side. Not in a creepy way, but in a respectful *you're one of the most beautiful women I've had the pleasure to lay eyes on* way.

I said I liked him, but if he doesn't take his eyes off her soon, I have no issue retracting my statement.

Unfortunately, we're close enough friends that I can't exactly call dibs by referring to Indy as my girlfriend.

"This is my roommate, Indy." I gesture towards her, possessively keeping a hand on the small of her back.

He takes her hand, shaking it, his eyes twinkling like he just found the future mother of his child. "I'm Kai, but you can call me Ace."

"Ace, huh? What's with the nickname?"

"Always been the best pitcher on the team. I've got good hands. The right touch. In case you were curious."

And those *good hands* are still holding on to my fake girlfriend's.

"Okay, that seems like enough of a handshake there, buddy." I separate them, putting my body slightly in front of Indy's and out of his eyeline.

Kai is basically a golden fucking retriever with his obvious good looks, black-rimmed glasses, and charming smiles. I don't need him showing Indy those smiles especially when I don't give her enough of mine.

He chuckles. "Got it."

And it's clear he does. What exactly, even I'm not sure, but he knows she's off-limits.

"How long are you here?"

"Just long enough to cover my contractual obligations." He shakes his head. "I gotta get home to release the nanny."

"I thought you fired the last one?"

"I did. I hired another one, who I'll probably fire soon too."

"You have a kid?" Indy's voice bursts with excitement.

"A son," Kai beams. "Max. He's eight months old." Pulling out his phone like the proud dad he is, he scrolls through the endless pictures.

I don't blame him. Max is one of the cutest kids I know.

"You don't have a kid. You have a *baby*." Indy's tone switches to soft and sweet, her smile beaming as she looks through Kai's phone.

"Yeah," he sighs. "And he's looking for a mom."

"Jesus Christ." I huff out a laugh. "Try to be a little more fucking subtle why don't you."

The 6'4" baseball player wears a not so innocent grin.

Indy's brows instantly furrow. "Where's his mom?"

And because I know how emotional she is, she's about two seconds away from glass-covered eyes, knowing there's a baby boy out there without his mom around.

Kai pats me on the shoulder. "Your *roommate* here will be happy to fill you in, I'm sure. I've gotta sneak out of here. How much longer you've got?"

We both look around the room. "An hour at best."

"You're better than me." Kai turns back to the woman at my side. "Indy, it was a pleasure to meet you. Make sure our boy over here has some fun, will ya?"

And with that, I watch Kai slip out the side door without being noticed and I couldn't be more envious of the guy.

"Ryan Shay, do you have an actual *friend*?" I don't respond to the dig but notice Indy watching his back. "So, what's with baseball's Clark Kent?"

Dark Hair. Dark-rimmed glasses. Tall. He fits the bill, not to mention he's a nice guy. I look for any interest in Indy's expression, but she just seems genuinely curious.

"He and I share an agent. He moved here last spring then found out his ex had his baby when she dropped him off at Kai's doorstep and skipped town."

"Wait, Max really doesn't have a mom?"

I roll my eyes. "Don't let him fool you. Kai is happy to be doing this without her. And Max could have any mom he wants. Multiple moms, but Kai is protective. He's pretty much the nicest fucking guy in the world as long as you're not the current nanny. He's firing them every other day, but other than that, they're good."

"What the hell kind of woman could leave their baby boy like that?" Indy's chin trembles before she looks over my shoulder and sucks in a sharp breath. "Hold that thought. It's showtime, boyfriend."

Her forced smile beams to who I'd assume is my GM. Inhaling a deep breath, I turn around.

"Mr. Morgan." I hold out my hand for his.

"Shay." My General Manager shakes my hand before motioning to the woman at his side. "You know my wife, Caroline."

"Of course. Good to see you, Mrs. Morgan." I turn to Indy with my hand hovering, not sure what amount of touching is appropriate or believable, so I end up patting her upper arm a couple of times like a middle schooler afraid to catch cooties. "This is my girlfriend, Indy."

Indy stares at me blankly and we don't know each other too well, but her look is unmistakable. *You suck at this. You have no idea what you're doing*. But then there's the Indy spin on it and I internally add, *are you really that afraid of girls*?

She forces a smile back on her face, turning back and holding her hand out to shake Caroline's. "So lovely to meet you."

"You as well."

I've always liked Caroline. She's sweet and brings Ron's intimidating edge down a few notches. Guy turns into putty when she's around.

"I love your dress," Indy compliments.

"I feel the same about yours. This pink is so much fun."

The two women fall into comfortable conversation, which I attempt to focus and join in on, but I'm too distracted by the penetrating stare coming from the man who signs my paychecks.

Ron watches me before his eyes bounce to the gaping space between my date and me. Clearly, he's not impressed, and my body language is practically screaming that I've never touched this woman outside of a hug or small innocent gesture.

Is it hot? It feels really fucking hot in here. Pulling at my collar, I try to loosen it, but Ron's disapproving gaze is burning me up. This little stunt isn't even about faking it in order to get him to approve of me anymore. It's about getting out of this colossal lie I created, unscathed.

The man spends a good amount of the team's budget on my salary and I've yet to bring him to the playoffs. How much longer is he willing to invest in me? At what point is he going to gamble with a younger guy who might be a diamond in the rough, but cost him a whole lot less? If he finds out this is some elaborate scheme to get him to like me, I can't imagine that option being too far off.

Indy's smile is radiant and warm as she converses with Caroline, and she doesn't look at me or break away from the conversation she's having, but she pulls my hand away from my collar and laces her fingers through mine, holding my hand.

"Did you go to the game last night?" Caroline asks.

"I couldn't." Indy crosses her other arm over her body, holding my single hand with both of hers. She's effortless and luminous and so fucking good at this. "I was traveling for work, but I watched it on TV. He's amazing."

Wait. She watched from her hotel room?

"Do you enjoy your job? Flying the Raptors around. That sounds fun."

"I love my job, but when I'm on the road, I miss home." She smiles up at me and it's soft and loving, but I know it's not real. I know this is all pretend, but fuck, I'd be lying if I said that didn't do something to my insides.

"Any chance you're in town next Thursday?" Caroline asks the woman at my side. "We were supposed to have dinner with Ethan and Annie this weekend, but last minute, Ron was invited to speak at his alma mater. We're headed to Hanover tomorrow, but if you two can join us next week, that'd be wonderful."

"Hanover? As in Hanover, New Hampshire?" Indy asks, turning towards Ron. "Did you attend Dartmouth?"

His brows lift. "I did."

She nods approvingly. "You seem like an Ivy League man."

There's a faint, almost indistinguishable tug at Ron's lips, but for a man like him, it's equivalent to a full-tooth grin.

Whatever Indy wants, she can have. I can't even begin to list all the ways I owe her for tonight.

"That was my dream school."

My neck almost snaps with how quickly I turn to look at her before remembering I'm her live-in boyfriend who should know these things.

"It's a tough school to get into. Low acceptance rate."

"Yes, that's true." Indy's radiant smile falters, but she recovers so quickly I may have imagined it.

At this moment, I'm realizing how much I don't know about this woman and how much I wish I did.

She turns back to Caroline. "I'm sorry. Huge conversation shift. I *am* in town next Thursday and we would absolutely love to have dinner with you two."

There are no scowls or hard lines on Ron's face besides the ones permanently etched in his skin from a constant state of disappointment. But this is the softest I've seen him look and it's because of Indy.

Though, she is being more formal than the chaotic girl I found crying in my apartment, and I hope she knows she doesn't have to fake more than our relationship here.

"She's lovely, Shay," Ron says to me and it's the first time I'm involved in the conversation.

Awareness floods me. Indy has been carrying this with grace and confidence, meanwhile I've been standing as stiff as a board, my fingers splayed wide with tension while Indy's are effortlessly curled around mine.

"How did you two meet?" he continues.

Shit. We talked about this. We knew this would come up, but we never decided.

"We—" Indy and I begin at the same time, but I pause and let her continue because I trust her enough to get us through this.

"We were introduced through his sister."

Perfect. Simple. To the point.

She looks up at me and I can only hope she can read my appreciation.

"Oh, I see that look," Caroline mews. "You two lovebirds. There's more to the story, isn't there?"

She has no fucking clue.

"There is," I tell her, clearing my throat because it's the first time I've really spoken in God knows how long. I slide my arm around Indy's waist, pulling her into my side, and when I speak, I keep my eyes locked on hers. "But we like to keep the details between us."

Indy's brown eyes shine with relief as I finally get one thing right tonight.

"You two are utterly adorable. Indy, I'm looking forward to seeing you at dinner next week. We're doing something a little different."

"I can't wait. It was so wonderful to meet you." She leans her head on my shoulder.

"Shay." Ron puts his hand out to shake mine and a bit of that disbelief and distrust has washed away. He's still skeptical, clearly, but he seems as if he's questioning the possibility of this being legitimate instead of outright believing it's a lie.

As they walk away, my chest deflates with a much-needed exhale. "You were incredible, Blue."

"And you were terrible. We have so much work ahead of us if I'm going to even consider taking you to that wedding."

"You know you can be yourself while doing this, right? You don't have to be so poised and perfect. They'll like you regardless."

She pops her shoulders. "I'm used to playing the doting girlfriend who always has the right thing to say. That was almost second nature."

"I can't believe you're still here." Ethan sets another glass of champagne in front of his wife, Annie, as he speaks to me. "This is the longest I've ever seen you at a work event."

"That's because he's got a stunning girlfriend to show off." Annie motions her flute in Indy's direction.

I find Indy by the bar, holding court, surrounded by a few of the guys from the Raptors. She's wearing that infectious smile, those kind brown eyes, that confident body-language. And I'm suddenly aware that she works with these men every time she's on the road.

God, they must love her.

Indy wasn't lying. She really is a social butterfly and I find myself a bit envious at her ability to be so open.

"It's not real, Ann."

"I know, I know," she brushes off her husband. "But a woman could dream. Imagine Ryan having a real girlfriend. I'd be in heaven having someone at team events instead of the flavors of the week the rest of your teammates rotate through."

"Sorry to crush your dreams, Annie." I smile into my whiskey glass, taking a swig. "Speaking of staying out late, you two are out past ten. Parents gone wild."

"We have an overnight babysitter."

"And a hotel," Ethan adds with a suggestive brow wag.

"So, daughter number four in nine months. Got it."

"Here's hoping." Ethan holds up his beer bottle in a cheers.

Annie smacks him in the chest. "Absolutely not."

"Ry, have you planned team dinner yet?" Ethan asks.

I lean back in my chair, casually sipping my whiskey. Of everyone on my team, Ethan is my closest friend and the guy I feel most myself around.

"What do you mean?"

"Team dinner," he repeats. "Team captain plans team dinner every other month. And we're almost a month into the season."

"Wait. That's a thing? I thought we went to your house every other month because your mom is an amazing cook."

Annie and Ethan share a laugh. Ethan's parents came to the states before he was born, and his mom would cook up a storm of authentic Korean dishes every month for the team to gather around their table and share a meal. She even taught me how to prepare my own kimchi last season. It's the one outing I genuinely look forward to.

"No, man. That's part of your duties as the new team captain."

"Well, fuck. Can't we keep doing it at your house? I need Mrs. Jeong's cooking."

"I think it'd go a long way with the guys if you planned something yourself. It'd be good for them to see who you are outside of basketball."

"What are you talking about? I've played with some of these guys for four years." I find a group of my teammates gathered around a high-top table, shooting the shit, and laughing with each other. "Then there's Dom who I've played with since college. They know me."

"They know the best point guard in the league. They know the guy who holds the record for the most assists in a single season, but they don't know anything about *you*. You're in charge now, man. You've got to connect with them off the court."

"You sound like Ron."

"Well, maybe he wasn't that far off. You want to prove him wrong? Team dinner is your first opportunity."

The idea of allowing fourteen guys into my apartment for dinner causes my skin to crawl. Ethan has been over a few times and Dom has stopped by here and there, but the rest of the guys, they haven't been in my space. I haven't allowed them to.

No one besides Indy.

"You're still welcome to come over anytime for my mother-in-law's cooking," Annie offers. "And bring that cute fake girlfriend of yours when you do."

"That secret stays between us three," I remind them. "No one else can know. I can't risk one of the guys slipping up and Ron finding out."

Annie motions as if she were sealing her lips and locking them up without saying a word.

# 10

# Indy

The bartender slides me a gin and tonic as I scan the room for Ryan or Stevie or Zanders or Rio. Or just about anyone really. I like company, crave connection. I truly am a social butterfly, but that's mostly because I've never been on my own and at twenty-seven, I'm afraid to learn that I don't know how.

Mr. and Mrs. Morgan walk by, offering a wave and I hope they don't find Ryan's absence suspicious.

If I were either of them, I'd call us out on his pathetic display of a fake relationship. Ryan was so awkward with me. His big moment of PDA was essentially a high five to my upper arm. What the hell was that?

If the beginning of the evening was any indication, I thought we were going to crush it. When I stepped out of my room, Ryan's eyes hooded, his lips parted. He spoke softly, intimately as I fixed his tie that was perfectly straight before I had ever pretended it wasn't.

In that moment, he looked like he wanted me, but his acting fell by the wayside as soon as we stepped out of the car.

I, on the other hand, felt far too natural holding his hand, leaning into his chest. I'm praying the show I put on was as convincing for Ryan as it was for his GM.

Because the truth is, I liked it.

It's a frustrating awareness to have when I realize how disloyal I feel. I loved Alex my entire life, and now for the first time ever, I'm enjoying the company of another man. Alex can fuck someone else and yet, here I am, still so loyal to that relationship and the love I had for him, that a pang of guilt flashes through me simply from enjoying another man's company.

"There she is," Stevie says, sliding into the space beside me, leaning her elbows back on the bar.

And just then, I find her twin across the room as he interacts with a few older men who are nothing short of enthralled by him. He stands straight, shoulders back and tight, nodding along with whatever they're saying. Their basketball icon is here tonight, professional and on edge.

"Daily update for you, Vee."

"No thank you."

"Your brother is hot as hell, and I'd happily let him bend me over this bar top." I pull my drink to my lips, keeping my attention on him.

"Could've easily gone through my night without hearing that."

"Has he always been this uptight or is it new since I've been around?"

"Don't take it personally. He's been this way since he got drafted, but I hadn't noticed how bad it had gotten until I moved here last year and saw it firsthand."

Two ocean eyes break away from the small group crowding the superstar and find me across the room, pinning me with a breath-taking stare. Ryan may be stiff and uncomfortable, but that man in a suit is any girl's fantasy. He's stunning and causes a blush to creep up my cheeks when his lips tilt in a small smile before returning his attention to the crowd in front of him, as if he simply needed to check on my whereabouts before continuing with his evening.

That Ryan Shay smile almost means more because I don't see it often, and I may be fantasizing about the man every free moment of the day, but no one else needs to know that.

In my periphery, I watch Stevie's attention bounce from her brother to me and back again.

"Are you sure this is a good idea?"

I turn to face her. "What do you mean?"

"Faking it while also living together. It seems messy."

"Well, we both know how much Ryan hates a mess," I tease.

Stevie turns back to face the bar and I join her.

"To answer your question," she continues. "He's not uptight per se, but he is aware of the countless eyes watching him, waiting for him to mess up. Ryan doesn't show his emotions very often because it's safe for him. It's safe for his brand."

I can't imagine that, altering your life, holding back to appease everyone around you. Not too enthused, but not too solemn either. Not too stoic, but not too animated. What a terrible way to go through life.

*Maybe tone it down tonight, Indy. These guys, they don't like loud women.*

*These are my coworkers, so sit back and let me do the talking.*

*You look gorgeous, Indy. All you need to be tonight is pretty.*

Alex's previous words ring in my mind, so maybe I *can* imagine that.

The bartender interrupts us with a fresh beer in his hand, sliding it across the counter. "This one is on me," he says to Stevie, with a grin that can only be described as "panty-melting."

A tattooed hand slides around Stevie's waist from behind. "Absolutely not." Zanders' venomous glare is focused on the soon-to-be dead bartender. "Abso-fucking-lutely not."

The bartender's face pales. "Sorry, man." He holds up his hands in surrender before taking off to serve another patron.

"Yeah, that's what I thought." Zanders keeps his attention on his back before leaning down and dotting kisses down Stevie's neck. "I can't take you anywhere," he murmurs against her skin.

"Ind, you look great." Zanders turns my way. "This is fun, having you at events with us and not just on the airplane."

"Well, take a good look. It might be your one and only shot."

"No way. Your pretend relationship is already on the rocks?" Zanders' phone dings and he pulls it out while continuing our conversation.

The statement catches me slightly off guard. Of course, Stevie told Zanders that her brother and I are faking it, but I hope it's not much more than our small circle who knows. The less people who are aware, the safer our lie is.

"Your guy has practically ignored me since we talked to his boss. I could make another one of these athletes my *real* boyfriend and I'm fairly certain he wouldn't even notice."

"I'm pretty sure he'd notice." Zanders' chest bubbles with an arrogant laugh while holding his phone out to me.

**Ryan:** *Keep an eye on Indy for me. She has no clue that these guys are eye-fucking the hell out of her in that goddamn dress.*

Finding him again, his back is to me as he chats with more fans, and I wouldn't believe he sent that text unless I saw it with my own two eyes.

"Indigo!" Rio exclaims, holding me out at arm's length. "You look so…"

I don't fill in the blank for him. Instead, I give him a moment to choose his descriptive word. Rio is lovable, excitable, and young, but he needs a little coaching when it comes to his approach with women, and we've been working on it.

"Bang…" He catches Zanders' raised brow. "eautiful."

"Bangeutiful?" I ask.

"Beautiful. You look beautiful, Indy." He turns towards my friend. "Now, Stevie, you look smoking hot. I'm talking drop-dead gorgeous. Every guy in here is probably thinking about—"

I slap a palm over his mouth, trying not to laugh. "You've got a death wish," I inform him as Zanders arches a challenging brow in his over-confident way.

Rio's green eyes shine with mischief because he's a bit of a shit disturber, though always in good fun. He enjoys getting under his team-mates' skin and Stevie is the easiest way to do it.

"Kidding. Kidding. But this blue dress does look great on you, Stevie."

"Thanks, Rio," she laughs.

Zanders wraps two possessive arms around her. "Yeah," he mumbles under his breath. "And it's going to look even better on *my* bedroom floor tonight."

"Rio, come on. Let's go dance before the Raptors lose two of their best players tonight. One to murder and the other to a prison sentence."

Rio and I take the crowded dance floor. With a small pull of his wrist, he brings me into his chest where I place a hand on his shoulder. He's different on the dance floor. He leads with grace and confidence, completely opposite in his approach with women.

"Where did you learn to dance?"

"Six years of ballroom lessons. I was a terrible skater when I was a kid, believe it or not. I had two left feet, so my mother put me in dance lessons to learn balance. I was the best skater on my team a year later."

"And yet, you kept dancing for five more years?"

He pushes me out, spinning me with complete control. "Do you know what the girl to guy ratio was in my dance class? I had numbers on my side."

As usual, Rio makes me laugh.

"That," he continues. "And I may have enjoyed it."

I cock my head with a thoughtful smile. "Regardless that we love to give you a hard time, one day, someone is going to be very lucky to land you."

That olive skin tints with a shy smile. "Thanks, Ind."

We stay on the dance floor for two songs, chatting and catching up. I thoroughly enjoyed myself tonight. Even though Ryan is stiff as a board, and probably blew our cover, I had fun seeing my friends outside of work. It was nice to dress up, go out, and socialize.

But as the beginning of song number three begins to fill the space, Rio's expression drops, that typically goofy smile falling into a flat line.

"Are you okay?" I ask.

He swallows, looking over my shoulder as we continue to sway along the dance floor. "I'm pretty sure your fake boyfriend wants to very real kill me."

I still. "Geez. Does everyone know it's fake?"

"Stevie told Zanders and Zanders told me because, Indy, I was freaking the fuck out."

"Rio. You and I, we're friends. We've been over this."

He scoffs, his head jolting back. "I'm not talking about you. I thought one of my closest friends was dating Ryan Shay. Ryan *freaking* Shay. You know how I feel about him."

I roll my eyes before peeking over my shoulder to find Ryan sitting at a table, leaning back in his chair, legs sprawled like a king as he mindlessly sketches the rim of his glass. His stance might seem informal, but his stare is venomous, pointed right at Rio.

"Don't worry, it's not you. He didn't want to stay long, and I think I lost track of time."

"Indy." Rio stops moving completely. "I might be inexperienced when it comes to women, but I'm still a man. That right there is jealousy."

"No, it's not."

"Trust me. I know that look."

"Well, then he's doing his job. *Pretending* to be my boyfriend."

And finally knocking off *something* from his bucket list. Would've been a good night for a slow dance, but I'll take the jealousy.

"Give the man a fucking Oscar then." Rio's eyes continue to flicker to my roommate. "As much as it'd be an absolute honor to be punched in the face by Ryan Shay, I don't know that a fundraiser is the best place for that."

"I should get going." I slide my arms around him in a hug. "I'll see you on the plane."

As I make my way to Ryan, he doesn't look up at me. Instead, his eyes track Rio as my friend leaves the dance floor, and it isn't until I take the seat directly in front of him, blocking his view, that he breaks his stare.

"Well, hi there." Ryan's middle finger traces the edge of his whiskey glass with cool indifference.

"Are you okay?"

I'm acutely aware that my knees are between his sprawled legs as I sit facing him.

"I'm good."

"Are you ready to go?"

"Do you want to stay?"

"You said we were only staying for an hour and a half, and I'm pretty sure it's been much longer than that."

"I know what I said, but do you want to stay? Are you having a good time?"

He sits up, bringing his legs in, and trapping my knees between his. The shiny pink satin of my dress contradicts his thick legs in black suit pants, but I won't lie, I like the juxtaposition.

"I *am* having a good time."

"Then we'll stay." He takes a small swig of the whiskey in his glass.

His previous hard glare is now soft as he looks at me, and the slight tilt at his lips is a sight I'll never get sick of.

Without looking away, he lifts his hand to push a few fallen strands of hair behind my ear. The pad of his thumb skims the skin of my throat, gentle and delicate but with all the confidence in the world for a man who has been nothing short of uncomfortable with faking it.

I find myself relaxing into his touch. "What are you doing?" I whisper lazily.

His eyes softly trace my face before he discreetly nods his head to the side. "Pretending."

Oh.

His GM must be here, watching us.

My roommate stands, slipping out of his suit jacket and slinging it over my shoulders.

"Ryan—"

"Your dress has had its moment. Trust me, no one has kept their eyes off you, but you're shivering. You're taking my jacket."

*I'm not shivering because I'm cold.*

Regardless, I tug the lapels together, covering me with the jacket's warmth and Ryan's scent—crisp and refined.

Ryan retakes his seat, his legs trapping mine once again. "Remind me of that guy's name."

I feign innocence. "What guy?"

"You know which guy."

"Rio? He plays for the Raptors. You've met him before."

"So, you see him every time you're on the road for work?"

"Yes."

He nods, those ocean eyes staying calm, cool, collected—a Ryan Shay signature. "Is there something going on between you two?"

"What?" I burst with a laugh. "No."

He doesn't respond, waiting for me to elaborate.

"He is a good friend, though."

"Just a friend?"

"Yes, Ryan. Just a friend. What's with the lineup of questions?"

"You're supposed to be my girlfriend. I figured I should know if you're seeing someone."

"Well, I'm not. You're the only man I'm seeing. Pretend or otherwise."

Ryan's set shoulders drop slightly, and the movement is so minor that I could've imagined it. He nods. No words, simply a head movement to end the conversation.

"Are you sure you're all right being here, or do you want to go home?"

At that moment, Stevie and Zanders take two more seats at our table, but don't pay us any attention. Ryan's change in posture and the ease in his eyes is unmistakable from having his sister around.

"I'm all right. Tonight is kind of fun, actually."

He leans his elbows on his knees that bracket mine as his fingertips begin to softly dance along the satin of my dress, mindlessly tracing the fabric.

*Acting. Fake. Pretend.*

"You're a different guy when your sister is around."

"What do you mean?"

"You're relaxed because she's here tonight."

Ryan looks across the table to where Stevie sits. "Yeah." He clears his throat. "Yeah. I guess you're right."

"It's nice to see you like this."

His fingertips freeze on the satin as he watches me, lips slightly parted. After a moment, he slides his hands, taking up more residency on my legs.

Black suit, a Rolex on his wrist, and those cuff links create a daydream I can't stop thinking about. I wonder what he looks like peeling off that suit. Does he have a specific place where he likes to store those accessories? Knowing Ryan, yes, of course, but does he organize his things even when there's a woman waiting for him on his bed?

I think I'd like that view. Watching him slowly peel off every layer with precision while I'm sprawled out on my back.

Clearing my throat and my mind of those daydreams, I whisper, "Can I tell you something kind of ridiculous?"

There's a tilt of his lips, but he tries to suppress it. "Please do."

"I know this isn't real, but this is the first date I've been on."

"You mean since the breakup?"

"No, I mean ever."

Eyes widen. "How is that possible?"

"Alex and I had just kind of decided we were together one day. There was no first date or any date really. When we went out it was with all our friends. Sure, we lived together, but this is my first proper date, one-on-one. Ironic that it's fake, huh?"

Ryan's confused brow softens. "Indy, I wish I had known."

"Why?" I laugh. "It wouldn't have changed anything."

A moment of silence lingers between us, and I wish I had something to say, something to break the tension and the wave of awkwardness after admitting to my superstar athlete roommate that I've never been on a date.

Ryan speaks before I can come up with something. "So, Dartmouth, huh?"

"Yep."

I find his palms on my thighs, wishing I could put my hand on his, to feel our fingers intertwine as they did earlier tonight, but I don't want him to stop tracing mindless designs on my legs either.

"Where did you end up going since you didn't get in?"

"Oh, I got in."

His head jolts back slightly. "But you didn't attend?"

Ryan's hands slide again, his palms now living on my upper thighs with authority. I should look around and find Ron Morgan, reassuring myself this is all an act, but there's the romantic part of me that wants to continue living in the fantasy, even if it is a lie.

"Alex and all our friends were staying in Chicago, and we weren't quite together yet, but I knew we would be. He didn't feel comfortable with us doing long distance." I laugh without humor. "I should've listened to him back then. The second I started traveling for work, he got with someone else."

Pity covers Ryan's face. "Blue—"

"Don't feel bad for me. Yes, I stayed near Chicago to be closer to Alex, but I'm privileged. I still went to a great school, and I still got my MBA. Sure, I don't use it, but I can't exactly complain."

Ryan's brows find each other, creasing his forehead. "Why didn't you say that when Ron brought up Dartmouth? That's impressive as hell. *You're* impressive."

"Because I've learned over the years that sometimes people, especially men, are more intimidated than impressed by intelligence. I was valedictorian of our class, but I wasn't given a second glance until I grew into my body. Some men don't want to feel like they have someone to compete with, so I play the game. I'm trying to get your boss to like me, not feel like I'm overstepping."

I'm good at reading people. I know how to make them feel comfortable around me. I know how to adjust who I am depending on the person I'm with. As much as I love people, sometimes they suck and what makes them comfortable is for you to appear to be inferior.

I did it plenty in my last relationship.

"Indy—"

"Please, Ryan, don't say anything. I know everything you're thinking right now."

"No. That's not how this is going to go. When you're with me, I want you exactly as you are. That includes letting people know just how fucking smart you are. You're not going to cater to anyone's toxic masculinity bullshit. You're not going to be quiet and appeasing when you're with me. If Ron, or anyone else for that matter, has an issue with you being smarter than him, then we're going to have a far bigger problem than him thinking I'm not a good leader."

"Ryan, it's fine. I've done it for years."

"Yeah, that's another thing. How fucking small was Alex's dick that he let you do this? Or should I say, *asked you* to do this. That shit is manipulative and controlling because, let me guess, he didn't like that you were smarter than him, possibly more successful. Did he ask you to tone it down in front of his friends? Did he want you to stay quiet and look pretty so his colleagues wouldn't think less of him?"

What the hell? There's a strong prick in my eyes, a quick burn of my nose because Ryan is right. He's never met him, and yet, he knows everything I tried to ignore.

"Don't." Ryan sits forward. "Don't you dare cry."

I suck in a breath, shaking my head and stopping any emotions before they really start. "Sorry. We're at your work event."

"Indy." Both his large hands cup my face. "I don't give a fuck where we are. You could cry all you want at this fundraiser. You could scream, laugh, throw a temper tantrum in front of these people for all I care. I don't give a fuck, but you're not crying over him, here or anywhere else."

He needs to stop. He can't be demanding and caring in the sexiest way while he's wearing that suit. He should know by now that I'm a romantic and I'll end up kissing him for it or something stupid like that.

And as much as I've fantasized about the way his mouth would feel against mine, how soft and pliable his lips would be, we're putting on a show. I can't forget what this is and confuse my idealistic heart.

This isn't one of my romance books. This isn't a fairy tale. And even if it were, I'd be the worst main character because I am nowhere near able to feel anything other than broken even for this man who is sexy and controlling in his own way.

"Ryan," I say, breaking the spell I wish I could allow myself to fall under.

"Hmm?"

"You're really good at pretending when no one else is around. Now we need to work on it for when we have an audience."

Ryan sits back in his chair, creating a needed distance between us. "Right," he says before finishing off his whiskey. "I'll work on it."

# 11

# Ryan

Blonde hair and lilac-painted toes clouded my mind all practice. Imagining what that pink satin would've looked like on my bedroom floor last night instead of Indy's.

I haven't fantasized about a woman like this in years. Typically, if I'm attracted to someone, it fades within a few hours once I remember who I am and why someone would want to be with me. That thought alone douses any fire. But lately, I've barely recognized myself through the carnal thoughts invading my brain—Indy on her back. On her knees. On her stomach, ass in the air.

Fuck, I can't stop thinking about every position I could take her in and I'm a piece of shit for it because she's getting over a guy who only cared about the trophy on his arm. The last thing I want is to be compared to him.

There's a nervousness thrumming through me as I open the door to my apartment, the one place I'm able to find peace and solitude. But today, the peace is gone, replaced instead with uncertainty. Part of me hopes Indy is home so I can know whether she's wearing her hair in a braid or a bun. Whether she's wearing socks around the house or letting her bare feet enjoy the heated floor. Whether she's still in the clothes she slept in or if she's ready for the day.

And part of me hopes she's gone so I can't have any of those questions answered. They're dangerous to our arrangement and they're dangerous to me.

But every single one of those questions is answered when I walk into the apartment and find Indy sitting at the kitchen island with her laptop open in front of her.

Braid slung over her left shoulder.

Bare feet dangling off the stool.

Oversized sweatshirt and cotton shorts that she clearly slept in.

"Oh, Ryan is home," Indy says to the computer, all while she moves her hands in quick motions. She turns towards me. "Ryan, come meet my parents."

Again, her hands move and this time, I pick up on the four letters of my name from my very minimal knowledge of American Sign Language.

Stepping behind her, I find the camera, allowing her parents to see me. "Hi. I'm Ryan," I say with a wave.

I find those four letters that make up my name in Indy's hand movements once again.

"Lovely to meet you," her mom says, using her hands to speak as well. "I'm Abigale."

Her dad waves and speaks with only his hands.

"This is my dad, Tim," Indy says, signing as well. "Geez, Dad!" she says after her father signs something else. She turns towards me. "He said, 'We hope our daughter hasn't been too much of a pain in the ass.'"

She wears a post-giggle smile, awaiting my response. Indy must notice my hesitation. "Speak clearly," she reassures. "He can read lips and I'll sign for you as well."

I've never met a woman's parents before, not that this is a "meet the parents" type of moment, but their daughter does live with me and between that and the inappropriate images that have been flashing through my daydreams, it's a bit terrifying.

But Indy's parents seem kind and welcoming. Her dad must be where she got her height. I can tell he's a tall man even as he sits on his living room couch in Florida. On the other hand, her mom is a petite woman, but that blonde hair and those warm brown eyes make me feel at home in the same way I do with her daughter who shares the same attributes.

Leaning forward, I split the screen with Indy. "She's only a pain in the ass when she leaves her dishes in the sink or forgets her clothes in the dryer for days at a time."

Indy signs all while wearing a gaping mouth in mock offense.

Her parents laugh. "Just wait until you realize she never screws the lids back on all the way or forgets to close cupboard doors behind her."

"Mom! God, you guys, I'm right here."

"Honestly, though," I continue. "I've enjoyed having her here. You raised a good woman."

Indy's attention darts to me before she looks away, signing my words as she does.

"Thank you." Even though Indy translates for her dad, I know the very basics of ASL. She clears her throat uncomfortably. "He asked if you'll watch after me."

I look back at Indy, but she won't make eye contact. She seems nervous for what I'll have to say and maybe she's wishing her dad didn't ask that at all.

But regardless of his request, I've been watching out for Indy since she moved in. I hate what she's going through, and my understanding is partly why I've been so accommodating, but I think selfishly I've wanted Indy to be here since the first night she slept in my spare room. Why else would I buy her a bed to sleep in and add vegetarian substitutes to my order every time I get groceries delivered?

"Yes, sir. Always."

Through the laptop screen, I watch Indy bite the corner of her lip, either to keep a smile contained or to hide a small tremble. You never know with her. Emotional girl, my roommate.

"He watched your game against Boston," Indy continues for her dad. "He says you had an amazing third quarter. He's a big basketball fan."

"Oh, yeah? Well, I'll be sure to get you some tickets next time you come for a visit or when we head down to Florida for a couple games."

A pair of brows and a smile lift on Tim's face before he signs once again.

"He would love that."

"Ryan, we like you in case you couldn't tell," Abigale laughs.

Tim signs again, a small gesture I've noticed a few times already, but before Indy can translate, I ask her, "What does that sign mean?"

"Which?"

I repeat Tim's hand motion. It's a fairly simple one—a fist with a pinky extended, motioned in a small circle around his chest.

"Oh, that's my name. My sign name."

"Sign name?"

"It's a special sign to identify someone," Indy says, her hands continuing to move for her dad in the most beautifully elegant way. "That way we don't need to spell out our entire names every time we speak. Not everyone has a sign name. My dad chooses who gets them and what their sign is." She balls her hand, but her pinky stays straight up then rubs her hand in a small circle over her heart. "'I' for Indigo and my dad says I'm his whole heart." She repeats her sign name. "Indy."

Her mom speaks up. "And I'm Abigale." She uses her hand, forming the letter "A" and tapping it to her head. "Because Indy's father first noticed my blonde hair."

"He typically doesn't give a sign name right away, but he did with my mom." Indy smiles thoughtfully, her hands moving. "They've been together for almost thirty years, and I think he knew she was going to be in his life from their first meeting. Isn't that right, Dad?"

A nostalgic smile lifts on Tim's mouth, nodding to agree with his daughter.

Indy, the romantic. Of course, she would assume that, but watching her parents on the computer screen, I'm not sure that I can argue. They seem utterly in love even after all this time, and it's no wonder my roommate has these idealistic notions of romance. She grew up watching this.

But most people aren't like that. Most people can't be trusted with your heart, and I'd assume she quickly learned that after losing the life she built with her ex.

We chat for a few more minutes, all three of the Ivers speaking a language I didn't realize was so intricate and beautiful to watch until now, getting to see it in action. The way they make each other smile or laugh with simple movements of their hands. I find myself envious that I can't participate, and instantly wish I knew more than the basics so Indy's dad could speak directly to me without his daughter having to translate.

Once Abigale ensures I have her number in case of emergencies, Indy hangs up the call.

"They seem great."

She smiles. "They're the best. I miss them."

"It's only you? They didn't have any other kids?"

"They couldn't. It was a small miracle they got pregnant once. My mom had fertility issues."

"Oh. I'm sorry."

"Don't be," Indy brushes me off. "They got one perfect child out of the deal."

"Mm-hmm," I hum suspiciously, attempting to keep my wandering eye off her long legs and pajama shorts. "Did you just wake up?"

"Yes." She yawns with a stretch, her hands in the air. "How was practice?"

The short answer? Terrible.

I've never had so many turnovers in a two-hour span, never missed so many free throws in a single practice. And it's all because I couldn't stop thinking of what might have happened if I knocked on Indy's closed bedroom door last night instead of going to my own.

After hesitating with my hands on her doorframe, my chest moving with heavy breaths, and the overwhelming desire to end our night doing something that would be anything but pretend, I did the right thing and turned around. I went back to my own bedroom, back to my own shower where I took care of myself as I have for the last couple of years.

"It was fine."

She stands, circling the kitchen island to my side and I automatically round in the opposite direction, needing to maintain distance when all I want to do is touch her.

"Have you always known how to speak like that?"

"ASL?" she asks. "I guess so. At home we've always signed. My dad was born deaf, and my mom learned the language when they met."

"How would..." I hesitate uncomfortably. "How would an adult learn the language?"

Her head snaps around to me. "You want to learn how to sign?"

Oh fuck. Those glossy brown eyes are back. Indy, the romantic. "I want to be able to speak to your dad without you having to translate. That way I can let him know when his daughter is being a pain in my ass."

A quick, non-feminine laugh bubbles out of her. It's lovely.

"There are classes you could take. Or I could help teach you if you'd like."

She doesn't make eye contact, as if she's new to the topic. As if no one else in her life has ever asked her how they could learn to better communicate with her family.

Indy opens the fridge, quickly shifting the subject. "Are you hungry? I can make you some—" She takes her pink coffee cup out of the refrigerator and holds it up to me. "What is this?"

"I uh…" I rub my hand on the back of my neck. "I made you coffee before I left for practice and put it in the fridge to cool so it wouldn't get watered down when you added ice."

Her head drops to the side. "Ryan, that's really sweet. Thank you."

I look away from the girl who probably assumes this is some grand romantic gesture. "It was nothing."

She rifles through the fridge, her blonde braid cascading down her back. Those bare feet and long legs distracting me once again.

"Where's the regular bacon?" she asks.

"I haven't been ordering it. I've just been getting the vegetarian stuff."

She looks over her shoulder at me for an explanation.

"I think it tastes pretty good. No need to order both."

Another thoughtful smile pulls at her lips.

Dammit. I know she's going to think this is deeper than it is. She's going to romanticize me buying fucking breakfast meats because that's who she is, but it's nothing. Really.

I just want the fridge to be stocked with things she can eat. I want her to feel at home here because it's her home too.

The realization rams into my chest.

*I want her here. I want her to* want *to be here.*

Fuck, when did that happen?

# 12

# Ryan

"We had too many turnovers in the third and we couldn't recover. That's something we're going to work on in practice this week."

At least thirty hands shoot up, but I can barely make out the reporters' faces thanks to the blinding camera lights.

"That's enough questions for tonight," our media coordinator announces in the post-game press conference.

I stand, fixing my suit and offering my most diplomatic wave and smile after making sure my answers were perfectly poised for the media. "Thank you, everyone."

The buzz of chatter is behind me as I make my way back down the tunnel to the locker room. The rest of the team is gone. Only Coach and I had to stay back to be drilled with questions about why we played like shit on our home court. I had my worst game of the season and since I lead my team with the way I play, we collectively played like garbage.

I'd like to say my lack of focus was a random one-off, but the truth is, I know where my head was tonight.

It was stuck on my roommate who I was texting with pregame when she dropped the bomb that she was driving rideshares tonight. She was stoked it was going to be busy thanks to the drives to and from the arena. However, all I could think about is her being stuck in her car with strangers. Doesn't she realize how potentially dangerous that could be? Doesn't she understand how drunk some of these fans are after a game?

Worse than that, she hasn't texted me back since I got to my phone.

"Ry."

My zoned-out daze is broken to find Zanders casually leaning on the wall outside my locker room, one leg crossed over the other.

"Hey, man. Were you here for the game? I thought Stevie said you were out of town for some sponsorship deal."

"Just landed and headed here."

I push the door open. "Want to come into my locker room?"

"You mean *my* locker room?" He wears a smug smile.

"Not until tomorrow night."

The Raptors and the Devils share the United Center, so on nights where I'm not playing, there's a good chance you could find my sister's boyfriend on the ice.

"Are you picking up Stevie or what?"

Zanders takes a seat in one of the locker stalls as I collect my phone, wallet, and keys, still frustrated from the lack of Indy on my phone.

"No, she's home already, and doesn't know I'm here. I wasn't sure if Indy was at your place, and I was hoping to talk to you alone."

Well, that catches my attention. I turn around to find Zanders' expression completely serious, an uncommon occurrence for the defenseman.

"Everything okay?" I take a seat in my stall, elbows on my knees.

"I wasn't at a sponsorship deal. I was in Nashville."

Stevie's and my hometown.

"To talk to your dad."

Oh. Oh shit.

"Do you remember the night we met, and I told you I wasn't going to ask for permission to date your sister?"

I attempt to hold back the slight tug on my lips remembering the charity gala where I formally met the arrogant hockey player. Going into that night, I hated him. He was a walking stereotype, but here we are, almost a year later. The guy sitting in the stall across from me is one of my best friends and loves my sister in the way she deserves.

"I'm all for Stevie making her own decisions, so again, I'm not going to ask your permission, but this time, I do care how you feel."

"Zee, you're being sappy as fuck about this," I laugh. "Spit it out."

"Ryan Taylor Shay." Zanders gets on one knee in front of me. "Will you be my brother-in-law?"

"You're an idiot."

"I'm kidding." He retakes his seat, laughing. "But I would like to know how you'd feel my asking Stevie to marry me. You're one of my best friends, but I also want both of you to be my family. Officially."

I'm not an emotional man. I don't cry often. I've shed a few tears in my younger days if I didn't make a game-winning shot or if I felt like I let my team down. Now, the only time emotions hit me is when my sister is involved. She's my gray area in a world of black and white. I want her happiness more than I want my own and knowing the guy across from me makes her happier than she's been in her whole life causes a slight burning in my eyes.

I exhale a deep breath, centering myself. "You're about to make me lose it, man."

"Good. You can get on my page. I was a crying mess talking to your dad today."

I can picture that perfectly. My dad is a sweet man, caring and kind and Zanders is as in tune with his emotions as I've seen almost anyone. Well, maybe besides Indy.

"So, what do you think?"

"What do I think?" I contemplate for a moment. "I think if you hurt her, I'll kill you." I stand with a smile on my face, repeating the phrase I used the first night I met my future brother-in-law. "But yeah, I'd love for my sister to marry you."

He stands as well, both of us throwing our arms around each other in a hug. I smack his shoulder a couple of times before pulling away.

He holds me at arm's length. "You played like shit tonight, by the way."

A silent laugh heaves in my chest. I almost forgot about my terrible game, but it's one of eighty-two and I'm not going to let it ruin my night any longer.

"Thanks, Zee. Always supportive." I exit the locker room with him following behind.

"Just keeping you in check. At the very least, I need you to make the playoffs because I've got a Stanley Cup win under my belt and it's becoming a heavy burden to be the only champion in this family."

"I'm so glad I make more money than you." We head to the players' parking lot. "Do you need a ride?"

"Nah, I drove."

As we find our cars, I hesitate, knowing I'm going to sound like a complete stalker, but fuck it. This guy is about to be my brother. If I can't ask him, who else can I ask?

"Hey, Zee." He turns to face me, his hand lingering on the handle of his G-Wagon. "When you're on the road, Indy…She's good?"

His lips lift mischievously. "Is she good at her job? Yeah, the best."

"No."

"Oh, you mean is she good at getting hit on in every bar we walk into? Yeah, she's fucking great at that too."

"Fuck you."

He laughs from his core. "She's good, man. She usually comes out and grabs a drink with Maddison, Rio, and me if we have the night off, but other than that, she's in her hotel reading or sewing or whatever the fuck she does with her shoes."

"The guys though, they don't mess with her?"

"Ryan, if you're asking if any of my guys are getting with her, the answer is no. Are they trying? I'm fairly certain a few of them have tried, but she's not interested in the slightest. But if you're asking if she's good as in, is she happy? She seems happier than she has been in a long time."

A quick nod of my head. "Thanks, man." We both get into our cars that are parked near each other, but I roll down my window to add one more thing. "And keep your teammates in check. If I hear that one of them tries anything with her again, I'm coming to you."

Zanders folds over his steering wheel in laughter. "Ryan, my guy, you're so completely fucked, and you can't even see it."

"Indy!" I hang my keys on the hook by my front door. "Blue, are you home?"

All the lights are off in the apartment which means I was the last to leave. Indy leaves a symbolic trail of breadcrumbs behind her in the form of open cabinet doors and unnecessary lights on whenever she exits a room.

I quietly walk by her open bedroom door to be sure, but it's empty. Her pillows are still stacked on one side of the mattress from last night, yet to work on her bucket list.

Grabbing my phone, I dial her again, which makes it my third call since I left the arena twenty minutes ago.

"You've reached Indy!" her voicemail repeats once again. "You can leave a message if you want but I probably won't call you back. Bye!"

Typically, I'd find her voicemail charming just like her, but tonight it's frustrating beyond belief.

"Call me back, Ind," I mutter into the receiver, pacing the length of the living room, continuing to check my phone.

Surely, she's got to be done driving by now. The game ended two hours ago.

What if she picked up a trip that took her hours out of town? Or what if her car broke down? Fuck, I don't even know what she drives. Is it safe for a Chicago winter? She's a Midwest native, so I assume it is, but what if it's an old car?

I'm self-aware enough to know I'm avoiding the real question. What if something worse happened to her? Fans can be belligerent leaving the arena, I've seen it firsthand.

Where the hell is she?

"Stevie?" I ask as soon as my sister answers her phone. "Have you heard from Indy?"

"No. She's driving tonight. Is everything okay?"

"She's not home yet. She should be home by now."

"It's only eleven thirty. Maybe she's still working or maybe she met up with friends."

"What kind of friends?"

She laughs. "Oh my God. Male friends, I'm sure. The kind with lots of money and huge di—"

"Vee."

"I'm kidding. Friends like girl friends or Rio."

"Why are you not concerned at all?"

"Because she's a grown woman who's working. Will it make you feel better if I text her?"

"Please."

My sister softens her tone. "Ryan, I'm sure she's fine. I'll text as soon as I hear back."

Another twenty-five minutes goes by. I pace the kitchen. I pour myself a scotch. My collar feels too claustrophobic, so I change out of my gameday suit before wrapping a bag of ice around my shooter's shoulder.

Stevie is probably right and I'm being over-dramatic, but the idea of Indy being alone in her car with strangers in the middle of the night sends a reaction through me that I haven't felt in quite a while—concern.

My emotions haven't taken over in years, including this one. I've kept them locked down, controlled, but right now they feel entirely unmanageable thanks to my blonde roommate I can't stop worrying about.

I know how overwhelming it can be with the public. She's not me, but what if fans recognize her from the photos of the banquet?

My phone pings, and you'd have to believe I was a professional athlete by how quickly I snatch it off the kitchen counter.

**Blue:** *Sorry, still working! I've had nonstop rides tonight. Be home late. Going to keep driving until the bars close.*

What the hell? Is she trying to force me into cardiac arrest? As if the fans after a home game weren't rowdy enough, I can't imagine how sloppy some of them get when they hit the bars afterward.

**Me:** *Can you please come home?*

**Blue:** *Can't. I need to make a little more $$ before calling it a night. Got a ride! Got to go. See you tomorrow.*

See you tomorrow? Is she out of her goddamn mind? In what world does she think I'm going to bed and will just *see her tomorrow*?

**Vee:** *Indy is good. Still working.*

**Me:** *What the hell is so important that she needs to be working these kinds of hours? Did the airline do a pay cut?*

**Vee:** *No, but it's also not my business to talk about. If she wants to tell you she will. Heading to bed. Love you.*

I exhale a deep, resigned sigh.

**Me:** *Thanks for getting ahold of her. Love you too.*

Indy's obnoxious yellow curtains are pushed to the wall, letting Chicago's midnight skyline filter into my living room. Stevie and Zanders' penthouse is across the street, and I watch as their lights go out for the night.

I'm glad someone is getting some sleep because I'll be sitting on this couch, wide awake until Indy comes home.

It's 2:57 when the front door quietly opens, and I'm sitting in the living room like someone's father, disappointed by a missed curfew.

"You're awake?" Indy whispers as if there were someone asleep in this apartment.

"Clearly."

Shedding her coat, she slips off her high-top white Converse, the ones that are covered in embroidered designs. "What's wrong?"

I take a long sip of my scotch, shaking my head. "Nothing."

"Okay. Want to try that again without lying this time?" She stands opposite me in the living room, her arms crossed over her chest, pushing her tits up in the most distracting way.

"I can't say what's wrong, otherwise, I'll sound like a controlling dick."

"Control is kind of your thing, Ryan. Are you upset because you had a bad game?"

Scoffing, I stand from the couch and head to the kitchen to rinse out my glass. "I don't give a fuck about my game."

She follows me, palms on the kitchen island opposite me. She's wearing a pair of 90s denim jeans that seem too short on her long legs, but she of course, pulls off the flooded look in an intentional way. Her T-shirt is worn beyond belief, a soft pink cotton from an old-school Brittney Spears concert.

God, she's fucking adorable and that pisses me off.

Because this version of her, the real one where she's not putting on a show for my GM or her ex-boyfriend and his friends. The version where she's not toning it down to be appropriate or appeasing. This is *my* version of her. The one where she's comfortable and casual at home and I don't want to share her.

"Then what's wrong?" she presses.

I set my glass down on the drying rack, bracketing my hands on the edge of the sink as I exhale a deep breath. "I was thinking about you the whole game."

"Aw, Ry." A hand splays over her chest. "I'm flattered. Truly."

"I'm not kidding, Blue. I don't want you picking up and driving random strangers around."

"Well, that's not really your say, is it?"

"What if Ron Morgan called a rideshare and you happened to be his driver? How would we explain why you're driving rideshares while your millionaire boyfriend is playing a game?"

"Okay." Indy laughs. "The chances of that happening are almost nonexistent, so why don't you tell me what your real issue is."

Her brown eyes are soft with patience, not that I deserve it. I'm acting like a possessive caveman right now, but I don't know how to fake it.

"I'm…I don't know." I look down at the sink where my knuckles are white with restraint. I haven't cared about another person besides my sister in God knows how long and I have no idea how to feel or express it.

Her voice is kind. "You're what, Ryan?"

"I'm…worried about you, Ind. I was worrying about you the whole game."

Her lips lift mischievously, her tone teasing. "Ryan Shay, do you *care* about me?"

"No."

"You care about me."

"No, I don't, but I'd rather you not get kidnapped while I'm playing a fucking basketball game."

She moves her shoulders, dancing around the island. "Ryan Shay cares about me!"

"You're annoying."

Her hands go to her knees, and she sticks her ass out, twerking in my kitchen. "Yeah, but you still care about me."

Shaking my head, I try my hardest not to laugh. "I'm going to bed."

"Say it."

"Not saying it."

"Well clearly, words of affirmation are *not* your love language."

I turn around to face her, continuing to walk backwards to my bedroom. "None of this has to do with love."

"Ryan Shay cares about me!" Hands on her hips, she circles them, continuing to dance in my kitchen.

"How much caffeine did you have tonight? Jesus."

"None. I'm high on life, baby!"

"You're not paying rent anymore, by the way. So that should solve the whole driving random strangers home from the bars thing."

Her dance moves halt. "Ryan!"

I roll my eyes. "I was saving it for you anyway. So just...put it towards whatever you're saving for."

"You don't have to do that."

"I know I don't." I lean back on my bedroom door, not quite going inside yet. "Knowing you're not out there alone driving drunk dudes home at two AM is worth far more to me than five hundred dollars a month. Besides, you should probably start coming to my games when you're in town. You are the point guard's girlfriend after all."

"I'm not going to cry over this."

"Congratulations." I motion to Britney Spears on my twenty-seven-year-old roommate's chest. "Cute shirt by the way."

"You know it'd be a whole lot cheaper to just tell me you care about me."

"Good night, you weirdo. Oh, and by the way, the dinner with the Morgans tomorrow night is an hour outside of town and we're spending the night. So, pack something to sleep in."

"Do footy pajamas work?"

"Yes, please. I want nothing more than to share a room with you while you're wearing fucking footy pajamas."

I go to close my door, but she stops me, putting her hand out and blocking me.

"What happened?" She nods towards my shoulder.

The ice has long melted, but I've yet to unwrap the pack from my sore muscles.

"Nothing. I'm just banged up from the game."

"Can I see?"

Hesitating, unsure of what she's looking for, I cautiously unwrap the ice from my shoulder and put the pack in the sink. Reaching up, Indy's dainty fingers run the length of my shoulder blade, her thumb following behind and digging in.

I wince, pulling away slightly.

"Ryan, you're really tight."

"I'm fine."

Indy's hand glides down my bare bicep and forearm until it slides into mine. She begins pulling me to the couch. "Take a seat on the floor. Let me rub this out."

*Let me rub this out.*

Jesus. Inhaling a deep breath, I pray away the erection. Ever since the banquet, I can't stop remembering how good she felt to touch, how natural it felt to have her with me. The fantasies have been on overdrive, and I've done everything in my power to will them away, but how the fuck am I supposed to do that with her soft hands rubbing my skin?

Taking a seat on the ground in front of the couch, Indy sinks into the sofa behind me, sitting on top of her crossed legs. Her hands find my shoulders, kneading and manipulating my sore muscles into relaxation. Instantly, I close my eyes from the sensation.

"This is your shooting arm?"

She takes her time on my right shoulder, thumbs pressing into the sore flesh. I can feel my face contort with pain, but it's equaled out with pleasure.

"Yeah."

"How'd it get so bad?"

"Repetition, I'd assume. I'm shooting a few hundred shots a day between scheduled practice and my own time on the court. That, and, sometimes I'm not given the same respect as other guys with protective calls, so I can get thrown around in games."

"Why not?"

"I don't have a championship or an MVP yet and I'm one of the smaller guys in the league. It's all politics."

"You're 6'3"," she laughs. "And it's only a matter of time for the other things to come your way."

I don't respond, but also don't miss the blind confidence she has in me.

Her latest read sits on the coffee table in front of me. As usual, it displays a shirtless man right there on the cover.

"What's this one about?" I ask, holding it up.

"The female main character hooks up with her ex-boyfriend's dad."

"What the fuck?"

"Trust me. The little shit deserved it."

I'm glad she's behind me and can't see the smile pulling at my lips. She's fucking ridiculous sometimes and I kind of love it.

Her warm hands work into my skin, loosening my muscles. Her

fingertips move over the tendons of my neck, creating slow circles before the edges of her nails lightly scratch against my hairline.

My head falls forward with a low moan.

"Does this feel good?"

"So good."

So fucking good. Yes, my muscles feel loosened, but being touched by her feels borderline euphoric.

Indy's voice is soft and a bit hoarse when she asks, "Do you want to come up here with me so I can get a better angle?"

It's a bad idea. It's a terrible fucking idea. It's three in the morning, I'm half naked with a half-hard dick, and my stunning roommate is asking me to get on the couch with her.

"Yeah," I rasp.

Standing, I stretch my neck, already feeling some of the tension dissolving. I know of another way to dissolve some tension that involves a soft, flat surface like this sofa, and a lot less clothes on us both. My body is too aware of the option and the awareness only heightens when I sit on the couch and Indy sandwiches her body behind mine.

Her long legs open around me and fuck if that doesn't send an image straight to my lusting brain.

Digging the heels of her palms into my back, she whispers, soft and low, "Does this hurt?"

Moaning, I shake my head. "No. It feels so good, Blue."

I can feel her breath on my neck, her scent on my skin. She's almost holding me in this position, her chest to my back, her legs wrapped around me.

I haven't been held in years.

"Did you do this for Alex?"

She pauses her movements.

I don't know why I asked. Maybe because I wanted to hear that I'm special. Maybe I wanted to hear that she treats me differently than she did him.

Or maybe I need to hear that her attentive doting is nothing out of the ordinary.

"No. He got plenty of attention from other people. He didn't need mine."

With her legs slung around my hips, I find one of her thighs, pulling her leg into my lap, and slowly running my palm from her ankle to her knee.

Even down to her toes, this girl is pretty. Slender bones and soft skin.

Indy's touch is no longer a massage but wandering caresses up and over the slopes of my shoulders. They're careful and exploratory, roaming my body.

The apartment is dark. It's the middle of the night. Her mouth is inches from mine.

"Do you think you'll ever be able to love someone the way you loved him?"

"I don't know," she says with honesty for no one else to hear but her and me. "Right now, it feels like he took everything. Like I don't have anything left to give someone else."

I swallow, hating that answer.

"I know I need to move on," she continues. "I know I joke around a lot, but I'm really messed up, Ryan. As if that wasn't clear from the night I moved in." Her light laugh rumbles against my back. "How can I go from being with someone for six years to jumping into something with someone else? It feels wrong."

"He did," I remind her.

"I know." Her forehead falls to my shoulder. "It feels disloyal, as ridiculous as that sounds, but that's how long I loved him for. I never imagined loving someone else. But at the same time, if I'm being honest, when I think about the time we had, the overall feeling I come away with is that he made me feel like I wasn't enough yet too much all at the same time."

I shake my head, inhaling through my nose because well…I hate this guy. Indy would never question how magnetic, how *distracting* she is if she saw herself the way everyone in her orbit sees her. The way *I* see her.

"You can't stop being who you are because someone else thinks it's too much, Ind. He can go find less."

From the sounds of it, that's exactly what he did. You don't get much better than Indigo Ivers.

"Do you think I'm a trainwreck, Ryan?"

I huff a laugh. "You're more like a cute little fender bender."

Feeling her smile against my skin, I pull her other leg into my lap as Indy wraps her arms around my neck from behind.

"Do you think he loved you the right way, Blue?"

"I don't know. He loved me loudly. I think the romantic in me thought that was the right way. The grand gestures. The big love confessions. He wasn't afraid to touch me in public but being away from him for the first time in my life, I'm realizing there are a lot of ways in which I thought he was showing me love, but really he was just showing me off."

Leaning back, I push her into the sofa, which only makes her body close around mine even more.

"I thought he loved me loudly, but when I found him with someone else, you were right when you said he practically screamed that he didn't want me. That was the loudest he's ever been."

My breathing turns shallow and rushed with the knowledge of her proximity.

Turning, my lips almost graze hers with how close we are. I can feel the erratic beat of her heart thumping against my back, her breasts pressing against my bare skin.

I want to kiss her, but I don't know if I'll be able to stop.

She whispers, low enough that if I weren't inches from her lips, I wouldn't hear. "Sometimes, I think I just need to move on in a different way. In the only way I can."

In a *physical* way.

*She's your sister's best friend, and you couldn't handle just one night even if she weren't.*

"Indy, it's late."

"Ryan—"

"I should go to bed."

Her voice is a low rasp, the whisper sending goosebumps over my skin. "Please don't."

Oh, fuck me with that gentle plea, those begging eyes. Indy sweeps her tongue across her bottom lip and my attention is glued to it. Glistening pink, pouty and what I can only imagine as pillow soft.

"Ry."

Clearing my throat, I stand from the couch and untangle our bodies in the process. "Good night, Blue."

Like the coward I am, I rush to my room, closing the door behind me.

Indy is not the type of woman you can simply flush from your system after a single night. She's the kind to seep into your veins and rewire your brain, making you do and say things you swore you never would. Whether she believes it or not, Indigo Ivers is the type of woman you keep forever, and even though I can pretend to be her boyfriend, there's no way in hell I could pretend that one night with her wouldn't completely fuck me up.

# 13 Ryan

"Camping? Who the hell goes camping in Chicago in the middle of winter?" Indy asks while adding two more sweatshirts into her overnight bag.

"I don't think it's real camping. Annie called it glamping, whatever the hell that means, and Ethan said the whole place is heated. We're just going to do dinner on the grill and eat outside."

"I can't believe you, of all people, are down for this. Do you know how dirty it is to camp? Are you sure you want to get in with these people? What if you have to start doing this kind of stuff all the time?"

"I take it you're not big into camping."

"Ryan," she deadpans. "Look at me. Do I look like I'm *big into camping*? I was hoping for a nice dinner where I could dress up and wear some cute shoes. I like having central heat and a place to plug in my hair tools. Are you positive you want to go?"

I place my duffel by the front door. "Yeah, I do. This might sound pathetic, but I miss being outdoors. I'm looking forward to being outside of this apartment without people watching everything I do."

Indy's expression morphs with understanding. "No, that's not pathetic. You're right. I'm sorry. That will be nice for you."

She takes a seat on the bench in the entryway, slipping her feet into her white converse that are covered in stitched doodles.

"What's with all the stitching on those shoes?"

She holds up one to examine it. "I like sewing and one day, I thought it'd be cool to sew a pattern onto the canvas. They're little doodles of things from my life. My friends, places I've been. That kind of stuff."

As Indy ties them up, I take a closer look.

An airplane is sewn by the outside ankle of the left shoe. There's a hockey stick and a Stanley Cup on the right. An ocean and sunset which I assume is Florida. A head of chestnut curls and I could recognize that as representing my sister even from a mile away. A number thirty-eight is nestled into Boston's skyline for her friend Rio, I guess. I don't let myself think too far into that because I'm just grateful there's nothing regarding her shitty ex that she would quite literally be walking around with.

I'm not sure how you'd sew a jackass who made the biggest mistake of his life, but I'm confident Indy could figure it out if she really wanted to.

I've always found Indy's Converse random and a bit strange, but now I find myself wondering what I have to do to get myself added to them.

"Ready?" she asks, wearing a much brighter smile than she was twenty minutes ago when I reminded her she's going to be sleeping in a tent tonight.

I grab both our bags, sling them over, my shoulder and follow her out of the apartment.

"How many cars do you have?" Indy asks as I drive at a snail's pace through the campgrounds, looking for our camping site's number.

"Two. This one and the Audi."

"Don't get me wrong, both a Range Rover and an Audi are way out of my price range, but you've got *money* money. I thought you'd go more extravagant."

"Indy, what part of my lifestyle seems extravagant to you?"

"That's true." She nods. "But why? You have more money than you'll ever know what to do with."

"It seems wasteful. I save and invest. I have a whole college fund set up for Stevie's kids if she decides to have them, but I doubt she'll be using it now that those kids are going to be half the most over-the-top, extravagant guy I know."

"Zanders' children are going to be wearing Tom Ford and Prada to school."

"Unless Vee gets them to love thrifting as much as she does."

Peeking over to Indy, she wears a soft smile as she leans back on the headrest.

"Half of my income though..." I continue. "I donate to charity."

"Really? Where to?"

"Well, currently I'm housing this flight attendant who is terrible at cleaning up after herself. Total charity case. Tragic story, really."

She lightly smacks my arm, laughing. "Shut up."

"I donate to Zee's foundation, Active Minds, but my main focus is Chicago's public school system. Making sure kids have the textbooks they need for class and food for lunch. And part of my shoe deal is that every year my sponsor has to match my donation in gifting said shoe to kids who need something to wear in order to be active. But there's so much more that needs to be done. It feels overwhelming."

Keeping my eyes out for our campsite, the silence begins to take over. Eventually, I look over to find Indy staring at me with the softest brown eyes I've ever seen.

"I didn't tell you that to make you think I'm some great guy. I don't really tell anyone about it for that reason alone. Just assume it's for tax purposes so you don't get all sentimental over it."

Biting her lower lip, she shakes her head, but my emotional roommate's eyes can't help from shining. "I don't think you're great. I have no opinion about this whatsoever. I. Feel. Nothing."

"You should work on your acting skills before we get to the campsite."

Indy heaves a broken breath. "Okay, I'll try."

I pull into our numbered lot and park next to Ethan's truck. About twenty feet ahead of us sits three tents on individual platform decks with stairs leading to each one. The tent itself shouldn't be referred to as a tent at all. It's more of a tiny house made of glass walls and canvas covering the sides and back to give the illusion of camping outdoors when in reality, you're completely indoors.

"Damn," Indy exhales. "So, this is how rich people camp."

Luckily, it's an unseasonably warm day for this time of year, but even if it weren't, the fire is roaring in the middle of the site, and the cabins seem to be plenty warm.

Ron stands at the grill to the left of the cabins wearing cargo pants, a flannel shirt, and a goddamn puffer vest. Maybe there was a better way to get on my boss's good side rather than having to spend the night out here with him and his wife and *oh, dear God*. I'm going to have to see what he looks like when he wakes up in the morning.

"Maybe we should go home." I switch the gear into reverse.

"Are those cargo pants freaking you out as much as they're scaring me?"

"It's like we drove an hour outside of Chicago and he became a different person. This is a bad idea. We should've waited for a normal dinner invite. We could lie for the course of a dinner, but a whole fucking sleepover?"

"Come on." Indy sits up with excitement. "This looks fun."

"What happened to 'I'm not big into camping'?"

"This is hardly camping, and I'm always down for some social interaction. Plus, there are no fans around to stare at you like you're some sort of magical all-powerful being."

Indy reaches for the door handle, but I click the lock in place before she can get to it. Brown eyes roll with exaggeration when the door refuses to open for her.

Call me old-fashioned, I don't care, but I have yet and will not let her open her own door.

Rounding the car, I unlock it on the key fob and open the passenger side to find Indy wearing an unimpressed expression. "You're so weird about that."

"I'm not weird. You've just never had someone take care of you before, so you may as well get used to it."

I sling both our bags over my shoulder when Ron waves us over. "Welcome! Did you find it all right?"

"We did. Thank you for inviting us."

I allow Indy to walk ahead of me, but before she takes too many steps, she reaches back to place her hand in mine. It's small but reassuring, so I wrap mine around hers and hold on in hopes we can pull this off.

"This is so amazing. I had no idea this was out here," Indy says as Caroline exits her tent.

"Oh, you made it! Ethan and Annie just arrived too," Caroline bursts. "How was the drive?"

"It was beautiful."

"Nice to get out of the city, huh?"

"Yeah," I interrupt, exhaling. "It really is."

Ethan and Annie come out to greet us and after all the hellos are said, Ron points us in the direction of our cabin. With our bags in tow, I follow Indy up the steps.

"This is...*revealing*," she says.

"Remind me not to go outside unless Ron and Caroline have their canvas pulled down. The last thing I need is to see my boss wearing his pajamas and spooning his wife."

"You think he wears pajamas? He seems more like a bare-ass-naked kind of guy."

"Jesus, Ind."

Before I'm fully inside, I'm releasing the cord to the canvas that covers the front of our cabin, giving us a moment of privacy.

Indy stops in the doorway. "Cozy."

While yes, the inside of the cabin is comfortable and warm, the coziness she's referring to is the single bed that takes up seventy percent of the room.

"You take the bed. I can sleep on the floor." I drop my bag on the three feet of floor space I'll be sleeping on tonight.

"Don't be ridiculous." Indy plops her duffel bag on the mattress. "I'm going to pile the other side with pillows anyway, you may as well sleep next to me. But don't worry, Shay, I don't have cooties."

Cooties are not what I'm worried about. Indy loves to give me shit that I'm afraid of girls, but the truth is the only woman who has ever truly terrified me is her. Her intelligence, charisma, and sharp little attitude are the most frightening things about her, because I've never felt as weak as I do when I'm around her.

Indy gets her toiletries organized in the world's smallest bathroom while I layer up in preparation to eat dinner outside, slipping my wool coat over my hooded sweatshirt.

"Here, let me help you with that," she insists, situating my hood on the outside of my coat. I turn around to face her as she begins slipping the buttons on my jacket through the holes. "You can work on your bucket list tonight. It would be a good night to work on casually touching in public."

"Oh, you'd like that, wouldn't you?"

"Watch it or I'll work on *my* bucket list by kicking your ass out of bed and sleeping alone."

I bite my lip to hold back my smile while Indy mirrors me.

Tucking my ears into my beanie, I slip Indy's lavender one over her head. The color looks nice against her blonde hair and brown eyes, but then again, she looks nice in just about anything.

"Let's go help with dinner before they think we're in here fucking."

She raises a brow. "Trust me. If we were fucking, they'd know. I'm not very quiet."

Instantly, I turn away from her, putting my hands on top of my head, and attempting to keep my blood from flooding south. "Jesus, Blue. Not funny. Are you trying to make me go have dinner next to my GM with a goddamn hard-on in my pants?"

"That's one way to convince him you're into me." She giggles mischievously.

*No one needs to be convinced. It's fairly fucking obvious.*

Curiosity laces her tone. "Did it work?"

As I turn around, her eyes immediately drop to my crotch. Her smile falls and I watch that pretty, slender throat of hers move in a deep swallow.

"What do you think? I can't exactly think about how loud you might be in bed without all the blood rushing straight to my cock."

"Oh," she breathes.

I rub my palms over my face. "I'll be out in a minute. Good god, woman."

# 14

# Indy

**Me:** *Daily update—I just want you to know, I saw the outline of your brother's dick and I very much want to have sex with him. But I'm not going to. Aren't I such a good friend?*

**Stevie:** *If I could have one wish, it'd be that your campsite didn't have Wi-Fi so I never had to read those words.*

**Me:** *Blame your brother for that one too. Only rich people have Wi-Fi while camping.*

**Stevie:** *Gonna go throw my phone against the wall now! Have fun!*

I'm sure there's a blush covering my cheeks as I head down the stairs to dinner, and I'm not embarrassed but I am flustered. He blatantly brought up sex on a night we have to share a bed, and I ran with it.

*If we were fucking, they'd know. I'm not very quiet.*

What the hell is wrong with me? As if the other night, tangled up on the couch when he rejected me after I hinted that I was ready to move on physically from Alex wasn't bad enough, here I am, telling him how loud I am in bed.

"Indy." Annie waves me to the fire that's roaring in the middle of the campsite. "I'm having a hot toddy. Can I make you one?"

"That sounds great."

Annie pours from her thermos to a mug before adding some lemon and a cinnamon stick. "I know you're just pretending," she whispers for no one else to hear. "But you two look good together."

I take a sip of my cocktail, warming me from the inside out. "Ryan would look good with just about anybody."

Annie raises her brows, unimpressed. "Mm-hmm. Whatever you say."

"Where's your boyfriend?" Ethan calls out as he stands at the grill with Ron.

"He's uh…taking care of something." *Subtle.* "He'll be right out."

"I hope hamburgers sound good tonight." Ron's voice drips with pride as he mans the grill with a metal spatula in his hand. "These are going to be a perfect medium-rare."

"That sounds great," I lie, hoping there are some sides I'll be able to munch on. I'm here to make a good impression on Ryan's boss, not offend him by refusing to eat the dinner he's so proudly prepared.

Caroline comes out of her tent with a plastic piece of Tupperware, shaking it to show us. "And I hope you like s'mores!"

I don't know what Ryan's deal is with Ron Morgan, but he seems nice enough to me. Sure, I've only met him twice and he was with his wife both times, but the guy seems like a total softie. Ryan is far more intimidating than him.

Speaking of my fake boyfriend, I hear his car beep in the lot behind me before he emerges with a cooler in his hand. The sun is setting, leaving a slight golden glow to illuminate him and he looks fucking gorgeous in those fitted black jeans. His beanie is a navy knit which does nothing but make his eyes glow strikingly blue.

*Good God, Indy. Get it together. It's a goddamn beanie and jeans.*

"Ron, would you mind throwing a few of these on the grill too?" Ryan asks, putting his cooler on the picnic table and fishing out a box of frozen veggie patties. "Indy is a vegetarian."

He didn't.

"Oh, I had no idea." Ron's voice drips with apology, looking at me.

"It was my fault," Ryan cuts in. "I should've told you. I brought some veggie sausage for her breakfast too. Do you have somewhere to store them?"

"I do!" Caroline bursts, pulling Ryan into their makeshift kitchen where they have a much larger and fancier cooler than his.

"Hmm," Annie hums.

"What?"

"Nothing. Don't get me wrong. I love Ethan, but my real husband is nowhere near as thoughtful as your fake boyfriend."

"He's just trying to convince them that we're legitimate."

At that exact moment, Ryan looks over his shoulder, offering me the sweetest smile that man could give.

Annie takes a long drink from her cocktail. "They're not the only ones he's convincing."

In true Ryan fashion, he takes the liberty to wash the dishes after dinner. It's not quite the same setup he has at home, but a single sponge and a waterspout seem to work just fine for him.

Four tree stumps circle the campfire, acting as seats. Ron, Caroline, and I each take one while Ethan shares his lap with his wife.

"Annie, how are the girls?" I ask while leaning forward to roast a marshmallow over the fire. "Did Gemma's piano recital go well?"

It might seem like I'm asking to appear close to Annie because any girlfriend of Ryan's would be friends with his closest teammates' wife. But the truth is I genuinely like Annie and enjoyed getting to meet her at the fall banquet.

"It did!" Annie adjusts in her husband's lap. "She got a little case of stage fright in the beginning, but Ethan gave her a pep talk and she was good to go. She did great."

Ron cuts in. "What did you tell her, Ethan?"

"The usual. How if I have to play basketball in front of thousands of people, she could handle a room of fifty. I also added that the only person she needed to impress was herself. That sort of stuff. Oh, and I bribed her with post-recital ice cream if she got on stage and performed."

Through the glow of the fire, I can see the smile on Ron's face. "You're a good dad." He turns to me. "What about you two? Any kids in the future?"

My cocktail goes down the wrong pipe, turning me into a sputtering mess, but somehow, I still find the mental wherewithal to pull my marshmallow from the flame before it burns. All while replaying Ron's question if I'm going to have Ryan's babies anytime soon.

Annie and Ethan chuckle into each other, finding this entire scenario hilarious.

Ron cocks his head, as if he's testing me for the answer, quickly reminding me that we've yet to fully convince him of our relationship or Ryan's drastic and sudden change.

"I uh…we…" I stumble.

A blanket settles around my shoulders. "We haven't talked about it yet," Ryan says with full honesty. In fact, it might be the most honest thing we've said to Ron tonight.

"Settle down, Ronald," Caroline condemns. "They're new and young and in love. Let them enjoy it. They're in the exciting stage, when your bellies fill with butterflies from the prospect of seeing each other. Although, that stage may have already passed for you two since you live together."

"Well—"

"It's still like that." I cut Ryan off, looking up at him over my shoulder. "Very much so."

Keeping his lips pressed together, he smiles down at me, those freaking dimples concaving with the glow of the fire lighting his face. "Can I sit with you?"

I look to either side of me, but between me and all my winter layers there's no room left for Ryan on my seat.

He bends down, speaking quietly. "You can sit on my lap, Blue."

As his girlfriend, of course I would. As his roommate who is forming an unhealthy crush, it's a terrible idea.

I finish my cocktail for liquid courage and stand with the blanket still wrapped around me, my skewer and sad marshmallow in my hand. Ryan takes a seat, one palm lingering on my hip and guiding me down to sit on his lap. He situates the blanket over me, then pulls me closer, my back flush with his chest and the warmth of his breath lingering on the skin of my neck.

"Good?" he whispers.

"Good."

Good doesn't do it justice. I'm great. I'm fan-fucking-tastic. This man is huge and warm and these goddamn thighs are pure muscle.

Under the blanket, his hand slides from my hip bone, curving inward, palm covering my thigh. His fingertips slip between my legs, dangerously close to a spot I need them, before he kneads my flesh as if he were holding back from more.

*Acting. Fake. Pretend.*

But the blanket is covering us, and this little show of restraint is for no one else to see.

There's a light pounding on my back—his heart rate speeding up and God am I tempted to rock my ass back a touch and see if—

"Indy," Annie interrupts, holding out the Tupperware. "For your s'mores."

"Oh. Thank you." I smile what I'm certain is the guiltiest looking smile she's ever seen.

Concentrating on roasting my marshmallow, I attempt to ignore the stunning man underneath me. More chatter about kids circulates between the two couples, and I need to join in before I do something impulsive like grind my ass against my roommate to see if he's still hard from earlier.

Turning towards the Morgans, I ask, "What about you two? Do you have any children?"

Caroline reaches out to squeeze Ron's hand. "We wanted to," she says. "But it wasn't in the cards for us. We have nieces and nephews who we treat as our own though. Ron and I are lucky to each have a handful of siblings, so we still got the family we always wanted."

I swallow. "I'm sorry to hear that."

"Don't be. Life has a funny way of fulfilling you, even when it isn't in the way you assumed it'd be."

Can't argue there. Lately, life has been anything but what I assumed.

Looking at Caroline, I might be seeing my future self. Although, I don't know that I'll be as lucky to have a husband that loves me the way Ron does her. There's a high chance kids won't be in the cards for me either, but unfortunately, I'm an only child with no prospects of nieces and nephews to sublimate my need for a family.

There's always fostering or adoption, and I'm thankful for those possibilities, but I'm not sure how many adoption agencies are going to pick a single woman over a dual parent household.

"Blue." Ryan lightly shakes my leg, pulling me out of my trance. "Your marshmallow is black."

"Oh shit." I pull it from the flame, blowing out the fire it brought with it. Ryan quietly laughs at me but pulls me in closer at the same time.

Typically, I'm the one to carry the conversation. That's my self-assigned role in our phony relationship, but I can't seem to come up with something to talk about after what Caroline said.

Ryan takes the cue. "So, we have Houston tomorrow night. Easton's been on a roll these past couple of weeks. We should think about double teaming him in the back court. Try to break his rhythm."

Ethan clears his throat, eyes bouncing from Ryan to Ron in warning.

"What?"

"We talk enough about basketball during the week, don't you think?" Ron asks. "We like to keep family dinners to that. Family. We came out here to get away from the city. To have a break for the night."

Ryan stiffens beneath me, and not in the way I want. We're here, supposedly showing Ron that Ryan cares about more than just the game he lives and breathes. That he understands relationships and camaraderie are what make a great leader, not just the score at the end of a game. And he just walked into basketball talk without realizing.

"Oh," Ryan hesitates. "I know. I didn't—"

"I haven't seen Ryan play in person yet," I blurt out, hoping to save him.

"What?" Caroline bursts, lightly smacking her husband on the arm. "Ron, did you hear that? Oh my goodness, you have to! He's so talented."

"He is amazing," I agree.

"Are you in town tomorrow night?" Ron asks. "Caroline and I are missing the game. It's her brother's birthday. Our seats are yours if you'd like them. Take a couple of friends and enjoy the game."

"Really? I'd love to. That's so generous of you."

"You better dress up!" Annie cuts in. "Courtside at your man's game. You'll be photographed for sure."

"Can you come sit with me?"

"I wish I could, but I'm officially at the stage of Ethan's career where the girls are going to sleep in our family box by halftime, and I'm trying to stay awake long enough to finish the game."

"Damn." Ethan laughs. "I've really lost my appeal, huh? Falling asleep watching me play? Don't let me keep you up, Ann."

Annie pats Ethan's chest. "I don't."

The energy has shifted once again, and Ryan's little slip-up is in the past. As chatter continues, I refocus on my s'more, adding twice as much chocolate as I probably should, but needing it to cover up the fact I burnt my marshmallow to shit.

Ryan rests his chin on my shoulder as I sandwich the graham crackers. "Thank you," he whispers for no one else to hear. "You saved me out there."

"We're a team. I'm here to help you out."

"I like the way that sounds."

Turning, I smile at him.

"Does that mean the team shares s'mores too?"

I shake my head in disagreement. "They're reserved for the MVP." I make a dramatic performance of the giant bite I take right in front of Ryan's mouth, letting my throat release a low moan in show of how good it is.

"Don't make those little noises while you're sitting on my lap." He grabs my thigh, his lips dangerously close to mine while he speaks. "Otherwise, you're not going to be able to get up for a while."

It's all a show, but goddamn, this version of Ryan is not the same fake boyfriend I went to the fall banquet with. He's sexy and confident and comfortable out here. I like it far too much.

"You mean *you* won't be able to get up for a while."

"Same thing."

Turning around in his lap, I swing both of my legs to one side of his, offering him some of my s'more. His lips wrap around it, taking a generous bite, all the while keeping his ocean eyes penetrating mine.

Wow. It feels claustrophobic in this open air.

A bit of marshmallow falls onto his chin, and without thinking, I wipe it off with my thumb. But before I can clean off the mess, he grabs my hand and takes my finger in his mouth to suck off the remnants.

I'm entirely out of breath when the warmth of his tongue swirls and flicks my thumb, very similarly to how I'd imagine he'd swirl and flick something else.

*Acting. Fake. Pretend.*

He's getting good at this fake boyfriend thing, and if I don't keep reminding my romantic heart of exactly what this is, I'm going to be in trouble.

# 15 Ryan

While Indy is showering inside, I make sure all the canvases are down to cover the glass walls for the night. Needing, at least, to sleep in privacy. The walls are built into an A-frame, the highest point of the ceiling aiming straight to the sky. A separate drawstring is attached to the canvases on the roof, so I test one, tugging to see what happens. The fabric covering one half of the ceiling opens, giving the cabin an open skylight to watch the stars from bed. I do the same to the other half before heading inside and locking the door behind me.

Before I can look up to see the view, I find a much more spectacular one standing naked in the center of the room wearing only a towel and looking up towards the sky.

"Wow," Indy exhales, her head thrown back. "That's beautiful."

I honestly couldn't care less what's up north. If she saw how stunning she looked with a light layer of moisture coating her body or the slight flush to her cheeks from her warm shower, she would understand my disinterest in looking away.

"The stars are so bright out here," she continues. "I never see them in the city." Brown eyes track me. "Ryan?"

I nod. "Stunning."

Every fiber in my body wants to close the gap between us and kiss her right now. And if she asked for more than that, I don't think I'd be able to hold back. It's a terrifying revelation to have, especially when we're minutes away from crawling into bed together.

*She's your sister's best friend. She's going through a nasty breakup. She's your roommate, for fuck's sake.*

This room is too fucking small to share with her when she's naked and smelling clean and tropical from her soap.

"I'm going to take a shower."

Head down, I take two quick steps in that direction, needing to get behind a closed door, only to run into a soaking wet blonde. Our bodies collide, the impact dropping her towel to the floor. I know this because my hands are around her bare back to steady her, and two hard peaks are pressed into my upper stomach.

"Oh my God." She freezes. "Oh. My. God."

My eyes are locked on that scenery I refused to look at before, even though the temptation could not be greater to see what's in my hands. "Indy, what the hell are you doing?"

"I'm sorry! I was going to get my things out of the shower for you."

Calloused fingers curl into the soft, warm flesh on her back, and my teeth clench together. "I need you to very carefully pick your towel up off the ground. Right now."

If I thought I had strong self-control before, nothing compares to the restraint I'm experiencing at this moment because as she slowly bends to the ground, she brushes against my cock. I hiss an inhale, as if all my blood wasn't already headed in that direction before she grazed it.

Her laugh holds an awkward edge. "Oops. Sorry."

As soon as I sense her body is covered once again, I take the final step into the bathroom and close the door behind me.

What the fuck sort of evil thing did I manage to do in order to earn this kind of temptation? I've gone years, *years* without giving a woman as much as a second glance, and now the one I can't stop thinking about is living in my house.

Fuck. The bathroom smells like her. *I* smell like her from holding her in my lap all night. Part of me doesn't want to wash her off my skin, but most of me knows I need to take care of the painful erection I've tried to hide all night before I crawl into bed next to her.

I let the water pound against my back as I brace my palms on the wall. I shouldn't do this, but the need is too strong. I won't picture her, though. I won't picture anyone.

But as soon as my fist wraps around my cock, an image invades my mind. Indy on her knees, soft brown eyes begging for my dick.

*No. No, stop picturing her.*

Indy's lips form a pretty little "O" as she bats her lashes, looking up at me from the shower floor. Her lilac-painted fingers are clawing at my thighs and hips, needy and begging for me to let her work.

My fingers entangle in those blonde tresses, pulling her hair the way I've pictured since the day she walked into my apartment. A quick lash of her tongue heats the underside of my tip, all the while she keeps her attention on me.

Fuck, I wish this were real. I stroke myself, imagining it is. Her coconut body wash sits on the ledge, and without thinking, I pour some into my palm, rub it against my skin, and create a lather before using the slickness on my cock. Her scent invades my nostrils, creating an even more convincing picture.

"We shouldn't do this," I remind her, tugging her chin down with my thumb, opening her mouth.

Her pink lips form into a pout. "But I want to. I *need* to. Please, Ryan."

Goddamn, I love the way she says my name and imagining her voice when she says it brings me that much closer to the edge.

"I know how to make you feel better." She swirls her tongue around the head. "Please let me make you feel better."

"You want it, Blue?"

She nods, all doe-eyed and innocent. It's one of my favorite things about Indy, how confident and charismatic she is to the outside world, but then she's soft to those who know her.

I pick her up off the ground, slinging those long legs around my waist and pushing her back to the tiled wall. "Then let me give it to you."

I tighten my hand around my base, pulling and stroking, keeping my eyes closed as the water beats down on me.

My cock slides against her pussy and she lets out the prettiest little whimper.

I want to fuck her so badly it hurts.

"You feel…" Her chest pounds against mine, trying to catch her breath. "God, you feel so good, Ryan."

She does too, according to my imagination. I pick up the speed and tighten my grasp, imagining it's Indy's body clenching around me and not my own fist.

"Put it in. Put it in. Please," she begs. "I need you. Please."

She bucks her hips off the wall, needing to meet mine, and as soon as I imagine pushing into her, jets of cum hit the shower tile with force. My release is almost blinding as I come harder than I have in a very long time. Continuing to stroke myself, I let every last drop fall and swirl down the drain, allowing the water to wash away what I just did.

With an acute awareness, I realize how utterly and completely wrong I was, thinking that would get Indy out of my system. Now, my body is begging for the real thing, wanting to know what she sounds like when she comes.

If I were any other man, I'd go find someone else to sleep with and get a quick fuck out of my system, hoping it'd fix the issue. But seeing as I'm me, and I can't allow myself to be vulnerable enough, even for a one-night stand, I'm left dreaming of the blonde living in my house.

If I'm being honest with myself, I know no one else would do it for me right now. No one else *has* done it for me in years, but that doesn't change that this can't happen. I won't allow it. Tomorrow, I'll wake up and the first thing I'll think about is my game. My day will continue that way, until I wake the following morning and do it all over again. Rinse and repeat until my mindset is back where it should be—my career.

This fucked-up daydream—the one where I can't seem to think about anything other than getting into bed with Indy—ends the second we leave this goddamn campsite.

Indy's back is towards me when I leave the bathroom, wearing only my towel. The cabin is small and she's everywhere. Her clothes. Her smell.

"Enjoy your shower?" she asks.

Best fucking shower of my life. The teasing tone of her voice tells me I could bet good money that she heard me and already knows the answer.

"Yeah, it was very—"

"Wet."

*Fuck me.* Just hearing the word *wet* pop out of her mouth has me gearing up for another round with my hand.

"Yes, Blue. The shower was wet."

She giggles at the innuendo, and I drop the towel, slipping into a pair of shorts while she's still facing away from me.

"No pillows?" I round the bed to find my side empty.

"Not tonight. I guess you'll do." She eyes my chest, those brown eyes appearing more hooded than usual. "You're not wearing a shirt."

"Lucky you."

She softly laughs and as I lift the cover to slip under her sheets, I ask, "Is this okay?"

Shyly, she nods her head.

Dipping between the sheets, I'm cautious to leave some room between us. I lay on my side to face her. "Thank you again. For helping me out tonight."

"I had fun." She tucks her hands under her cheek as we maintain a good foot of space between us.

"Yeah?"

"Yeah. You're getting better at faking it. We might have a real shot of pulling this off at the wedding."

The realization of why it might come more naturally to me now is terrifying.

"Good." I offer her a slight lift of my lips before turning around to face the wall. "Night, Blue."

"Good night." She exhales a long breath, and I can feel the dip in the bed as she turns around too.

I need to sleep. I have a game tomorrow, and the sooner I can pass out, the sooner this outing is over. I know I should be looking forward to this evening ending so I can refocus on the purpose for this charade—to prove I can be a good leader, to actually *lead* this team to the playoffs—but I don't want it to be over. I like that people believe she's mine. I like how it feels to have her in my bed.

Flipping on my back, I get a glimpse of Indy's blonde hair cascading down her pillow, her back to me. Maybe it's more torture than anything, having her so close, but still maintaining the boundary of her being my roommate and sister's best friend.

Indy flips onto her back as well, and as she does, her hand accidentally falls into my open palm between us, but she pulls it away instantaneously, a wave of awkwardness washing over us. Even though we've touched and held each other in public, this is different. No one is here to witness and therefore, it's no longer an act. It's simply two roommates who technically have no reason to share physical contact.

There's a heavy silence in the room, and not the kind when two people are trying to fall asleep, but the type that's buzzing with anticipation because you're both aware of just how awake you are.

A beat passes between us before hesitantly, Indy slips her hand back in mine. It's soft and small, and I close my fingers around hers before she can leave me again.

I can almost hear my nervous heart beating in the silence until her thumb skims mine in a gentle stroke, and fuck if I don't want to yank her on top of me and kiss her right now. But I can't. For a multitude of reasons, I can't, so I keep our hands as the only point of contact.

I aim my eyes up towards the sky, basking in the stars, being outside. I missed this freedom.

"Hey, Ind?"

"Mm-hmm."

"About last night. I didn't say it, but I do care about you. You know that, right?"

She lightly squeezes my hand. "I know you do. But it's nice to hear it. Words of affirmation and all that."

"Right. Now, this is the part where you tell me how much you care about me."

She yawns—forcibly. "Oh, man. It's getting late. So tired."

"You suck."

The bed moves from her quiet laughter. She turns to face me, her hand still in mine and her other tucked under her cheek. "I care about you too, Ry."

Even though I'm looking at the night sky, I can see her watching me in my periphery.

Her voice is barely a whisper when she asks, "Do you trust me?"

In theory, it's a simple question with a simple answer. But trust is the most complicated belief in my world of black and white. If most people asked the question, it'd be an easy no, but with Indy, after only weeks of knowing her, the answer is undoubtedly, "Yes."

Looking over at her, her expression is soft, hopeful.

"What?"

She shakes her head. "Nothing. I just know how big that is coming from you."

I stroke the back of her hand with my thumb as I turn my body to face her, the only remaining space between us is where our hands are connected.

"Will you tell me a secret?" she asks quietly. "Something no one else knows."

Without hesitation, Marissa and the month following my college graduation runs through my mind. It's my biggest secret. Only my sister knows what I lost, but as much as I trust Indy, I'm not sure if I'm ready to share.

Instead, I offer her another secret, something just as true. "You make me feel relaxed. Like I can be myself."

She holds eye contact, reading me before breaking into a laugh. "Don't lie to me, Shay. You constantly complain about how messy I am. No way in hell do I relax you."

"You're chaotic as fuck, Blue, but you bring me more peace than anyone else."

She stops her giggling.

"Yes, I worry about you and that stresses me out. And you've practically shit a rainbow all over my apartment which almost gave me an ulcer, but when you're home I don't feel like I have to put on a show. I have a hard time with new people. I'm sure you know that by now. But with you, I can be myself, and that might seem like nothing to anyone else, but to me, it's everything."

Silence lingers between us, but I wish she'd just fucking say something.

"Stop being nice to me or you're going to make me cry."

I smile at that. "You always cry."

"I know! But that was really nice to hear, Ryan."

Fisting my free hand, I keep it at my side, holding back from touching her. I don't want her to misinterpret my reasoning for being vulnerable. I did it simply because she deserves to hear how special she is.

"Since you didn't give me the secret I wanted, I'll just ask. You can decide if you answer."

Pausing, I give her time to ask the question I inevitably know is coming.

"Why don't you date?"

Exhaling, I scrub my free hand over my head.

Fuck it. I already know I'm going to give her the not so pretty details one day. "The last woman I was in a relationship with tried to get knocked up so she'd get eighteen years of child support from me."

Indy stays eerily silent.

"As if she *did* get pregnant with my child, I wouldn't be involved." I chuckle without much humor behind it.

"Ryan—"

"I'm fine."

"No, you're not. You won't date because of that. That's why you have a hard time trusting people? This is the woman from college?"

I nod, silently answering both questions.

In a rare moment, Indy is speechless, maybe picking up on the fact I don't want to talk about this any longer. But she gives me her silent support through the squeeze of my hand.

"Will *you* tell me a secret now?" I ask.

"I don't have many secrets. I'm kind of an open book if you couldn't tell."

"What are you saving money for?"

I can almost see the wheels turning in her head, contemplating this conversation.

"You don't have to tell me."

"No. No, it's nothing to be secretive about and it's nothing exciting. Just…promise me you won't laugh."

"Well, now I'm intrigued."

Even through the darkness, with the stars illuminating her face a bit, I can see her looking away from me.

"I'm saving money to have my eggs frozen."

*Huh?*

My brows are creased in confusion. "Why? You're still so young."

"I know I am, but my ovaries aren't. Thanks to my genetic line, at twenty-seven, I've got some old-ass eggs. All I've ever wanted is to be a mom, and I don't care how. Stepmom. Foster mom. Adoptive mom. But if I want to keep the very slim chance of being a biological mom, this is my only hope. It might be too late already, I don't know, but I need to try."

Okay, now I can't help but touch her. Grazing my fingertips across her cheek, I push her hair behind her ear. "Why would I laugh at that?"

"I don't know. I've been told I sound desperate. Maybe I do, but I don't care. It's the one thing I've always wanted in life. It's just unfolding a little differently than I pictured. I refuse to ask my parents for help. It's *my* potential family and I want to do this for myself, but that means working more to make some extra cash."

"Who called you desperate?"

"I don't remember," she answers far too quickly.

My little lying roommate. It was her ex. That's clear as fucking day.

"I don't want you to take this the wrong way because I'm genuinely just being curious. But why did you wait so long? If you're worried it's already too late, I mean."

She exhales. "Ryan, I'm pretty sure you already know the answer to all these questions. I didn't do it sooner because the man who I thought was going to be the father of my children told me he wanted to start trying. Soon, I mean. It was always 'soon.' It wasn't that I wanted to have kids right then. I was young. I'm still young, but I did need to make a decision or a plan, and his plan was to continually dangle 'let's try soon' in front of me. It's my fault for not taking action, so that's on me."

I let go of her hand and instead, tuck one arm under her body, pulling her into my chest. She hides in the crook of my neck, so I speak softly, my lips to her ear. "There's nothing desperate about going after what you want most in life. So, fuck him for saying it because even if you don't want to tell me, I know it was him."

"It might end up being a waste of money."

"Money comes and goes. This is your life. Be selfish for once, Ind. You spent six years catering to that guy's timeline. It's about time you do something for yourself."

She buries herself deeper into my neck.

"And ironically, you want a child so you have someone else to take care of and therefore you're not being selfish at all."

Her body shakes against mine with quiet laughter. "God, what's wrong with me?"

"Nothing. You're a nurturer. It's who you are."

"I think you're a nurturer too."

An awkward laugh escapes me. "I don't know about that."

"Yeah, because you're not caring and protective and sweet at all. You're just a selfish basketball player who only thinks about himself and his career."

Her voice carries a sarcastic tone, but she's not far off. That's who I am.

"And you're probably mentally agreeing with me, but you're wrong. One day, you'll see it."

I run my palm over her back, quickly learning that Indy didn't bring those footy pajamas she threatened me with. She's wearing some kind of silky sleep set and I could not be more thankful I can't see underneath the blankets. Because I know it looks as good as it feels in my hands, and I'm over here trying my fucking hardest to be a gentleman while sharing a bed with my biggest weakness.

Indy lifts her head from my neck to look at me. The subtle glow of the stars outlines the slope of her nose, the fluttering of her lashes, the soft pillows of her lips. She wets the bottom one with a slick slide of her tongue.

Fuck me, I want her, and even though she's made it clear she's got nothing left to give, I find myself desperate to take even the scraps if they're offered.

What I'm not sure I can do is separate a physical relationship from the rest the way she wants, so instead of taking her mouth, I brush her hair behind her ear and place my lips on her forehead.

Indy yawns, repositioning herself as I lay back on the bed. She rests her cheek on my bare chest and slings an arm over my waist.

"To be honest, my stack of pillows is much more comfortable than your chest, but I guess you'll do." She readjusts. "Seriously, Ryan, it's like sleeping on a goddamn boulder."

"You're awfully whiney for a girl who's practically burrowing her way into my skin right now."

"Shut up."

Wearing an amused smile, I pull the blankets higher over our bodies before wrapping both my arms around her to make sure she can't get away. With my fingertips, I trace invisible designs over her ribs, memorizing the way she molds against me.

Her breathing slows after some time, but I don't think I'll sleep a wink. I can't recall the last time I shared my bed with a woman, and as sad as it sounds, I don't want to miss a moment of this.

She inhales deeply. "Ryan?"

"Hmm?"

"Why do you smell like coconut?"

# 16 Indy

If there's anything I know how to do it's to play a part. Whether it be the happy-go-lucky friend or the girlfriend who shines brightly on her partner's arm but knows when to dim her light for him to excel in front of his peers.

But tonight, I'm playing the point guard's girl, and I've got to admit, it's my favorite role thus far.

Skin-tight black leather pants, red strappy heels, and an itty-bitty Devils tee create the perfect costume for the act. My hair is in a slicked-back ponytail, and I finished my makeup with a swipe of red across my lips which I'll chalk up to team spirit and is in no way meant to distract number five.

"Indy, you've got the tickets?" Zanders asks as we exit his G-Wagon, and even though he's not the one playing tonight, he still has the luxury of parking in the players' lot.

"Yep." I hold my phone up. "Ryan sent them."

"Look at us. Going to your fake boyfriend's game like a happy little family." Stevie slips her arm through mine, her other hand threaded with Zanders' as the three of us walk towards the arena. "Ryan's plan must be working if the Morgans gifted you their court-side tickets."

"What can I say? I'm quite the actress."

Zanders gives the older man at the door a hug before leading the way down the long hall that stretches past the locker rooms.

"That's the visitor's training room." Zanders points out as we follow along on his tour. "Visitors' locker room and home training room. And here"—he stops us in front of one of the two team portraits on the wall —"are the Stanley Cup champs."

I lean in close to the picture, examining all the guys I work for covered in confetti after their Stanley Cup win. I didn't get to see the team after they won at home last season so this is a cool insight.

Maddison's kids are both in the shot with him. Rio's goofy grin is splitting, and his green eyes are shining as if he maybe shed a few tears. Then there's Zanders, who seems less arrogant than he typically is.

"Zee, you look kind of sad in this picture."

"Understatement, Ind. I was devastated. That was one of the best and worst nights of my life."

He looks down at Stevie, the two of them sharing an understanding smile. They weren't together when the Raptors won the Cup and from what I understand, Zanders assumed that was the night he lost her for good.

He pulls her in tight as we continue our tour. "Home locker room," Zanders says and suddenly I'm hyperaware that Ryan is just on the other side of those doors.

The idea of seeing him in the space which he excels most has been consuming me all day. As if I wasn't already intrigued by him in every other aspect of life, I now have the privilege of watching him be the best at what he does while I sit front row. That's not going to fan the flame of my attraction or anything.

I woke up with my leg slung around his hips, his grip holding me tight, and his nose buried in my hair. There was a wave of awkwardness as we untangled from each other, but I won't lie, it was the best night of sleep I've had in months.

Skin warm to the touch. Chest bare and broad. Hand overpowering but gentle.

He's everything I've never had in a man before and everything I'm finding myself desperate for, but as soon as we got home this morning, he grabbed his bag and headed to his morning shoot around, entirely refocused on basketball. I haven't seen him since.

Zanders leads us through the underground tunnels of the arena, where no other fans have access. I guess that's the kind of perks you get when you're the alternate captain of the reigning Stanley Cup champs.

And for the first time in days, Alex runs through my mind. It's quick and unexpected, painful still to think of him because he would've loved this. Alex is a huge sports fan, especially of our local Chicago teams, and call it childish or petty, but a sly smile slides across my lips knowing I'm the one that gets to be here and not him.

The arena is deafening as we exit the tunnel on the courtside, partly from fans who are excited for the game, but mostly because Zanders is recognized instantly. Eager supporters bend over the railings, calling his name, cheering, hoping to touch him or get his signature. It's odd to see this side of it. To me, Zanders and the rest of the Raptors are normal guys I work for, not idols who finally brought a championship back to Chicago.

Even as we find our seats, fans that have courtside access still approach Zanders while the two basketball teams on the court warm up.

"This is crazy," I whisper to Stevie. "Is it always like this?"

She pops her shoulders. "This is the worst of it. He'll get recognized out in Chicago, but it's not with hundreds of fans in one single place like it is here."

"Does it get tiring for you?"

"Not really. I'd rather they like him so much they want his autograph than enjoy hating him the way they did before. Besides, this is nothing compared to what it's like when I'm out with Ryan. It's hard to go most anywhere with him."

The bucket list hanging on our fridge passes through my mind. How I asked him to make our practice dates public events instead of private the way I know he'd rather. I should amend those when I get home because even I, an extrovert, would be overwhelmed with this kind of attention, let alone someone as isolated as Ryan. It's no wonder he rarely leaves his apartment unless it's work related.

Stevie nudges me in the shoulder, gesturing towards the court. "There he is."

I don't know how he wasn't the first person I saw as I exited the tunnel because Ryan commands attention, even in a crowd of 23,000. He's got a Devils long sleeve on instead of his jersey, a pair of tearaway pants, and he's by no means the tallest man on the court. However, there's something about his humble confidence, the way he's focused that makes it almost impossible for me to look away.

In the same way I saw on my television weeks ago, Ryan secludes himself from the rest of the players, off to the side with two basketballs in his hands. He dribbles them with ease, crosses them over one another, and even as fans scream his name asking for attention, he stays focused on his task.

Much in the way he conducts the rest of his life, Ryan works alone.

Warm-ups end, starting lineups are announced, and the national anthem is sung.

Ryan has yet to look in our direction, and with the attention Zanders has garnered since we sat down, there's no way he doesn't know where we are. However, he pays us no notice. Instead, every part of him is dialed into the game, concentrated on the next couple of hours.

As the lights expand over the court, illuminating the arena, Ryan tears away his pants, revealing his basketball shorts underneath, but then he slips his T-shirt over his head, and I'm blessed with a naked chest.

It's only for a moment, but he's shirtless long enough for me to catch the cascading beads of sweat dip into the crevices of his muscles, to watch his chest heave much like how I'd imagine it does during a different kind of physical activity.

I had him just like this in bed last night and every fiber of my being ached with the need for him to grab me and kiss me. Just once. My body is burning to know what it'd be like, but Ryan has made it perfectly clear that kissing in public is off the table, so I'm going to assume, unfortunately, that means in private as well.

But my God, that man had no idea what he did to me last night. He may have slept next to me simply because it was the only bed in the room, but I was awake for hours more, hyperaware of how perfectly I fit tucked into his body.

Sometime in the first quarter, a gin and tonic is delivered to my seat as giant sweaty basketball players rush past me, so close I could reach out and touch them.

"Basketball games are the best. I can't believe I've never been to one."

Zanders laughs from two seats down. "You're sitting courtside in the General Manager's seats. It's a little different in general admission."

Stevie keeps her eyes on the game as she speaks. "We probably should've gone to a game and sat in normal seats before this. It's almost as if flying first class for your first ever flight then having to sit coach every time after."

"Well, I guess I'll need to convince the Morgans to bring me again." I take a sip of my G&T.

Stevie smiles. "From the sounds of it, I don't think they'd need much convincing. Ryan said Mrs. Morgan loves you."

Ryan takes his time dribbling up the court, holding up three fingers and calling out a play. And as always, he's perfectly calm, cool, and collected as he does his job, even as countless fans eagerly watch his every move.

Houston's point guard isn't on Ryan's level by any means, but he is good. Not as effortless, his moves are choppy and brutish, but I've noticed his team makes up for passes that might not be perfect or plays that might not be fully executed. However, he's a shit talker if I've ever seen one. In Ryan's face every chance he gets, holding on to his arm or jersey while on defense. He's loud as if his words will make up the difference in talent levels between the two point guards.

I lean into Stevie. "Who is that? The guy guarding Ryan."

She can't hold back from rolling her eyes. "Connor Easton. He's a jackass. Played for Duke while we were at North Carolina and he's in the same draft class as Ryan but went in the fourth round. I'd say they've had a rivalry since freshman year, but the truth is, it's one-sided. Ryan has never once said a word back to him on the court, but Connor can't shut up."

She's right. Connor hasn't stopped talking, getting in Ryan's face every chance he gets. He seems like he plays a little dirty, and still, Ryan doesn't say a word.

*Calm. Cool. Collected.*

Connor guards Ryan tightly at the top of the key, swiping at his arms and jersey, but Ryan protects the ball with ease as he dribbles around the perimeter. I can't hear a word Connor says, but his lips won't stop moving. You'd think after all the years they've played against one another, he'd figure out that it's impossible to rile up the guy.

Even after living with Ryan for a short time, I know it's rare to get him to show his emotions. It takes more than some adrenaline and shit talking to throw him off-kilter.

Ryan fakes right, throwing Connor off-balance, before he pulls back and hits a three over him. He doesn't say a word, doesn't wear a deserved smug smile, he simply turns around and jogs back on defense, completely in control of this game.

I have to cross one leg over the other, because it's really fucking attractive.

The first half goes by in a blur, and I get my second drink of the night sometime in the third quarter. I could get used to this, watching my hot-as-sin roommate while sipping on a cocktail, wearing my red strappy heels, and sitting courtside.

Probably shouldn't though. This fake relationship has an expiration date. He'll get his GM's support, I'll get through my friends' wedding, and eventually I'll have to move out.

My chest hollows at the prospect.

No one has distracted Ryan this whole game, not the fans, not Connor Easton, and not me. Call me needy, but I wouldn't mind those ocean eyes looking over here once. Wouldn't mind knowing I have that man's attention even if it's only for a split second.

Then the basketball gods smile down on me when the ball gets knocked out of bounds right next to my seat. Ryan walks towards me, directly in my path to inbound the ball, but still, he keeps his eyes down on the floor, utterly focused. The area around me explodes with screams and desperate cries of his name, hoping for a high five or a wave, or even just some eye contact. But what they don't know is that if his own twin who was sitting at my left can't get a small look from the guy, there's no hope for a single fan to garner his attention.

Ryan stands just to my right, so close that if I spread my legs out even a tiny bit, they'd knock into his. The fans around me are quick with their phones, documenting the moment Ryan Shay was breathing the same air as them.

The referee holds on to the ball as both the teams substitute players, and my roommate takes a moment to bend over, palms on his knees, catching his breath.

Corded arms, decorated with veins. Long fingers, big hands. And holy hell, that ass.

His sweaty body smells oddly heavenly to me, and—*what the hell is going on? Get control of yourself, woman.* His sister, my best friend, is thankfully using the restroom at the moment, but what is wrong with me? I'm in public and trying to smell my roommate mid-game like an addict needing a hit of his pheromones.

"Blue." My attention is torn away from Ryan's backside to find blue-green eyes amused and watching me. He's still bent over but looking back. "Are you checking out my ass right now?"

A flush ghosts my cheeks and under normal circumstances, I wouldn't be embarrassed, but this guy has thousands of fans' eyes on him, and many more watching from home.

"It's a nice ass." I shrug unapologetically.

His chest rumbles, his voice lowering. "Trying to distract me tonight? With those heels and those lips? Because you look fucking stunning."

Before I can answer, the referee blows the whistle. Ryan's focus is instantly back on the game. However, the man directly across from him on the inbound, Connor Easton, has his mischievously glinted eyes on me.

His stare is uncomfortable and unrelenting. I offer him a small smile, hoping to pacify the weird sudden interest he has in me, and thankfully the game restarts and he's gone.

"Jesus," Zanders laughs. "So, you and Ryan are sleeping together, huh?"

"Define *sleeping*."

His hazel eyes narrow with annoyance. "Fucking, Ind."

"No," I quickly answer, but there's not much conviction behind the word. "Do I want to?" I cock my head to the side. "Very much so."

Zanders' amused laugh shakes his chest as we lean over Stevie's empty seat to talk.

"I can't though," I continue. "Stevie will be upset. I tell her I'm planning to bang her brother all the time, but she knows I'm joking. Well, she *thinks* I'm joking."

"Nah," he reassures. "She wouldn't be upset. I don't know that she'd be cool with you using him as a rebound, but if it's more than that, I'm sure she'd be supportive."

Is that what this is? Is this unrelenting attraction simply the rebound I've been needing to get out of my system for the last seven months? Possibly. The last person I was with is Alex and now Ryan is a part of my daily life. It'd make sense if it was my body's form of begging for a release. Would he want that? Do I want that? Yes, I want to sleep with him, but I also want to have breakfast with him every morning. I want to sit on the couch and read with him. I want to spend my days off work holed up in that apartment. I'm not sure those are *rebound feelings*, but I might need a rebound to figure it out.

By the time Stevie's back in her seat, Ryan has a game high forty-two points, but the Devils are still losing by three in the fourth quarter. Connor Easton has continually tried to knock Ryan off his game, to get him to react to something, anything he says, but to no avail. The guy is a brick wall of emotions, and though I give him a hard time for his sometimes stoic and robotic personality, I can see why it works so well for him on the court.

That is until the final few minutes when Houston has a bad pass, and the ball comes bouncing over to where I sit on the sideline. It's already out of bounds by the time Connor dives for it, and there's truly no possible way he could save it. I don't know why he'd even attempt to. His giant body falls into my lap, spilling my drink all over my chest. The crowd around me yelps, and the heavy blow to my body is a bit painful.

"I'm so sorry," he says as he stands from my lap. He holds on to my shoulders, bending down and making himself eye level. "Are you okay? Let me get you another drink." He slides a thumb over my cheekbone. "You're far too pretty to be covered in—"

"Get your fucking hands off her." Ryan shoves Connor. "Fuck you! You could've hurt her."

I'm front row to watch Connor laugh as the ref blows the whistle and awards Ryan with a technical.

"Oh, bullshit!" Ryan protests. "He's diving into the crowd for no goddamn reason! The ball was already out of bounds."

"Technical foul. Chicago. Number five."

"Whoa," Stevie exhales. "Ryan's never been tee'd up before." She turns to me. "Are you okay?"

I nod in silence, hoping to regain the breath that was knocked out of me.

Connor saunters past Ryan on his way to the free-throw line, knocking his shoulder as he goes. "Finally found a weakness, Shay."

"Fuck you, Easton." Ryan charges at his back, but one of his teammates holds him back.

The typical calm, cool, and collected basketball player I've come to expect is nowhere to be found at the moment.

He stays as close to the sideline as possible while Connor shoots his free throws. Ryan watches the court but speaks to me over his shoulder. "Are you okay?"

"Yes," I quickly blurt out. Because I am and that was a far bigger scene than it needed to be. "I'm fine. I'm sorry."

"Don't apologize. You're not hurt?"

"No."

"Promise me."

"I promise."

Ocean eyes sweep up my body, taking me in as if he's double checking that I really am okay. I am, it just scared me a little. Finally, his eyes glide to mine and a soft smile graces his lips, those sweet dimples concaving into his cheeks.

"I like having you sitting so close."

I laugh. "Ryan, I just caused you to get a technical foul."

Connor makes both of his free throws.

"Worth it."

The game continues, everyone's attention back to the court.

Leaning over to Stevie, I speak quietly. "Daily update—I hope your brother wears his jersey when he fucks me." I pop my shoulders. "Or I could wear it."

Ryan's teammate, Ethan, hit two back-to-back threes in the final minute, and the Devils pulled out the victory by one. It was thrilling to watch, seeing my roommate excel at the thing he's best at. I knew he was good, even from my minimal knowledge of the sport, but *talented* and *gifted* don't suffice.

He was *magic*.

There's an odd sense of pride flowing through me as Zanders, Stevie, and I wait for Ryan outside the players' parking lot. Some admirers have found their way down here, but the game ended long enough ago that most of the crowd has gone home, leaving only a handful of fans hopeful for a glimpse of Chicago's basketball team.

Zanders is once again asked for photos and autographs to which he obliges, pulling Stevie along with him as well.

"Indy?"

The voice stops me in my tracks because I know it. I've memorized the way my name rolls off his lips, but I'm not ready for this. No part of me is prepared. There's a wedding date on the calendar that I need to be ready by, and that day is not today.

"Indy," Alex repeats when I don't turn around the first time.

Unfortunately, there's no out for me so I turn on my red heels and face him. "Alex," I exhale in disbelief.

Kevin and two more guys from our friend group stand a few feet behind him, but they're not who I'm looking at.

Blonde hair, brown eyes, the boy I loved my entire life stands in front of me. I haven't seen him since the night I fled our apartment, so why does he look so goddamn good? Shouldn't he be profusely apologizing or something other than smiling that fucking megawatt smile like he's running into an old friend? As if I'm not the woman he's known for twenty-two years and dated for the last six?

He shakes his head, still smiling. "What are you doing here? You've never been a basketball fan."

"I um…" I swallow, words stuck in my throat as I throw a thumb over my shoulder to where Stevie and Zanders are entertaining fans, entirely unaware of the way my life has turned upside down in the last thirty seconds.

"That's right. Your old coworker is Ryan Shay's little sister."

"They're twins."

Really? The first words I say to him after all this time are to correct him on my best friend's birth time?

"Right." He nods, hands in his pockets, looking me up and down. I've still got a wet spot on my T-shirt from my spilled drink, and I'm frozen in shock. Not exactly the impression I wanted to make the first time I saw him again. "So, what's new with you?"

Is this really happening? How is he so casual right now? Am I the only one in this situation who feels completely thrown off-balance?

He always hated when I wore my heels because we'd be the same height, or in his opinion worse than that, I'd be taller. He's six feet on his best day, but we all know that means somewhere around five-ten. And right now, he's standing on a curb to give himself the added inches to be able to stand over me.

Metaphorically I feel about two feet tall, as it is.

"Indy, what's new with you?" he repeats.

"Flying."

He nods again. "Always on the road." The insinuation is heavy in the air, and there's something about the inflection in the way he says it that speaks volumes. *I cheated because you were always on the road. It's your fault there was someone else in our bed.* "Will you be at Kevin and Maggie's wedding or are you flying during that too?"

What the hell? It was Alex's suggestion for me to become a flight attendant. The financial firm he's a part of offered me a job right out of college with a much higher salary than his. Even though I went to school for business, the kind of work he does wasn't for me, so I detoured to a completely different route. One that would allow me to travel and socialize. He was stoked for me when I got on with the hockey team last year, or so I thought.

"I'll…um…yeah, I'll be there." This is going horribly. I'm a fumbling mess. "Will you…will you be there too?"

"Of course. I'm with the group almost every day. I can't wait." He looks down for a moment, kicking the cement with his shoe. "Maggie said she's giving you a plus-one. I have one too. I'm planning to use it, so I thought it'd be the right thing to give you a heads-up."

I wasn't aware I was so forgettable. It's a humbling and humiliating revelation. Alex has etched his way onto my heart, and I assumed that sentiment was mutual. I'd rather he regret our relationship or maybe even wish that we had never crossed paths. But to look at me as if I'm the most forgettable woman in the world hurts more than the rest ever could.

"Are you bringing someone?" he continues.

"Blue."

Somehow the name pulls me into focus to find Ryan standing outside of the players' entrance. Gym bag slung over his shoulder, hands in his pockets. His eyes bounce to Alex then back to me, as if he were studying the situation.

"Holy shit," Kevin whispers. "Ryan Shay."

In my periphery, I can see Kevin, Alex, and two of my old friends, lightly smacking each other to ensure everyone sees who just walked out of the arena.

Ryan's eyes dart between Alex and me again, and maybe it's the fact that I'm about two seconds away from crying or that he can physically see that I'm living out my worst nightmare, but he drops his gym bag and in a few quick strides, charges towards me.

Before I can think any further, his palms cup my face, long fingers threading into my ponytail, and his lips are on mine.

Soft lips, warm to the touch. Commanding yet measured, as I'd expect any kiss from Ryan Shay to be. My mouth yields to his, parting to take him deeper and his tongue ever so slightly sweeps across mine in an electrifying slide. One of his hands drops, curving around my throat to bracket the back of my neck as the other pulls my hips to his.

His imposing touch makes me feel small and the deliciously domineering way in which he kisses me makes me feel entirely out of control.

I knew I'd like it. I knew it would be good, but what I didn't expect was to feel light as a feather from my fingers to my toes. To fall completely under a spell just from feeling his mouth, especially when he told me I'd never have it.

My palms find his shoulders, sliding over his broad frame to hook around the back of his neck. A small, unpermitted moan creeps up my throat and I feel Ryan's lips curve up against mine before pulling away.

Moving his hand to my lower back, he presses my body into his. His lips dot a map of soft kisses along my jaw, until his mouth ghosts my ear, whispering. "Are you okay?"

My chest is heaving uncontrollably so no, I'm not okay. What the hell was that? And when can we do it again?

I lie, nodding my head against him.

He breaks our connection to look around me. "Hey, I'm Ryan."

Oh my God, Alex is here.

Then Ryan continues. "How do you know my girlfriend?"

An uncomfortable breath escapes Alex as he steps off the curb to his natural height. "I uh…we used to…"

Now who's fumbling?

Ryan slides a forearm around the front of my shoulders, holding my back to his chest. He nods towards Alex's jersey. "Oh," Ryan says sweetly, patronizingly. "You're a fan of mine."

I didn't notice the Devils jersey he had on, but I especially didn't pick up on the fact there's a number five on the front and my fake boyfriend's last name on the back.

I have to bite my lip to keep it from curving.

"Were you waiting for an autograph?" Ryan continues.

Is it too soon to tell him I love him? Because I think I might love him in this moment.

"Yes!"

"Kev," Alex quietly scolds.

"It's Ryan fucking Shay." Kevin rolls his eyes, pulls out a Sharpie, and turns around for Ryan to sign his jersey.

He continues to autograph the other two guys' as well, but Alex goes on to claim the jersey he's wearing isn't his and doesn't want to return it to the "owner" with Sharpie on it.

"We should get home." Ryan slides his hand to my lower back, turning me towards his car. "See you at the wedding, huh?" he calls to the guys over my shoulder before placing another lingering kiss on my temple for them to see.

He opens the passenger door for me and once I'm inside, he gets down on his haunches, making us eye level. "Are you okay?"

No. Yes. What the hell just happened?

I nod. Quickly, maybe too quickly, but I'm more okay than I ever thought I would be just five minutes ago.

My gaze drops to Ryan's lips and the bucket list item he refused. *I don't feel comfortable faking intimacy.*

"What was that?" My words are low, breathy, hopeful for him to lean in and kiss me again.

He tucks a piece of my hair behind my ear. My slick ponytail must've gotten messed up while his fingers were threaded through it and his mouth was on mine.

"It was acting, Ind."

Oh.

The balloon filled with reckless hope pops in my chest.

"I thought kissing was off the table. You didn't want to fake it."

"I made an exception. You were drowning out there. Besides, I owed you a rescue after I bombed at the fall banquet. Call it even?"

Call it even? He just gave me the best kiss of my life and it was to settle a score?

"Yeah," I breathe out. "Sure. We're even."

"Good." He offers me a smile and a reassuring squeeze of my thigh. "Let's go home."

# 17

# Indy

**Me:** *Daily update—that kiss you saw last week was fake, but I still had to change my underwear when I got home. So, kind of real?*
**Stevie:** *If I help you move out, will the daily updates from hell stop?*
**Me:** *I'm too far in, sis. Reminder—I warned you.*

"And you're sure?"

"I am. I checked with our provider yesterday. Our insurance policy doesn't cover fertility treatments, and that won't be changing at the beginning of the year. That will have to be an out-of-pocket expense."

Falling back onto my bed, I sigh a defeated exhale. "Thank you for looking into it."

"Of course, Indy. Have a good day."

The head of the airline's human resources department hangs up the phone before I grab a pillow off the side of my bed and silently scream into it.

Goddammit. I knew I shouldn't have gotten my hopes up.

Last week, I went to dinner with the flight crew while on the road for work and spilled the details of why I was wanting to earn some extra cash. One of my coworkers could've sworn our insurance packages were changing with the year to include fertility treatment benefits, but unfortunately HR finally got back to me this morning to snuff that hopeful flame.

I'm making enough with my salary now that Ryan isn't allowing me to pay rent, but it'd be nice to offer him something. Honestly, I wish he'd take even a little bit so I could maybe go shopping for a new outfit and not feel guilty that my best friend's brother is giving me a free ride while I blow some cash on fun.

Heading into the kitchen, I turn on the sink and get to work. Ryan's been on a weeklong road trip, and I somewhat cleaned the mess I made of the apartment, although I'm sure it's not to his standards. But last night I got burnt out and left the dishes until this morning. Honestly, I'm surprised Ryan didn't start doing them when he got home from the airport around three AM.

He left on a road trip the morning after that kiss, and if you think I've thought of anything else since, you'd be sorely mistaken. The way his hands took charge, claiming me, one on my hip, one through my hair. The way his lips were commanding, but soft enough to yield to mine. Most of all, the reason he did it—because he didn't want Alex to think he'd come out ahead.

Sure, it was all for show, but good luck trying to convince my body of that. If that was a fake kiss, I'm not sure I could handle knowing what a real one feels like.

Seeing Alex was a painful dose of reality. I had the privilege of forgetting about him until that night. Well, maybe I didn't completely forget about him because the damage he's done feels like a deep scar that'll never heal, constantly opening for the rest of my life, but he has moved to the back of my mind over the last few weeks.

That night though, seeing him, realizing he views me as disposable, as a forgettable piece of his life when he had been my priority for so long, has made me desperate to try to move on the way he has.

If he can live his life like I didn't mean anything to him, why can't I? Why is he the last man I've been with? Why shouldn't I be able to disconnect sex and love? I've never done it before, but I need to try. It's only been seven months since I was living the life I thought was my forever. My heart shouldn't be ready to move on, but that doesn't mean my body can't.

Maybe a physical relationship will flush him out of my system and there's only one man I want to test that theory with.

As if he could hear my carnal thoughts summoning him, Ryan's bedroom door opens while I'm mid-load of the dishwasher. I'm bent over, ass out, but since everything has been so fake between us, it shouldn't be a problem for him. The attraction is all *pretend*, right?

When I look back, I'm pleasantly surprised to find his blue-green eyes hooded over and staring at my ass. My shorts are a little too short, but that's what he gets.

*That's right, take it in, Roomie. And good luck blaming the drool dripping down your chin on acting.*

But then I see the rest of him, my eyes coasting down his bare chest because the motherfucker is in nothing but a towel, water still dripping down his body, fresh out of the shower.

He leans against his doorframe, corded arms crossed over his damp chest, stupid fucking dimples concaving with a smirk. "Indigo Ivers, are you doing…*dishes*?"

I roll my eyes. "Is this what your wet dreams look like, Shay?"

"Essentially."

He pops off the doorframe, sauntering into the kitchen, and the rarely seen smug smile across his lips tells me he knows exactly what he's doing.

"Where are your clothes?"

"In my room?"

"Why aren't you wearing them?"

"Because this is my house."

I feel him behind me, watching me as I swirl a sponge around a dirty bowl. His hands brace the counter on either side of me, his chest to my back, and the heat from his shower radiates off him, warming me.

He's naked under that towel, and every part of me wants to lean back and feel his body on mine.

Clearing my throat, I ask, "Adding this image into your spank bank for your next lonely night on the road?"

His chest rumbles. "Yes." His palm glides against my lower back as he backs away, giving me space. "Good morning, by the way."

I swallow down the low moan from his simple touch. "Morning. How was your road trip?"

"It was all right. We split. Two wins, two losses. You're leaving on yours today?"

Putting the last of the dishes in the dishwasher, I close it and turn to face him. Perfectly lean muscles across a broad chest, obliques tight and curving downward, creating a visual path I'd love to follow. Dusting of dark hair under his navel and—*dear God, get it together, woman.*

He laughs, breaking my trance. I love the sound but hate the haughtiness of it.

"Go put some goddamn clothes on."

"You were the one who was obsessing over me being shirtless the first time you came over here."

"Yeah, well, that was before I realized how annoying you were."

A thumb dusts his lower lip as his wandering gaze works its way over my bare legs. He must know what he's doing to me, and honestly, it's not fair. He's already turned me down once.

"Ryan." I cock my head. "Really. What are you doing?"

"Just playing the game you started." He pushes off the counter, taking two steps towards me. His index finger hooks under the hem of my shorts, igniting my skin with goosebumps. "Wearing these itty-bitty shorts and bending over in my kitchen. Don't act all innocent, Blue."

He turns away from me, grabbing a yogurt from the fridge while I inhale a needed breath. How is he so unaffected? My entire body is on fire because I need to get laid and the only person I want to do it is my fake boyfriend who is currently walking around our apartment in nothing but a towel.

Did he truly feel nothing from that kiss? Is he not sexually attracted to me in the slightest?

I slide in front of the silverware drawer before he can pull out a spoon.

He sighs. "Indy, what are you doing?"

"Do you think I'm pretty?"

He rolls his eyes.

"Do you?"

Ryan levels me with a look, serious and stoic. "I think you're smart."

Oh.

"Kind. Chaotic. A bit of a smartass and too charming for your own good."

Oh, wow. I like that answer much more than the one I was expecting, but I divert because his response is far too detailed and knowing of who I am. "So, you don't think I'm pretty, then."

He chuckles. "Indy, I'm not blind, but even if I were, I'm pretty sure I could touch your face and understand just how fucking stunning you are, but it's not the first thing I see anymore."

Well, *fuck me.*

Stepping towards him, still blocking the drawer he needs to get into, my breasts press against his stomach, taking away any space between us. He can't answer a question with that much sincerity after claiming he faked a kiss with me the other night.

I watch his throat bob in a swallow. "What are you doing?"

"Pretending." I inch into his personal space, snaking my arms over his shoulders, my nails scratching the tight fade around his hairline. "Acting. Just how you pretended the other night when you kissed me."

"Oh, yeah?" His neck bends, his lips ghosting over my jaw until his forehead falls onto my shoulder. "Mmm, that feels good," he murmurs into me as I pull him closer.

*Acting my ass.*

My hips move into his, voluntary or not, I can't exactly say, but I'm quickly reminded that this man is wearing only a towel.

A gasp escapes me as he easily swoops me up with one arm behind my back, hoisting me on the kitchen counter. Large palms hook under my bare thighs, jerking me towards the edge and while his face is still pressed into the crook of my neck, he spreads my knees apart.

He's suffocating, crowding me like this, but in the best way possible. I pull back slightly so I can watch the pads of his broad thumbs languidly trace their way up my inner thighs. He takes his time, patient and frustrating as he pushes my legs farther and farther apart. Once he's halfway up my upper legs, as he dots my throat with warm wet kisses, I close my eyes, head falling back and heat rushing south.

I want him.

I especially want him a few inches north. His thumb preferably, creating stiff little circles.

I'm lost in the feeling, my legs open around him, his breath and mouth on my neck. Involuntarily, my hips grind into the open air, searching for him.

A gentle bite of my ear sends a shockwave to my clit and a moan slips from my lips.

"You don't want to play this game with me, Blue." Pulling away, he bops my nose with a spoon. "I will always win."

He grabs his yogurt once again and heads towards his bedroom.

Looking down, I find the silverware drawer pulled out between my open legs. That motherfucker distracted me and opened the goddamn silverware drawer between my spread thighs.

I'm hot and flustered and kind of pissed off. The audacity of this man to leave me on the counter panting for more. "How are you so certain you'll win?"

His brows lift, sending me a pointed glance that screams *you're about thirty seconds from coming on the kitchen counter and you think I'd be the first one to cave?*

Holding his stare, I don't accept the silent answer.

Turning away from me, he heads into his room, but before he closes the door behind him, I hear him say, "I'm celibate, that's why."

"Shay, you're buying right?" Dom shouts from the other end of the table.

I have to laugh to myself because the guy can afford his own dinner just fine if he were the one paying. "Yeah, man."

He turns towards the server. "I'll have your most expensive red then."

Motherfucker.

Ethan, sitting to my right, leans in. "This is a nice spot." His attention wanders the private back room of one of the most exclusive restaurants in Chicago. "Fancy."

Hell yeah, it's fancy, but more importantly, it's private. Back door entrance, paparazzi are banned, and apparently the waitstaff has all signed NDAs. If every public outing was like this, maybe I'd leave my apartment for more than just practice and games.

Ethan's critical gaze coasts the room again.

"Okay, what's wrong with this place? You said I had to host team dinner. I'm hosting team dinner."

"I also told you to use it as an opportunity for the guys to get to know you. Kind of hard to do when half the team is a shouting distance away."

The back room consists of black walls, low lighting, and a table so long that it sits fourteen comfortably—if you're not trying to speak to half of your guests.

To be honest, I knew it was a bullshit excuse for team dinner when I booked the restaurant two weeks ago. Ethan's home is always warm and inviting. His wife and mother have taught some of the guys their famous Korean dishes over the years, and his daughters are usually running around or sitting on one of the players' laps, teaching professional athletes how to color within the lines.

But I'm not Ethan. My apartment is bare and admittedly somewhat cold. I don't have a wholesome family waiting at home to welcome the team, and even if I did, I can't stomach the idea of letting this many people into my space, regardless that they're my teammates.

Only a few have penetrated my circle of confidence—Ethan, Zanders, and now Indy, but I don't blindly trust most people, including my teammates. Sure, I've known most of them for four-plus years, but they're strictly my coworkers.

Trust is earned, not given, and if I said any of that out loud, Ethan would chew my ass out and remind me that my lack of trust in my team is probably why we're on a four-game losing streak.

Halfway through dinner, the guys seem like they're having a good enough time. The other end of the table is much louder than my end, shooting the shit, and drinking on my dime.

One of the rookies sits to my left. "Leon, do you want another glass of wine?" I hold the bottle up to offer him a pour.

He keeps his stare down on his plate. "No, thank you."

"Are you sure?"

Hesitantly, his eyes find mine, trying to read me.

Ethan laughs. "It's not a test, Leon. You're not going to get reamed for having a second glass of wine. We have a travel day tomorrow."

Leon's lips tilt slightly, though he looks at Ethan while he smiles, but his eyes are back on his plate when he says, "Sure. Okay, I'll have one. Thank you."

I pour Leon another glass. That was fucking weird.

By the time dessert is being served, I can't help it any longer. I pull out my phone to text Indy.

She flew home from a road trip this afternoon, so I haven't seen her in five days. And before that, I was gone for six. Which means for the last eleven days the only thing I've been able to think about is that kiss.

It was perfect, consuming, soft. Fuck, it was intoxicating, and I want to do it again. I think I might *need* to do it again before I combust. Is there a study out there that tests the limit on how many times you can jerk off before creating a long-lasting problem? Because every languid stroke of my cock has come with the image of her long legs around my hips, her soft hands touching every crevice of my body, and those lips. Those goddamn lips exploring every inch of my skin.

Was it as fake as I claimed? Not in the slightest.

As I told her, I don't feel comfortable faking intimacy, so I didn't. My body was boiling when I saw her standing with him outside the arena. I knew who he was the second my eyes landed on him, and my suspicion was confirmed when I noticed the frozen yet fumbling mess that was my roommate. Her kind brown eyes were shining with unshed tears, and yeah, that pissed me off because he deserves no part of her.

I'd never let him see her cry over him, so you could blame the kiss on that, but the truth is when I walked out of the players' entrance all I saw was *Blue*. My perfect fucking Blue with those strappy heels, leather pants, and an attitude consisting of the strangest mix of welcoming and sharp.

But when I noticed him, all I saw was red.

Call it possessive, protective, or straight-up caveman tendencies, I don't care. There was no part of me that would allow for that sorry excuse of a man to think he "won." So, yeah, I kissed her to prove a point.

But I also kissed her because I'd been wanting to do it for weeks now.

**Me:** *How's bridal shower planning going?*

My sorry attempts to find any excuse to text Indy are getting more obvious. Sending her pictures of my lonely breakfasts without her, asking her the name of certain flowers I stumble upon, or just texting her to complain about how she's not very good at cleaning up after herself, though I've grown used to my apartment being a bit more frenzied these days. Seems like I find a reason to message her at least once a day, and we've already talked about this bridal shower all week, but fuck it, I want to talk to her.

Don't get me started on how I feel about her childhood friends taking advantage of Indy's ingrained necessity to do anything for those she cares about. They went dress shopping without her, but conveniently need her to plan a bridal shower. She would never say no, and she'll knock it out of the park, but that's not the point. I wonder when the last time one of those friends planned something for *her*.

**Blue:** *It's coming along! I ordered the flower arrangements today. How's team dinner?*

**Me:** *It's fine.*

I wait just thirty seconds before I text again and tell the truth.

**Me:** *No, it's not actually. It kind of sucks. When we used to do it at Ethan's house, everyone was happy to be there.*

**Blue:** *Well, what do you think the difference is?*

**Me:** *I don't know. I picked one of the most expensive restaurants in Chicago. The food was good.*

**Blue:** *You can't see me, but I'm rolling my eyes. The difference is that Ethan let the team into his life. Maybe you should too.*

**Me:** *Jesus, did he tell you to say that?*

**Blue:** *No, I'm simply that brilliant on my own.*

The bill is discreetly handed to me, and I slip the server my Black Amex.

**Me:** *I'll see you when I get home?*

Glad that was just a text, because if I said that out loud, I'm pretty sure my voice would've cracked like an excited middle schooler getting to see his crush.

**Blue:** *Yes, but I'll be home late or maybe tomorrow. I have plans tonight.*

What the hell? What plans? And with whom? And excuse me, but "maybe tomorrow"?

It takes all my restraint to keep my thumbs from typing out each of those questions, not that I'm in any position to deserve the answers. I'm just her roommate. She doesn't have to tell me anything.

But goddammit, I've been looking forward to her coming home all week. I even had the guy who owns her favorite flower stand down the street drop off a bouquet for her today, simply because I knew she'd be excited for a fresh one. That and because I killed the last arrangement she left me with.

And now I'm feeling petty and annoyed and for no real reason other than I wanted her to want to stay home with me. Isn't she tired from working all week? Yes, it's a Friday night, but why'd she make plans?

I'm asking myself these questions as if I haven't gotten to know the girl across the hall. Indy is a social butterfly who loves people. Of course, she made plans on a Friday night. She's a single woman, stunning and too smart for her own good. Just because I have a hard time leaving the apartment doesn't mean she does. Hiding away with me would never be enough for her.

**Me:** *Okay. Let me know if you need anything.*

God, I'm pathetic.

**Blue:** *Thanks! Have a good night.*

Highly unlikely that'll happen at this point.

One of the rules of team dinner is that if there's going to be alcohol, no one gets behind the wheel. So as the last of the guys pile into a rideshare, Ethan and I wait for our respective drivers to pull up.

"That went okay, don't you think?"

He pops his shoulders. "Yeah, it was nice. Food was good."

"But..."

"But did you notice how Leon couldn't look you in the eye? Or how half the team was having their own conversations? Team dinner is about team bonding. Gives us an excuse to get out of our uniforms and get to know each other as people not players. That didn't really happen tonight."

I'm self-aware enough to know my team dinner was lacking in comparison to the ones Ethan used to host. "Yeah, what the fuck was up with Leon anyway?"

Ethan narrows his eyes. "You can't tell? The kid is scared shitless of you."

"Of me?"

He laughs, sarcasm dripping in his tone. "Shocking, right? Because you're just the nicest guy on the court."

"That's work. Who I am on the court while I'm working is not who I am in my free time."

"Ryan, you're my guy, you know this, but you're making the exact point I've been trying to prove this whole time. No one else knows you outside of basketball, so of course the guys think you're some domineering dickhead that's going to chew them out if they do the wrong thing. Leon's afraid to be on the same team as you during practice. Did you know that?"

I scoff. "That's ridiculous. There's no reason he should take what I say or how I act while I'm working personally."

"Guys are afraid to drop a pass from you. They're afraid to miss a shot instead of giving you the ball and letting you shoot instead. We're never going to make the playoffs if they can't trust themselves and even more so, if *you* don't trust them."

Goddammit, I swear this man is a mind-reader. I know all of this. I see the fear in my teammates' eyes when they fuck up, and of course, I'm aware of my own trust issues.

Ethan's blacked-out sedan pulls up. "I'm not trying to be a dick—"

"No, you're right," I interrupt. "You're right. I need to work on it."

He gives me a quick slap on the back. "Thank you for dinner. I'll see you at the airport tomorrow."

"See you then."

The drive back to my apartment is silent. Sometimes I'll chat with Harold, but tonight the quiet is necessary. I know what it takes to bring home a championship—I won two national titles while in college—but I'm a different man than I was then. Trusting my teammates, trusting anyone isn't nearly as easy.

"Welcome back, Mr. Shay."

"David?" I ask as I step out of the back of the car. "Why are you working the night shift?"

David, my usual daytime doorman, holds the lobby door open for me. And even though I've requested for him to call me Ryan, it's evident he doesn't feel comfortable being so casual with me while at work, so I let the formality slide.

"My granddaughter had a piano recital this afternoon. I couldn't miss it."

David is a good man with a big family. He's also discreet and I appreciate him more than he probably realizes. He's been a constant in my life since I moved to Chicago, so last year when he told me his granddaughter had to stop her piano lessons because their family could no longer afford it, I found a scholarship foundation to support her and pay her way for as long as she wants to keep playing.

He doesn't know that said scholarship is simply my personal bank account, but the details aren't important.

"How was it?"

His eyes sparkle. "Magnificent. Remi is getting good."

I give him a pat on the shoulder. "I know you have a video. Show me tomorrow?"

"You got it. Your flowers were delivered. As well as your bookshelf. Should I have someone come up and assemble it for you?"

"I got it but thank you." I'm halfway through the lobby when I turn back to the door. "David, did you happen to see Indy tonight?"

A smile slides across his lips. "Sure did. She looked beautiful, didn't she?"

I swallow. "I'm sure she did. Did she mention where she was going? Did she take her own car?"

"She didn't say, but she took a rideshare."

"Got it. Have a good night."

Before I step into the elevator, David stops me. "She's a good one, Mr. Shay. Kind heart."

I soften at his words. "She is a good one."

The apartment is admittedly depressing. Friday night and the city outside is booming with music and people and life. Here I am with a night off work and self-confined to these four walls. Even if I wanted to go out and enjoy my weekend, maybe call Indy and try to meet up with her, I can't. That's not a luxury I have. Privacy is a privilege I gave up when I signed my contract with the Chicago Devils four and a half years ago.

Stevie and Zanders took a quick trip back to Indiana to see Zee's dad, so I truly am alone for the night. It's nothing new. In fact, this is what I've wanted, needed, but ever since my colorful roommate moved in, being alone hasn't felt quite as appealing. The silence is screaming without Indy here.

I want the comfort of privacy, but I want her to be with me while I have it.

The flowers I had delivered are shades of light purple and pink, so I know she's going to love them. It's impractical, constantly spending money on flowers that will die shortly after bringing them home, but every cent is worth it when I get to watch that beaming smile bloom when she sees them. The girl deserves to be spoiled, and I want to be the one doing the spoiling. I trim the stems down the way she taught me before adding the flower food to the water, trying to situate them like the professional florists do. Mine doesn't look nearly as nice, but fuck it, I tried.

Changing into a pair of sweats and a tee, I grab a beer from the fridge and get to work on the bookshelf I ordered. I easily could've purchased a custom-made one or even a bookshelf that was already put together, but the idea of building this myself sounded nice, normal even.

It seemed like something a normal man would do for a girl he likes. Because at the end of the day, that's who this bookshelf is for.

I reclaimed my own, my books now in their rightful spot—organized by author's last name without shirtless dudes crowding them, but Indy's romance novels have been stacked on the floor in the living room since the week she moved in. As much as I tease her, I've found her crying, laughing, or even crossing her legs during certain scenes, and it's beyond endearing that the love between fictional characters can bring her so much joy.

The instructions call for two people to build this, but it's only me, so I take a swig of my beer, throw the directions away, and get to work.

Okay, so I may have had to disassemble and reassemble it a few times. I also may have had to watch a YouTube video or two to figure it out, but Indy's bookshelf is finished and somewhat stable. My beer is still full and warm, essentially untouched by the time I'm done, but I think she's going to be happy.

I leave her books stacked on the floor where they are because even though I have a particular way I like to organize, Indy doesn't live by the same code and this area is hers.

My ringing phone cuts the music playing on my surround sound. Shuffling through the discarded cardboard, I find my sister's name scrolling across the top.

"Hey, Vee. What's up?" I sink back on my couch.

"Are you still at team dinner?"

"No, just hanging out at home."

"Okay, good," she exhales. "I need a favor. Well, Indy needs a favor."

That causes me to sit up. "What's wrong?"

"She's going to hate that I called you. It's not a big deal, but…"

"Stevie, what's going on?"

"She called Rio for a ride, but he's been at home drinking while playing Xbox with some guys from the team. Rio called me, but I'm two hours away in Indiana to see Zee's dad and rideshares are taking close to an hour for pickups downtown."

"She needs a ride?" I'm already off the couch, grabbing my keys, and headed to the door, thankful I was too distracted to drink that beer earlier. "I'm on my way. Where is she?"

"Don't freak out."

I stop in my tracks, my hand on my doorknob. "Well, that's one way to get me to freak out."

"She's on a date, and the guy is being a creep, making her uncomfortable. She's at Sullivan's on eighth."

She's on a date?

My mouth goes dry as rage seeps through every pore of my body. Don't get me started on how I feel about her being on a date, especially after she told me *our* date was the first one she'd been on, but if he so much as laid a fucking finger on her without her consent, my sister may as well start driving back to Chicago so she can bail me out of jail tonight.

"Ryan, are you there?"

I swallow, lubricating my parched mouth so I can speak. "I'm on my way."

# 19 Indy

He's celibate.

Ryan Shay is celibate.

What did we, as the female population, do to deserve this?

In the oddest way, I feel robbed, like I'm missing out one of life's greatest experiences because I don't care if he's been celibate for one year or eight, I know that man knows what to do between the sheets. There's not a soul on earth that could watch the way he plays basketball with precision, fluidity, and control then tell me Ryan Shay is bad in bed. You can't convince me that his kiss was a one-off and it doesn't translate in other ways.

All those times I gave him shit about being afraid of naked women, turns out I wasn't far off. He may not be afraid, but he's avoiding them at all costs.

"Indy, did you hear what I said?"

No, *Jason*, I didn't hear what you said because you haven't stopped talking about yourself all night and I fully tuned out around the time you mentioned you slept with your buddy's girl on prom night.

"Yep," I lie. "That's fascinating."

"I know, right? She was batshit, wanting me to go with her to her grandma's funeral, but I told her the day we met, Saturdays are for the boys. If you can't get on board with that, I don't want you, you know?"

Jason orders us another round.

"No, I'm good. Thank you."

"Stop. Have another. You're drinking so slow. I'm on my fourth one already."

No shit, and each one makes him more handsy. He won't stop touching the back of my barstool, my shoulders, and his leg won't stop pressing into mine. I would scoot further away if I could, but I'd be in the girl's lap next to me if I did. Honestly, that doesn't sound half bad at the moment.

"Gin and tonic?" the bartender says to me. "I got you."

"No, I'm—" My words die when I catch the bartender's discreet nod of her head.

If I knew I was going to have less than one drink, I would've driven myself and left an hour ago.

I've never dated before, and if this is what the dating pool has to offer, my future is looking bleak. My first real date. God, it's tragic.

I'd rather claim the fall banquet with Ryan as my first date, even though it was all pretend.

As Jason continues to spill his entire dating history, I tune him out. The guy clearly loves the sound of his own voice that he doesn't notice me on my phone instead. I swallowed my pride and texted Rio fifteen minutes ago, but the last thing I heard was that he was working on a ride for me.

I'm aware that if I would've called Ryan, he would've been here in a heartbeat, but I couldn't do it. He doesn't need to know I'm on a date. Either he's not going to care in the slightest and that'll hurt my feelings, or he's going to be upset and that will hurt even more.

Besides, I only downloaded Tinder and swiped right on Jason because he was attractive. Unfortunately, he hasn't shut up and his personality has made him the least attractive man in the room.

I haven't had sex since Alex. I haven't gotten off since Alex and it's beyond time for it to happen. I'm a twenty-seven-year-old woman who hasn't had an orgasm in almost eight months and I'm afraid my body will forget how to if I don't have a release soon. My fingers, toys, none of it has worked. I'm too in my head when I'm alone that I've come to the realization I need someone with me.

Of course, Ryan is my first choice. You could say I've developed an unhealthy crush on my roommate, which is the last thing I need. I shouldn't have real feelings for someone else so soon after I was with the man I thought I was going to marry. Right?

I truly thought there was a possibility I might have sex with my basketball star of a fake boyfriend until that morning last week when he dropped the news that he's celibate.

He's fucking celibate. I didn't see that one coming. I knew he was private. I knew he hadn't dated since the woman in college who tried to use him. I knew he didn't have women over, but I figured it all happened on the road in his hotel room. I assumed he had the women he was with sign NDAs or something drastic like that, but no, he spends every night on the road alone. Just how he spent every night at home before I moved in.

I scroll through the pictures of our text thread—the one of the empty seat next to him at the kitchen island after he made breakfast for only himself while I was out of town. The bouquet of flowers he wanted me to name in the hotel lobby while he was staying in Denver for a game. And then there's the ones I've sent him of my travels—the bookstore I stumbled upon in Columbus. The outdoor basketball court I walked by in Minneapolis.

I've looked for any excuse to talk to him this week and I can't blame it on being lonely. It's because I truly enjoy talking to him more than I do most other people. I never thought my recluse roommate would become the person I most look forward to seeing, but here we are.

And here, in this crowded bar, I'm lonelier than ever because he's at home and I miss him.

The bartender sets my drink in front of me. "Cheers!" Jason says, taking a long swig of the whiskey and Coke in his hand before I've even lifted mine off the bar top.

Taking a small sip of my drink, I'm pleasantly surprised to find its only sparkling water. The bartender shoots me a wink and I secretly hope she charges him for a double.

"So, what do you say?" Jason asks, his hand sliding onto my thigh.

I pick up his sleeve with my thumb and forefinger, as if he might have a disease, and move him off me. "What do I say about what?"

"What do you say about coming back to my place? It's a ten-minute walk from here."

"Actually, I'm going to call it a night."

"Why?"

"I'm tired."

He laughs without humor. "Sure, you are. Fine. I get it. We'll stay here for now." He takes another swig of his drink, but then his eyes fixate on the door behind me. "Oh my God, that's—"

His words tune out when I turn around to find Ryan standing in the doorway of Sullivan's. His angry eyes wander the room, until they soften slightly, landing on me. He takes me in, his shoulders dropping until his attention lands on my knee, and he stiffens again.

Jason's hand is back, and I didn't realize.

Ryan's strides are big and commanding, as if he wasn't already drawing the attention of the entire room simply by being who he is. I can't believe he left the apartment, and it's quickly dawning on me why he typically doesn't. Every pair of eyes is on him, and the whispers are low but discernible.

"Is that Ryan Shay?"

"Oh my God, it's Ryan Shay."

"Quick! Get your phone out!"

His anger is palpable by the time he reaches me, but the controlled venom of his voice is the scariest part. "Get your fucking hands off her."

I stand, removing Jason's hand in the act, but also putting my body between Ryan and him.

"Whoa, man." Jason laughs like the unaware man that he is.

The quick flash of a camera phone reminds me who Ryan is, his reputation, and what's about to happen if I don't get him out of this bar.

"Ryan, it's fine. I'm fine."

He looks around me, as if I'm not there. "Did you touch her?" He turns towards the bartender. "Did he touch her?"

"Ryan," I attempt to interrupt.

"I had an eye on her," the bartender says.

"Ryan, people are watching."

Finally, his angry stare breaks away from my date. "I don't give a fuck, Indy." Just as quickly, his attention swings back to the man behind me. "Did you fucking touch her?" His nostrils flare and if I wasn't so wrapped up in what's happening in this moment, I'd give him a pat on the back for pulling off that whole "jealous book boyfriend" thing.

"Not in any way she wasn't asking for."

Oh God, he's revolting.

I'm not looking at Jason, but I'm sure his smile is smug, and the quick lunge Ryan takes towards him ensures me that it is.

An alert movement keeps my body between them. My fists ball in Ryan's shirt, tugging him down, hoping to get in his line of sight. "Let's go home, Ryan. I want to go home."

Finally, he looks at me, his chest thumping against my hand. Cupping my face with his palms, he checks me up and down as if he could tell from my outward appearance. "Are you sure you're okay?"

"I'm fine. I promise. Take me home."

His hand slides to my back, ushering me to walk ahead of him, but I'm cautious to move my body from the space between these two men solely because people are recording on their phones. Eventually, I step towards the exit because I truly want to get the hell out of here, only to hear Jason laugh and say, "Did Ryan Shay just steal my date?"

Ryan halts, and I'm praying to God he shows his typical controlled restraint. Any other time, I'd love to see him pummel this guy, but whatever Ryan decides to do in this moment has the potential to end up on the front page of the newspaper tomorrow.

He takes a centering breath and turns around. "Trust me, she was never yours."

His blacked-out Audi is parked illegally in front of the bar, and I rush towards it, wanting to get us away from the chaotic scene I caused. Reaching for the door handle, I barely open it only for Ryan's palm to slam it back closed.

In surprise, I find him staring down at me, his chest rising and falling in rage, his nostrils flared, and his mouth set in a hard line. But then I look up. Brow creased and ocean eyes swimming in a world of…*hurt.*

I hurt him. Oh my God, I hurt him.

We face off, and I can almost see the words on the tip of his tongue. He wants to say something, but doesn't, letting the silent anger radiating off his body do the talking for him.

I want to say something too. *That was nothing. It didn't mean anything. Thank you for saving me.* But we both stay silent, watching one another, and waiting for the other to break the tension-filled void.

Finally, he looks away from me, as if he can't bear the sight of me any longer and opens the door for me to get inside.

The ride is silent, but the car is filled with so much tension I'm afraid the windows are going to bust from the pressure. Ryan's left arm is leaning on the doorsill while he drives with his right, his knuckles turning white around the steering wheel.

"Ryan—"

"Not right now, Indy," he bites back.

"Yes, right now. Why are you so angry?"

He inhales a breath through his nostrils, running a palm over his mouth, but stays silent.

"Fine," I huff, turning towards my window, watching the lit-up skyline of Chicago pass by me. "We won't talk. That seems like a mature way to handle things."

The ride consists of the loudest silence I've ever experienced. By the time we make it home, my lungs are hungry for fresh air, needing space from this man who is suffocating me with his presence. Ryan pulls into his parking space, cuts the engine, and is halfway out his door before I have a chance to leave first.

"Don't," he commands when I reach for my door handle.

I follow his gorgeously sculpted body as it rounds the car, and even as I will eye contact through the glass window, he won't look at me. It isn't until he reaches my side that he unlocks the car and opens my door for me to get out because even as angry as he is, Ryan Shay can't help but be a gentleman.

Stepping out, I keep my attention on him, but still, Ryan refuses to look at me. As he holds my door open, I lightly grasp his chin and force him to meet my eye.

Yes, he's angry, but there's a mixture of wounded feelings in there, and for a man who doesn't let himself get emotional, there's a whole lot of emotion going on at the moment.

He exhales, his voice softer. "Let's just go home, okay?"

More tension builds on the silent elevator ride to our floor, and once we're inside the apartment, he wastes no time before beelining it for his bedroom.

"Ryan," I plead, attempting to stop him.

It works, but he keeps his back to me, standing at his door.

"I didn't mean to hurt your feelings."

He scoffs, turning my way. "My feelings? You didn't hurt my *feelings*. I'm upset because you did something reckless. You're out in Chicago with another man. Why? Anyone could've seen you. People *did* see you. We had a deal."

I take a step towards him, and instantly regret it by the way his body retreats. "It wasn't like that. I'm not *seeing* anyone. It was just going to be one night, and I'm sorry, I didn't think anyone would recognize me."

"One night?" His brows crease. "What was just going to be one night?"

I feel the heat rising on my cheeks because now he decides to hold unwavering eye contact—in the exact moment I wish he wouldn't look at me.

"I just…" I fiddle with the hem of my dress.

"You what?"

"I need a night with someone who isn't Alex, okay? Not that it's really any of your business."

His laugh is dry and humorless as he rounds the kitchen island and pours himself a shot of whiskey.

"I'm sorry, Ryan, but a woman has needs."

"Then take care of them yourself!"

My head jerks back, a few palpable seconds passing between us.

"It's really not that fucking hard, Indy. How do you think I've gone so long without?" He releases a harsh breath before grabbing our bucket list from the refrigerator. He scribbles quick, angry words before sliding the paper across the island to me. "Here, I'll even add it to your bucket list."

*Number 6. Have sex with yourself.*

"Screw you, Ryan. What if I added that to your list? For you to have sex with someone?"

He blinks. "Is that what this is about? Because I told you I'm celibate?"

I falter, hating where this conversation is going. No part of me has judged his life choices and I don't think of him any differently for them.

But deep down, yes, this is because he's celibate. Because I want him and even though there was an invisible line that kept him somewhat off-limits, now it's clear as day. I can't have him and maybe someone else would be able to help drown out that realization.

"No. No, it has nothing to do with that, but I've been single for eight months. I haven't been with anyone in eight months—"

"So, you were going to let that piece of shit be the first man to touch you?"

"It's just sex! It doesn't mean anything!"

"Yes, it does!" He's desperate, pleading for me to understand. His tone lowers to almost a whisper. "It means something, Indy, and you may have blown our cover for some jackass who doesn't even deserve to breathe the same air as you."

"Ryan," I say softly. "All my life I've been told I'm too emotional, that I feel too much, so for once I'm trying to be the girl who is unattached. Look what happened to me the last time I loved someone."

The truth is, I've never had meaningless sex in my life. I lost my virginity to Alex. I truly have no idea how to be unattached.

Ryan pounds back his shot of whiskey. "You're right." His glass hits the counter. "Do what you want. I'm just your roommate, right? It doesn't matter how I feel about the situation."

*How he feels about the situation?* If he's upset his GM could've caught me, that's one thing, but if he's hurt because I didn't ask him to be the first man post-breakup, that's another. Does he not remember that *he's* the one who rejected *me* on the couch a few weeks ago? And now that I know that he's celibate, I would never ask him to change his lifestyle for me.

"Maybe do it in private next time, you know, to keep up our little ruse."

I should tell him the truth—*I don't want just anyone's help. I want his help*—but it'd probably make things worse. Besides, Ryan knows how attracted I am to him, so I doubt he'd be shocked to learn what I want, and he already told me where he stands.

Instead, I give him as much of the truth as I can muster, stopping him before he makes it past the threshold of his room.

"You want the truth?" I swallow as he looks over his shoulder at me, bright eyes pleading for me to say something that'll make the situation better. "The truth is I haven't gotten off in eight months." I throw my hands up in defeat. "You think I haven't tried to take care of it myself? I have. Countless times. And every time I get close, an image of my ex-boyfriend pops into my head and suddenly, I'm back in our old apartment walking in on him fucking his coworker. He cheated on me and now I can't even have an orgasm because of it." A half-hearted laugh escapes me. "I'm pretty sure my body is broken, so yeah, I thought I'd test that theory by having someone else there to help distract me. I didn't think about being seen in public, so I apologize for that, but I'm not going to apologize for having needs and being desperate to take care of—"

Ryan's hand brackets my throat, pinning me to the wall with his hips, stealing the rest of my words when his mouth takes mine.

Instantly, I'm compliant, pliable, letting him take me however he wishes. On the other hand, he's commanding in his standard controlling manner, but there's a juxtaposition in the way he kisses. Rough but thoughtful. Hurried but enjoyed.

This…this can't be fake. There's no one else to witness it and therefore that insecurity has vanished from my mind.

A whimper crawls up my throat when his tongue sweeps into my mouth.

He groans, pressing his forehead to mine. "Fuck, Ind. Make those little noises again and I don't know that I'll be able to stop."

"Good, I don't want you to."

Hesitating for a moment, eyes bounce between mine until his lips are back where they belong.

The whiskey he drank burns my senses in the most delicious way, like I could get drunk on it, simply from tasting it on his tongue. His body falls into mine with a low grunt and his hand releases my throat, instead finding the wall behind me with whatever restraint he has left.

I've never been kissed like this. Desperately. Longingly. As if he's needed to do this since the day I walked into the apartment in the same way I have.

I have no idea how long it's been since he's been touched. This lonely man, who is so stunning and controlled, hasn't been intimate for far too long and I get to be the woman to change that.

Fingertips sliding up his chest, I touch every crevice and ridge, his heart beating against my palm at an erratic pace. Though Ryan is great at appearing controlled on the outside, his heart tells a different story.

The pads of my fingertips glide up his neck, cupping either side of his skull, holding him to me.

He whimpers at that, and I don't know if it's the feeling of simply being touched or knowing someone else has got him that breaks him, but either way I plan to recreate that sense as long as he'll let me.

Every kiss is wetter, needier than the one before, my body burning with how badly I want him. How achingly sweet the pain is between my legs, needing something to rub against.

With his hands bracketed above me, he moves from my mouth to my jaw, peppering hot slides of his lips until he takes my neck, working his way down the column of my throat.

"You're not broken," he rasps against my skin. "You just didn't have the right distraction."

He might be onto something because right now, with him touching me, kissing me, I'm not thinking about anything other than how he would feel between my legs.

Ryan nips at my collarbone, leaving a precious sting before licking it to soothe.

Head falling back, I offer him better access, my tits flush against his chest. My hard nipples press into the softness of his shirt. There's nothing I wouldn't give for him to rip this dress off me and take one in his mouth.

Instead, his lips are back on mine, eager and wanting. Giving me just enough to placate my neediness. Even in his giving, he's controlled. I want him to unravel, to lose himself in the way I feel lost right now.

My lower body grinds into nothing, searching and throbbing. Pulling at his forearms, I ask him to touch me without having to beg for it, but he stays strong, his palms bracing the wall above my head.

Instead, his foot slides between mine, urging them apart.

"Oh," I cry out, followed by the most desperate of moans when he positions his thigh to hit against my clit. "*Oh God.*"

On instinct, I grind against him, rocking my needy body and chasing a desperate release.

It feels good. Too good.

Pulling back, Ryan watches me, his eyes locked on where we're connected. Dilated pupils zero in on his leg. He slightly lifts my dress, not enough for him to see all of me, but just enough to note the glistening wetness I'm leaving on his thigh.

I could give two shits that my arousal is all over his leg. I haven't been this close in months.

"Look how pretty that is, Blue."

"Please don't stop." The words are more desperate than they've ever been.

"Never, baby."

Building and building, reaching for my climax, I rub, needy and frantic, as he grinds into me with the tempo I need.

That is until I'm distracted once again, my attention falling on a little white bookshelf sitting next to Ryan's. An empty cardboard box and single screwdriver lay tossed aside on the floor.

"Did you build me a bookshelf?" I squeak out, trying to swallow down the emotion sitting in my throat.

He was home, thinking of me, while I was being selfish, thinking of me too.

Blue-green eyes dart up from where they were mesmerized on our connection, finding me staring over his shoulder.

He grasps my chin, forcing my attention back on him. "Focus on me." That's met with another searing kiss, my body rolling against the muscles in his leg. "Focus on us. *Fuck*," he exhales against my lips, sharing breaths before his eyes drop south. "Are you going to come on my leg, Ind?"

Grinding, I moan into his mouth.

Yes, I'm going to come because if I wasn't close already, now I'm teetering on the edge, ready to fall. I'd love to think I could disconnect sex from emotion, but I can't, and knowing Ryan was thinking of me tonight, has me coming undone.

I pull his shirt up, needing to feel the warmth of his stomach, my fingers whispering against the hard planes of his muscles until they tighten and coil under my touch.

He hisses an inhale through his teeth. "Keep touching me."

His words are just as desperate as mine, silently begging me to want him.

My palms slide around his back, under his shirt, holding him to me as close as possible. He's warm and hard and so perfect it hurts.

In reply, Ryan presses his thigh firmly against my clit, rubbing, and my body's response is immediate and electrifying.

His name rolls off my lips like a desperate prayer as the beginning waves of my orgasm rip through me. Needy fingers turn into white knuckles grasping at his shirt, hoping it has the strength to keep me upright. Euphoria sparks in the back of my eyes, stringing me along as wave after wave flutters through me.

I can barely focus on Ryan's admiring gaze watching me work through my release, but it's there, nonetheless, watching me unravel for him.

Catching my breath, my head falls, finding the wet spot I left on his pants but unable to care in the slightest.

After almost eight months, all it took was Ryan's fucking leg to make me come.

Grasping my chin once again, he kisses me more tenderly than before. Reverently. Passionately.

"Next time you decide you need help with your...*situation*," he murmurs against my lips with an aching rasp. "Ask me."

With that, he leaves me dazed and satisfied, slumped against the entryway wall before he closes his bedroom door behind him.

# 20
# Ryan

As of the last four years, basketball has been my entire existence and I have the privilege to play in the NBA. I'm grateful for my opportunities, yes, but I've never disliked my job more than I do right now.

My profession took me away from home and put me on an airplane just twelve hours after my Indy came all over my leg. Twelve hours after I told her the next time she needs to come, I want her to ask for my help.

It's been three days and we haven't spoken since.

I'm not sure if I freaked her out or got her thinking, but we've been flirting in our own way for weeks. She's blatantly told me she's attracted to me multiple times, so I'm not going to lie, I was half expecting her to knock on my door and ask for another orgasm right then.

I've been celibate for more than two years, but I've imagined how her legs would mold around my waist or how it'd feel to slide against her sweat-soaked skin since the day she walked into my apartment, so there's no way in hell I was going to let someone else get the job without throwing my hat in the ring.

Making sure she gets hers doesn't have to change that for me. I can take care of her in that department without compromising on the rules I've set in place for myself. In fact, we could add her orgasms to our fake dating arrangement if she wants. I'll make sure she comes so many times she won't be able to see straight as long as I'm the only one with the privilege.

Because trust me, after the night I pinned her to the wall and made her come, there's no way in hell another man is going near her without me losing my goddamn mind.

Or going to prison.

She thinks she's broken. *Broken*. As if her ex-boyfriend wasn't already the first name on my shit list, the fact that he made this woman think she's anything less than perfection personified has me close to seeking him out and destroying his life by any means possible.

An afternoon game in San Antonio got us to Dallas early enough for the boys to take it easy and have the evening off. I, however, have been in my hotel room watching game film since we landed, and I'll stay right here until our morning practice tomorrow, inevitably checking my phone every thirty minutes for a text from my roommate.

A page full of notes and a quarter and a half into some Dallas film, my hotel phone rings. The sound is obnoxiously loud, and there's no way to really silence the thing without answering. Unfortunately, even as secure as these hotels are, at least once a road trip, someone from the front desk will call, needing absolutely nothing other than wanting to hear me speak on the other end.

Exasperated and wanting to get this over with, I answer the phone. "Yeah?"

"What a greeting."

"Ethan? Why are you calling me on the hotel line?"

"Because you ignored me on your cell. The boys are grabbing a round at the hotel bar. Let's go."

"I don't—"

"Private bar. No fans. I'll even threaten the bartender with an NDA if you want."

"I'm in the middle of watching game film."

"And it'll still be there after you hang with the team for an hour. Ryan, this is the kind of stuff Ron is talking about. It's the perfect opportunity to bond with the guys and you're at the hotel. You can go back to your room when you're ready."

Before I can deny him one more time, my cell begins buzzing on my bed. With the hotel phone tucked under my cheek, I reach across the mattress to find Indy's name on the caller ID. I haven't heard from her in days, and she's never once called me.

"Ethan, I've got to go. Indy is calling me."

He laughs without humor. "Oh, so you'll answer your phone for her but not for me."

"Yeah, well, she's a lot cuter than you. Talk to you later."

Simultaneously, I swipe to answer my cell while hanging up the hotel phone.

"Indy?" There's too much excitement in my voice, so I clear my throat and settle myself. "Is everything okay?"

"Yes. Hi. Sorry. Are you busy? Am I bothering you?"

A chuckle escapes me. "No. But why are you being so formal?"

"I don't know." She hesitates. "I guess I'm nervous."

Taking a seat on my bed, I lean against the headboard. "Why would you be nervous?"

"It's just… I haven't heard from you in a few days."

There's a small smile sliding across my lips from the unsure tone in my confident roommate's voice. Nervous Indy is endearing.

"I haven't heard from you either, Ind. I was giving you some space. Putting the ball in your court after I offered to help you come. After I *did* make you come."

"Ryan!"

"What? Don't tell me that finally having an orgasm has made you shy. It's just sex, remember?"

She whispers, indicating she's in public. "I'm not…*shy* when it comes to sex, but I thought *you* might be."

"Just because I'm celibate doesn't mean the subject makes me uncomfortable."

There's a pause on her end of the line, so I continue for her.

"So, you called. What's going on?"

Her voice brightens and I can almost imagine her squaring her shoulders in excitement. "I'm working on my bucket list, and I thought you should know."

"Oh yeah? Which one?"

"I'm at the grocery store and I'm buying whatever I want. My cart is halfway full already. I'm getting three different coffee creamers I want to try. One is Fruity Pebbles flavored. Did you know that was a thing? I hope there's room in the fridge. Do you think there's room in the fridge for them all?"

I can't help but smile at the overwhelming joy coming through the line. "We'll make room. What else are you getting?"

"My favorite dessert are these raspberry turnovers in the frozen aisle. Alex liked the apple ones better so I always bought those, but today I'm getting the raspberry ones."

"Mmm. Yeah. Those do sound better."

"I'll save you a couple. Maybe one. I'll *try* to save you one. Actually, do you need anything while I'm here? I can get some things to make dinner when you're back. Anything you're in the mood for?"

"Indy," I sigh. "That's the opposite of what's on the bucket list. You're only allowed to buy what *you* want. And I can cook for myself. Breakfast is different because it's…well it's…"

*It's special.*

"It's our thing," she says for me.

"Yes. It's our thing and we trade off, but the whole point of this bucket list is for you to be selfish for once."

"I know, but I'm not paying rent anymore. Shouldn't I contribute in some way? I can feed you. If you need help with laundry—"

"Absolutely not," I scoff. "You're not my mother."

"I'm just used to taking care of someone."

"Trust me, Ind. I know, and you're still taking care of someone. Only now the person you're taking care of is *you*."

"You're right." She sighs into the phone. "Make your own goddamn dinner, Shay."

A content laugh rumbles in my chest. "There's my girl."

*What the fuck did I say?*

My eyes are wide with regret as I listen intently, sitting in uncomfortable silence.

"I mean—"

"So, what are you doing tonight?" Indy shifts. *Thank God.*

"I'm in my hotel room. Watching game film."

"Why? Don't you have the night off? Go hang with Ethan or something."

"He's headed to the hotel bar with the team."

"You should go! It's the perfect opportunity to spend time with the team outside of practice."

"I swear you and Ethan have a text thread going about me because he said the exact same thing to me five minutes ago."

"I should've added this to your bucket list." Her tone changes, as if she were writing it down. "Become friends with your teammates."

"Except that has nothing to do with becoming one of your book boyfriends before the wedding, which is the point of the bucket list."

"No, but it has everything to do with becoming a good captain."

I flip over, burying my face into the pillow, and mumbling into the fabric. "*Fuuuuck.*"

"Don't you just love when I'm right?"

"No," I quickly answer. "But fine, you win. I'll go down for one drink."

"Send me a picture when you get there. For evidence."

"Well, speaking of the bucket lists, I have one I'm ready to knock off."

"Oh yeah? Which one?"

"There's a party I need a date for next Saturday night. You're home. I checked the Raptors' schedule, and I'm fairly certain there will be some dancing involved. I'm confident we can get a slow dance in."

The truth is, I didn't need to check the Raptors' schedule because Zanders purposefully planned this party on a night he and I are both off work and in town.

"This sounds fun. And intriguing. What's the party for?"

"I can't say just yet, but I think you should buy yourself a new dress."

"How fancy are we talking here?"

Knowing Zanders, fancy as fuck.

Her pink satin dress floods my memory. How soft the fabric felt under my touch. How fucking stunning she was in it. "Something similar to what you wore at the fall banquet would be perfect."

"I'll just wear that dress again."

I've taken Stevie shopping multiple times but making sure my sister is all dressed up would be less suspicious if her best friend took her with the same goal in mind. Not to mention, Indy won't say it, but I know my girly roommate is dying for a new dress.

"I think you should buy a new one. There's a credit card stored in the top drawer of the entryway table. Take Stevie and make a day of it."

"Ryan—"

"Don't pull that 'I can't spend your money' bullshit. We both know you want to go, and you told me you were an expensive girlfriend, so prove it."

"You're sure?"

I laugh. "Stop acting like you're not excited to spend my money. Yes, I'm sure. And pay for Stevie's too, please. For this party, I want to be the one to buy her dress."

There's a pause on the other end. "What's so special about this party?"

I stand from the bed. "I gotta go meet up with the team."

"Hey, Ryan, just so you're aware, you're the absolute worst, and I'm buying a new pair of shoes with your money too."

A smile spreads once again. "Kind of says a lot about you since you like me so much."

Her soft chuckle invades my ears.

Slipping into my shoes, I grab my hotel key with my phone still pressed to my cheek. "Hey, Blue, I kind of missed talking to you for three days. Let's not do that again."

"Deal."

"Add it to the fridge. With all the other deals we've made."

We both stay silent for a moment, neither of us hanging up just yet.

Indy clears her throat. "See you at home."

And fuck do I love the way those words sound rolling off her tongue.

"See you at home."

The hotel bar is hidden from plain view, quietly tucked on the twentieth floor. The double doors are inconspicuous, though the noise of chatter from my fellow teammates is a dead giveaway to the crowd inside.

I keep my head low until I reach the security guard standing with his hands behind his back, guarding the entrance. Looking up, he tilts his head in an approving nod and lets me inside.

Ethan was right, it is a private bar. This very rarely happens, and instantly, this particular hotel shoots to the top of my list. As blessed as I am to live the life I do, I can't just go out for a beer after work like most people do. I'll be recognized, photographed, and if I have a bad game the next night, accusations of playing hungover will litter the internet.

Having a social life isn't worth the headache that comes with it. So, while yes, my apartment can feel like a personal prison at times, it keeps me and my reputation safe.

"Shay!" Dom bursts as soon as I remove my hood. "Hell yeah, man. Get over here."

He pushes a rookie out of the barstool next to him and pats it a couple times as if it's been open all night and waiting for me.

Dom is a party boy. There hasn't been a team gathering where he's not the center of attention, but he's also a good guy who loves his mama. He was in the draft class ahead of me, but we spent three years together in college playing for UNC. He went in the second round to a team in Los Angeles, but a year into his contract, his mom had to battle cancer and he requested a trade to his hometown of Chicago, taking a pay cut, simply to be close to her. She's doing well, but ever since, he hasn't wanted to leave the city he grew up in. He's talented. Could go play for any of the championship contenders, the same way I could, but he stays for his family.

For some reason I forgot this about him. Probably because I've been selfish as fuck and haven't thought about any of these guys outside of basketball for far too long. The thirteen guys around me all have their own stories, but I've been too worried about my own to care.

Dom holds his beer out to cheers me as we sit at the bar, leaning forward on our forearms.

"How's your mom?"

Dom's head jerks back and an instant pang of guilt rams into my chest. I can't even ask the simplest of questions without causing suspicion.

"She's good. She had her bi-yearly scans two weeks ago and she's still in remission." He nods as if trying to remind himself of the good news. Then he pauses, his brows furrowing in confusion. "Thanks for asking, man."

"I've got to admit, I feel like an ass for not checking in for so long."

"You're a big shot now. You've got more important things on your plate than my mom's health."

He's not wrong. Well, he's not wrong in that I've acted that way, but the excuse is bullshit. Back in college, I knew every one of my teammates' parents by their first name even though I always called them by their last. I knew their siblings. I checked in on their grades to see if they needed help maintaining our team required grade point average.

I knew how to care about other people, how to think about other people. How to *trust* other people because I made sure they could trust me. Allowing Indy into my world has made me painfully aware of the selfish bubble I've been living in.

I've been wearing blinders for the past four years since everything happened, and I haven't looked up once. I haven't seen that my teammates are just like me—normal guys playing the game they love, while living in the spotlight. Sure, it might not be as bright as mine, but it doesn't mean the pressure feels different.

"That's bullshit," I admit. "I mean, you're completely right that I've treated everyone that way, but it's not okay. I should've checked in. I've been an ass since I joined the league."

Dom chuckles. "Okay, softie Shay. We're cool. You're still my guy." He cheers his glass with mine once again. "That Disney princess you've got at home is getting you all emotional."

I laugh. "Her name is Indy, you dick."

"Oh trust me. I haven't forgotten your girl's name. Pretty sure I moan it in my dreams sometimes."

I shake my head, but an amused smile lifts on my lips. Even though Dom pulls more than any other guy on my team, something about the night Indy went on a date shifted our dynamic. With every fiber of my being, I know she's not stepping out on this fake relationship.

"Not a chance in hell, Dom. She's not going anywhere near you or your overused dick."

His laugh is deep and full. "Fuck, I missed you, Shay."

I've nursed the hell out of my single beer, but two hours into hanging with the guys, and I've genuinely had a good time. Ethan headed out an hour ago, but not before giving me the proud dad eyes from across the room. As if I hit my first home run in t-ball instead of simply drinking beers with my teammates in a hotel bar.

My phone buzzes in my pocket with a picture from Stevie of Zanders and their dog Rosie passed out, cuddling on their couch.

**Stevie:** *Look at my cute little family. Also, I miss you.*

That family is going to be official real soon, and she has no idea. I've been a bit distant since having this secret on my shoulders, simply because I don't want to ruin the surprise. But my sister and I can't go a day without talking, so I remind her via text how much I miss her too.

Then I find a text from Indy in my messages. She sent it well over an hour ago, but I had been too distracted hanging with my teammates to check my phone. Even though my knee jerk reaction is to apologize for missing the picture she sent me of the Chinese takeout sitting in front of all her groceries on our kitchen island, most of me thinks she might be proud of me for having such a good time that I forgot to check my phone.

**Me:** *Would you hate me if I told you I completely forgot to send you a picture of me at the bar with my team?*

**Blue:** *Sorry, who is this?*

**Me:** *Cute.*

**Blue:** *My ego, Ryan. We only have so much space in the apartment.*

I send her a picture of my empty beer glass with my teammates blurred in the background.

**Blue:** *Who is that tall one? Is he single?*

**Me:** *They're all tall.*

**Blue:** *Perfect, any will do then.*

**Me:** *Are you trying to make me jealous?*

**Blue:** *Is it working?*

I know flirting with my sister's best friend is very much blurring the lines of my fake relationship, but I can't exactly help it with Ind.

**Me:** *I'm trying to get along with my teammates, and now I'm fighting the urge to get them all traded just from imagining you giving any of them the time of day. Jealous enough for you, Blue?*

Three gray dots dance along my screen then disappear. Reappear. Disappear.

**Me:** *For someone who always has something to say, I like making you speechless.*

Her response is almost instantaneous.

**Blue:** *I can think of another way you can make me speechless.*

Oh, *fuck me.*

Well, now I'm the one without words. In true Indy fashion, she says whatever the hell is on her mind, and I can barely catch up let alone catch my breath.

**Blue:** *I hope you and your right hand enjoy the rest of your night. See you at home, Roomie.*

All the ways I could make Indy speechless flood my mind, but I think I'd rather make her scream. My name, preferably. Goddamn, and now I'm remembering how fucking pretty she is when she comes. But imagine more than just her dry-humping my leg. Is that chaotic girl even more wild when she fully unravels? Would those lilac fingernails dig into my back and maybe draw blood? Would her bare legs wrap around my waist, her ankles twisting together to pull me tighter? Fuck, I hope I get to find out.

There's a shit ton of blood rushing to my dick and I'm in a bar of my colleagues. Not exactly the moment I need a fucking hard-on to make an appearance. Indy's not wrong. That little image she put in my head is begging for my right hand to get to work.

I tell Dom he's paying for my beer and I'm halfway out the door when I see one of the rookies, Leon Carson, towards the perimeter of a crowded half circle the team is making around the bar. The last time we hung outside of work was at team dinner where Ethan so kindly pointed out that the kid feared me.

Yes, I want respect, but I don't want anyone I play with to be *afraid* of me. That's reserved for any guy wearing a jersey other than Chicago's.

"Leon."

He stands straighter, eyes bouncing away from my face, having a hard time connecting. "Hey, Shay."

Jesus. Even when I was a rookie, I was never this timid. I came into the league with humble confidence, knowing what I was bringing to the game. But Leon is a bench guy. He's our backup point guard and only plays in the fourth quarter if we're blowing out another team or getting blown out ourselves.

"On Tuesday I'm going to stay late after practice and work on some footwork drills. Get some shots up. Do you want to join?"

"For real?"

"Yeah, a couple of the guys on the coaching staff usually stay late with me once a week to work on individual stuff, and if there's anything you're having trouble with we can go over it together. If you need some pointers on—"

"Yeah! Hell yeah. That would be incredible."

He's looking me in the eye now, a bit more self-assurance coming through.

"Good." I nod towards his empty beer before heading towards the door. "Get yourself another beer. Dom's buying."

# 21

# Indy

**Me:** *Daily update—this is a few days late, but I gotta tell you something. I dry-humped your brother's leg like a dog in heat.*
**Me:** *Stevie, why aren't you answering?*
**Me:** *AM I BLOCKED?!*
**Me:** *Stevie Renee Shay! You were the one who wanted me to live with him!*
**Me:** *Kidding. This isn't your fault. I LOVE YOU!! Are you mad at me?*

It's been a week since Ryan offered to *help* me out. It's taken as many days for the words to sink in, for my body to come down from the hurried orgasm thanks to his thigh pressing into me. I've been fantasizing about that man since I moved in. Hell, I've been fantasizing about him since the day we met—the same day I caught Alex with someone else.

I'm not sure what it says about me or our relationship that I was looking at another man hours after my relationship ended with the person I thought I was going to marry, but I'm beginning to wonder if the love I had for Alex was genuine and true, or simply a convenient avenue to the life I wanted.

If I'm being honest, the notion has rocked me this last week because even though I've flirted with Ryan since I met him, it all became too real the night I went on a date with someone else. That date was meant to get me out there again. To prove to myself whatever I was feeling towards Ryan was fleeting. I couldn't have genuine feelings for someone else only eight months after who I thought was the love of my life. Anyone would make me feel the same way as I was feeling towards the man across the hall.

Alarmingly enough, it proved the opposite.

Ryan came home this morning, but I haven't seen him yet. He dropped his bags, made a coffee for me and stuck it in the fridge to cool down, then headed to get some shots in before interviewing with the media all before I was awake. A typical Saturday for superstar Ryan Shay. I wonder if he gets tired of it all. His life might seem glamorous to an outsider, but seeing the daily grind, I'm exhausted for him.

Stevie and I went shopping two days ago and I've been dreaming of the scarlet-red satin hanging in my closet ever since. Red isn't typically my shade, but I'm in need of the boldness the color brings. Straps wrap into bows over my shoulders, and the hemline ends mid-shin. Conveniently, I need a second pair of hands to zip the dress up all the way, so I throw on my new pair of nude pumps until I can ask Ryan to help with the rest.

This secret party he refuses to discuss is in an hour and across town so when I hear his bedroom door open, I give myself one last long look in the mirror, take a deep breath, and head to the living room.

The click of my heels against the hardwood floor gains his attention, mid-drink with a glass of scotch in his hand.

Blue-green eyes follow a path up my legs, taking their time gliding up my body, lingering on my chest, not that I have much in that department, but this dress is doing a fantastic job of displaying what I've got. Ryan's kissable lips part, wetting the bottom one in a slick slide of his tongue.

I watch his Adam's apple bob in a swallow when he finally meets my eye. "Wow."

"Hi."

He nods, reminding himself to speak, and I've got to admit, having his undivided attention like this is quite the ego boost. "Indy, you look incredible."

I turn around, giving him my back. "Could you zip me up?"

There's a slight rattle in my knees from adrenaline coursing through me and my palms are sweaty with nerves. I don't consider myself a nervous person, but the idea of seeing this restrained man lose control has had me on edge all week.

Gathering my hair above my neck, I hear his glass touch the counter before one, two, three leisurely steps pad towards me. Heat instantly warms my back from his proximity, and we share a sharp inhale of breath when Ryan's palm slides against my hip.

The shift between us is evident, a new energy in the air around us. What was once a flirty friendship has turned into an awareness that there's more going on. It's only a matter of time before one of us decides to act on it.

Ryan's fingertips dust the skin of my neck, pushing away any stray hairs. The sensation instantly floods my body with goosebumps and the bastard begins to chuckle from it.

"I hate you," I tell him, though my breath is slightly labored.

"Mm-hmm. Seems like it."

The fingers that were on my hip dig into my skin, the fabric of my dress bunching in his grasp. He zips me up with his other hand, tracing the column of my spine with his fingertips, and taking his time as he does. When the zipper reaches its destination, holding me secure, the pads of Ryan's fingers snake around my back to my neck before curving around my throat.

A firm chest is molded to me now as his thumb traces the thrumming pulse point in my neck. "Did I buy this dress?"

I nod.

His throat releases a gravelly noise in satisfaction.

"Has anyone ever told you that you're a little possessive, Shay?"

His chest rumbles against my back in a silent laugh. "Never. But then again, no one else has ever made me feel quite as greedy as you do."

Oh God. I like him controlling like this.

Arching my back, I'm about two seconds from asking him to blow off this party, take me to bed, and take care of my every ache and need.

Ryan must sense my thought process, because he interrupts it to tell me, "We've got to go."

I turn to face him, chest to chest with his navy-blue suit and white pressed shirt. He looks good in a lighter color than black. His blue-green eyes are leaning towards sapphire in this outfit.

"You look handsome tonight."

His tongue sweeps out to wet his lower lip before it's pulled between his teeth in a smirk. Attention darting to my mouth, I suck an anticipatory breath before Ryan steps back to create some distance.

"We can't be late," he reminds me.

"Can you tell me what this party is for yet?"

He checks the Rolex on his wrist, but then he looks back to me, hesitating for a moment. "Zanders is proposing to Stevie. This is their engagement party."

"What?"

Ryan eyes me with concern.

"He's asking her tonight?" I cover my mouth with both hands.

"He's asking her right now. They're on a plane headed back to Chicago."

My chest heaves with a broken sob. "Oh my God."

Once again, Ryan looks at me like I'm a fragile doll about to break. "Are you okay?"

My eyes burn with tears because even when I'm so overwhelmingly happy, crying is my emotional outlet of choice.

"Hey," Ryan says, hands cupping my face, thumbs gently swiping under my eyes. "Don't cry. You're going to ruin your makeup."

"I can't help it."

"Are you upset?"

"What?" I pause. "Why would I be upset?"

"I don't know."

"Why would you say that?"

He holds eye contact and understanding floods me.

"Because it's not me?" I surmise.

Ryan's lips lift in an apologetic smile. "Everything is still so fresh for you, Ind. You're going to a bridal shower tomorrow and now an engagement party tonight—"

"I'm happy. I'm so fucking happy for them. This isn't about me."

Every word is the utter truth. I don't know if it's the time I've had since Alex and I broke up, or if it's simply that seeing my best friend happy holds no room for selfishness, but no part of me is upset from what I lost out on.

Ryan tucks my hair behind both ears before giving a final swipe under my eyes. "You're a good friend to her, Blue."

"Well, she's a good friend to me. You could've told me. I could've helped with the party. I could've—"

"I know. Zanders thought about asking for your help, but I told him not to. I wanted you to have fun without worrying if everyone else is too."

That's my role, though. I'm the party planner, the host. I make sure people are taken care of and having a good time.

"Yes, Ind. You're going to spend an entire night enjoying yourself without taking care of a single other human being. Shocking, I know, but I think you can do it."

"Fine," I resign. "But if this party sucks, I'm giving Zee shit for not asking my opinion."

"It's Zanders we're talking about. This is going to be extravagant as fuck." He pushes the hair out of my face, both palms bracketing my cheeks. "You're sure you're okay?"

I nod in his grasp. "Yes, but thank you for asking."

Once again, my attention darts to his lips, but just as quickly, he clears his throat.

"We should get going."

Ryan opens my door for me once his driver drops us in front of an inconspicuous building with nothing but a small dimly lit sign over a black door. There are no paparazzi or media outside, which is something I was prepared for, and only a large man stands by the front entrance with a clipboard in his hands.

Zanders did a good job of keeping this under wraps. Even I had no idea this was happening tonight, let alone the local media.

Ryan's hand slides against my lower back, leading me towards the front door.

"Indy Ivers," he tells the doorman. "And Ryan—"

"I know who you are. This is wild." The doorman's brooding expression softens into a smile as he shakes his head in disbelief because even a bouncer who is getting paid to be discreet can't help himself from fanboying when it comes to Ryan Shay.

He opens the door for us, leading us into a dark hallway, and Ryan's hand continues to protectively overwhelm the small of my back.

Shedding my jacket, I turn towards him before we enter the main room. "Since your teammates and GM aren't here, I guess we don't have to pretend we're together tonight."

Ryan hangs both our coats with the rest of the guests'. "I guess we don't."

Neither of us hold much conviction in our tones.

"But," I begin, and Ryan's eyes dart to mine, a bit of hope flickering through them. "It could be good practice."

"Right, and the wedding is coming up."

"Right," I quickly agree. "So, we should pretend tonight? For practice."

"Yeah, that seems like the right thing to do."

Without further hesitation, Ryan's hand is in mine, fingers threaded together, leading us into the main room.

The space is small and quaint, just large enough for Zanders and Stevie's closest friends and families to fill the room. But in true Zanders fashion, the lighting is moody and expensive, the bar is fully stocked with the best beer and liquor money can buy, and there's a DJ and a dance floor waiting to be occupied.

Rio, Maddison, and the rest of the guys from the Raptors are the first faces I see. Rio's green eyes go wide with excitement, his hand waving me over. Though I'm not so sure if he's stoked to see me, or if he's hoping the man at my side, who he's utterly obsessed with, will join too.

"I want to go say hi to the team."

"And my parents are here," Ryan says. "I should go warn my mother that you're not my actual girlfriend before she gives herself a heart attack from excitement."

I would join him to say hi to my best friend's parents, but Mrs. Shay isn't my favorite person. Ryan and Stevie's dad is a gem, a sweet and loving man, but their mom wasn't great to Stevie for a lot of years. They've been in family therapy and are repairing their mother-daughter relationship, and clearly, things have been better between them otherwise Zanders wouldn't have invited her here today.

I may be too lenient in my own life, but if you cross my friends, I've been known to hold petty-level grudges. So, for Ryan's sake, I'll skip out on speaking to his mom tonight, especially after I have few drinks.

"See you soon?" I ask.

"I'll come find you."

We pull away, but not before fingers linger a little longer than they should for two people who are pretending.

"So, you *are* fucking my celebrity man crush," Rio says as he wraps me in a hug.

"We're not fucking. We're using this as a practice run. He has to be my believable boyfriend in front of my childhood friends in a couple weeks."

Rio turns away from the group of his teammates, keeping his voice low. "There's absolutely no way to convince me that you're not sleeping with your roommate. Have you told Stevie yet?"

"No, because we aren't. At least not yet. He did offer to help me with that problem I told you about."

"Are you kidding?" Rio's eyes widen. "That was a volunteer thing? I would've offered months ago!"

I shoot him a blank expression.

"Yeah. Yeah. I know."

"How wild that we're at Zanders and Stevie's *engagement* party. Did you know?"

"Maddison filled us when we got here."

I say hello to Maddison and his wife as well as the rest of the guys I fly around the country for work while we wait for the guests of honor to arrive. Ryan is still hanging out with his parents by the time the main doors open, and the place erupts with cheers and celebration.

Stevie looks absolutely radiant walking through the door, and I'm sure her smile is splitting across her face, but I can't tell due to her palms covering her mouth in surprise.

Even from across the room, I can see the rock on her left hand and it's fucking huge. The man who loves nothing more than to spoil her wraps her up from behind, endlessly proud that he pulled off this surprise and gets to show off his girl in the process.

I take a step towards them, but hold myself back, wanting to let their families congratulate them first.

Stevie's eyes track the room, looking for one person in particular and when they land on her twin brother, she instantly takes off towards him. Ryan meets her halfway with quick strides, picking her up in a hug.

Surprisingly, I've kept my emotions in check. Instead of tears, I've channeled them into giddy smiles and bouncing toes, wanting to go wrap my girl in a hug. But when Ryan pulls away from his sister, wearing the most stunning smile, he also wipes at his eyes.

My roommate isn't an emotional man. That much is clear, but Stevie is always his exception. He loves her fiercely, and the fact he's unguarded enough to shed a few tears for her in public, gives me hope that maybe one day, someone else will make him just as vulnerable.

When he goes in to hug her once again, I have to shift my attention to Zanders so I don't break my ten-minute-no-crying streak. Zanders embraces his sister and dad, quickly followed by his best friends, the Maddisons.

Rio urges a gin and tonic in my hand, swinging an arm over my shoulders. "You good?"

"I'm good."

"That's what I like to hear."

There's a lull once Stevie hugs her dad and she looks my way. I take that as my cue, setting my drink down and as quickly as I can move in my heels, I throw my arms around her shoulders in a squeeze.

"Did you know?" she asks in our embrace.

"I had no idea! Did you know?"

"I had no clue!" she bursts with a laugh.

"Is this why you didn't text me back?"

"Yeah, about that—"

"Let me see that rock." I take her hand in mine, interrupting because this moment is about her and not her brother and me. "Dear God, Zee."

At that moment, Zanders swings an arm over my shoulders. "Do you like it?"

"I would've preferred you to ask for my help, but even if you did, I don't think it could be any more perfect."

Stevie is pulled in another direction, so I turn to hug her new fiancé. "Congratulations."

"Thanks, Indy." Zanders wears a content smile on his face, but it morphs to concern as he lowers his voice, speaking for no one else to hear. "Are you doing okay?"

"Why does everyone keep asking me that?"

"Well, because when we met a year ago, you had a ring picked out and a potential wedding date set. Don't get me wrong, I couldn't be happier you're not with that guy, but it hasn't been *that* long." He eyes me with caution. "Ryan said you'd be happy, and I don't doubt that you are. I just want to check in, is all. I don't want to be inconsiderate here."

"Oh God, no." I brush him off. "This has nothing to do with me. I could not be happier for you two. I promise. I'm good."

"Good." Zanders eyes my outfit. Of all my friends, he understands my appreciation of fashion. "Love the dress."

"Love the suit."

Stevie and Ryan are pulled back into their own little world as they clink their bottles of beer together, sharing a moment. Zanders and I watch the Shay siblings from across the room.

"You don't think eight months is that long?" I ask.

"I think eight *hours* was too long to grieve for that idiot, but I know you, Indy. You feel things more than most people, so no, I don't think eight months is that long. You're loyal to a fault and when you love someone, every fiber in your body feels it."

"But what if that sense of love and loyalty was all a lie? What if the feelings I thought I felt for Alex were simply pushed by my own narrative because I thought we would build the life I wanted? In that case, is eight months long enough?"

Zanders chuckles. "If you're asking me if eight months is long enough to understand Alex didn't deserve you, and maybe, just maybe there's someone else you're realizing might, then yes, I think eight months is eight months too long."

Looking up, Zanders wears a knowing grin. "Now, I'm going to go dance with my fiancée. There's another Shay over there who I know for a fact wouldn't mind spending his evening with you."

I chuckle. "Okay, matchmaker."

"What can I say? I'm in love!" Zanders takes off, hands out to the side, but he turns around to walk backwards, facing me for a moment. "Just have fun, yeah?"

*Just have fun.*

Fuck it. That's exactly what I need to do. Stop overanalyzing this whole situation. Stop wondering if I've honored my past feelings long enough to move on. Just have fun.

And the person I enjoy spending my time with the most happens to be here tonight looking like an absolute snack in that navy-blue suit.

I follow Zanders to the twins.

"We're dancing," he says to Stevie, taking her hand and leading her to the dance floor.

Rounding Ryan, I lean my elbows back on the bar table, facing him.

His eyes take a lazy trail down my body. "And what are *we* doing?"

"Good question." I take a swig of Ryan's beer. "What *are* we doing?"

The question masks a far more important one: How much of this is going to be pretend?

He chuckles, one side of his lips tugging upward as the music shifts to something a little more sultry. "We're dancing."

Ryan holds out his hand for mine and as soon as my palm is in his, he ushers me to move ahead of him. He wraps an arm around my waist from behind as we walk together to the dance floor.

Over my shoulder, he leans in close to my ear. "You're stunning, Ind. In case I haven't mentioned it in the last five minutes."

I cover his arm with my own and lean my cheek into his.

The most confusing part of tonight is wondering how much of this is fictitious. Sure, we agreed to act as if we're together in order to get some practice in, but why does everything feel so authentic?

The dance floor is crowded already, but Ryan and I find our way in. Turning me to face him, he drapes both my arms over his shoulders, running the pads of his fingertips against my skin as he does. His hands overtake my waist before they curve around my hips and settle lower than I expected them to.

As he pulls me in closer, I can't help but notice how well we fit together, how perfectly we mold even though we're opposites in every other way.

I'm disorganized. He's a clean freak.

I'm a romantic. He's a cynic.

I'm an extrovert. He's the dictionary definition of a recluse.

I want my future to involve love and family. He's adamant about spending the rest of his days alone.

But here, with him holding me, we don't feel all that different.

Tracking Zanders and Stevie on the dance floor, I rest my head on Ryan's shoulder, swaying with him as I watch the newly engaged couple. They light each other up, brighter than I've ever seen two other people shine.

"What are you thinking about?" Ryan asks softly.

"They're so in love."

I feel Ryan's neck turn to find who I'm watching. He chuckles. "I think that's an understatement, Ind."

"It looks nice."

Knowing my roommate, who refuses to acknowledge any form of love, platonic or otherwise, I fully expect him to ignore me or give me a hard time for romanticizing my friends' lives. Instead, he exhales a nostalgic sigh and says, "Yeah. It does."

Pulling away to better look at him, I keep my arms around his shoulders, my fingers mindlessly tracing the fade of his haircut. "Have you ever been in love?"

"Once."

"In college?"

He nods.

"Did it feel like that?" I motion towards his sister and soon-to-be brother-in-law.

"No, it didn't."

Ryan rarely talks about his past, and I don't want to fuck it up by prying more, but at the same time, I want to know everything about him.

My laugh puts a small smile on Ryan's lips. "What's so funny?"

"All this time I thought you didn't believe in love."

"I believe in love, but I'm a realist. You could love someone with your entire being, but it doesn't guarantee they'll love you in return. It's a gamble, and I don't like to make bets I might lose."

It's his version of control, I realize, never letting himself feel deeply enough to wager getting hurt. Never letting himself feel at all. I, on the other hand, just went all in and lost on a single hand, but I'm already thinking about taking a seat at the table for another round.

Did she not love him back? Is that what happened? Clearly not, knowing how she attempted to use him. I'm not sure how anyone who was given the opportunity to know this man, to be loved by this man, wouldn't love him in return.

Did she realize how special she was to be chosen by him?

Did Alex not feel special to be loved by me? It sure seems that way, otherwise, why else would my unwavering love be thrown by the wayside?

Loving someone doesn't ensure that sentiment is reciprocated, but even though I've tried and failed, I hope one day I find it again. I hope one day Ryan will wish it for himself too.

His thumb draws mindless circles on my lower back. "How are you still such a romantic, huh? After everything."

"I've got to believe that there's more than what I had, if you can even call that love anymore. And that's exciting, hopeful even, to believe there's better out there. Call me a dreamer. Call me naive, I don't care. I call myself optimistic."

He stills us on the dance floor, feet no longer moving. His ocean eyes track every inch of my face, lingering on my lips. "There is better out there, and if anyone deserves to get everything they want in life, it's you."

"You deserve to have your dreams come true too."

"I don't dream, Indy. I plan, and my life is going according to that plan. I have the career. It's what I always wanted."

His eyes can't connect with mine as he says the words because I'm not sure even Ryan finds them true. I see the toll the sky-high expectations take on him. He might still love the game, but the pressure to be perfect weighs on him, stealing a bit more of him every day. He's confined to the walls of the apartment unless he's prepared to be scrutinized and idolized at the same time. He lives in a million-dollar prison on the twenty-second floor. I can't imagine he wished for that part of his career.

Ryan pushes me out in an elegant spin, disconnecting our moment before I can pry any further. He's surprisingly graceful on the dance floor, and for a man who hasn't held a woman in years, he has no issues leading me here.

"I can say we've crossed this one off your bucket list. I'm sure we can pull off a dance or two at the wedding."

A soft smile runs across his lips.

The DJ shifts into the next song, which keeps the same slow and sultry vibe. "We should maybe practice a little more. Don't you think?"

I love this type of practice. All of it. The dancing. The living together. The fake relationship. "Yeah. Practice is good."

We move around the dance floor, our hands intertwined and held out to the side, our cheeks pressed together, suffocating but comforting. Once again, I spot my best friend on the other side of the room, radiating with so much happiness.

"Do you think they'll have kids? Zanders and Stevie?"

"I'm not sure," Ryan admits. "Stevie never talked much about kids. I was the sibling who always wanted them. My sister was too busy saving every stray animal she could find." He chuckles lightly. "But I think they might. Zee wants them."

I don't miss the sentence he threw in nonchalantly. *I was the sibling who always wanted them*. Layer by layer, Ryan lets me see a bit more of him, as more of his confusing backstory pushes forward, eager to come to light. I want to see it. I want to know everything, but I don't want to scare him off either, so I stay silent.

He eyes me cautiously, as if for the first time realizing he's walking through a minefield talking about marriage and babies with a woman who might not get either but wants nothing more.

Thankfully, the music shifts, filling the room with a beat you can't help but dance to.

Ryan peels off his jacket, tossing it on the back of a nearby chair before rolling up the sleeves of his white button-down shirt. It's decided at that moment, with the veins running down his forearms and the watch on his wrist, that it's just about the sexiest thing a man can do.

"Enough talk." He taps my ass, steering me to the center of the dance floor. "Come on, girl. Let's have fun."

Countless songs in and I'm a sweaty mess. We all are. Most of Zanders and Stevie's teammates and friends haven't left the dance floor, and the DJ finally caught on to the fact that all we want to hear is ass-grinding music.

My shoes have been long discarded, and I hope I find them again. They were cute. Expensive too.

The dance floor in general is a chaotic mess of music, sweat, and grinding bodies. This once black-tie affair has quickly turned into a personal nightclub of overdressed guests.

Even through the madness, I track where Ryan is, whether that's on the outskirts sharing a drink with his dad or taking a quick step outside for air. He only lasted two songs before he took off and call me needy, but I want him out here again.

"Dance with me, Indigo!" Rio grabs me, slinging my arms over his shoulders, keeping his hands at a respectful height on my back.

Our hips move together, but it's completely platonic. There's enough distance between us to make that clear.

Through the dim lighting, loud music, and over Rio's shoulder, I find Ryan watching me from the edge of the dance floor. Drink in one hand, the other in his pocket. The last time he caught me dancing with Rio was at the fall banquet. This time, even though I can see the heat flaming in his eyes, it's matched by a self-assured stance.

He watches me with suffocating intensity, bringing the rim of his glass to his lips, and even as I move with Rio, I keep my attention locked on him.

Are we still pretending? I'd love to know.

His gaze rakes my body, slow and sweeping, not missing an inch and all I want to do is tempt my jealous fake boyfriend enough to get him out here. So, I do it. Turning around, I put my back to Rio's front, swaying my hips to the beat, all while keeping my eyes locked on Ryan.

"Just so you know," Rio says into my ear, loud enough to hear over the music. "I'm well aware you're using me to make him jealous and I'm perfectly okay with that."

I chuckle. "I was hoping you would be."

"Fuck it." Rio grabs my waist, pulling me into him. "But if he hits me for this, he better at least give me an autograph too."

His hands overtake my hips, his mouth next to my ear, and not even ten seconds pass before a pair of expensive dress shoes stop in front of me. I track the legs they belong to, long and muscular, finding an unimpressed stare on Ryan's handsome face.

"You can go," he says to Rio, keeping his intense ocean eyes on me.

Rio's hands shoot up in surrender. "She made me do it."

"Oh, I'm well aware."

"I'm gonna…" Rio tosses a thumb over his shoulder. "Yeah," he says, taking off.

"Nice little show."

"Thank you. Got you on the dance floor with me, didn't it?"

I step my bare feet onto the tops of his shoes, slinging my arms around his neck. And even though this music is meant to grind and shake your ass to, he begins to move his feet, slow dancing with me once again.

"Do we need to add this to our deal? Put it on the fridge? Because as far as I'm concerned no one else gets to touch you."

"Does that mean *you'll* touch me?" *Jesus. No filter tonight apparently.*

Brows lift in surprise. "Do you want me to touch you?"

Yes. Yes, please.

"I've told you before," he continues. "All you've got to do is say the word. Ask for my help, Indy."

As tempting as it is to let the words slip out of my mouth, I hesitate.

"What's wrong?"

"Just trying to figure out how good you are at acting."

"You think I'm acting?"

"I don't know what's what anymore."

His palm slides down my back, cupping my ass, and pulling my hips into his where I'm met with a bulge hitting just above the apex of my thighs. "Does this feel fake to you?"

My breath catches. "Jealousy turns you on?"

"Nah. No need to be jealous when I know what's mine. I'm the one you're going home with."

As if every last feminist bone has left my body, I melt into him.

A beat passes, stares bouncing between eyes and lips. Fuck it, I don't want to wait to get home.

Leaning up on my toes, I move towards his mouth, and I can sense him slanting down partway to meet me before my drunk best friend grabs my hand.

"Our ride is here! There's room for you guys. Let's go."

Stevie.

*Fuck.*

I was about two seconds away from kissing her brother at her engagement party, and I've yet to tell her about my feelings for him. Sure, she gets my daily updates, but I doubt she realizes how serious I am in the majority of them.

As Zanders said, I don't think she'd be upset, but Stevie has a track record of shitty friends using her to get close to her brother. I refuse to let her believe I'm one of them. I have to speak to her first. My friendship with her is far more important than the crush I've developed on my roommate.

Ryan's expression matches mine, as if the exact sentiment went through his mind.

He steps back, creating distance. "I'll grab our jackets."

I say goodbye to the guys from the Raptors before heading out with Stevie.

"I barely saw you tonight," she drunkenly reminds me, leaning her head on my shoulder.

"I know. I'm sorry. You were a little popular."

"And you and my brother were a little obsessed with each other."

I halt us in our steps, looking over to her, thankful to find a humorous glint in her blue-greens. "We were practicing. For Maggie's wedding."

"Mm-hmm," she hums, unconvinced. "Dry-humping his leg was practice?"

"Now you take them seriously?! You never listen to my daily updates!"

She laughs. "Seeing you two tonight made it pretty clear that your daily updates are genuine. And in case tonight wasn't just some pretend practice for Maggie's wedding, and not that you need my permission, but I'm cool with it."

"You are?"

"Yeah." She pops her shoulders.

"I don't want you to think that I'm violating our friendship or anything."

"Oh God. Our friendship was violated from the first daily update." She throws her hip into mine. "Of course, I don't think that. You don't have a bad bone in your body. You're my best friend, Ind. All I want is for you to be happy. Just be careful with him, okay? He's sensitive, even though he tries to hide it."

Hearing the person who knows Ryan best call him sensitive, reaffirms what I already knew. He feels things. He's emotional, even if he tries to play it off.

"I'm going to come over this week so you can give me all the details but give your girl a Cliff Notes version. How'd your flashy fiancé propose? I know it was extravagant as hell."

"So over the top. Rented a private plane and flew us to different cities that mean something to us. Cities where we fell in love last year. Then in the most perfectly understated way, that felt as if it were meant just for me, he popped the question at home because he wanted Rosie to be there too."

"Good God." I throw my head back. "Book boyfriend material."

"I have no idea what that means."

"Just agree with me."

Partway towards the exit we connect with Zanders, Maddison, and his wife. And all the way down the hall, in front of the exit, Ryan waits with my jacket slung over his shoulder and my heels dangling in his hand.

I wish I could take a picture and keep it forever, because he looks absolutely stunning with the slight neon glow of the exit sign illuminating above him. He helps me put my coat back on, delicately pulling my hair from the collar. Eyeing the heels in his hand, we silently and mutually agree that there's no way in hell they're going back on.

I'm completely sober, but I refuse to stuff my feet back in stilettos at this time of night.

The blacked-out SUV pulls up to the curb outside and without a moment of hesitation, Ryan scoops me up with one hand, my legs wrapping around his hips. I hold on to his neck to keep steady while he carries both me and my shoes to the car.

Leaving the third row to Zanders and Stevie, Maddison and his wife as well as Ryan and me pile into the middle. There are only three seats for four of us, so as soon as Ryan closes his door behind him, he pulls me onto his lap. Maddison's wife is hauled into his, leaving the center seat empty.

"There's room for you now, Indy," Maddison says before distracting himself with the red-haired beauty he's married to.

The engine starts and as we take off down the road, I move to slip off Ryan. But instead, one large hand grips my hip, keeping me in place.

"Don't," he grounds out in my ear.

The rest of the car is too distracted to notice I have yet to move, so I settle back into his chest. His palm slides over my thigh, and as I lean back, I turn to face him, finding hooded eyes and parted lips.

He's turned on and goddamn so am I. This entire night has felt like foreplay.

I glide a hand around the back of his neck as he ever so slightly rocks my hips against him, pulling the softest, almost silent whimper from us both. His lips are centimeters from my own, and no part of me cares that others are in this car to see.

"I just want everyone to know," Zanders announces from the backseat. "I joined the mile high club today."

The car erupts with drunken laughter and congratulations.

"Dear God," Ryan mutters for no one else to hear, shaking his head. "That's one way to kill an erection."

I giggle, leaning back into him.

"He got down on one knee, so I got on two," Stevie cuts in with a casual shrug.

"That's my girl!" I exclaim.

"Sir." Ryan leans forward to the driver. "I'm going to jump out real quick so if you could pick up speed that'd be great."

I give him a playful swat in the chest before he leans back into his seat, pulling me with him.

"That was a good pickup line, Vee."

"Thank you." She pops a shoulder. "I've been waiting all year to use it."

"Do you have any pickup lines?" I quietly ask Ryan for no one else to hear.

He shakes his head. "Nah. I'd rather pin you down than pick you up."

My mouth gapes because that wasn't cheesy at all. Not with the confidence in which he delivered it. Holy hell.

His laughs from my blatant shock.

"You have an early morning tomorrow?" he whispers.

"Yeah, and a long day."

He exhales a deep sigh before placing a soft kiss on the top of my shoulder, leaving his chin to rest there. "Okay."

By the time we make it home, I understand what that "okay" meant.

He's not going to try anything. He's going to let me sleep.

What he might not understand is that due to the hours of foreplay and only a single orgasm in eight months, there won't be any sleeping for me tonight. At least, not unless something happens.

He closes and locks the apartment door behind him, leaving my shoes by the entryway. We shed our coats, hyperaware of the other's proximity, standing in tension-filled silence.

"So, I um…" He tosses his thumb towards his bedroom. "Good night."

He hesitates in the entryway for a moment, and like the coward I am, I stay silent.

Head down, he takes a step in that direction.

"Ryan," I interject, halting him. "My dress. Will you unzip me?"

He takes his time moving the zipper down my body, as if knowing this is the end of our night and wanting to make it last. His breath lingers on the back of my neck, his fingers skim the spine of my back, and my body is ignited with goosebumps once I realize his proximity.

With the back of my dress hanging open, Ryan curves his palms around my hips, fingertips digging in. "There you go."

He doesn't leave, doesn't move until I stay silent for far too long.

What am I doing? Why am I hesitating? If I'm being completely honest with myself, as much as I openly talk about sex, I haven't been properly touched since Alex and that scares me. Getting naked, being at your most vulnerable with another person, can be terrifying, but I'm tired of Alex being my last and only. He doesn't deserve the title of the last man to have that part of me.

"Ry." I stop him at his door. He looks back to me, eyes desperate and begging. "Will you help me?"

His head falls back, exhaling a sigh of relief. "Fucking finally."

# 22

# Ryan

In two quick strides I have her pinned against the wall, legs slung over my hips, and the straps of her pretty red dress falling over the slopes of her shoulders. Chests pressed together, I can feel her thumping heart as I work my mouth over the length of her neck. I kiss and lick the delicate skin, feeling a soft whimper work its way up her throat and against my lips.

Moving south, I brush my wet mouth against her collarbone as her chest becomes pink and flush. Her nipples are perfect little peaks, showing through her bra, and lifting the red satin away from her body. God, I want to put them in my mouth and suck and bite, maybe see if I can make her come from that alone.

Because tonight is all about her. She's going to come harder than she's ever come in her life.

I'm unbelievably hard from the lead up of our night. Fuck, the lead up of the last couple of months, but the fact I'm going to make Indy come until she can't see straight doesn't change the promise I made to myself. I can do this. I can touch her and lick her and make her scream all without fucking her.

"Ryan," Indy pants. "My room. Take me to my room."

She moves, grinding her pussy over my erection and with her dress bunched up around her hips, there's only a couple of layers of fabric between us. I hiss an inhale from the friction, precum already leaking from the tip because well, I haven't been touched in years. I haven't been touched in *years* and now I have the most gorgeous woman, who's incredibly smart and caring, in my arms, her pussy seeking my cock with every rock of her hips. She's hot already, and I could bet good money that she's wet too.

I turn towards her room, but I can't do it. I avoid that place at all costs, and it sure as hell won't be the first place I make her come tonight.

Instead, I carry her to the couch, dropping her on her back, my mouth still latched to her neck, ear, chest. Anywhere I can taste her other than her mouth.

I didn't lie when I said I don't like faking intimacy. Last time my jealousy wouldn't let me hold back from tasting her mouth with mine. I know how I feel about Indy, and fuck, I've wanted to kiss ever since the she first time she opened that pretty mouth and spoke, but she's blatantly told me this is all she can give me, and the idea of getting invested in another woman who doesn't reciprocate my intentions is terrifying.

She asked me to help her come. She didn't ask me to get attached and kiss those pouty lips until I can't think straight. Until I can't *walk* straight. God, I want to though.

Her long blonde hair pushes back into the pillows beneath her, arching her back and pushing her chest into me. Her fingers grab for the buttons on my shirt, undoing them as I kiss my way along the soft slopes of her shoulders. Finding the bows holding her dress straps together, I take the satin between my teeth, pulling at the fabric until it falls open. By the time I've undone the other as well, Indy has my white dress shirt completely open.

Her soft hands and red-painted nails rake down my abs and fuck if that doesn't make me grow ten times harder.

"I touched myself thinking of you," she admits.

*Fucking hell.* My dick is aching, crying against my zipper from the six hottest words I've ever heard in my life.

Chocolate eyes peer up at me from behind dark lashes, waiting for me to say something.

"What did you think about?"

"Your hands."

"Oh yeah?" I palm her breast through her dress, gliding my hand up, my fingers and thumb gripping the edges of her throat. "What else?"

I lightly squeeze the sides of her neck, testing to see if she's into that sort of thing.

Her agreeable moan vibrates against my palm.

"This," she exhales. "You on top of me. How it would feel to be under you."

With my knees between her thighs, I hook my index finger into the neckline of her dress, pulling it down to her belly. My eyes immediately drop to her chest. Hard nipples pull taut under her bra which happens to be strapless and black, subtle yet devastatingly sexy.

"Your favorite color."

*Good God.*

I'm going to be the guy who comes in his pants from a few words. Granted, they're the perfect words coming from the most kissable mouth, but if I don't take back some control, this night is going to go very differently than I planned.

"You didn't come when you thought about me, Ind? Because every time I've touched myself while thinking of you, I've come so hard I almost black out."

"You touch yourself while thinking of me?"

I exhale a humorless laugh. "That night we went camping? I thought about you while I was in the shower and just about every time since."

Her hands rake down my stomach again, every muscle in my abdomen contracting. "Why didn't you do something about it when you came back to bed?"

"I didn't know you wanted me to, but I've dreamt of seeing you like this. On your back, your legs around me."

She reaches for the buckle on my belt, unfastening it. "Well, you've got me here now, so what are you going to do?"

"Nothing."

Her movements halt, brows forming the most adorably frustrated scowl. "What?"

I run both my palms over her stomach and waist, loving the way she feels under my touch. "I'm not going to do anything. You're going to. You're going to make yourself come."

"But I can't," she protests. "It doesn't work. Please, Ryan. You said you'd help me."

"I am helping. I'm going to distract you, and you're going to touch yourself." I take her hand, guiding it to her lower stomach. "Do you trust me?"

"Of course, I do." Her eyes soften. "Do you trust me?"

"Yes," I say without hesitation, and the realization that I've never trusted another woman more than I do Indy has me real close to finding a condom and saying fuck it to my two-year celibacy streak.

There's a fierce surge of possessiveness running through me, screaming *mine*. Her legs are spread on *my* couch. She lives in *my* house. She wants *my* cock.

But I internally scold myself. Tonight is for her.

"Touch yourself, Ind. Make yourself feel good." Sitting up on my knees, I peel off my shirt, tossing it to the ground. "But first, for the love of God, show me what's underneath."

Falling over her, I keep myself hovering her body with one arm, my dick gliding against her center. I almost come right then, and the painful buildup worsens when Indy arches her back in pleasure, giving me just enough room to unclasp her bra with my free hand.

Fabric in my favorite color loosens around her bust before she drops it to the ground. Her tits are fucking wonderful, tempting and needing to be sucked.

"Ind," I breathe out in disbelief, leaning back to get a better view. "You're fucking beautiful. I mean, I knew you were, but dear God."

"You should probably touch me then, don't you think?"

Little smartass.

I nod. "Probably."

Her tits are less than a handful, but when I grab one and squeeze, it feels perfect in my palm. I run my thumb over the hard pebbled peak with so much tender appreciation. Thanking her for letting me see her body, for letting me touch her.

She whimpers the most angelic cry.

Her palm curves around the back of my neck, pulling me down, and without further hesitation, I take her nipple, sucking the rose tip before flicking it with my tongue. Taking her flesh between my teeth, I gently bite, letting her precious cries fill our living room.

Her lower half is squirming with anticipation, her pussy finding friction against me. I take my time moving on to her other breast, giving equal attention and admiration.

Between us, I move her hand back to the hem of her dress, using my own to guide it upward. "Show me."

I lick a path between her tits, my eyes locking on hers. She's dilated and dazed, soft under my tongue. I love seeing her like this. My chaotic girl is even more disordered, unable to breathe in a steady rhythm, unable to let her mind wander to places it shouldn't.

Looking down, I watch our hands bring her dress up, slowly sliding the satin against her soft thighs. It gathers around her hips, and she lifts her ass off the couch to bring the material to her waist.

I've never loved the color black more than I do now, seeing it wet and between Indy's legs.

I want to bury myself in her, in her scent. I want to lick and suck and tongue what I know is going to be the prettiest fucking pussy I've ever seen, but tonight is about her remembering she can take care of herself.

I bury my head into the crook of her neck, looking down between us. My erection is desperate for relief, but I'm trying my hardest to show some restraint.

That control I'm so good at? Yeah, it's about to fly out of the fucking window. I'm two seconds away from ripping that thong off, needing to see all of her.

"Show me," I beg once again, fisting my hands on the couch. "Please show me."

She toys with the string on her hips, her fire-engine red fingernails running the length of the fabric covering her center.

"Don't tease me, Blue." It's a warning. "Fucking show me."

My hips are rocking into the air, waiting impatiently. Ever so slightly and ever so tediously slowly, she pulls the black fabric to the side, showing me the glistening folds of the most beautiful cunt I've ever seen.

"Jesus, Ind," I choke out in admiration. "How are you real? You're fucking stunning."

"Thank you," she says softly.

There's a small patch of trimmed hair just above the cleft. Dark pinkish-purple folds gleam with her arousal. Her slit is tempting and teetering me on the edge of flat-out giving up years of practiced celibacy, solely to find out what it would feel like to have those lips slide over my cock.

I want to touch her, spread her, see every part of her, but she's supposed to be touching herself. She's supposed to be learning, my little Ivy-League student.

Taking her hand, I guide it south, covering her fingers with my own. I use our index and middle fingers to rub the length of her core before opening her and letting me see that perfect pink bud, tight and wet.

She's soaked, her arousal not only coats her fingers, but mine too. I want to put it in my mouth, lick every inch of her off me.

Her body stiffens, interrupting my carnal thoughts. Peering up, those soft brown eyes latch on to mine, giving me all the trust in the world and fuck if I don't melt on the spot.

"You okay?" I ask.

She nods, her throat moving in the prettiest swallow, my mind racing with dirty ways I'd love to see her swallow again.

"I'm nervous."

Brows pinched, I ask, "Why?"

My confident roommate, nervous?

She laughs uncomfortably. "I feel like a virgin. It's just been a long time."

"Tell me about it."

She smiles at that, that kissable bottom lip sliding between her teeth.

"If you want to stop, tell me. But you don't have to be nervous with me. God, you're fucking perfect, Blue. Pretend you're alone, in your room, touching yourself."

"I don't want to pretend I'm alone."

Of course, she doesn't. She never does.

"I like knowing you're here. That you're watching me."

"Then I'll just be here, eternally grateful that I get to watch you make yourself come." I move her hand once again, forcing a bit more pressure and together, we find her clit.

I show her how to rub a circle around the bud, how to flick, how to squeeze it just the way I would if her hand wasn't between me and her body.

"Oh God, that feels good." Her head falls back into the couch below her and I continue to help her work herself up.

Her chest is moving rapidly, her tits begging for attention. I take one in my mouth, continuing to move her hand.

"What's your thing, Ind, huh? Do you like to be called names in bed? Do you like to be talked down to?"

She lets out a tiny moan, but I think it has more to do with the pull of her nipple between my teeth and the flick of our fingers coasting over her clit, and less to do with what I said. Because I know this girl and there's not a world in which she wants to be called a degrading name. She likes to be told she's lovely and smart.

"No, that's not it. My little valedictorian likes to be praised, doesn't she?"

A whimper. The prettiest, sexiest sound I've ever heard comes from her throat.

"Clever girl like you, you want to hear how good you're doing. How perfect you are. How well you're taking it."

I feel our fingers getting wetter the more I talk.

"Well, Blue, you're doing so fucking good. Do you feel us touching your pretty clit? Do you feel how swollen we're making you? How wet you are? So good, baby."

An audible gasp escapes her as she drops her head back, her tits pressing into my face. Her legs are shaking around me. Her toes are bunching against the surface of the sofa.

God, I want to fuck her. I'm scared to, but at the same time, I can't think of anything better.

Instead, I slide off the edge of the couch, letting my cock rub against the sofa, pacifying practically none of the burning need.

Fuck, the view from down here is dangerous. She's breathtakingly bare. Her thong is pushed so far to one side, I'm able to memorize the entirety of her pussy. Every silky fold. The glistening slit.

"Prettiest pussy I've ever seen."

Her muscles clench at that, and all I want to know is how fucking tight she is.

"Ryan, make me come," she begs.

"Make yourself come."

Moving her fingers, I slide them through her folds, prodding at her entrance. I guide her to press inside herself. Her middle finger disappears. In and out. Slick and wet.

The noises between her panting breaths, her incredible whimpers, and her soaked skin are going to do me in. But then she says a few more beautiful words and I could swear I've been transported to heaven.

"Yours too," she pleads. "Put your finger inside me."

"Fuck, Indy. You keep talking like that and I'm going to come before you do."

"Wrap your hand around your cock then put your finger inside me. If this is the only way I get to have you inside of me, then please."

If this is what it feels like to give up control and have a stunning woman tell me what to do, I need to let go more often.

"Do you have any idea how much I want you, Ryan?"

*How much I want you, Ryan.*

I let the words wash over me, basking in them. I can't remember the last time I was truly wanted.

Pulling my cock out, I give it a quick tug, then pinch it at the base, needing to stop before I explode. When her finger comes out again, I cover it with mine, both of ours breaking the entrance.

She's so goddamn tight. Our fingers are a snug fit, her walls already pulsing. And all I can think about is my cock in my hand. How deliciously constricted it would be inside her.

I stroke our fingers from the inside, playing with her and finding the spot against her front wall.

Indy's a squirming mess, her head tossing back and forth. Her cries filled with "yes, right there," "oh, how does it feel so good," and my personal favorite, "I'm going to come."

Her heaving body resists the impending orgasm, not letting go just yet. Typically, I love a bit of orgasm control, building her up, easing her back then up again until she releases. But tonight, I just want her to come. She's been held back for far too long.

"Let it go, Ind. I need to see you let go."

"Are you going to come?"

Am I going to come? The cock in my hand is leaking and angry that it's not inside anything other than my fist. One quick tug and I'll be coming all over the edge of this couch.

"Yeah, baby. I'm going to come."

"Can I watch?"

Holy shit. That's hot, and if that's what she needs, who am I to deny her?

Removing my finger from her pussy, I'm back on my knees and between her legs.

Indy's dazed gaze finds my dick as it moves between my languid strokes.

"Oh," she breathes out. "Wow, that's big."

I chuckle. "Ind, how about you come before you start inflating my ego."

"Yes, sir."

*Jesus. Not helping.*

I hover over her, cock in one hand, the other finding her throat. My muscles contract at an erratic pace. I watch as Indy fingers her clit, so much of her arousal covering her hand, and like the dirty bastard I am, I want to coat my hand in her and use it to get off.

But I don't because I'm already crossing way more lines than I intended to tonight.

She keeps her attention on me. "Come on me," she begs. "Oh fuck. I—"

"There it is. Good girl, Blue. You're doing so fucking good."

Her reaction to my words is immediate, her feet digging into the sofa, her stomach stiff and her tits pebbled with goosebumps. Her lips fall open as her entire body contracts, and when she closes her eyes and says "Ryan" like a prayer, I come with her.

Avoiding her red dress, I come on her stomach, covering her in me. We ride it out together, ecstasy and euphoria buzzing between us.

As I catch my breath, I watch her recover. I see the dazed and thankful glint in those mocha eyes. The unadulterated bliss in her expression. The flush of an overly needed orgasm warming her skin, and I'm ruined.

I'm fucking ruined.

If I thought I was fucked after the last time she came on me, this time, with my fingers contributing to the bliss, I'm done for. In what world did I think I could touch her, watch her touch herself, come all over her body and act like I could live another day without doing it again? How could I live another day without being inside of her?

As the post-coital fog lifts, realization hits me. This is my sister's best friend. My sister who doesn't have many friends because of who I am. Not only that, but Indy needs to live here. She needs to save money, and this could easily ruin our living situation.

But those aren't the real reasons why my anxiety is settling in.

Quickly, I stand from the couch and tuck myself into my pants, grabbing a dish towel and wetting it under the sink.

"Are you okay?" she asks from the sofa.

Gripping my hands on the edge of the sink, I take a deep breath.

*Get it together. This is fucking embarrassing.*

Panic begins to run through every nerve in my body. It prickles against every inch of my skin.

I exhale, long and slow, hoping to calm myself down. "Yeah."

Back at the couch, I avoid eye contact as I clean up the mess I made.

Indy grabs my hand to stop me. "Ryan," she says, forcing me to look her in the eye. "What's wrong?"

"Nothing," I blurt out too quickly.

I clean Indy up and fix her dress, pulling it both up and down to cover her beautiful body.

What is wrong with me? That was amazing and wonderful and fucking terrifying. I know why I'm panicking, and I was hoping that being with Indy in this capacity would fix it for me. That I could get over it.

It's a fucking joke, thinking I'd be able to do that without wanting to have sex with her. As if abstaining from kissing her would help placate that fire. But all I can think about is the reason I've abstained for so long. The crushing feeling of being lied to by someone I trusted. The dark depression it dropped me in.

She curves a palm around the back of my neck. "Hey, look at me."

I can't. I feel like an asshole and a coward all wrapped into one. I place a swift kiss on her palm. "I'm sorry, Ind. It's not you. I just need a minute."

Without looking at the blonde beauty, I rush to my room, closing the door behind me. I drop my head back against the door and catch my breath.

Why am I like this? I'm a twenty-seven-year-old man who is panicking over sex. It's a horrible combination of knowing what we just did isn't enough for me, coupled with a fear to go further. It's not sex that scares me. It's the blind trust in another person that's petrifying.

I was head over heels in love with a woman once, until I learned it wasn't love at all. She lied to me. I trusted her more than anyone and she was trying to use me in the worst way possible. Clearly, my radar is off if I could fall for someone like that. Who says that's not happening again?

A soft knock at my door startles me. "Ryan?" Indy says, hesitating for a moment.

I stay silent because I'm a fucking coward.

Her voice is soft and low, tenderly patient behind the door. "Thank you."

It's at this moment that I hate myself. I just made a kind, funny, beautiful naked woman come on my couch then left her there because I can't get past my own shit. She doesn't deserve that.

I have to fix this, and I have no fucking clue how.

# 23 Indy

Every muscle in my body aches the moment I stepped out of bed. Chills take over as soon as I finish my morning shower, and a numbing headache is fast approaching behind my eyes.

I feel like shit.

Only a few hours ago I felt amazing. Euphoric. Satisfied. But waking up this morning my body is done with me. After too many red-eye flights, a late-night engagement party, and stressing over ensuring Maggie's bridal shower turns out perfect, the exhaustion is catching up with me.

You'd think my body would be thanking me for giving it the hardest release of my life last night. It should be grateful the eight-month dry spell is behind us, but no. It's rewarding me with a cold.

At least my dress is cute. Purple floral fabric flows away from my body. *Thank God.* The thought of anything touching my aching skin makes me want to cry.

I hope the girls like it.

Translation—I hope they like *me*.

I've spent so much time and money planning this bridal shower, partly because I want it to be perfect for Maggie, but also because I feel like I need to impress my friends. Which is odd, seeing as I've known these women my entire life. We've seen each other through every awkward phase. Every tragic and happy moment. But ever since the breakup, I've felt left out, and I miss being included.

Does that make me pathetic? Desperate? I'm sure it does, but I can't explain how excited I was that the girls asked me to help with Maggie's shower. It seems like a step in rekindling our friendships that have been lacking as of late.

I heard Ryan leave early this morning while I was lying in bed and not getting any sleep. Last night was incredible and confusing all at once. It hurt my feelings, if I'm being honest, seeing him run away from our moment to hide in his room. For him, maybe it wasn't a moment at all. Maybe it was just a weak instant as he finally caved on the mutual lust. Or maybe he took pity on me and did his poor roommate a favor by helping her come.

Does he regret it?

It's not lost on me that he didn't kiss me last night. He doesn't like faking intimacy, he said so himself. And even though his fingers were coated in my arousal, and even though he came all over my chest, maybe that wasn't intimacy for him. It was getting off hurriedly and hard. Nothing about it was tender or loving, not that I needed it to be.

But as more of the post-orgasm fog lifts, the clearer our night becomes.

Did I romanticize what happened on the couch? I must have. How embarrassing.

Another humiliating moment on display for Ryan Shay to witness, and the realization that I grossly misjudged our night has my already sick and aching body feeling even worse.

January in Chicago is bitter cold, but the restaurant where Maggie's shower is being held is only a few blocks away from the apartment. It seems wasteful to drive, even though my feet are aching with every step I take.

I've been gathering the endless decorations, table settings, and gift favors over the last few weeks and dropped them off yesterday. I even placed a hefty order with the guy at my favorite floral stand to create the most beautiful centerpieces of peonies, roses, and carnations to give that "fresh from the garden" feel. I spent more than my budget allowed for this party, but I want Maggie to have the best time.

Stevie comes barreling through the doors, curly hair pinned under a beanie, ripping off her winter coat, and ready to get down to business. All because I completely fucking forgot to tell her she didn't have to come. If I knew she was getting engaged yesterday, I never would've asked her to help me set up this party in the first place.

She doesn't even know Maggie and yet she's here for me only hours after her own celebration.

"What can I start with?" she asks.

"Vee, I'm the worst. Please go home. I completely forgot to tell you not to come. Go home and have post-engagement sex like a normal new fiancée."

She waves me off. "We've been going at it all night. An hour break is needed. Put me to work."

I want to stand up and hug her, but I'm in so much discomfort I don't think I have enough energy to move.

Staying seated, I point around the room. "The balloons need to be tied off. I need to light all the tea lights and arrange the floral centerpieces. There's a mimosa bar going over there, and I need—"

"Whoa, Ind." A heavy crease forms between Stevie's brows. "You don't look so good."

"Don't say that. Look at how cute my dress is!"

She silently laughs. "Very cute, but you're sick."

"It's just a cold."

She eyes me suspiciously. "I think you should go home."

"I can't. Please just help me set up." I stand from my seat, the blood draining from my face as a wave of dizziness washes over me.

"Indy." Stevie grabs me, sitting me back down. "I don't think it's just a cold. You need to go home. I'll do this."

I bury my face in my hands. "I can't go home."

She pets my hair soothingly. "Why not?"

*Because your brother came all over me then bolted and I'm too much of a coward to face him.*

"I…I need to make this party perfect. It's important."

"Of course, it is, but you can only do so much when you're sick."

"Vee, Maggie asked me to be in her wedding while Alex and I were still together, and I'm worried she regrets it. At least with this, I have something to contribute."

"Indy," Stevie coos, sitting back on her haunches to look me in the eye. "Anyone who gets to call you their friend is beyond lucky and if you're here trying to convince them of that, well then honey, they aren't your real friends."

"I just want to impress them."

Because I'm the butt of the joke. Alex cheats on me, yet they're all great friends with him still. But maybe if I can make today perfect and maybe when they see me at the wedding with Ryan on my arm, they'll be impressed by how well I'm doing. Faking it or not.

My eyes burn with tears because yes, I'm an emotional person, but I'm starting to realize just how sick I am and how much my body is hurting. I'm also starting to realize she's right. I'm holding on to my old life and my old friends with an iron grip, but why? Because it's what I've always known? Because they were part of the picture I painted for myself?

"Do I want to know why I didn't get a daily update today?" she asks, suspicion lacing her tone.

"Probably for the best if you don't ask questions."

She chuckles. "All right. Sit your pretty self in this seat and drink some water. You can bark commands and tell me what to do from here then I'm taking you home."

"I can't leave."

She lets out an exasperated breath but doesn't fight me on it any longer.

The balloon arch is more like a short, stubby tower, but it'll do. The candles are lit, the banner is hung, and the flowers are arranged. Stevie went home, leaving me here, much to her reluctance.

Maggie, her family, and the bridal party shower me with compliments, taking in every detail of the space. The food is delicious, at least from what I'm told, and the mimosas are flowing. It's taking every ounce of strength I have just to sit down and stay awake, let alone try to eat or work the room as the hostess.

Conversation flows in the seats around me, the rest of the bridesmaids speaking on the plans for the combined bachelor and bachelorette party taking place in Miami next weekend, but I won't be able to attend due to a work conflict.

A year ago, I would've been ecstatic to vacation on the beach with my boyfriend and our closest friends. We always had a good time together, and I'm up for any opportunity to socialize, but inevitably there would come a time in the weekend where Alex would ask me to quiet down or not correct him while the guys are chatting about their finance bro talk, even though I typically know more than them about the subject.

Now, I can't think of a better weekend than holing up in the apartment with Ryan. I could talk as much as I'd like, or we could sit in comfortable silence while reading next to each other. I wouldn't have to be anyone I'm not because Ryan likes me for me far more than Alex ever did.

"It's beautiful, Indy." Maggie sinks into the seat next to me.

"I'm glad you love it."

"You've always been good at this kind of stuff." She smooths her white-chiffon dress. "I wanted to talk to you," she hesitantly begins. "Kev and I have been spending a lot of time with Alex, and I miss you."

"You don't have to miss me. I'm right here." I put my hand on her knee. "I always want to see you. Whenever you want to hang out, I'm in."

"You know what I mean. I miss you *together*."

"Well, we aren't together."

"What if that were to change? I've never seen Alex as torn up as he has been since he saw you with that guy."

Her words have me rearing back. What in the world is she talking about? Last time I saw Alex he made sure to let me know how well he was doing. "It doesn't really matter if he's torn up, does it? He made the choices that led us to where we are today."

"He made a mistake. *One* mistake."

"You can't be defending him."

"I'm not defending him. What he did was not okay, but it's *Alex* we're talking about."

Taking a deep breath, I attempt to calm myself as saliva pools in my mouth. Even my teeth are aching at this point. I need to go home but can't even find the strength to stand. I'm running on empty, trying to make today perfect, and now I have to sit and hear this? I've been doing my very best to let my nonexistent future with Alex lay to rest.

"You cannot be serious right now. What if Kevin did this to you? You'd just forgive him?"

"I don't know, but I wouldn't write us off so completely. Twenty-two years of friendship because of one night? And it's not just with him, it's with all of us." She motions to the other women in the room. "You can't deny the dynamic has changed."

"Of course, it's changed! You all stopped inviting me to things because you wanted Alex there." Taking a deep breath, I try to keep my volume down. "If having me in the wedding is your attempt to get me to rekindle things, I don't think I should go."

"Indy, he wants everything you've ever wanted. He had a moment of weakness. He wants the marriage, the kids. There's no way you're close to that with that basketball player. Are you really seeing that guy?"

"Ryan!" I burst. "His name is *Ryan*."

She looks around and lowers her voice. "If that's all for show you need to tell me."

"Why would you say that?"

"Because," she laughs half-heartedly. "You've loved Alex your entire life and you're the most loyal person I know. Regardless of what he did, I can't imagine you moving on to someone else. It's always been *him*."

I'm far too sick to be having this conversation. It's the same words I've repeated to myself for months, assuming it was too soon to move on. But things have changed. I'm not sure when my heart and head decided to finally get on the same page, but they did. Now, there's someone else who has my loyalty, and it isn't Alex.

"I need a minute."

Slowly standing, I head to the drink station for some water. My hands and forehead are clammy, my muscles are sore, and I'm desperate to go to bed. Resting my palms on the edge of the drink table, I close my eyes and inhale a deep breath, trying to swallow down the aches and pains.

The front door to the banquet room swings open as Ryan bursts in, halting in place when the eyes of twenty women land on the only man in the room.

"Hellllo," an older woman catcalls from the back of the room. I'm not sure who it is, and I don't have the strength to turn around and find out who's hitting on my roommate.

Ryan scans the room, finding me in the corner. His ocean eyes widen with shock as his strides pick up pace to meet me. He's beautiful and commanding, but I have no idea what he's doing here.

Is this part of the deal? Him acting like a protective boyfriend in front of my old friends?

His warm fingers push my hair away from my face before testing the temperature of my forehead with the back of his hand. I brush him off without much authority, but he ignores me and checks again.

"What are you doing here?" I ask, finally giving in and leaning into his touch.

"I'm taking you home. You're sick, Blue."

"I'm fine, and your sister is a little snitch."

He chuckles a warm laugh. "Yeah, well her stubborn best friend wouldn't listen to her."

"Who says I'm going to listen to you?"

I don't know why I'm acting as if I have the energy to put up a fight. I'm about two seconds away from falling into his chest from exhaustion.

"You don't have to."

In one simple motion and with one single arm, Ryan swoops me up, chest to chest with my legs slung around his hips. Without fight, I wrap my arms around his neck and drop my head to his shoulder.

He carries me to the exit, grabbing my coat on the way and covering my body with it.

Ryan doesn't give me time to say goodbye to anyone, but I find myself perfectly okay with that.

The cold Chicago air hits me as soon as we exit the restaurant, but I welcome it, hoping it calms my burning skin. I close my eyes, needing to rest as Ryan walks us back to the apartment.

"You left the house for me."

He exhales a sigh. "Yeah, I seem to do that quite a bit for you."

His hands are hooked under my legs, keeping me from sliding down his body. I'm not much help, I have almost no strength left, but Ryan seems to be able to handle me just fine.

I pull back slightly to look at him. He's as beautiful as ever this afternoon, but his eyes are narrowed with concern, seeing me.

"Why aren't you at practice?"

"I called out."

"Why?"

"Why do you think, Ind?"

"Can't you get in trouble for skipping practice? Or fined?"

He places a hand on the back of my head, ushering me to lay on his shoulder once again.

"I guess it's a good thing I'm rich then."

Inhaling sharply, Ryan's clean scent invades my nostrils and even though I'm frustrated about last night, I can't help but relax into him. "I told you I was going to be an expensive girlfriend."

"Welcome back, Mr. Shay," I hear our doorman say. "Miss Ivers."

"Thank you, David."

"Should I have some chicken noodle soup sent up?" I can picture the look of concern painted on his face as he eyes the dead weight in Ryan's arms.

"I've got it handled," he reassures. "But we appreciate it."

"Bye, Dave." I give him a weak wave over Ryan's shoulder, reminding myself to bring him a coffee soon for being the sweet little angel he always is.

In our apartment, Ryan sheds my jacket by the front door, hanging it on the rack next to his keys. He continues across the living room, headed for his bedroom door.

"My room, please."

"No."

"Ryan, I'm still mad at you."

"Okay, you can be mad at me all you want while you sleep in my bed."

I have absolutely no fight left in me, which really is a shame. It's one of my favorite things to do, volley back and forth with him.

Through the threshold of Ryan's room, he carries me to the mattress, laying me on the side opposite his. His bed is big and luxurious, and I sink into it, both in pain and reprieve.

A clammy sweat lingers on my forehead as he begins untying my shoes. "This is how I know you're really sick. You didn't even wear heels today."

I nod quickly. "That should've been my sign."

He places my embroidered sneakers on the ground, grabbing a pair of his sweatpants from his dresser. Guiding my feet through, he slides the pants up my legs before folding them down a few times around my waist.

"Do you mind if I get you out of this dress?"

I shrug. "It's nothing you haven't seen before."

Typically, I'd add some humor in my tone, but my feelings are hurt over last night and I'm too tired to try to hide that.

Ryan exhales as if the words punched him in the gut. He lifts my dress up and over my head, before pulling off his own t-shirt, leaving himself bare-chested. He slips his worn tee over my body, enveloping me in his warmth and scent.

"Do you want your bra off?"

A smile spreads across my closed lips. "Well, if those aren't the six sexiest words in the English language strung together."

I open one lid to peek at him. He's shaking his head at me, but that kissable mouth is tugged up on each side. "I think that fever of yours is going to your head."

"I don't have a fever."

"Actually, you do. You're burning up and I'm fairly certain you have some kind of flu."

Without hesitation, Ryan slips his hand under my back and unclasps my bra with a single motion, sliding it out from under the shirt. I watch his backside as he hangs my dress in his closet, draping my bra over the hanger, and before he returns to me, he places my shoes neatly by the door.

My little clean freak.

He pulls the comforter up to my chin. "Try to get some sleep. I'm going to make you something to eat." Brushing my hair away from my face, he places a soft kiss on my damp forehead.

"Ryan," I call out, stopping him in the doorway. "Why are you doing this?"

"Because I like taking care of people. You, especially." He closes the door behind him.

Alone in his room for the first time ever, I allow my eyes to wander, taking in my surroundings. There are no photos in here, no color. Only the large window showing off downtown Chicago. His room is minimal, just as the rest of his apartment was until I moved in. It's as if he's passing through, though he's lived here for four-plus years already.

It's sad when you consider it. You'd think he'd want to set down some roots. To come home and have it *feel* like home.

My fever must be causing hallucinations because I could swear there's a pop of green on his dresser. I recognize it from the terracotta pot I replanted it in. A succulent plant sits in plain view, and I can't help but smile from the small sign of life in his otherwise lonely room.

With a grin on my lips, a fever running through my veins, and his clothes on my body, I fall asleep looking at the tiny pop of color he stole from our living room.

Sometime later, after I've eaten some of Ryan's homemade vegetable soup, with a sweat lingering on my forehead and chills running rampant over my skin, I find the strength for a shower.

Ryan sets me up in his bathroom, grabbing my shampoo and conditioner from my own before checking the temperature of the water and leaving me. I take my time, anchoring my palms on the cool shower tile and allowing the warm water to fall over my back. It takes me far longer than normal to wash my body and hair, but I soak in every second, letting the heat of the shower seep into my bones and by the end of it, I feel a tad more like myself.

Finally, once I redress, I open the bathroom door to find him sitting on the floor, his head leaning back on the wall right next to the doorway as if listening to hear if I might need him.

He looks up at me. "Are you okay?"

I nod and he stands, handing me my hairbrush he was holding on to while camping outside of the bathroom.

With shaky hands, I run it through my strands, but I'm tired and weak, and I honestly don't care that my hair will be a matted mess if I don't brush it.

Ryan's brows are creased with concern as he watches me struggle. "Let me do that, Blue."

I give in without a fight. Ryan ushers me to sit on the ground in front of the chair he has in the corner of his room. He takes a seat behind me, legs spread on either side of my body.

Gently, he begins to brush my hair.

The slight tension pulling at my scalp feels far too heavenly that I can't help from falling into his leg, resting my head against his knee.

"Why'd you go today?" he softly asks.

"I had to."

"Why'd you go today, Ind? The real reason."

"Because." I close my eyes, leaning into him. "They're my friends. They *were* my friends. I don't know anymore."

He pauses his movements and I refuse to turn around and see the disappointment on Ryan's handsome face. He knows, the same way I know that I'm holding on to those friendships as if I'm holding on to the life I had with Alex.

As I replay Maggie's words of how Alex regrets the way things have played out, an unexpected peace washes over me.

Because I don't regret it at all.

If Alex hadn't done what he did, I never would've had the opportunity to know Ryan the way I do. I never would've had the chance to be immersed in this man's world and realize how *right* it feels. How *at home* I feel.

It's an overwhelming realization to have, that I truly want no part of the life I once wanted.

Softly, Ryan uses the pads of his fingertips to guide my head to lean against his opposite knee so he can brush the other side of my hair.

Ryan doesn't make me feel like a burden. He doesn't make me feel like I'm too much.

I've offered him absolutely nothing other than exactly who I am, and he's embraced every part of me, good and bad.

I don't think I fully understood that until today.

"Indy," he whispers from behind me. "What you offer in a relationship, as a friend, a woman, a partner, by simply being who you are is more than enough. And if someone can't see that you're *everything*, then it's them who's missing out. I know you're faithful. It's one of my favorite things about you, but there has to be a limit. Some people don't deserve your unwavering loyalty."

Tears leak from my closed eyes, partly because I'm sick and partly because I've never had someone take care of me like this, body and soul. Today's realizations are overwhelming me, and in true Indy fashion, crying is my favorite outlet.

"No one has ever taken care of me," I squeak past the lump in my throat. "Thank you, Ryan."

He halts once again, so finally, I look over my shoulder at him. "What?"

He shakes his head, resuming his task of untangling my hair.

Ryan doesn't like faking intimacy, but this, him brushing my hair and taking care of me while sick seems far more intimate than anything we've ever done.

I'm certain the fever must have stolen my filter when I ask, "Are you faking it?"

"No, Blue. I'm not faking anything."

Then I feel his fingers slip into my wet hair, separating the strands into three equal parts.

"Are you braiding my hair?"

"Yes."

*Jesus. This man.* "Where did you learn to do that?"

He chuckles quietly. "My twin sister has a head full of natural curls and you're asking where I learned how to braid?"

And now I'm picturing a little Ryan helping a little Stevie with her hair and I'm sick and swooning and I want to cry all over again.

I lean into the moment of vulnerability. "Did I do something wrong last night?"

"No. God no. You were perfect."

"Then why'd you leave me?"

He exhales a long sigh. "Because I'm fucked up, Blue."

"No, you're not."

"I am," he bursts. "I had…" He pauses, his long fingers holding onto my partially braided hair. "You're a fucking gift, Ind, and I cannot believe I made you feel anything less than that. I'm so sorry. I truly am."

Turning back, I look at him. There's a world of apology in those blue-greens and I've come to learn though Ryan is sometimes sparse with his words, the ones he does say are intentional.

"I don't know how to be casual with you, and that scares the shit out of me. I'm trying to. You've made it clear you don't have anything left to give, and at the same time, I'm still so fucked up from things that you don't even know about." His face screws up in pain, quickly reminding me that I've barely scratched the surface of Ryan's past. "It all hit me like a freight train last night."

It's evident this is weighing on his shoulders, maybe more than it's affected me since last night. This conversation is important, and as much as I want answers, I know I don't have the mental strength to give it the attention it deserves. The attention *he* deserves.

I turn back around, wrapping my hand around his calf.

"We can talk about it another day," I suggest. "When I'm feeling better."

Hand slipping around my neck, he palms my opposite cheek and drops a desperate kiss to the top of my head, lingering his lips there for a moment.

Then he resumes braiding my hair, leaving that conversation on hold.

His words were laced with desperation and honesty, but he is wrong about one thing. I do have something left to give. I've quickly learned that when I'm not putting on an act, when I'm encouraged to be unapologetically myself, the exhaustion from wearing a perfect mask is gone. I have the energy to love someone, and my heart has the space to accept it in return.

Alex may have drained the old me, but the real me, I have plenty left to give.

And I think I'd like to give the real me to Ryan if he wants it. I think he'd treat my heart with kindness.

Morning shootaround was relaxed but filled with reporters waiting to talk to us the second we stepped off the court. I did my job, giving them enough of an inside scoop before I was back behind the microphone for pre-game interviews answering more probing questions.

This afternoon, I went home for a quick pre-game nap, finding Indy packing for another road trip. I was hoping she'd call out and give herself more time to rest, but she promised she was feeling like herself again. Her fever broke in the middle of night and the twenty-four-hour bug seems to have come and gone.

She freaked me out when I saw her at that party, clammy skin and sunken eyes. I didn't realize she'd need someone to remind her to take care of herself, but I shouldn't have been surprised. She spends so much time making others happy that I'm learning she tends to pass over her own well-being in the process.

"Shay." Ron stops me in the hallway after I've finished my pre-game interviews. "We missed you at practice yesterday."

He stands in his tailored suit, hand outstretched to shake mine.

"I'm sorry, sir. Indy was sick, and I didn't feel comfortable leaving her alone. I know you have to fine me for an unexcused absence. I completely understand."

"A family emergency qualifies as an excuse."

"But she's not my family."

"Is she not? You live together. You clearly love her enough to miss out on time in the gym. I'd call that family. She's good for you, Shay. You never would've skipped practice last season or any season before that."

He's not wrong. I wouldn't have dared miss precious time on the court. My opponents sure as hell wouldn't and how am I supposed to be the best if I'm taking days off while my competition is working hard?

But when Stevie called to tell me Indy was too sick to stand, I wasn't thinking about my competition or the game at all. I was thinking about the blonde across the hall who I'd give up almost anything to take care of.

"As my boss, don't you want me at practice?"

"I want you to have a balanced life, and for a player at your level, you've never had that before. I won't lie, I was skeptical about the whole thing. I thought you were trying to pull a fast one on me, but I know you. You'd never give up time in the gym for a ruse. I like this version of you, Shay. Keep it up."

My stomach churns with unease at the accuracy of his words. I knew Ron was suspicious of me and my fake relationship, and come to find out, the part where we weren't faking it at all is what got him to believe in us.

The whole thing is starting to feel messy, and I hate a fucking mess. How much of it is even pretend anymore?

I care about Indy much more than I've allowed myself to care about anyone in years, and at the root of it all, it's centered around me using her. It's a sickening realization.

"Caroline was looking at the schedule, trying to find a road game she wanted to fly out for. The Raptors are going to be in Phoenix at the same time as us. Would Indy want to catch your game with us?"

"Oh. I'll have to see if she's free and if it works for her schedule."

Yet another night I need her to use her. What the hell is she getting out of this deal? A wedding date to impress a group of friends that don't deserve a second of her attention?

"But," I continue. "She'll be working, so I'm not sure if she can make it."

"Of course," Ron says, clapping his hand on my shoulder as we begin walking through the players' tunnel to the home locker room. "I wanted to mention, there's been a lot of chatter behind the scenes. I know it's only January, but there's only one name floating around for league MVP and it's yours."

I stop in my tracks. "No shit?"

"You act so surprised." He laughs half-heartedly.

"I am. I didn't expect them to consider someone from a non-playoff team."

"We're making the playoffs. At the rate you boys are playing? There's no doubt in my mind. You're doing good, Shay. You're exactly who I needed you to be this season. A good return on my investment." His phone rings in his pocket. He pats me on the shoulder one more time and finishes with a, "Good luck tonight, kid."

It's what I've wanted to hear all season, that he believes I'm the right man for the job. That's what this whole ruse with Indy has been about, proving the team made the right decision when they named me as Captain. Sure, a lot of them still go to Ethan when they need something, but I'm two months away from getting us in the playoffs, something that hasn't been done in the organization in years.

I allow Ron's praise to wash over me as I warm up, and I carry his words into the game. I don't necessarily need someone else to tell me I'm doing a good job. I know I'm doing a good fucking job. I'm on pace to break my personal records in both assists and points in a single season, but I won't lie and say gaining the approval of the man who signs my paychecks isn't a total ego boost.

It's what I've been working towards. It's what I've been lying for.

Middle of the third period, up by eighteen, the home crowd of Chicago fans electrifies the building. The boys have been playing great, completely in sync. No one is in foul trouble, and all our starters are hitting double digits in scoring.

If we can keep up the tempo, I'll be sitting my happy ass on the bench for the entirety of the fourth quarter, as Leon takes over as point guard for the rest of the game.

My arms are covered in angry, red scratches thanks to driving the lane and the refs not calling anything. My body is sore from the constant fight to stay on my feet against guys way bigger than me. I'm quick, though, and can usually outmaneuver the punishing blows to my body.

However, sometimes, I get caught in the middle of something that any other MVP nod would be given a whistle in order to stop the play.

Not me. I don't know if it's because of my size or that my fingers aren't decorated in championship rings yet, but I'm rarely given the respect of a protective call.

Taking my time coming up the court, I hold my hand in a fist above my head, calling for a motion offense.

Our power forward sets a screen on the backside of my defender, giving me room to move before he rolls off towards the basket. I feed him the ball just in time for Ethan to swing around to the corner off a screen in the paint from Dom. The ball is kicked out to him, then passed to me, open at the top of the key where I sink a three.

The crowd erupts as we lead by twenty-one. Plenty of space for me to take the rest of the night off, and after staying up late, taking care of Indy, I couldn't be more stoked to get pulled from a game.

"There he is!" Ethan shakes the back of my head as we jog back on defense.

"Jesus," Dom huffs, running by. "You get laid or something? You just hit a triple-double for the second game in a row."

I laugh, turning around to play some defense, wondering just how accurate that accusation is. I'm relaxed, that's for goddamn sure.

Coach stands from the bench, edging towards the court and I know the second there's a dead ball, he's subbing me out.

"On your left!" Dom shouts and I tighten my defense on Memphis's point guard.

I get so close to him that when their center tries to set a screen on me, I'm able to slip around his giant body, keeping me one step ahead of my opponent. Their big man rolls off his useless screen, and Dom is quick enough to get in front of him, knocking the ball and disrupting the pass.

I take off the second Dom gets his hand on the ball. Ethan picks it off, and just like that, we're in transition with a clear lane from me to the hoop. Memphis's point guard is hot on my trail, but Ethan passes the ball out ahead of me, giving me space to control it and get to the basket.

A quick glance over my shoulder confirms how close he is, so I give myself one dribble before I'm off my feet and putting the ball through the hoop in a self-assured dunk. Nothing too flashy, we are up by twenty-one after all, but just enough to snuff any hope of closing the gap on our lead.

As soon as my fingers grip the rim, I'm coming right back down. Sure, these fans paid for a show, but there's a fine line between confidently putting the ball away and being a dick to a team now down by twenty-three.

I don't see it happen.

I don't see him coming because why would I expect another player not to slow down after I've already scored an easy bucket?

Memphis's point guard barrels underneath me as I'm coming down, swiping my legs, and flipping me in the air. I watch myself falling headfirst into the hardwood, but I keep turning, sheets of color zipping past me, as I hope to God my body finds the right side up.

Somehow, the balls of my feet and my toes hit the ground first. The unprepared smack to the hardwood shoots a burst of sharp pain through my right knee. There's an unmistakable pain in the joint and the immediate knowledge of what happened provides a deafening ring in my ears, even over the rowdy crowd.

My body is thrust forward, falling to the ground as I grab my knee, the pain shooting through me, my joint instantly throbbing.

And as I see the team doctor sift through a few rows of seats, running towards me, I know in that moment, I'm entirely fucked.

# 25 Indy

Rolling my suitcase through our private terminal at Chicago's O'Hare International Airport, I offer a wave to the office staff, ready to get this overnight trip to Columbus under way.

"Hi, Margie." I lean over the front desk. "I need to get to the plane." I show her my badge as if she doesn't know who I am.

"The pilots are out there already." She clicks the button to unlock the door that leads to the tarmac. "Go ahead."

"Thank you! Have a great week."

Taking my suitcase and flight bag, I head outside.

"Oh, Indy!" I hear behind me. "I'm so glad you're here. I was going to call you."

Yvonne, the one-woman show that is our HR department, races out of her office to meet me.

"I have some good news," she says quietly, pulling me away from anyone else who could hear. "Our insurance package was adjusted at the beginning of the year and now they cover—"

"Fertility treatments? Are you serious? How much of it is covered?"

"One-hundred percent."

"Are you kidding me?"

With a smile tugging on her lips, she shakes her head to tell me no, she's not kidding in the slightest. "Amazing news, right?"

I bend down and swoop her into a hug. I barely know this woman, only through passing hellos in the hallway, but she's delivering the best news I've received in a long time.

"Oh my God," I exhale in relief, pulling back to look her in the eye and make sure she's not lying to me.

"I'm so glad I got to tell you in person." She pops her shoulders. "That was fun. Have a great trip."

I heave out a disbelieving laugh. "I will. Thank you!"

In a daze, I make it to the airplane to find our two pilots performing their pre-flight checks. I give them a silent wave, entirely stuck in my head about what just happened.

This can change my entire situation. I don't have to pinch pennies. I could offer Ryan some rent money.

I could *move out*.

The somber realization stops me in my tracks.

I hate the idea of leaving that apartment. I knew there would come a time when I would have to move out and Ryan was adamant about me saving for my own place, ever since our first morning together. But the thought of waking up and not having breakfast with him, not finding a coffee cooling down for me in the fridge, and not tossing out the remnants of another bouquet he killed by trying his hardest to make it thrive feels like the worst-case scenario. Not being suffocated with his presence every second I'm at home seems…lonely.

And not in the way I've felt loneliness before by simply not having others around, but by being without the one person who makes me feel valued and worthy of the space I'm occupying. That my voice is worth hearing.

Should I tell him about the news? Will he want his apartment back if I do?

Sticking my purse in an overhead bin, I get to work organizing the plane for our trip. Sometime later, the other two girls join and the team staff begins to arrive. I find my way to the front of the plane, my station to work, welcoming the passengers on board.

"Welcome!" I say with a small wave as each person boards the airplane.

The players arrive last, filtering on one by one.

Excitedly, I see Rio's dark curls bounce with him as he climbs the stairs, carrying his signature boombox at his side. "Hey, Ind," he says much more solemnly than his typically goofy tone. "Have you talked to him?"

"Talked to who?"

"Ryan."

Huh? How the hell does Rio know I need to talk to him? He has no idea what happened on the couch the other night.

"How's he doing?"

"Good, I guess?"

Zanders comes barreling up the stairs behind him as Rio hangs in the front galley with me.

"Ind, I've been calling you," he breathes heavily, as if he sprinted from his car to the airplane.

"My phone is in my purse." I grab it out, finding countless calls and texts from both Stevie and Zanders. "What's wrong?"

In that moment, Rio realizes how lost I am about our conversation. He looks to Zanders to fill me in.

"It's Ryan. He got hurt in his game."

Time stills as I repeat his words over and over again until they sink in.

"How hurt?"

"He's at the hospital now. Stevie's with him. He's getting an MRI on his knee. They're worried he tore his ACL."

No. No, that's impossible. Ryan is steady. Constant. Unbreakable.

I don't know enough about sports injuries to understand the severity of what Zanders is trying to tell me, but with his hazel eyes pleading unspoken words, it's clear that this moment is critical enough that I shouldn't be on this airplane.

"I should go, right?"

He nods. "Yeah. You should go."

With shaky hands, I gather my things, looking around the front galley, and completely lost.

"I um..." What am supposed to be doing right now? I've never left a flight before. I stick my head into the cockpit, speaking to the pilots. "I uh... I have to go. I need the standby flight attendant to cover me for this trip."

The captain turns back over his shoulder to look at me. "Is everything okay?"

"No, it's not. I mean, it will be. Yes." How the hell am I supposed to explain Ryan's and my complicated situation? *My roommate is hurt? My fake boyfriend is injured? The guy who I'm very much falling for is in the hospital right now and I need to see him?*

Composing myself, I try again. "It's kind of a family emergency." I don't know how true the words are, but they feel right coming off my tongue.

"I'll call dispatch and have them swap the crew."

"Are you sure?"

"Yes. This is why we have a standby flight attendant on call. Go take care of yourself."

Turning back to the rest of the full airplane, I call one of the other girls up to the front and put her in charge, debriefing her with all the information she might need for the trip.

Zanders carries my bag down the steps of the aircraft for me. "It might be hard to get inside the hospital. I'm sure there's a media frenzy outside. Call Stevie when you get there. She'll get you in."

"How's she doing?"

"She's okay. She's worried about him, of course, but with the way Ryan got hit, he probably should've landed on his head and not his feet. So, all things considered, she's all right."

He hands off my suitcase, gives me a hug, and returns to the plane, but before he's too far away, he turns back.

"Indy, I don't want to freak you out, but if it's torn, he's done for the season, and more than anyone I know, Ryan believes this game is all he has. Take care of him, okay?"

I nod in agreement. It's what I'm best at.

Zanders was right. The hospital is a zoo of reporters camping out front, hoping to be the first to hear the prognosis for superstar Ryan Shay. As if the Devils organization won't be the first to release a statement. I can guarantee the team doctor is inside right now.

As I wait for Stevie to text me back and tell me where to go, I sit in my car parked out front. Pulling out my phone, I search his name.

Endless articles litter my screen with speculation of his injury, including countless video replays of the event. Bracing myself, I pull one up and press play.

It isn't until the third attempt to watch that I'm able to make it all the way through without turning away. It's hard not to avert my eyes when I see the player in gray charge right below him just as his fingers leave the rim.

Zanders is right. Ryan should've landed on his head, but somehow, thanks to his athletic ability, he was almost able to find his feet again. I want to feel relief for that, but it's almost impossible when I see him writhing on the ground in pain.

He's strength personified, and I hate seeing him in a moment of weakness.

As the team doctor reaches him on the screen, a text from Stevie comes through with directions to a private entrance. As stealthily as I can, I find the secret door and wait for her to meet me on the other side.

She cracks it open, allowing just enough space to slip through.

"How's he doing?" is the first thing I ask.

She pops her shoulders. "It's Ryan. He's trying to be stoic about it, but he's a shitty diagnosis away from losing it." She halts in the hallway to hug me. "You didn't have to come."

"Yes, I did," I say into her embrace.

She wears a knowing smile as she pulls away and we continue to his room.

"Are you feeling better?"

Right now, I'm feeling fairly sick. "I'm not sure how to answer that yet."

The hallway is littered with countless staff members of the team. They're still in their Devils polos, looking up things on their laptops, some on their phones in the mists of heated conversations, and a couple pacing the hallway.

Ron spots me while on the phone with a scowl. He offers me only a tight-line expression and a half-hearted wave.

It's in this moment I realize the entire organization is riding on these MRI results. Riding on Ryan himself. A weaker man would fold under the pressure, but I can guarantee when I open the door to his room, I'll find him calm, cool, and collected.

Stevie opens the door to prove I'm right. Ryan sits in a private hospital room with his knee propped and covered in ice, eyes closed, leaning back on the pillow behind him, headphones in, blocking any outside noise.

I can see the layer of old sweat drying to his forehead that he hasn't been able to shower off yet, and his freckled cheeks are still a bit tinted from exertion. Besides that, you'd have no idea he's just experienced something potentially season-ending.

"Ryan." Stevie shakes his arm, gaining his attention as he takes out his headphones.

He opens his eyes to look at her, blank and rigid, not showing any sign of emotion until she moves out of the way so he can see me.

That emotionless expression instantly shifts when Ryan furrows his brows as deeply as possible, then bites his lower lip in an attempt to hide the tiny tremble that passed through it.

"I'll um…" She throws a thumb over her shoulder. "I'll be in the hall."

As soon as Stevie closes the door behind her, Ryan drinks me in with his eyes, lingering on my work uniform.

"What are you doing here?"

"Zanders told me what happened."

"But why are you here?"

His blue-green eyes are begging, pleading for me to give him the right answer. Because besides his sister, not a single soul in that hallway is here for him. They're here to check on their asset, not him as a person.

As soon as I open my mouth to answer, the door opens and a man wearing a white coat sneaks inside, followed by Stevie and who'd I assume to be the team doctor. They pinch their way through the door, quickly leaving the chaos in the hall behind them.

Stevie rounds Ryan's bed on the opposite side of me as the doctor puts his MRI images on the screen which lights up from behind. We all stare at the pictures as if we have any idea what we're looking for. Even as I squint, I can't make out anything from the black and white images.

"Clearly, this is your knee…"

The doctor begins his spiel, but I accidentally tune him out when I feel Ryan's hand reach for mine that's dangling next to his bed. Looking back, I watch him thread our fingers together all while keeping his attention focused on his doctor.

I give him a slight squeeze of encouragement before concentrating once again.

"As you can see here"—he points to a specific part of the image—

"the anterior cruciate ligament has been stretched, but there are no visible tears."

Ryan exhales a deep sigh of relief, laying his head back on the bed and closing his eyes.

"It's a grade one, but you're very lucky. If your legs weren't so strong, we'd be looking at a complete tear, surgery, season-ending injury. You need to be careful on it."

Ryan quickly nods in agreement before the team doctor takes over.

"We're looking at three to four weeks off the court if you're taking proper care. We'll be doing physical therapy every day. I'll set you up on a treatment plan, so you don't have to think about anything other than getting back on the court."

I look down at Ryan with bright eyes. This is good news, but he doesn't seem to be taking it that way. His severe and stoic expression is back.

"A month?"

"A month," his doctor confirms.

A heavy silence lingers in the room.

Ryan unlaces his hand with mine. "Can I go home now?"

The room shares nervous glances before Stevie cuts in. "Your agent is working on making sure there's a safe way to get into your building. Media is everywhere, including the apartment."

He shakes his head in annoyance. "Of course, it fucking is."

"Ron is going into a press conference to make a statement. Once the word is out, the chaos will die down," the team doctor says, handing Stevie a note explaining tonight's at-home treatment. "Let's stay here for a few hours and once the coast is clear, you can head home."

I've never seen more people crowded outside of a building as I did when I got home from the hospital. Even poor Dave was being bombarded with questions about Ryan's injury when he was only manning the door, trying to do his job.

I watched Ron's press conference on the television while I changed out of my work uniform and unpacked. There seems to be an equal sigh of relief from fans as well as speculation of what this will mean for the team's playoff prospects with their star out for an entire month.

I don't really understand how it all works. All I know is the expression Ryan wore when he asked us all to leave the room so he could be alone, was not one of reprieve. It was one of disappointment and frustration.

I've tried to look up ACL sprains online to know what to expect as far as recovery, but there's not much on the matter when it comes to a professional athlete, especially one as in shape as Ryan. Through my minimal research I've learned he's really fucking lucky it wasn't worse.

A few hours after I got back, the crowd outside our building was cleared and Stevie got the okay to bring her brother home.

What I didn't expect was for him to barrel in the front door on crutches.

"Hi." My stare lingers on his wrapped knee.

"Hey," he exhales, unable to look at me, hobbling to his room. "I'm going to bed."

Stevie and I share a knowing look. In true Ryan fashion he wants to be alone when the last thing he needs is to mentally beat himself up in silence.

"Actually," I interrupt him. "I set up the couch for you." I gesture towards it. A pillow is fluffed on the ottoman to prop his leg, and his latest read is sitting on the armrest.

He eyes me. "I just want to be alone."

"And I don't." I motion towards the couch once again. "Shall we?"

Reluctantly while rolling his eyes, Ryan hobbles over to the couch and plops down on the spot I made for him, lifting his foot onto the pillow with caution.

"Wonderful." I clap my hands together.

Stevie silently giggles from the doorway before setting the note from the team doctor on the kitchen island. "I'll leave this with you, Ind. I'm going to go check on Rosie, but I'll be back later once Ryan's meds are filled." She closes the door behind her while throwing out, "Love you, Ry!" over her shoulder.

Checking over my assignment for the night, I grab an ice pack from the freezer and hesitantly unwrap Ryan's knee to find it looking more like a balloon than a body part.

"I know," Ryan groans. "It's fucking horrible."

Securing the ice pack over his injury, I take a seat on the couch next to him. "It could be a lot worse. You got good news today. I don't know why you're so upset."

"Good news?" He huffs out a disbelieving laugh. "You call this good news? I'm out for a month, Ind."

"Well, you could've been out for the season," I shoot right back. "Or worse, you could've landed on your head, and I don't even want to think about what those consequences would've looked like."

He shakes his head, looking away from me. "You don't get it."

I turn his chin, forcing him to look at me. "Then explain it to me."

He closes his eyes for a moment, inhaling through his nose. "I was one wrong move from an ACL tear. That's a whole year of recovery, and you know what happens to most guys who try to come back from that? They snap their Achilles tendon the next season because their leg strength is shit. Now we're looking at a *two*-year recovery. By then, I'm almost thirty. There's no way in hell I'd ever be able to make it back to the level I'm at now. My career would be over."

"Okay? But none of that happened."

"But it could've. Just like that." He snaps his fingers. "My career could've been over, and basketball is all I have. That's it. It's my entire life."

I attempt to hide the hurtful sting his words cause.

"I'm out for a month. That might sound like nothing to you, but a month in my world may as well be the rest of the season. I'm the reason we're on a playoff track. I miss a whole month's worth of games? We're fucked. We may as well call it now."

"Well, that sounds awfully conceited for a man I've only known as humble."

"It's not being conceited, Indy. It's knowing the facts. This entire team, this entire *organization* is relying on me, and I just failed everyone." He shakes his head in disappointment. "Every fucking news outlet has my face plastered on it, has that fucking play on repeat."

I stand from the couch, ready to spend the rest of my night alone in my room.

"Where are you going?"

I shrug my shoulders. "I don't really want to listen to this. Yes, that sucks, Ryan, but the way I look at it, you're lucky. Sorry if I don't understand all the basketball talk, but as my…" I wave my hand, motioning towards him. "Whatever you are, I'm just happy your brain is intact."

"My brain doesn't do shit for me in this game. My body does."

Other than that statement being entirely absurd, he's wrong. I don't know much about the sport but from what I've seen, he's always the smartest guy on the court. He anticipates every play, every move. He sees it all before it happens. His brain is the most special part of him as a player, and along the way, his body happened to catch up with that talent.

I slip past the couch, but he grabs my wrist to stop me.

"I'm sorry. I…I don't know how to go a month without this game."

He pulls me down towards his lap, and I take a seat across it. His hands drape over me, holding me tight as if he can't stand the thought of me trying to leave the room again.

"Why'd you come to the hospital?" he asks softly.

"Because you were hurt."

"Was it because Ron was there, and it would look suspicious if you weren't?"

I jolt back slightly. "Is that what you think?"

He shrugs, looking away from me.

"I was there to see *you*. Believe it or not, I don't give a shit about your boss, and I couldn't care less who you are to anyone else. To me, you're…well, I don't know what you are, but you're…*important*. You as a person, not the player, are important to me."

I run my palm down the side of his face soothingly, but once again he can't make eye contact as he fully turns towards the kitchen.

Shifting a bit, I catch his eye. They're covered in a glossy film, making the color even more vibrant.

I've never seen Ryan cry besides a few tears over Stevie's happiness. I've seen him reluctantly show other emotions—hurt, jealousy, concern, joy, playfulness. But I've never seen sadness.

He swallows down the tears. "I think you should catch a flight and meet up with the hockey team on the road. Stevie can take care of me."

"No."

"Indy, please," he begs, refusing to make eye contact. "I don't want you to see me like this."

"Like what?"

I gently grasp his chin, making him meet my eyes. Tears well at the base of his lashes, but they don't drop.

"Like what?" I press. "Human?"

"I'm not allowed to be human."

Those tears fall, but I quickly wipe them away with my thumbs before he freaks himself out too much when he feels them on his cheeks.

"I'm not allowed to mess up. I'm not allowed to step out of line. I'm not allowed to get injured and take a month off. I'm not allowed to turn it all back on. The amount of pressure on me,"—he sucks in a sharp, shaky breath—"feels suffocating. I feel suffocated."

His chest shakes as he tries to breathe without full-on crying. I've never imagined I would see him in this state, and I feel both honored and terrified to fuck it up and make him crawl right back into his emotionless shell.

"Turn what back on, Ry?"

"All of it. Wanting things I know I can't have. Feeling things I know won't be reciprocated. Wanting a future that has nothing to do with basketball." Tears continue to fall from the corners of his eyes. "That's all I have in this life, and it has to be enough for me."

*What is he talking about?*

"Ryan," I coo, running my thumbs over his freckled cheeks. "I'm not sure I know what you're talking about."

Looking at me with intentional eye contact, he takes a deep breath before angling his head and kissing my palm.

"Can I explain it to you?"

# 26 Ryan

Indy nods in agreement, offering her full attention.

Turning her waist, I open her legs around mine so she's not only sitting in my lap, but also looking at me straight on. I've run away from talking about this for so long and I can't keep it in anymore. She's overwhelmed me, walking into my life with her chaos and kindness and between realizing how much I want her and almost losing everything today, I'm wrecked. Emotionally undone.

It's unexpectedly liberating. For years, I've been emotionally numb and, in a way, refusing to feel anything— joy, sadness, love, or in this case, fear— felt like a death sentence.

I don't want to be numb anymore.

Inhaling through my nostrils, I attempt to compose what little strength I have left.

"When I was younger and I thought about my future, I saw myself playing in the NBA, but in equal measure I saw myself having a family alongside me while I did it. And I'm not referring to Stevie and my parents, but I wanted a partner. I wanted a wife, kids, all that white picket fence shit."

Indy's mocha eyes widen for a moment, before she catches herself, falling back to neutral.

"I know it doesn't seem like it now, but I was a lot like you when I was younger. I used to trust people, love people. Stevie always gave me shit about being a hopeless romantic because I saw the best in people and when I fell, I fell hard. I had a couple of girlfriends in high school, but it wasn't until college that I fell in love for the first time. Only time, actually."

I check on the pretty girl in my lap, looking for any sign of discomfort on the topic, but Indy seems as locked in on this conversation as I hoped she would be.

"You know what happened, but you don't know the full story. Her name was Marissa. We met at the end of my junior year, and I fell pretty quickly for her, but she didn't want people to know we were together, so we kept it a secret. To be honest, I liked that. My team had just won the national championship and people were starting to see me as the star basketball player and less as a normal guy. I noticed that people around me were wanting to get a piece of me before I entered the draft. But Marissa..." I shake my head. "She wasn't like that. She didn't want the attention that came with being my girlfriend, and her parents were extremely religious, so for those reasons, we didn't tell many people. But I knew that by the time we graduated I was going to propose and a lot of what she was worried about wouldn't be an issue anymore.

"You know she was trying to get pregnant. Well, she did. During my senior season."

Indy adjusts slightly, inhaling a quiet but sharp breath.

"I was stoked, and she was too. She was due that summer, shortly after the draft. I knew I'd be financially set to take care of them both, and this family was everything I ever wanted. The only person I could tell I was going to be a dad was Stevie. Marissa didn't want to tell anyone, didn't want her parents to find out until we had the baby, got engaged, and were living in whatever city I ended up playing for.

"The week of the draft, I went number one overall to Chicago. The next day I flew out here and bought this place in cash, furnished it, and got it ready for my soon to be fiancée and child to come home to. Then Marissa went into labor. I immediately caught a flight back to North Carolina and rushed to the hospital. I was too late to be allowed in the delivery room, so I was pacing in the waiting room with an engagement ring burning a hole in my pocket for what seemed like hours. Life was like a dream that week. I was going to get everything I had ever wished for in the span of five or six days.

"I remember this guy kept eyeing me in the waiting room, but I had brushed it off at the time. More and more people were starting to recognize me in my everyday life, so I chalked it up to that. I was bouncing, Ind. I was so fucking excited and nervous and happy and scared. Every emotion you could imagine feeling in that moment, I felt. A nurse came and got me once the baby came. She was healthy, Marissa was healthy, but as soon as I walked into the delivery room, something was off.

"Marissa could barely look me in the eye, but I was too overwhelmed to think much of it until she handed me her daughter, and the second I held that little girl, I knew she wasn't mine."

Indy sucks a sharp breath, covering her mouth with those red-painted nails.

"Marissa knew it too and I don't know what caused her to do it, but she spilled every detail right then and there. That guy in the waiting room? Yeah, that was her real fucking boyfriend. It was his kid. He was in on the whole thing. Our so-called relationship was all a scheme. They both played me, and she was trying to get knocked up. They were just trying to get eighteen years of child support out of me." I laugh in disbelief, hearing how absurd the words sound out loud as I recall that day four and a half years ago. "She was never afraid of the limelight and her parents weren't religious. She didn't want anyone to know we were in a relationship because she was playing me the whole fucking time."

I drop my head down between my shoulders. "I wanted it so badly, Blue. That whole scenario was my dream life. I was so ready for it. I thought I was going to be this cool, young dad who got to grab his kid from the stands and carry them around the court. I wanted to come home to them every day and I got fucking played."

Indy curves a hand around the back of my neck, soothingly rubbing the skin there. "Ryan," she says, not having any other words to add.

I stopped crying a while ago, but Indy took over in that department.

"That's one of the most horrible things I've ever heard."

I wipe at her cheeks. "It's why I have such a hard time trusting people. I was manipulated by the one person I thought loved me. Imagine how many normal, everyday people would try to use me if I let them close enough."

"You bought this place to start a family." She slaps a palm over her mouth. "Oh my God, my room is painted yellow. That room was supposed to be—"

"I fucking hate that room."

She buries her face in her hands. "Why are you living here? This apartment is like a prison for you. You can barely go outside as it is, then you're stuck in here. The place you bought for the life you planned."

I stay silent as I watch her put together more and more pieces of the puzzle.

"This is why you're…Have you not been with anyone since?"

With her hips in my hands, I run my palms over her leggings, trying to calm us both down. "I have. I tried to do the casual thing, but that's never really been my style. The two years after everything happened, there were maybe three women in total. Random partners. No one I knew."

I wipe at her cheeks.

"Please keep going," she begs, those brown eyes glossed with tears.

Exhaling, I continue. "It was too weird for me as a man in his mid-twenties not to be having sex, right? So, I tried, but every time I was with someone, I'd be in my head the entire time, trying to figure out how they were going to use it against me. I was so fucked up, Blue, that the few times it happened, I would take the used fucking condom with me and dispose of it somewhere else. That's how paranoid I was. It was to the point that none of it was worth it. I was doing it because I thought I had to, so I gave myself permission to stop trying."

"That's why you left the other night?"

I nod. "It scared me."

"You don't think I'd—"

"No," I cut her off before she can even form that sentence. No, I don't think she'd try to use me in any way, shape, or form. "I just haven't allowed myself to want someone in a very long time. *That's* what scared me."

She offers me a soft smile, urging me to continue.

"But, um…" I hesitate. "Even though that day was one of the worst days of my life, it wasn't necessarily her that messed me up. It was the wakeup call and realization of who I was to the world that fucked me up more than any of it." I look to the side of her, unable to make eye contact. "I've never really suffered from mental health stuff before, but I fell into a pretty dark depression for a solid two years afterward. Everything I had ever wanted was taken that day, but I also learned that I would never be able to have it."

She jolts back a bit. "Ryan, you can have anything you want. If you want a family, you can have that."

"Really, Ind? I can't even do what we did the other night without freaking out. How the hell do you think I'd ever be able to trust someone enough to have more? To have a family with them?" My head drops low. "God, this is embarrassing."

"Why are you embarrassed? You didn't do anything wrong."

"Because I'm not allowed to do anything wrong! No one can know about this. People expect me to be perfect, to not fuck up. But no one has any idea that for two years, the only thing that got me out of bed was a contractual obligation to be at practice and games. Other than that, I was sleeping the days away, eating when I was reminded to. My apartment"—I motion around—"was a fucking mess. Why do you think I'm as much of a clean freak as I am now? There was a two-year time span I was living in filth because I didn't have the mental capability to find the energy to clean it. I was in a never-ending loop of darkness, and not a single soul knew that after a game was over their precious golden boy of basketball was going home and living in misery."

My eyes finally meet hers. "Fuck," I exhale, bracketing her face and wiping the tears away with the pads of my thumbs. "Don't cry, Blue. I didn't mean to make you upset."

She falls onto my shoulder, hiding her face. I take the opportunity to wrap my arms around her back as she melts into my touch.

"I wish I had known," she whimpers. "I would've cleaned up after myself more. I thought you were just giving me a hard time about how messy I am. I don't want to be a reminder of those days."

"Oh, Ind. No, no, you're not. I'm just teasing you about that." I turn slightly, speaking quietly as I hold her. "I think it's good for me, maybe. Having you here has helped me let go of some of my control."

Indy wraps her arms around my neck, digs her face deeper into my shoulder, and tightens her thighs around mine.

"But I want to explain myself. When I say that basketball is all I have, I truly mean it. As pathetic as it might sound, it saved me even though it's the reason everything fell apart in the first place. I was spiraling until a couple of years ago when I leaned into it. I dug myself out of that hole, I got my shit together, and put on a sparkling smile for the cameras. I stopped letting new people into my life, but at the same time, I moved my sister out to Chicago so I wasn't alone. I started spending all my time in the gym because no one would be able to fuck with me there. I got my control back. The world expected me to be the best, so I became the best, but I wouldn't allow anyone close enough to get a piece of it. Of me."

Sitting up, she wipes at her face. "Why does it have to be all or nothing? Why can't you be the best and trust that there are people out there that want nothing from you, other than a front-row seat to support you?"

"Because it doesn't exist. I haven't had someone come into my life who wasn't just looking for what they could gain from me. Use me. Take advantage of me."

*Until you,* I want to add. *Until you walked into my apartment and flipped my world on its head, unraveling every notion I had convinced myself of. Erasing every belief I once held.*

"Oh," she chokes out, blinking rapidly. "Okay." She nods to herself. "Well, I guess this is good news for you then. That procedure I need to have in the summer, it's covered by insurance, so I don't need to save up for it anymore. I can move out."

"Wait. What?"

Clearing her throat, she tucks her hair behind her ears, composing herself. "I don't want you to think I'm taking advantage of you. God, that's the last thing I want, Ryan, but I do want to help you. That's why I pulled myself from my work trip. So, I'll stay for a few days if that's okay with you? Make sure you're back to walking without those crutches, then I'll find my own place."

"No. Fuck, no. Indy, that's not what I meant."

"Oh shit," Stevie says from the doorway, her eyes pinned on us. "I shouldn't be here."

My head snaps to her. Neither of us heard her unlock the door. Indy scurries off my lap, finding the other side of the couch.

*Fuck my life.* I haven't had a chance to talk to Stevie about my feelings for her best friend, and she just walked in to find her sitting in my lap. Not only that, but my roommate is over here telling me she's going to move out because I didn't get to explain that those insecurities of mine don't apply to her.

Stevie will understand. Hell, she'll even be on board with this, but right now, I need to explain myself to Indy before she gets in her head more than she already is.

"I'm going to go," Stevie continues, throwing a thumb over her shoulder.

"Good idea."

"No!" Indy interrupts. "Please stay."

She doesn't look me in the eye when I snap my head in her direction. Indy sits at the corner of the couch, knees tucked up to her chest, evidently overwhelmed by our conversation. I've never dumped all that information on anyone before and now she's sitting there with the belief that I think her living here is a form of her taking advantage of me.

It couldn't be further from the truth.

# 27 Ryan

Spending the day at the gym and being able to do nothing but watch was torture. The team's doctors and trainers poked and prodded at my knee while I sat my ass on a table and watched the team practice through a glass window.

Day one and I'm itching to be back out there. I'm not sure if I can handle four weeks of watching from the sidelines.

Ron and my coach gave me the option to stay home from road trips while I'm out, and I'll probably take them up on the offer. Even at home games, I don't know that I'll be able to be on the bench. It's too difficult, and honestly, my shitty attitude might be worse than my absence from the sidelines.

Stevie is waiting for me right out front of the practice facility in Zanders' car. I can't drive for a few more days, but the trainers were impressed with how well my swelling went down over the last twenty-four hours. I'll thank Indy for that. She was doting and caring and concerned, pulling a typical Indy move by taking care of everyone else around her. But I'm not going to lie, I enjoyed being the center of her attention for the evening.

I got the okay to put a little weight on my knee by walking without the crutches, but I'm slow as fuck, lifting myself into Zee's G-Wagon.

"Look at you! No crutches!" Stevie cheers from the driver's seat.

"I'm not sure that's much to cheer about, Vee."

"Okay, cranky. I got you a coffee." She gestures to the center console. "What did they say?"

"They were impressed by how much my swelling went down. They want me to walk on it a bit, but I won't start any major movements until next week."

"That's exciting!" She puts the car in drive and starts us towards home.

"Is it?"

"Okay. Clearly, nothing is going to be good enough for you at the moment." She shifts the subject. "What time do you need to be at team dinner? Do you need a ride or is Harold taking you?"

"I canceled it."

"What? Why?"

Keeping my eyes towards the passenger window, I watch as Chicago zooms by. "Why do you think, Vee? I'm not in a good headspace. The last thing I want to do right now is take the boys to dinner and pretend like I didn't let them all down."

She stays silent, eyes on the road, mouth set in a hard line.

"See," I continue. "Even my own twin is annoyed with me. Imagine how much worse I'll be with other people."

That puts a small smile on her lips. "I'm not annoyed with you, but your team still needs you. You're still their captain."

I brush her off. "Ethan is their captain. I just wear the title for the public."

Stevie doesn't elaborate or tell me how wrong I am, which is another sign that if my best friend can't get through to me, no one can.

"So," she shifts the subject. "Should we talk about last night?"

Stevie's twin brain is synced with mine as I look out of the corner of my eye, finding my mirrored expression on her face, knowing smirk and all.

"What do you want to talk about?" I ask, feigning innocence.

She laughs. "You're so full of shit. It's obvious you asked me to drive you home instead of Harold so we can talk about this, so start talking, Superstar."

Fuck, sometimes it's scary how well we know each other.

"I might have a little thing for your best friend."

"Ha!" she bursts out a laugh. "Good God, Ry. Want to try that again?"

I roll my eyes. "I might possibly be a little bit smitten by the blonde living in my house."

Stevie laughs to herself. "You were holding her hand while finding out the biggest news of your career. If you said you were completely in love with her, I'd believe you more."

"I told her about Marissa."

Thank God we're at a stoplight because my sister's head snaps around to me, eyes entirely leaving the road. "You did?"

"Last night. It's kind of what you walked in on."

"Ryan." Her eyes soften. "That's a really big deal."

I don't expand on the rest—what the years after looked like. I love Stevie more than anyone else in the entire world, but even she wasn't privileged to the dark days. Indy is the first person to know, and I want to get home so we can talk about the rest. She needs to know how much I want her to stay. How much I *need* her to stay.

"I want her, Vee. I don't know where she's at or what she's even capable of feeling after everything she's been through, but I'll take whatever she can offer." I look over to her as she continues driving, concentrating on the road. "Would you be okay with that?"

I can see a faint tilt of her lips. "You don't need my permission to be together."

"Well, I still want it. This is your best friend, and we both know it's my fault that other friendships haven't worked out for you."

"Look, you could be talking about anyone, and I'd just be stoked to hear you're opening yourself up again, but with Indy?" She peeks over at me. "There's no one I trust more to protect you as much as you'll protect her."

I offer her a faint smile. "Thanks, Vee."

"But you should lock it down. Have you seen that woman?" My sister teases. "The entire hockey team is in love with her."

"Okay. Okay. I don't need the reminder."

"I'm just saying. Get a move on it, buddy. You already live together, and I want another sister-in-law."

"Dear God," I huff out a laugh. "I'm never telling you anything. You have no chill."

Stevie parks in front of my building. "You don't need to tell me anything." She taps the side of her head. "Twin brain. I know it all already."

I can hear Indy speaking before I've even stepped into the apartment. My house is chaos the second I open the door, folding chairs stacked against the wall, two long foldable tables in the middle of our living room. The couch is pushed to the wall. Empty cardboard boxes litter the ground.

There's a phone propped up on the kitchen island as Indy speaks into it. She must not hear me because she doesn't turn around, though, her mom catches my attention through the phone screen.

"Hi, Ryan!" She waves.

Indy turns around to find me inside the doorway.

"Hey, Abigale. What are you two doing?"

"I'm passing a recipe to Indigo."

Indy motions towards the cutting board in front of her, my entire kitchen covered in food she's prepped.

Radiantly beaming, she's endlessly happier than we left things last night.

"How are you feeling?" her mom continues.

"I'm getting there. Hopefully I'll be back on the court by the time you and Tim come to visit."

"Well, we'll be supporting you either way. I'll let you two get to it. Talk to you soon, Ryan! Bye, honey."

Indy hangs up the phone. "Why does my mother sound like your new bestie?"

I pop my shoulders. "Mothers love me."

She eyes me suspiciously but doesn't catch on to the fact her mom and I are as comfortable as we are because I've chatted with her parents more than a few times since I first met them over a video call in this very kitchen.

"I know the apartment is hectic, but I'll clean it after tonight." Indy takes in my body. "No crutches? That's exciting!"

"Are you okay?" I ask with confusion. Last night she was overwhelmed and distant. Today it's as if our conversation never happened.

"Of course, I am. Why wouldn't I be?"

*Maybe because you took what I said the wrong way yesterday and thought I wanted you to move out?*

Looking around the crowded apartment, I ask, "What's going on?"

"We're hosting team dinner."

"Um, no, we're not."

"Annie called and said you canceled the whole thing."

"I did."

"And I had Ethan un-cancel it and invite the team here instead."

"Indy, why would you do that? You know how I feel about people being in my space. Not to mention, I let every single one of those guys down last night. I'm not ready to face them."

She drops the knife she's using to chop veggies as she tilts her head and softens her approach. "Ryan, you didn't let anyone down, and we had a deal. I'm supposed to help you be a better leader."

"No, you're just supposed to help me convince Ron that I am."

"Why not actually do it? You can't play for a month. Why not take this as an opportunity to shift gears and contribute in other ways? You're the smartest guy on the team. You can still use your brain from the sidelines."

I can't exactly argue the logic. It's what a good leader would do.

"I don't know about this, Ind. Having everyone over here."

Not to mention, I thought I'd have her alone so I could convince her not to move out. All night long. With my tongue perhaps.

"Will you trust me with this?" she begs. "If they get here and it's too much for you, I'll kick them out, but I think this could be great. I bought you all new dishes and silverware, so we have enough for everyone. Well, *you* bought them. I used your credit card, obviously."

A tiny smile spreads across my lips. "Obviously."

Her eyes squeeze shut with regret, as if she caught herself in the act. "I'll pay you back for them."

"Please don't do that. Please don't walk around here on eggshells. You're not paying me back for my own team dinner."

"And I rented a couple tables and chairs." She offers me a playfully cautious smile. "You need to stop treating this place like a personal prison and start living again. Tonight is a good start."

Of course, I should've known the second Indy learned everything about my past she would attempt to help me begin healing from it all. She's good like that, caring like that.

The house is prepped and she's clearly excited. Whatever is cooking in the oven smells phenomenal and knowing that girl's pure intentions, she believes tonight will be good for me.

I'll most likely be a ball of anxiety, having so many people in my safe space, but for her, I'll try.

I remove the magnets holding all our agreements to the fridge. I don't need my teammates finding out I have a bucket list in order to learn how to be a passable boyfriend, or that the woman who is supposed to be my live-in girlfriend has a lease agreement.

"I'll hide these." I hold them up, showing the random scratches of paper that make up our entire relationship.

She chuckles, but before she goes back to chopping vegetables, I catch the sad smile fall on her lips.

I want to kiss it off her and tell her she's not allowed to go anywhere. Not when she fits so right here, when she makes it feel like home, but the knock at my door keeps me from doing so.

Dom's mid-chew of the most incredible chicken parmesan I've ever had. His eyes roll to the back of his head as another loud moan escapes him. "Holy shit, Shay. She's only your girlfriend and you get all this? This is wifey material." Indy pours him another glass of wine, trying not to laugh. "Indy, if he won't marry you, I'll do it. Right now." He begins to stand from his seat as if he were to go down on one knee in front of her.

"Get your ass back in your seat," I command from the head of the table.

He ignores me, focusing back on the stunning blonde. He gestures between the two of them before silently mouthing, *"You and me. Call me."*

She giggles and it's my favorite sound.

Indy has barely sat down, constantly running from the kitchen to the makeshift dining room with more food and drinks for the team. I haven't seen these guys so relaxed since dinners back at Ethan's house. The food is phenomenal, but I wish Indy would take the open seat next to me and eat with us. She made herself a single serving of eggplant parmesan but has yet to enjoy it.

"Shay, your place is incredible," Leon says, much more outspoken than the last team dinner.

I was hoping to start working with him one on one, but now with my injury, that's off the table.

"Thanks, man."

"Why haven't you had us over yet? This food…" He shakes his head in appreciation. "Holy shit."

"I'm not sure. I guess it didn't feel right until recently."

My eyes wander back to the kitchen to find the reason why I'm so relaxed. Surprisingly, I haven't felt too much anxiety since the guys began showing up. They've been talking about upcoming games and girls they're seeing. No one attempts to snoop around my space. Instead, they just enjoy being together outside of work.

Both my room and Indy's are locked shut, keeping everyone confined to the kitchen and living room, and entirely unaware that we have separate bedrooms.

"How long have you lived here?" Leon continues.

"Four and a half years."

"Wow." He shakes his head. "I'd love to have a place like this one day."

A place like this makes sense for a guy like him. Single. Young. I guess I'm single and young too, but there's not much about my life that works in an apartment like this anymore. More and more I'm itching for a bigger place. Somewhere with land to be outdoors and unbothered. Somewhere that feels less like a reminder of the life I thought I'd once have.

"You get us through the next month and I'm sure there's a nice little raise coming for your next contract," I reassure.

He laughs it off. "Yeah, that's not going to happen. I'm not exactly ready to fill in for Ryan Shay of all people."

Ethan overhears our conversation, our eyes meeting.

I put my fork and knife down, leaning back in my chair. "You are. You have to be."

Leon looks down the table of our teammates before directing his attention back to me, his voice quieting. "I can't do it. I'm a bench guy."

Leon is my backup, only playing in the fourth quarters if a game is a blowout. I lean forward so only he and Ethan can hear. "Yes, you can. I'll help you."

"You'd do that?"

"We're a team and you need to be the leader on the court now. You and I, we're still gonna stay late after practice like we planned. I'll go through everything with you. I'll be on the sidelines during games to help. You can do this."

I hadn't realized I decided all that until it was coming out of my mouth, but I know it's the right thing to do. It's what a good leader would do. It's what the leader I was while in college who brought home two national championships would've done.

"You're going to get us to the playoffs and I'm going to help you."

Leon takes a self-assured breath, nodding his head.

"Then," I continue. "In a month, I'm stealing my spot back."

An easy laugh spreads through the three of us. I catch Ethan looking at me, nodding his head, his eyes soft with pride.

Offering a knowing pat on the shoulder, I walk past him and the rest of the guys having a good time at the table. I find Indy in the kitchen, plating more food for the endlessly hungry fourteen basketball players in our home.

From behind, I trap her body with mine, bracing my hands on the counter in front of us.

"Are you doing okay?" she whispers.

"I'm doing great."

Tilting her head to look at me, her lips almost brush mine. Her eyes dart to my mouth but before I can say "fuck it" and kiss her, she turns back to the food, giving it her full attention.

"I told you that you could trust me."

I place a kiss on her shoulder, not having much more to say other than being eternally grateful for her pulling me out of my shell tonight. In an odd way it feels liberating to have company over. I thought I'd feel out of control, paranoid, but I don't. I feel oddly…calm.

Covering her hand with mine, I still her movements. "Come eat with me."

"I can't yet. I need to get more food and drinks out."

"Everyone is happy. Take a break and come eat dinner with me."

Reluctantly, she sets her serving utensils down and follows me to the table where I pull the chair out for her between mine and Ethan's. I place more plated food on the table, family-style followed by a couple open bottles of red. They're big boys. They can serve themselves.

Sitting next to Indy feels good as it always does, but tonight as she chats with my team, there's a sense of pride flowing through me that they believe she's mine. She could be. I want her to be. Need her to be the more I watch how effortlessly she goes through life unguarded.

She's not just a happy-go-lucky girl with no perception of the terrible parts of life. She doesn't shit rainbows or believe in unicorns, but she feels everything. Every emotion good or bad and for that reason alone she's a breath of fresh air in my life. She's living and I both admire her for it and am envious beyond belief.

There was a shift last night as she sat in my lap, listening to me spill the worst part of my past that I realized I wanted her as my future.

"Indy," Dom calls from down the table. "You're convincing me that I need a girlfriend."

"You have plenty of girlfriends," she quips back.

I've only mentioned Dom once or twice in passing, but I've quickly learned that Indy remembers almost everything I say, the same way I do with her.

"No, I mean a *real* girlfriend."

A fit of laughter breaks out from the team because well…Dom is not a one-woman kind of guy.

"Fuck you guys. I can change. Shay changed." He motions towards me. "Look at that love-sick motherfucker. Now he has an absolute smoke show living in his house. I want an Indy walking around my house."

"Watch it," I bite out. "The girl's got her MBA and she's funny as hell."

Indy's cheeks flush, embarrassment washing over her from being praised for her mind and not just the way she looks.

Dom holds up his bite of food with a mischievous smile. "And she's an amazing cook."

"Damn right I am," she agrees.

"My house is much bigger than Shay's. You're more than welcome."

Fucking shit-disturber.

"She's not going anywhere." I say the words to Dom, but keep my eyes on Indy as they come out.

She won't look at me.

It's too right, having her here. This is where she belongs, with me, in this apartment. And if she thinks for a second she's moving out, she's out of her goddamn mind.

# 28 Indy

**Me:** *Daily update—I need to get away from the apartment. Can I spend the night at your house?*
**Stevie:** *Is everything okay?*
**Me:** *No.*
**Stevie:** *See you soon.*

I packed my bag while Ryan was at practice and had planned to be gone by the time he got home. But once Annie called to tell me Ryan canceled team dinner, I knew I couldn't leave yet.

I probably should've gone further than Zanders and Stevie's penthouse if I'm really trying to get away, but I don't know that I am. I don't know what I'm doing. All I know is that apartment is filled with him, and it's suffocating.

How much I want him is suffocating.

How much I care about him is suffocating.

How much love I have for that man after only a few short months is suffocating.

Call me dramatic, but last night's realizations messed me up. Ryan has lived through a pregnancy with a woman he thought he loved, anticipating their future and family. He spent nine months loving a child that wasn't his. How do you come back from that? It's no wonder he's guarded and untrusting.

It was excruciating for me, as only a bystander, to hear how someone tried to use Ryan in the most hurtful of ways, how he thinks everyone around him has tried to take advantage.

I very clearly heard the way he didn't exclude me from that statement, and I refuse to miss the blaring neon signs once again. I refuse to stay in a space that isn't meant for me, just like I stayed in a relationship that was no longer my future.

The last thing I want is to be compared to the woman before me. I care about Ryan far too much to let him believe that, so I'll prove it. I'll move out. That way, he couldn't possibly continue to believe I was using him.

As soon as Ryan was distracted and all but Ethan and Dom had left the apartment, I left too. But as I haul my duffel bag into the guest bedroom, and before I've even changed into my pajamas, I hear his voice from down the hall.

"Happen to see a mouthy blonde tonight? Mile-long legs and a banging brain?" Ryan asks his sister and Zanders.

I can hear the smile in Zanders' tone as he talks to his fiancée. "I love this for us, Vee. Watching your brother squirm like a love-sick puppy. Mushy motherfucker."

"Fuck you very much."

Stevie laughs from where she sits on the couch with Zanders and their dog, Rosie. "She's in the guest room. She'll be out in a minute, I'm sure."

I knew he'd come here or at the very least, call, but he was quicker than I expected.

I've only just pulled out my toothbrush to get ready for my night, so with it in hand, I sheepishly make my way down the hall.

Ryan doesn't seem upset, only slightly unimpressed. Leaning a shoulder against the corner wall of the living room, he keeps his hands in his pockets and one foot crossed over the other, casually unaffected.

"There's the runaway."

"Hi."

Eyes soften. "Hi, Blue."

Zanders squeals from the couch like a teenager.

"I was giving you some space," I explain before I'm asked.

"Why would I want space, and from you of all people?"

"Last night—"

"Last night, you didn't let me finish what I was trying to say."

He pops off the wall, quickly swallowing the distance between us and meeting me across the room. He crowds me with his beautiful body, stepping into my space as I retreat at the same pace.

His hooded eyes look down at me, bottom lip sliding between his teeth. "Can we finish our conversation now?"

I swallow, audibly, and with a simple nod.

"No one has ever come into my life without just looking for what they can gain from me," he repeats his words from last night, as if I could forget them. "Until you."

Backing up, my shoulders hit the wall where Ryan brackets his hands above my head, caging me in, and ensuring I hear his words.

"Until you walked your colorful, messy, and extremely tempting ass into my apartment. I've never once felt taken advantage of by you. In fact, if you remember, *I* was the one who didn't want you paying rent. I don't give a fuck if you don't need to save money anymore, you're not leaving."

"That sounds very kidnap-y of you."

"Don't tempt me."

Looking down, I find the bright pink toothbrush still in my hand. My romantic brain played this out a lot differently. Maybe this confession would come in the middle of a rainstorm or announced publicly in front of millions of people. Not while I'm holding my toothbrush in the middle of my best friend's apartment.

"We have an audience," I whisper, nodding towards the couple of eavesdroppers on the couch.

"Good. They can watch for all I care." Ryan gently takes my toothbrush and sets it on a nearby table before draping my arms over his shoulders. "After what they put me through last year? This is the very least they deserve."

A quick bubble of a laugh escapes me.

The sound causes a beautifully soft smile to tug at the corner of his lip, concaving his dimples. "So, are we done with the whole bullshit conversation about you moving out?"

Ocean eyes drop to my mouth.

"But I spend a lot of your money."

"Someone needs to."

"And I'm messy. You don't like messy."

"I like your mess."

"And I'm needy. I have no idea how to be alone."

"Good. I don't want you to be alone. I want you to be with me."

His eyes fall to my throat, watching it work its way through a swallow.

"Come home with me, Blue."

Apparently, half a second is too long to hesitate because Ryan continues. "And let me make this perfectly clear, even if you say no, I *will* throw you over my shoulder and take you with me. But I'm working with a knee injury here and would rather you come on your own free will."

His mouth twitches, trying to keep in a straight line to re-enforce his threat.

I don't think this man has any idea how funny he can be. He likes to think he's serious and stoic, but he makes me smile more than anyone else I've ever met.

"Take me home, Shay."

Ryan's lungs fill with a deep breath before he grabs my duffle bag, links his hand with mine, and leads me towards the door.

"Indy, to make this clear, I don't want a single daily update tomorrow!" Stevie announces from the couch.

"I'll text you in the morning with details!"

"I'm getting a new number."

"Aren't we the cutest family foursome you've ever seen?" Zanders pitches in.

"Love you all," Ryan finishes from the doorway, pulling me behind him. "Rosie most of all, of course." Which is ironic seeing as Ryan has to take an allergy pill every time he's with her, but happily does so anyway just to spend time at their place.

Across the street, he pushes through the doorway of our apartment, swiftly picks me up, and takes me to his bed, tossing me on the mattress. But not before I notice the scraps of papers that make up our relationship pinned back on the fridge.

His chest moves in relief as if seeing me in his house and on his bed has brought him peace. "Right where you belong." His gaze scans the length of me. "Thank you."

"For what?"

"For everything. For tonight. I think I've always wanted to have the team over, to have people over, but it scared me. To let people into my life has scared me." Leisurely, he begins to unbutton his shirt, standing over me. "But you, having you here, I want everyone to see how lucky I am to have you in my home."

While on my back, I watch Ryan hang his shirt in the closet. I thought about this countless times, knowing he wouldn't be able to undress without putting every little thing where it belongs, but understanding why he's like this gives me a whole new appreciation to his cleanliness.

The view isn't half bad either. All this does is give me more time to admire his rippling chest and lean, muscular arms.

He's so beautiful and protective and hardworking. How someone didn't appreciate him is beyond me.

Ryan returns, crawling onto the mattress like a starved man. His hands push my hair away from my face, palms to my temples. "So, thank you, Indigo."

My legs open around him without hesitation as I sling my arms over his shoulders. "You're welcome."

"Now, please, for the love of God, kiss me."

"Are you sure? Because the other night when we...well, we didn't kiss."

His eyes bounce away from mine as he hovers over me. "That's because I didn't know what you wanted. I didn't know if you just wanted to get off or if you wanted me."

My brows pinch together. How did I not catch this before? How did I not realize he needs to be told how wanted he is? When someone else pretends to love you, pretends to want you, of course you need reassurance.

Tugging his chin, I force eye contact. "I want *you*, Ryan. I've always wanted you, but I didn't know I could be so lucky to have you."

That stunning smile is back. "Then kiss me, Blue."

So, I do, soft and leisurely, nails raking over his neck. He cups my face, fingers threaded into my hair as we take our time more than we ever have before. For the first time, there's not a question whether this is real. I know it is.

But I ask anyway.

"Are you just pretending?"

He pulls away, laughing deep and full. "I stopped pretending a long time ago, Ind."

"I…I don't want this if I'm just a convenience. You know, because I live here."

Call me insecure, but I spent far too long in a relationship that was convenient and comfortable, and I refuse to do it again.

Eyes searching, they soften as he watches me. "I mean this in the nicest way possible, but Blue, you're the most inconvenient thing that's ever happened to me."

My heart flutters, words sticking in my throat.

"If I was looking for convenience, I wouldn't have gone years without touching a woman. Waking up and thinking of you, falling asleep and wishing you were there, it's been distracting, tiresome, and goddamn infuriating, but I wouldn't give you up for the world."

I've been told beautiful things, lovely and romantic things. But being told I'm inconvenient simply because Ryan acknowledged he couldn't continue living the lonely life he assumed was destined for him is one of the most romantic things I've ever heard.

His lips are back on mine, capturing and taking before they dot along my jaw, my neck, my chest.

"Thank you for listening to me last night," he murmurs against my skin.

Guilt racks me. "Don't thank me. I clammed up. You were telling me something incredibly significant, something essential to who you are, and I clammed up."

He lifts himself, placing his chest on mine, laying on my body with his legs extended off the bed. I make a mental note that he hasn't bent his right knee and soon, we need to stop so I can get an ice pack on it.

"You were perfect," he reassures.

"I want you to know, it wasn't your story that made me freak out. It was the thought that you wanted me gone."

"I know."

My thumb flutters over his freckled cheek. "How do you feel after talking about it?"

"Lighter. Like it matters less today."

It does matter less, in fact, I could argue that it doesn't matter at all. That just because someone made him believe his value is based on his income or his name and not him as a man, doesn't make it true. And maybe he's beginning to see that.

He bends down to kiss the smile off my lips. Mouths molding, our tongues tangle, my hands roam and my legs tighten around his waist. He keeps me still with a hand cupping my cheek while pulling my bottom lip between his teeth.

The way he kisses drives me feral. I couldn't tell you the last time I made out with someone but rolling around in bed with Ryan Shay has me feeling like a teenage girl who has finally gotten her first kiss.

In some ways, this is a first. I've never been seen the way Ryan sees me. I've never been appreciated the way his eyes worship me. I've never been encouraged to be myself the way Ryan praises me to be.

"What do you want, Blue?" His voice is a low husk, but without pressing more, I know what he's referring to. Our bodies grinding and writhing into each other know too.

I want him to fuck me. I can feel the bulge of his erection sliding against my leg, looking for friction. I want him inside of me, but more than anything, after last night, I'd rather we move at a pace that makes him realize I'm not her.

"I want you to set the pace."

He stills, brows furrowing before he drops his head to my chest and kisses me there. His fingers intertwine with mine, pushing my hands above my head and into the mattress as his body rolls against me. He continues down my stomach, placing lingering kisses over my dress, all the while pulling the fabric up.

Ryan's injured leg is unbent as it hangs off the mattress, using his other to support his weight. Hands hook under my thighs, keeping me steady while also spreading me wider.

"You have no idea, Indy." Another worshiping kiss on my covered stomach. "The power you have over me."

My back arches, squirming beneath his body as he lifts my dress up and over my ass.

"All I can think about is seeing you smile and trying to be the reason you are." This time his warm mouth meets the soft flesh above my panties. "Trying to water those goddamn flowers just enough so I can watch your face light up when you get home." He bites the edge of my thong, snapping it against my skin. "Making you come just to hear my name dripping from that smart mouth of yours."

Ryan places a deep kiss on the center of my pussy. A groan rumbles in his throat as he inhales my scent, lingering his face in my slit.

Pushing my hips into him, I can't help but seek more friction.

"You're soaked, Ind. Does my smart girl like being told how all-consuming she is?"

My thighs tighten around him, unable to use words to articulate just how much I like his doting.

"Words, Indy."

"Yes," I breathe out. "I do."

Not that I want to think about the man before him, but I was with that guy for six years and the only time he ate me out is when I begged him to. Apparently in his mind, a blow job doesn't require reciprocation. I quickly gave up on asking. He was never very good at it anyway, and I sure as hell never came from his mouth.

Ryan, on the other hand, has his face enthusiastically pressed between my legs, as if he could spend the entire night down there and be happy.

I hope he does.

"Ry, do you like doing that?"

"Do I like eating pussy?" His tongue slides against the length of me, the fabric of my underwear creating a delicious friction against my clit. "What if I told you that every morning we had breakfast together, I thought about throwing you on the kitchen island and making a meal out of you instead? Or that every time you wore one of your pretty dresses, I was dreaming about lifting the hem over my head, falling to my knees, and tasting my roommate's perfect little cunt." Sitting up, he peels the corners of my panties down my legs, exhaling an appreciative breath when his attention zeros in on my naked center. "So, sure, you could say I like eating pussy, but that's not what you're really asking, is it? Ask me the real question, Blue. You want to know if I like eating *yours*."

God, his mouth. Dirty talk does it for me regardless, but coming from Ryan, the man who only speaks when the words are needing to be heard, it hits differently.

"Ask me, Ind." His mouth hovers over me. "Or would my valedictorian like a hands-on lesson instead?" He places a soft, appreciative kiss on my bare clit. "A mouth-on lesson."

A whimper creeps up my throat, seeing his head buried between my legs, his full lips shining with my arousal.

He surrounds my bud, sucking it into his mouth, and instantly bucking me off the bed.

*"Oh, fuck."* I drop my head back into his pillows.

Looking down, I watch his lips slide into a smile as his tongue darts out, tasting my sensitive skin with appreciative licks.

He's smiling. *Smiling* while going down on me.

I've never felt something so all-consuming as Ryan Shay's tongue on my body.

Long but controlled strokes taste every inch of me. He groans, sucking, tasting, and teasing me. Hands over my thighs, he pulls me into his mouth, as if he can't get close enough. His tongue, with controlled precision, focuses its attention on my clit, alternating between flicking it and pulling it into his mouth.

I moan. I cry. I'm entirely under this man's control because I'm fairly certain I'm having an out-of-body experience.

Tilting me off the bed, his tongue forms a long, wet path from ass to clit.

I jolt in surprise, but find myself loving the sensation, never once being tasted with such detail. "*Fuck*, Ryan."

"Say it again."

"What?"

"My name. Say it again. I want to hear it while my tongue is buried inside of you. I want you to remember you're mine. So, say my name again."

Peering down, Ryan looks up at me, watching and waiting for my words, those hands I love so much hooked around my thighs.

I sit up, bending my knees to pull my dress over my head, gaining his undivided attention.

"Ryan," I draw out in as innocent a tone as I can manage. "I'm yours to do with as you please." Unhooking my bra, I drop it to the ground too. Slowly. Deliberately. "Use me however you please."

"You've got to be kidding me." His head falls in defeat, but not before those blue-green eyes darken to pools of navy. "You're going to make me come from humping the side of this bed and looking at you."

I find his hips, grinding into the mattress and can't help but smile from that.

Stroking his hair, I scrape my nails against his scalp. "Please make me come."

"So polite tonight, baby." He kisses my inner thigh, working his way back down to my pussy. A single hand reaches up and squeezes my tit, rolling my nipple before his index and middle fingers dust my lower lip, asking for entrance. "Open your mouth for me and suck."

I take them in my mouth, sucking them as if they were a different part of his body.

"*Yes.*" Ryan's jaw slacks, watching me.

Rolling my tongue down the length of them, I twirl it around his fingertips, then suck them all the way until they touch the back of my throat.

"Goddamn," he exhales in admiration. "You should see the picture you painted in my head. You're going to look so pretty on your knees for me." He pulls his fingers from my mouth. "But first, lie down and come on my tongue like the obedient girl I know you are."

As he pushes me back down to the mattress, his mouth finds me once again in sync with his wet fingers. It's the first time he's really touched me without my own fingers in the way, and the sensation is almost too much. He strokes me in tandem with his mouth before he slides them inside, curling forward and finding my G-spot without much effort.

I gasp when he strokes it at the perfect pace.

For a man who hasn't been with a woman in years, he sure as shit doesn't seem out of practice.

"You're so fucking tight, Ind." He admires his own fingers pushing in and out of me. "So fucking perfect."

A rush of heat floods to my lower belly, my pussy fluttering.

He feels incredible. Skilled. Beautiful between my legs and when his fingers slide inside and stroke my front wall once again, every muscle in my body contracts with my impending release.

I'm half a second from coming when Ryan pulls away, his fingers slowing in speed and easing my orgasm off.

"Ryan," I whine. "No. No, don't stop."

"Tell me you're not moving out."

"What?"

"You heard me. You want to come? Tell me you're not moving out."

I writhe in aching need, trying to push my hips into his single finger as I search for my release.

"Ryan, you need to ice your knee. Please make me come so I can take care of you."

"Tell me you're not moving out and I'll do exactly that."

Who am I kidding? I'm not going anywhere, especially now that I know how he looks between my thighs. How soft yet rough his tongue feels.

"Come on, Blue. Tell me what I need to hear."

He blows a breath against my clit, bringing me closer once again.

"I'm…" I struggle to breathe, my orgasm lingering on the edge. "I'm not going anywhere."

The bastard has the audacity to smirk.

"Please," I beg.

"Is this how I keep you polite? Teasing you with an orgasm?"

"Shut up and make me come."

His chest rumbles with a laugh before he adds a finger, sucks me into his mouth, and sends me free-falling into an orgasm-induced oblivion.

It's the sound coming from him that does it for me. The laughter, the ease on his face. The handsome smile he wears that I didn't see much of when I first moved in. Seeing Ryan relaxed with me is what drops me over the edge.

His mouth works me through it as my thighs tighten around his cheeks, my back arching off the bed. He doesn't stop. He continues to lick me, taste me as if he's fully prepared to stay there all night.

My body goes limp on the mattress, fully satisfied and sated. I can't help but smile when I think about the fact that just weeks ago, I thought my body was broken. It's sure as shit not broken, and it's not a distraction I needed, but it was him.

Ryan licks my arousal, tasting it from his lips with a proud smile and a slap of my ass. "My favorite kind of mess."

"Physical touch," I exhale, somehow finding the strength to speak.

"What was that?"

"Physical touch. I think your love language might be physical touch."

He blows out a sexy laugh. "Yeah, baby, I think you might be right."

His hooded eyes roam my body, and with that appreciative stare, I feel no need to hide. Truthfully, I've never felt the need to hide with Ryan Shay. Since the first day I got here, I've been unapologetically myself.

He stands at the end of the bed, palms coasting over my thighs.

"How's it feeling?" I nod towards his leg.

"Ind, you're still dripping, and you're worried about my knee?"

"Who said I was asking about your knee?"

An impressive little smirk tugs on his lip. "If you're referring to my knee, it's all right. If you're talking about my dick, it's painfully hard."

Sitting up on the edge of the bed, I keep my legs open around him. A single hand takes my face, fingers pushing into my hair as he tilts my chin up and kisses me, letting me taste myself on his lips.

He moans into me. "I fucking love kissing you."

I sweep my tongue into his mouth, swallowing his noises.

While we're occupied, I fiddle with the belt on his pants. My fingers graze the dusting of hair above his waistband and Ryan's stomach tightens from my touch.

Inhaling sharply, he pulls his lips away, resting his head on mine and looking down at my explorative fingers.

"Tell me what you want, Ind."

I run a palm over him, through his pants.

"Use your words, Blue."

"I want it."

"Where?"

"In my mouth."

"Mmm," he hums a satisfied noise, pushing my hair out of the way. "Then take it out and show me what you can do."

He unclasps his belt quickly, and as soon as his pants hit the floor, my fingers are in his waistband pulling down his boxer briefs and freeing his cock.

He winces when he has to stand using only his injured leg to get them past his ankles.

"Ryan, sit down for me." I nod towards the chair in the corner of his room.

A small flash of relief washes over him. I know he's trying to be in the moment. I know he wants to be in control, but he's also in pain.

Ryan takes a seat, leaning back, one arm resting on the top of the chair. His legs are sprawled out as if he were a king waiting to get his cock sucked, and in my mind, he is.

God, he's beautiful. All man. All mine. Thick legs, cut arms, shadows showcasing the concaves of his stomach muscles. He's big and smooth and hard and I've never wanted anyone more.

When my gaze finally makes it to his, he takes his lower lip between his teeth, smirking. "What are you looking at?" He wraps a fist around his cock, stroking it a few times.

I refuse to play games or make him unsure of how much I want him. "You."

His chest puffs. "You painted a pretty picture earlier, but now I want the real thing."

I glow under his appreciative stare as I make my way between his legs, falling to my knees. Palms running the length of his thighs, I watch him, memorize him. His size is intimidating from this angle, with his hard length protruding upwards and begging for a release.

My thumb swipes over the head, gathering the bead of precum.

*"Fuck."* Ryan's head falls back to the chair behind him.

His moans and whimpers remind me that he hasn't been touched in too long, and I'm the woman with the privilege to change that.

I'll savor every moment.

I allow my hands to roam his thighs and stomach, appreciating every dip and curve of his muscular body. Ryan watches me with hooded eyes as he runs his hands over my hair, stroking it softly, before gathering it all in a single fist.

Finally, I run my fingers over his length. It's hot and smooth, hard. Ryan groans from that alone. There's no way he's going to last long, and I don't want him to. He shudders when I wrap my hand around him, and when my red nails can't connect around his width, they're practically a flashing warning sign that he's bigger than I've ever experienced.

"Look how good your hand looks around me, Ind."

There's no denying that. I love the way I look around him, and even more so, I love the way he's watching, as if he needs to remember every moment.

Gently, I place a kiss on the head before licking him from base to tip.

*"Oh, fuck,"* he curses, and I can't help but smile around him, sensing this controlled man on the brink of becoming unhinged. "Your tongue looks even better."

My lips form a ring, taking him as deep as I can, sucking him all the way back up. His tip is already leaking, but I clean it up with a sweep of my tongue. Head bobbing, I stroke my lips down his shaft, swirling my tongue as I go.

His words are labored and raspy. "Eyes on me, Indy."

Looking up, I find him staring at me with dark eyes and a ticking jaw, attempting to maintain some semblance of control. His hips are twitching, holding back from letting loose and fucking my mouth without restraint. Hand splayed on his thigh, I hold on for balance, sensing it's coming soon.

"Goddamn," he exhales. "I knew you were going to look so pretty on your knees, Blue."

His praise has me moaning around him before sucking, twisting my hand around the base that can't fit.

Ryan's hands cup my cheeks. "You can take more." He flexes his hips slightly, pushing more of himself into my mouth. "I know what you're capable of. I had my fingers down your throat. Come on, Ind. You can do it."

He's bigger than I've seen, let alone had in my mouth, but with the way my body responds to him, it seems to be made for him, so I relax my jaw and take him further.

"There you go," he praises. "That's my girl."

I preen at the phrase. Melt under it.

I love this kind of control. He's a strong man, but weak for me.

Repositioning on my knees, I find just the right angle to grind myself against my heel.

"Yes, Indy. Make yourself feel good until I can take care of you. Just like that. Your mouth feels fucking incredible, baby."

I flick my tongue on the underside of his crown, wanting to see this man's control shatter.

Then it does when he fucks my mouth. Hard. All I can do is keep my eyes on him and let him use me in any way he needs.

"Blue," he warns, ushering me off him, but I claw to hold on to his hips and stay.

I watch as he begins to unravel. This man, who I've only known as controlled and domineering, begins to fall apart around me. The realization that he can't hold it together because of *me* has me pushing him further into my mouth, taking him as deep as I can.

"Goddamn, Indy." His fingers curl into my hair, keeping me where I am.

He pulses in me, hot streams hitting the back of my throat. Ryan watches until his eyes finally have to screw shut, his head falling back. I take every last drop he has to offer, loving the way he tastes on my tongue, needing him in any way he'll give himself to me.

Once he goes soft, I slide off him, keeping my mouth closed with him still on my tongue.

Heaving chest and slack jaw, he looks down at me. "Swallow," he commands.

He leans forward, his lips hovering over mine. "Swallow," he murmurs again. Gently bracketing my throat with a single palm, he runs the length of my neck as he helps me work my way through a swallow.

"That's my girl," he praises, eyes sparkling in admiration. "You did so well."

Quickly shifting from commanding to tender, he grabs my hand and ushers me to straddle his lap. His hands rub my hips and back, gliding along my warm skin.

"Thank you," he whispers against my lips.

All that does is cause me to grind my naked, needy body against his.

I'm obsessed with this man, would quite literally do anything for him and he just thanked me for a blow job.

I'm trying to slow down and move at his pace, but when he reaches around my back, sliding his fingers underneath me and finding my swollen clit, it's hard to think of anything other than wanting more.

"Ryan, if you want to stop, I think now is the time because you feel too good, and I want you too much and I'm trying to be respectful—"

"Blue, I have no intentions of stopping if you don't want me to."

"No?" Snaking my hands around his shoulders, I hold on to the back of his neck.

"No, Ind. You've turned it all back on and I can't go back to pretending I don't want you." He kisses me slowly, savoring the moment before smiling into my lips. "Just be careful with me, yeah?"

He's kidding, I know this, but there's no denying I will be careful with Ryan Shay's heart for as long as he lets me have it.

I nod against him.

"Now use your words and tell me exactly how you want me to fuck you for the first time."

# 29 Ryan

With my back against the mattress, I leave my legs sprawled on the bed because this is what she wanted. Her on top, riding me. I'll take her any way she wants, but I'm also well aware she's being cautious about my injury. Though in this moment, there is no pain, only an overwhelming need to be inside of her.

"Come here," I urge, my voice hoarse.

Indy is stunning, always has been, but now that I know her, seen the most vulnerable parts of her, I truly don't think I've laid eyes on a more beautiful human. And when she straddles her naked body on top of mine, I'm done for.

Thank God she just made me come because there's no way in hell I'd last more than ten seconds inside of her if she hadn't.

Using my thumb, I rub her clit in tight circles, giving myself time to be ready to go again.

"Is this what you want?" I ask for reassurance.

Indy's eyelids flicker, her palms braced against my chest. "I want you."

*I want you.*

I've heard the phrase countless times, but the words haven't held the same meaning until today. Teams have wanted me for my talent, agents have wanted me for my name, and women have wanted me for what I can provide.

Indy wants me for *me*.

"If this is what you want, then I do too," she continues, trailing hot kisses along my jawline as she rocks her hips against my fingers. "If you want to wait, we can wait, but Ryan, I've never wanted anything or anyone more than I want you." She punctuates the statement by cradling my cheeks, leaning down, and kissing my lips like it's the last time she'll get the chance to.

But after tonight, there's no going back. I'm all in.

I tried so hard to deny it. I had fully convinced myself there wasn't a woman in the world that would change me, distract me, remind me of everything I once wanted. But in walked Indy Ivers, my living, breathing distraction, and I'm too weak a man to pretend as if she's not single-handedly repairing all the broken pieces.

I thought I had loved someone once, but if this is what it's supposed to feel like, now I know my heart was never fully invested before. I loved the idea of the life I thought I was going to have, but with Indy, even if we spend the rest of our days just the two of us in this apartment, I'd die a happy man with an abundantly fulfilled life.

"Indy." I pull back to look at her, my brows pinched and eyes pleading. "I know you wanted this to be easy, but I can't do casual with you. I'm in way too fucking deep to pretend you're not it for me."

"I don't want casual." She quickly shakes her head. "I never have, not with you. I'm sorry I let you believe that. You've been like a flash of lightning straight to my heart and I've been done for ever since. It was confusing."

Those words have my cock hardening, growing against her ass.

"But you're not confused anymore?"

"No. Because it's become clear as day that you're meant for me."

"Fuck, Ind." I drop my head back to the pillow below me. "Those are the prettiest words I've ever heard coming from the prettiest mouth."

She glows under my compliment, once again grinding down on me.

Reaching into the nightstand, I grab the condom Dom gave me after dinner. I couldn't exactly explain that I didn't have one because I haven't had sex in a couple of years, so I told him I had run out and with getting hurt, I didn't have time to grab more. The guy's got plenty of stock on hand at all times.

Slipping my hand up her spine, I cradle her neck and pull her lips down to mine, exchanging a few wet frantic kisses. Her tits rub against my chest, her ass grinds onto my cock, and I need her.

"Please," I plead, urging the condom into her hand.

"Are you begging, Shay?"

"Yes," I laugh. "I'm fucking desperate for you, Blue."

"Good." She tears the foil packet open. "I like you controlled for everyone else, but I want you unhinged for me." She scoots down my body, sitting on my thighs. "Can you be that for me?"

"I can be anything for you, baby."

I like her speaking into existence what she needs. Indy has centered her life around appeasing everyone else, but with me, I want her to be selfish. I want her to take.

We both stare intently as she centers the tip of the condom, and I have to breathe through my nose when her fist surrounds me to roll it down.

"Go slow with me," she requests. "You're bigger than I've ever had."

"Keep talking, Ind. You're good for a man's ego."

She smiles, climbing back over my hips and I take the moment to run my hands over her thighs and appreciate her body. My thumbs roll her peaked nipples. My palms cover her stomach and hips. My fingers cup her ass.

She's so goddamn stunning and smart and she wants *me*.

Indy truly could have men falling to her feet if she were the type to ask for that, but instead, she wants *me*.

She lifts herself, rubbing her pussy against the length of my cock. That alone feels too fucking good.

I don't speak because I physically can't. My fingers dig into the flesh on her hips, and I wouldn't be surprised if they left marks for her to find tomorrow. The anticipation is almost painful, and when my tip nudges her clit, pulling out the loveliest moan I've ever heard, I have to imagine just about anything other than the sexiest woman I've ever seen sitting naked on my lap so I don't come before I'm even inside her.

I haven't had sex in years and this woman is going to be my undoing.

Lifting up on her knees, she finds my cock and centers it. Her head falls back as soon as the tip rubs against her entrance, but she pauses there for too long. Breaking my stare away from our connection, I look up to find her watching me, and knowing her, she's checking to make sure I'm okay.

I'm more than okay, so as we stare at one another, her brown eyes blazing into me, I hold on to her hips and push into her.

A shared gasp is the only sound in the otherwise silent room.

"So goddamn tight," I grit out, slowly filling her.

"Ryan, it's too much."

"You can take it," I reassure, but at the same time, I halt my movements, letting her adjust.

When she's ready, she braces the headboard behind me, lowering herself the final inches, until she's fully seated and stretched around me.

"There you go. Such a good girl for me, Ind."

Her chest falls against mine, both our chests heaving in unison as I hold her there.

"I knew it," I say breathlessly against her ear.

"Knew what?"

"That you were meant for me. Do you feel how perfectly we fit together?"

She nods against me, then rocks her hips slowly. She's taking her time, and I'll let her move at her own pace even if it kills me to not take more. I want her to know she's in charge because I don't know if she's ever believed that.

Brushing her hair away, I pull her mouth to mine as she picks up pace, lifting herself to the tip before dropping herself back down.

"Fuck," I exhale. "You feel too fucking good."

She moans into my mouth, and I swallow the sound, drinking it in like a starved man. To be honest, neither of us are very quiet between the whimpers and groans echoing off the walls around us.

Grasping onto my stomach and arms, she leans back, sticking her chest out, her head falling behind her and giving me the view of a fucking lifetime.

From below, I watch as Indy's tits bounce with her, her golden skin flushed and damp. Her blonde hair sticks to her forehead, her lips swollen and deep pink.

God, she's magnificent.

Watching her, an overwhelming sense of emotion burns the back of my eyes. I find myself on the verge of crying like a little bitch because for the first time in four years I'm not thinking about anything other than how much I want this woman.

I feel free.

I feel like myself again.

"Stay with me, Ryan." Indy's hands bracket my face, her thumbs fluttering over my cheeks. "Stay with me."

I wrap my arms around her back, pulling her chest into mine, sniffing away any lingering emotion. "I'm with you, Blue. You don't have to worry about that."

She gasps when I flex my hips and thrust inside of her, hitting at just the right spot, then she wraps her arms around my neck and hangs on for the ride.

The sound of wet skin fills the room as I hold on to her hips and ass, moving her up and down my length. A mixture of warm breath and hot kisses pepper my neck and cheek. I suck on her tits, and she scratches my skin while I fill her over and over again.

Every muscle is tight as I work our bodies together, but mentally I've never felt more at peace. Never felt so right as I do at this moment.

Never felt so in tune to another person as I do her.

There's no mistaking what's happening. No one is fucking. This is too special, too connected to call it fucking.

And as she whispers words to remind me of how much I mean to her, how she'll choose me at every given opportunity, how much she wants me, it's then that I know I'll never be the same.

"Ry," she cries with a strangled breath.

My thumb finds her clit between us, circling it, urging her to the edge with me.

"Wait. I want you to come," she says.

"Don't think about anyone else, Ind. Take what you need. I'm right behind you."

She tosses her head back, exposing her slender throat, begging me to suck and nibble, and when she comes, moaning and worshiping my name, I get to feel the rumble of words against my lips.

She clenches around me, her tight pussy gripping me even more and when her mouth falls open in ecstasy, I fall with her. My cock spills into the condom. I let loose. I fully unravel, giving myself over to someone else's control for the first time in too long. In combination with a few select curse words, her name falls from my lips like a grateful prayer because that's exactly what I am.

Grateful.

A soft, rhythmic patter flutters against my cheek, waking me up from the most restful night of sleep I've gotten in a while.

Orienting myself, I find Indy underneath me, arms around me as she sleeps. My entire body is draped on top of hers, needing her to hold me like the needy fucker I've quickly become, and I can't help but smile, seeing her messy blonde hair contrasted against my black pillowcase. Her swollen lips. Her flushed skin, still glowing from the four orgasms she had last night.

I'm a little bit proud of that one. For a woman who couldn't come once in the past eight months, I've had no trouble getting her there.

Her smell is like a fucking drug to me, and her taste is quickly becoming my favorite addiction. Which is why while she was playing nurse and icing my knee after we had sex, I pulled her to sit on my face and gave her orgasm number three. Then, in the middle of the night, with her body molded to mine, I woke her up, slipped my hand between her legs, and made her come for the fourth time.

It was entirely freeing, to spend an entire night with Indy in my bed and have my mind clear of anxious thoughts.

"Mmm," she hums, stirring awake. "You're heavy."

"I don't care." I nuzzle my face back into the crook of her neck, wrapping my arms under her back.

"Get off me." She pretends to shove me.

I hold her tighter. "Not a chance."

She bends her knees, tightening her legs around my waist and crossing her ankles to pull me closer. It does nothing but press my morning erection, covered only by my boxers, into the apex of her thighs, reminding me she's absolutely bare besides the T-shirt of mine she has on.

A deep guttural groan escapes me as I move my hips against hers again.

If I had time and a condom, we'd be going at it.

"When are you going to let me reciprocate?" she whispers into my ear, which only stiffens me even more.

With desperation, I lift my head, snapping my attention to the clock on my nightstand, praying to God I somehow woke up early enough to have the privilege of watching Indy's mouth slide around my cock again. She tried last night, but after she made me come twice, I wanted the rest of the evening to be about her.

In the morning light though, I'm feeling a bit more selfish, especially knowing that after my game, I'm jumping on a plane for another road trip.

I let out a desperate whine, dropping my head to her chest when I see the time. "When I don't have to get picked up for a press conference in less than twenty minutes."

She sighs beneath me. "Are you making breakfast, or am I?"

With my laptop open, I keep an eye on the eggs cooking on the stove.

"Hey, Ind. Will you come here for a second?"

I sense her walking around the kitchen in only my shirt, but she slides her hand around my bare waist, resting her cheek on my shoulder to let me know she's here.

"What do you think about these shoes?" I ask, nodding towards my computer where a mockup of this year's potential sneaker is blown up on the screen.

"I...*like* them."

"You're a terrible liar."

"Excuse me, I've been successfully lying to your boss for months."

"And how much of that has been lying?"

She gives me a playful swat on my ass. "Shut it."

I nod towards the computer screen once again.

"They're a little boring," she admits honestly. "I think they could use some color."

I can't help but smile at that. I knew my bright girl wouldn't be all that into a black and white sneaker. "Of course, you do. What color are you thinking?"

She cranes her neck thoughtfully. "Maybe red, like your team colors."

"Or blue?"

"Why blue? Red makes more sense than blue."

Turning my head, my lips brush the top of her hair. "Because blue is quickly becoming my favorite."

"Either one." She shrugs, clearly not catching on. "Whatever you decide will look nice."

She tilts, placing a single kiss on my upper arm before leaving me at the stove.

I stop her with a heavy hand wrapped around her waist, turning her into me again. Eyes bounce between one another because though we've shared breakfast in this kitchen countless times, today is different and we both know it.

With the need to make sure what happened last night continues outside of the bedroom, I thread my fingers into her golden hair, tugging to tilt her head back.

"Good morning," I rasp before pressing my mouth to hers, tasting the toothpaste on her tongue.

Drunken and loose, she melts into my side. "You have no idea how many times I've wanted you to kiss me over breakfast."

So I do just that, again and again until the veggie omelets I made are ready.

She pulls her coffee from the fridge, adding one of the atrociously sweet creamers. "Maybe it's acts of service. That could be your love language. Every morning you make sure my coffee is cold, so it doesn't get watered down when I add ice. I've always noticed that." She looks at me, cocking her head and speaking softly. "Thank you."

Maybe she's right. Maybe that is my love language because even though I could've easily bought cold coffee for the fridge, I like the smile I get to see when she pulls her cup out and realizes I made one for her.

At some point, I should probably tell her that my love language is whichever one she wants it to be so she can stop guessing. I'll make sure that girl feels loved however she needs.

Taking a seat next to me, Indy slides a folder next to my plate.

"What is this?"

A heat rushes her cheeks. "Ignore this if I'm overstepping, but that day we went camping when you told me you wanted to start your own foundation, I couldn't get it out of my head. You said it felt overwhelming, so I thought maybe I could help steer you in the right direction."

Opening the folder, endless papers detail the ins and outs of a new nonprofit. Startup costs, fundraising projections, description, and a thorough marketing plan. Every detail is carefully thought out and organized, only needing a name to round out the comprehensive business plan.

The knowledge of what this is swells my throat, keeping me from speaking.

Indy continues for me. "We start small. A lot of these kids, they don't have a place to go over the summers like they do during the school year. They don't have school-provided meals either and I'd imagine, because of that, maybe some kids don't get to eat those days. So, what if we run a summer camp, something to keep them in a scheduled environment? We provide meals and a safe place to play." She flips through the pages, but I'm not reading a word. I'm looking at her. "We get some of the outdoor courts around Chicago cleaned up. Your shoe deal includes sneaker donations. They have something to wear. As we grow, we move into the school year, creating after-school programs. Here's my projection." She motions towards a chart. "In five years, this is how many kids we should be able to help if this is the rate at which we grow."

I stay silent, mesmerized by every single word that comes out of her mouth.

Nervousness and ingrained insecurities take over. She pulls her hands into her lap, leaving the folder on the kitchen counter. "Only if you want to, I mean. And it's only a rough draft—"

I interrupt her with a searing kiss before her innate need to tone herself down comes into play. Her nerves melt away as she melts into me.

"You're incredible," I murmur against her lips.

"It's nothing."

"It's everything."

"Do you like it?"

Do I like it? I love it. I especially loved how many times she used the word *we* when outlining the plan.

"Like isn't a strong enough word, Blue. This means everything to me, truly. Thank you."

I don't miss the proud little smile that slides across her lips from being praised for her brilliant mind instead of being warned to hold herself back. It makes me want to spend every day of the rest of my life reminding her just how incredibly bright she is until I get to watch those insecurities wash away.

The detail and care she put into every single page bleeds into the words as I flip through the pages.

"This is what you went to school for?"

"Yep. My degree is in business with concentrations in finance and administration. I had planned to go into the field after I graduated."

"Why didn't you?"

"Because I quickly learned that most of the time, I would be working with rich people to make them even richer, and numbers got real boring that way."

Indy takes a bite of her breakfast, and I can't help but stare. She's more intelligent than she allows most people to see. She's wonderful at putting on a happy mask and making sure everyone around her feels good about themselves. I can imagine that it got exhausting when stroking the egos and pockets of the wealthy.

She's, as always, an interesting mix of idealism and logic, leaning towards the romantic side. The soft side. The loving side where she lets herself feel everything and care for everyone. I'm sure it was hard for her to find much feeling behind numbers.

But this, finding a way to help kids, you can see the passion she's put into this business plan.

"So you became a flight attendant instead?"

"Mm-hmm," she says with a happy hum. "I love my job. I'm with people all day and I get to travel the world. I wanted to see as much of it as I could before I settled down with a family one day." Eyes darting to mine, she swiftly changes the subject, clearing her throat. "Are you going to your game tonight?"

It's the first one since my injury and though I was given permission to skip, I promised Leon I'd be there to help him. I want to help him. I want us to win, regardless that I won't be the one putting up the points.

"I am. Are you?"

"Do you want me there?"

"I want you there."

*I want you everywhere.*

"Then I'll be there."

This morning's press conference was the first since my injury and easily the longest of my career. Endless questions that I answered, as always, as diplomatically as possible.

*When am I back?* Hopefully three to four weeks.

*How are you feeling?* Great. I've made progress in the few short days since it happened.

*Do you think the team will be able to pull off a month without you?* I have faith in my guys.

If I could be honest, I'd tell the truth—that I feel as if I let an entire organization, an entire *city* down. But I have to be perfect, on at all times, and that includes media interviews. I can't let them see me sweat.

I couldn't be more thankful that I'm not on crutches as I stand on the sidelines. The stares and speculation are enough. I can almost feel the cameras zooming in on me, reporters talking about me in their broadcasts.

I hate it.

"You doing okay, man?" Ethan smacks my shoulder.

"As good as I can be."

"It's big of you to be here. This is the time when you find out the kind of leader you are. You're not faking it for Ron. You're showing up for them." He motions towards the team.

I've spent the last handful of months curating my life in order to convince my boss that I'm a good leader. But today, he wasn't on my mind when I made the decision to show up, and for the first time in a long time, I'm beginning to feel like my old college self. The one who led his team to two national championships. The guy who trusted people without second-guessing their motives.

I miss the old me, but my body feels light with hope that I'm on the way back to him.

My chair is the first on the bench after the coaching staff and my feet have been bouncing with energy for the entire first quarter as I attempt to stay seated.

Leon started, but he's been struggling. More so on defense. He's a hell of a shooter and can create a play especially with the other talent he's got out there on the court, but he's up against one of the best point guards in the league with Toronto's starter.

It's much harder for him to see the court the way I do, but that's what years of experience earns you. For now, I can be his eyes.

Leon gets pulled at the end of the first quarter to start his first break of the game, and with a single domineering "move" to the guy next to me, suddenly the chair to my right opens for him to take a seat.

He leans in close, trying to hear me over the packed arena.

"You're doing good," I reassure.

He exhales heavy breaths. "He's a step ahead of me every time he drives the lane."

"That's because you expect him to go right, but he prefers the left. Every time. And yes, he's faster than you. That's just a fact, so take a gamble and cheat that way. Best-case scenario, you'll stop him from driving the lane. Worst-case scenario you let him take you on the right and you learn for the next time. He's also got a hell of a tell. Whichever way he's attempting to drive he slightly shifts his weight on the ball of that foot for half a second. Barely visible. Look for it." I pat him on the back. "You've got this."

The next time Leon is back on the court, he takes away the left and throws Toronto's point guard off-balance long enough to strip the ball. The time after that, he watches his opponent's feet with precision and the moment he shifts his weight, Leon is able to cut him off and get a hand on a sloppy pass, causing a turnover that the Devils recover.

I might not be out there, but holy hell this feeling is almost as euphoric as if I were the one making the plays myself.

The next dead ball, Leon looks over like an excited little kid who just made his first bucket. It's charming and sweet, and I'm proud as hell of him.

My coach walks by with a pat on my shoulder. "Nice work, Shay."

After the postgame interviews and celebratory speeches in the locker room, I head out with my suitcase in tow, determined to find Indy before getting on the team bus and heading to the airport. I want to see her in my space. She looks good here.

She looks good everywhere.

And as I turn the corner out of the locker room, I'm pleasantly surprised to find Indy outside of the family waiting room.

Stevie and my parents have been down here countless times, but I never thought I'd have someone else waiting for me. And Indy of all people, my sister's best friend. Fucking stunner wearing my jersey.

"I didn't know where I should go. Annie told me to come down with her, but she and the kids went home already, and now I feel like I'm intruding," Indy quickly explains as I swallow up the space between us.

"You're in the exact right place."

Leaving my suitcase, I swing my arms over her shoulders as she runs her palms over the column of my spine. "Good game."

"Thank you." I almost want to remind her I didn't play, but she knows. Instead, I take the compliment.

Pulling back, I brush her hair away from her face and press my lips to hers. She smiles into me, instantly reassured of how much I want her here.

I lean back slightly to check her out again. "You look good wearing my last name, Blue."

That megawatt smile blooms as Indy pulls me into her and deepens our kiss, her back hitting the waiting room wall, and I couldn't be more thankful that Ethan's kids are gone for the night.

Nothing about this moment is feeling very PG, but I couldn't care less. No one is around to see it and I have to get on a plane and leave her for the week.

"Shay," I hear from across the hall. Pulling away from Indy, I look over my shoulder to find Ron Morgan.

Clearing my throat and wiping my lips, I straighten. "Sir."

"Nice work tonight. Carson did a hell of a job thanks to you. That's the kind of leader I was looking for." He nods towards my girl. "Indy, good to see you."

She cowers, trying to hide her flushed cheeks from being caught mid-make-out by my boss. "You too, Mr. Morgan."

"All right, you two." He waves us off, turning his back and heading down the hall. "Don't let me keep you from going at it. I hope to see you in Phoenix, Indy!"

We chuckle into each other, her forehead falling into my chest. Ironically, for the first time, none of that was planned for Ron to see.

It was for us.

She sighs a happy little sigh, arms slinging around my neck. "What's in Phoenix?"

"You. Me. Our trips overlap there for the day. He and Caroline were hoping to get together if it works for your schedule."

"Do you want to?"

If she asked me this a couple of months ago, I would've said yes instantly. I wanted to impress my boss, try to show him I'm not as much of a loner as he made me out to be. Now, I still want to say yes, but only because it means more time spent with her.

"I want to only if you're up for it. I know you'll be working, but if you're free, then yes, I'd love to see you."

"And the Morgans."

I roll my eyes. "And the Morgans."

Looking down, I catch Indy wearing her embroidered Converse tonight. I love her in heels and a dress, but equally love her dressed down.

Slipping my foot between hers, I nudge her feet apart to find a new addition to her shoes. Right there, inside of the left ankle is an embroidered basketball with my number and a heart stitched into the center of it.

"When did that get there?" I ask, loving the way my name and number look all over her.

"This afternoon. I thought it was about time."

My stare breaks from her feet to find her smiling proudly, wearing my favorite emotion of hers—joy.

"It was about damn time."

Leaning down, I take her mouth again. I don't think I'll ever get used to having the privilege of kissing this girl. I hadn't kissed a woman for so long that being touched by her, wanted by her is almost too much. What in the world did I do to deserve her wanting *me*?

"Walk me to the team bus?" I take my suitcase in one hand and hers in the other.

We're barely out of the back entrance of the arena, and I hear him long before I see him. He tugs at Indy's arm before I can register what's happening.

"Indy."

Her hand tightens in mine at the sound of her name. "Alex," she breathes out. "What are you doing here?"

He's still holding on to her elbow, gently. Longingly.

I brush his hand off her, keeping my voice calm and even. "Don't fucking touch her."

Instinctively, I shift my body, putting myself between them.

Metaphorically and physically, I want to be between them. He will have to get through me to get to her and that won't ever fucking happen.

"Okay." He puts his hands up in surrender before redirecting his attention to the blonde beauty behind me. "Indy, we need to talk."

"No, you don't," I speak for her, like a deranged caveman. She can speak for herself, but she shouldn't have to when it comes to him. There's nothing that needs to be said.

"Ryan, it's okay," she soothes, her hand rubbing at my side. "Alex, I don't think we need to talk. Now or ever."

"We've never spoken about that night. I need to explain myself."

She laughs, but I can hear how much it hurts her as it comes out. "Explain what? Why you slept with someone else?"

Alex looks down towards the ground, hands in his pockets. "Well, yeah, exactly. But I'd like to speak to you alone."

"Yeah, that's not going to happen," I interject.

"Indy. Twenty-two years. You owe it to yourself to hear me out."

Manipulative piece of trash, using history as a chess piece with the most loyal woman I know.

Indy inhales a deep breath and I know he's got her. I hate it.

"Fine. Five minutes."

"Blue," I protest over my shoulder.

"It's okay, Ryan." Her focus is back on Alex. "It means nothing."

I refuse to move, to allow any open space between them, but it doesn't matter because Indy rounds my body, facing me.

"It's okay. I'll call you when I can. Have a safe flight."

The daggers shooting from my eyes fall to the prick behind her. *Touch her and I'll kill you. Say something that makes her upset and I'll ruin your life. Look at her inappropriately and I will beat the living shit out of you.*

I don't know that he was able to gather that all from my stare, but here's hoping he understood.

My hands cup Indy's face as I silently beg her to just go home instead, but she holds her ground, determined to have this conversation.

I'm a possessive man when it comes to her, there's no denying that, and even though I'm controlling in my own life, I'd never control her or her decisions.

Relenting, I press my lips to her temple and linger there as long as I can.

"Ryan!" Ethan calls out from the team bus behind me. "We've gotta go!"

There are so many things I want to say to her right now, but mostly I want to know if what she feels towards me is enough for me not to worry. I also want to know if she's really okay to do this. It wasn't all that long ago she was crying in our living room before throwing a shoe at my door after being stranded without a place to live because of him.

But I don't have time to ask a single question with a bus waiting for me and a plane sitting on a tarmac, ready for our road trip.

"Call me when you can?" I ask, walking backwards towards the bus.

She nods, and I keep my eyes on her until I have to climb the steps on the bus, where I practically sprint to my seat and look out the window, finding the two of them taking a seat on the curb outside the arena.

*Why are they sitting? They don't need that much time. In fact, they don't need any time at all.*

No part of me is calm, cool, or collected. I'm entirely out of control. In a sense, I've been out of control ever since that girl waltzed into my apartment, but this time, the powerlessness doesn't feel freeing. I'm spiraling as we drive away.

Whatever is going on between us is so new. We haven't had the opportunity to fully discuss it, and at the time it felt weird to throw a label on something so organic.

But now I wish we had. That way she could tell him, but more importantly, she could tell *me* where we stand.

Every single insecurity of mine floods my body, overtaking any reasonable senses I have left.

*Do I mean enough to her?*

*Will she go back to him?*

*Was it always him?*

*Does she want me at all?*

Those four questions consume me, blind me as they repeat over and over while I watch the girl I'm completely gone for with another man. And I have to get on a plane, leave Chicago, and pray that I'm enough.

It's a twenty-minute drive to the airport and I give her that much time before I call her.

"Hi," she says, swallowing.

And I know her well enough that she's swallowing down emotions.

"Are you okay?"

Exiting the bus, I linger on the tarmac as the rest of the guys board the airplane.

A sob breaks free from her chest. "Yes."

"Indy." I close my eyes, sighing. "Fuck."

Not only do I hate hearing her upset, but not knowing exactly why is eating me alive.

Scrubbing a hand over my head, I pace the quickly cleared tarmac and listen to her broken breaths and sniffling nose.

Finally, she says, "I'm fine, Ryan."

There's a bite to her words and I'm not sure if she wants me to leave her alone or if she's simply trying to sound unaffected.

Tension lingers on the line.

"He wants you back, doesn't he?"

She doesn't answer, and my heart plummets from her blaring silence.

"What exactly did he say?"

"It doesn't matter."

"How could you say it doesn't matter, Ind? It clearly matters to you. You're upset."

"I'm processing. That's a lot of years to say goodbye to."

Fuck. None of this is what I wanted to hear, but I'm not sure what I expected. Did I really think she was going to answer the phone and tell me she told him to fuck off or that he didn't affect her at all?

Indy is sensitive. Initially, it turned me off, but it's what eventually made me fall so hard for her, her openness to feel. Of course, that conversation would affect her. She wouldn't be her if it didn't.

But what I need her to tell me is that nothing changes between us and clearly, she can't.

"Shay, let's go!" one of the team staff members shouts from the top of the aircraft stairs.

"Blue…" I begin but can't seem to find the words.

I need to tell her how much I want her. I need to tell her I can give her the life she's always wanted if she would let me. I need to tell her anything that will make her forget about that fucking conversation with the guy who's done nothing but make her feel like she's not enough, yet too much all at the same time.

"You have to go, Ryan."

"Shay!" I hear again.

"Goddammit." I inhale a deep breath, beginning up the stairs to the plane. "Take all the time you need, Indy. I understand, or at least I'm going to try to. Have a safe flight tomorrow."

I hang up the line because I care about her enough to understand this moment isn't about me. Yes, the lack of control and the unknown might just kill me, but how fucking selfish would I be if I didn't give her a moment to process?

But even though I'm trying to be a good guy, the overwhelming realization that I may have misread everything, like a love-sick fool, just as I've done before with another woman, eats at me as I slip into my seat for takeoff.

# 31 Indy

**Me:** *I need a daily update from you. Is Ryan okay? He's barely talked to me.*
**Stevie:** *I think he's scared, even if he doesn't want to admit it.*
**Me:** *He's got nothing to be scared of and he would know that if he would talk to me.*
**Stevie:** *I know, Ind, but insecurities don't exactly work that way.*

It's been a lonely few days, regardless that I've been on the road for work, surrounded by friends.

It no longer matters if I'm in a room full of people. If Ryan isn't around, I'm lonely. And right now, not only is he not around, but he's also not talking to me much either.

He's not mad at me, and he's not shutting me out, he's simply giving me space to process the conversation with Alex. I don't need space. I've told him exactly that, but the times we have talked over the last few days haven't lasted long enough for me to explain what happened.

Part of me genuinely believes he thinks if he gives me enough time to explain, I'll end up telling him I'm going back to my ex. But if Ryan gave me the time of day, I'd tell him how proud of myself I am for how I handled that conversation and reaffirm just how obsessed I am with the man I'm living with.

I would tell him that when Alex started crying, the old me would've jumped in to save him the second I saw he was upset, would've done anything in her power to make him happy, but the new me didn't feel the burden of that responsibility anymore.

I would tell him that when Alex explained why he slept with someone else—because we were together for so long, because we had been best friends since we were five, and I was the only girl he had ever been with. Because he wanted to explore before settling down for good, and it was the biggest regret of his life. I would tell Ryan what I told Alex—it was the best thing to ever happen to me.

I would explain that when Alex asked me if he was the last person I'd been with because for him, there was no one before or after the night I caught him, I told him he asked the wrong question. He should've asked if he was the last person I loved, but regardless, the answer to both would be no.

And I would let Ryan know that when Alex asked me to go home with him, I told him my home is on the twenty-second floor of a building downtown. It's an apartment that up until a few months ago was stark and sad, but now bursts with breakfasts shared over the kitchen island and more books than either of us have time to read.

I would also tell him that I was completely emotionless while sitting on that curb, but I was overwhelmed when he called me. I wasn't sad per se, but for the first time since things ended, I had the chance to mourn that relationship. The answers I'd been given gave me the opportunity to officially close that chapter in my life. In that moment I grieved for the sad girl from months ago who needed those answers so badly, even though the woman I am now doesn't care about his why's. The tears didn't mean I wanted that life back.

"This is my first time at this arena." Caroline claps her hands in excitement, pulling me out of memory lane as we sit courtside at Ryan's game in Arizona.

"It's my first game outside of Chicago." I force a smile, as if I'm not zoned out and staring at the visitors' tunnel, waiting for Ryan to come out.

Both the Raptors and the Devils are in Phoenix and playing tonight. Ron and Caroline called and invited me to sit with them, but I can only stay for the first half. I'll have to get to the airport during halftime to prep the plane so I can fly the hockey team home tonight.

Ryan assured me I didn't have to come. That just because I missed one invite from the Morgans, they wouldn't question it. But I didn't come for some ruse or to convince them of our authenticity. I came for him.

Finally, both teams come out for warm-ups, the court swamped by giant basketball players stretching and running through layup lines. But behind the blur of them, I find Ryan across the court, standing in front of his team's bench, dressed in his normal clothes with his eyes locked on me.

He's such a good man, and my heart aches seeing him so concerned. He doesn't look happy. He seems stressed.

Arms crossed over his broad chest, Ryan's lips lift in a slight smile, but it's not big enough to show off his dimples.

"Is Ryan doing all right?" Caroline asks from beside me.

"I'm not sure." I keep my attention on him, but he refocuses on his team and the game he can't play in. "I had a conversation with someone from my past a few days ago, and I haven't had the opportunity to explain to Ryan that it didn't mean anything. I think he's been stressed over it."

"Well"—she puts her hand over mine and squeezes—"that's because he loves you. He doesn't want to lose you."

An awkward chuckle bubbles out of me. "He hasn't told me that yet."

"No?"

Oh shit. Maybe I shouldn't have admitted that to Caroline. Here she thinks that Ryan and I are happily in love and living together. Things have moved backwards for us. Living together, pretending to love each other, then developing real feelings.

Maybe I shouldn't have said that out loud, but I feel too vulnerable to lie right now.

"You know, Indy. Ryan doesn't strike me as the type of man to be loud. He might not say it, might not scream it from the rooftops, but I could bet good money that he says it without words every single day."

Cold coffee waiting for me in the fridge.

Fresh flowers, though sometimes dead because he tried *too* hard to keep them alive, sitting on the kitchen island for me at home after every road trip.

Making sure I have food I can eat.

Even giving me time to process my conversation with Alex.

"Sometimes the quietest love is the loudest," she continues.

A sharp burn stings my eyes and nose as I sit courtside, surrounded by eighteen thousand fans. I've never thought of it that way. I once assumed that Alex's loud declarations of love, showing me off, and saying it daily was what it meant to love someone. But that belief was quickly diminished when his actions no longer lined up with the words.

As much as I'm a hopeless romantic, I no longer need the over-the-top declarations. I don't even need to be told. I simply want to feel it, be consumed by it. And Ryan has consumed me since the day I moved in.

That realization overwhelms me as warm-ups end. Ron finds his seat next to Caroline and after the team introductions, about twenty elementary-age kids are led out to the court.

The players, including Ryan, are each paired up with a student, ranging from ages seven to eleven. Apparently these twenty kids are from a local elementary school and are being honored for making their school's dean's list.

The students are given a jersey by each player they're paired with as a photographer goes around the group and captures the moment.

It's pretty adorable if I do say so myself. These men are huge, ranging from 6'3" to well over seven feet. Some of these students' heads don't even reach the players' hips, but the awkward poses, to get both people in a photo, makes the moment even cuter.

Ryan is paired with a little girl who looks to be the youngest of the group. She doesn't say a word to him as she stands at his side, doesn't tell him her name or ask his. She only stares at his face with wide eyes. She could very well be nervous. How intimidating to be seven years old and standing in front of a crowd of thousands next to Ryan Shay of all people.

But when the photographer continues to call for her attention and she doesn't turn to face him until Ryan points in his direction, it's then that I realize her wide eyes are set on his lips, prepared to read them when he speaks. She's deaf.

Surprisingly, Ryan picks up on it too.

As soon as the photographer gets his shot, Ryan crouches down on his haunches, making himself eye level with her.

He does the sign for "hello" with his hand touching his forehead and waving outward. He follows that up with a hand on his chest before the index and middle fingers on each hand cross over one another and tap twice, saying "my name."

Then Ryan fingerspells his name. Slowly and cautiously.

Anyone in the Deaf community would pick up that he's a beginner as he takes his time remembering each sign, but that's not what matters.

The little girl's face lights up as she watches him, catching on to how new he is when she slowly signs her name back.

*Sarah.*

He repeats her name with his fingers, also mouthing the word to confirm.

Her smile widens as she nods with so much excitement.

He points at himself again, followed by a motion that looks as if he were taking information from an open palm to his head, finished with the sign for "sign"—index fingers circling each other backward.

*I am learning sign.*

He mouths the words as well, but his sign was so clear that Sarah understands with no problem.

She grabs his hands, hopping around on her toes, unable to contain her joy, then gives him a double thumbs-up to tell him he's doing a good job.

Ryan's stunning smile beams, the two of them sharing a moment. I don't know how much he's communicated with a deaf person. I didn't even know he was learning the language, but this moment is special for him, I can see it. The pride in his eyes, the joy radiating off him, successfully speaking to another with his hands.

"I didn't know Ryan knew sign language," Caroline says next to me.

"He doesn't. He *didn't,* I mean. I didn't know he was learning." My stare is locked on him. "I offered to teach him, but we hadn't gotten around to starting yet." I take a sharp inhale, attempting to compose myself. "My dad is deaf."

"Oh, Indy." She places her hand on top of mine, the both of us watching Ryan and Sarah. "That man loves you. That right there is quiet love."

Refocusing, Sarah is partway into telling Ryan something as I rejoin their conversation. With her open number five hand, she signs at her chin then brings it up to her forehead. Ryan is confused, not yet understanding the signs for mom and dad, so she tugs at his sleeve and points to the sideline of the court where her parents stand, waving and so excited for their daughter.

"Excuse me." I quickly stand from my seat, rushing off the court and to the bathroom before I start crying in front of eighteen thousand people and Ryan's boss.

With my hands bracketed on the sink, I lose it. Tears stream down my face from the overwhelming knowledge that I've gone twenty-seven years without being loved the way Ryan Shay loves me. And now I have the privilege to be loved so selflessly, so attentively.

No one in my life has made an effort to communicate with my dad in his language. Not my life-long friends and not my boyfriend of six years. And in comes this man who I've only known for a few months, turning my life upside down and proving what it means to be loved.

He doesn't need to say it and I don't have to hear it. I already know. It happened so quietly, so effortlessly.

And he's in there questioning whether I'm back with my ex. How could he ever imagine I'd want to be with someone else after I've spent months being loved the way he loves me?

I'll take responsibility for that because even though I haven't done anything to have him question my loyalty since things developed between us, I know Ryan is working with some major insecurities. Insecurities that, though I've experienced similar things, never impacted me quite the way they do him. And I need to be the one to reassure him, to remind him how wanted he is until he no longer has to question it.

Maybe words of affirmation are his love language. Maybe it's quality time. I'm not sure, but I'm going to become fluent in them all until Ryan understands just how much I love him. How much I want him for his heart and not for his name.

Though, one day, I wouldn't mind taking that too.

It isn't until well into the first quarter, I'm able to compose myself enough to leave the bathroom. My eyes are so bloodshot and my skin so puffy, there's no way to hide how hard I've been crying. My makeup is completely gone, but if I feel like it, I'll redo it before my flight.

Ryan spots me as soon as I take a seat. His brows are creased, but his eyes are soft as the game buzzes around him. Sitting on the first chair after the coaching staff, he leans forward, knees to his elbows, mirroring the rest of the guys on the bench, but unlike them, he's not watching the game unfold before him.

I offer him a slight smile to placate him.

*"Are you okay?"* he mouths from across the gym.

Nodding, I smile a bit more, holding myself back from screaming *"I love you!"* at the top of my lungs or even mouthing it back to him. I want to tell him when I'm standing directly in front of him. I want him to see it in my everyday actions. I want him to feel the intention behind the words.

Ryan bites his lower lip as if he wishes he could say more, but instead, he refocuses back on the game.

At halftime, I quickly leave for the airport, with the knowledge that the sooner I get back to Chicago, the sooner I can tell him.

# 32
# Ryan

I'm a coward.

I've avoided Indy's calls for days, unable to find the strength to answer, knowing there's a chance she's calling to tell me she's back with her ex who doesn't deserve to even stand in the same room as her.

But seeing her two nights ago, sitting courtside at my game was enough of a reminder that I need to grow a pair and make sure she knows. Even if she doesn't want me, even if she decides to go back to the life she had before me, I wouldn't be able to live with myself without telling her how important she is. Both to me and to the world.

Indy, the romantic.

She deserves the gesture. She deserves to be loved loudly. She deserves to be loved in any way she wants.

And if I can be conceited for a moment, she deserves to be loved by me.

I will put her first. I will give her the life she's always dreamed of. I will make sure she knows how special she is, that she doesn't need to put on the show for everyone else. I like her chaotic and emotional. I like her messy.

But of course, I haven't had the courage to say those things, afraid that in response, she'll tell me the one thing that will break me.

Were the tears she shed while rushing to the bathroom at my game due to guilt, knowing it's going to hurt like hell when she ends things with me? The insecurities ramming into my chest want to scream at me that they were.

I should've stopped her from speaking to him. I should've reminded her that it took her absence from his life for him to understand what a gift he had, while it was her presence in mine that opened my eyes to everything I've ever wanted.

Indy left for her friends' wedding yesterday after she landed back in Chicago a day before me. The rehearsal dinner was last night, and it's not lost on me that I was too much of a coward to tell her how much she means to me before she spent an entire day with Alex.

As if I needed anything to add to the anxiety rushing through me.

The drive to the hotel where this wedding is taking place took me two hours out of town, and I was almost late thanks to my physical therapy appointment going over. But the good news is, I'm cleared to start low intensity practice next week and if things go well, and my knee continues to heal properly, I'll be back on the court shortly after that.

A few wedding guests quickly make their way past my parked car, rushing into the hotel, afraid to be late. On the other hand, I stay seated in my Audi, inhaling deep breaths and trying to calm my nerves. I didn't give Indy the chance to tell me she doesn't want me here, so I truly have no idea what I'm walking into.

The urge to put my car in reverse and get out of here is thrumming through my body, but we made a deal. I would be her date to this wedding, and though she may no longer need me to prove a point, or convince her friends she's doing okay, I made a promise to show up. I will always deliver on my promises to her, even if she doesn't want me in the same way I want her.

Keeping my head down, I enter through the lobby of the hotel before finding my way to one of the large banquet halls in the back. I might be the last guest to arrive, everyone already in their seats as I attempt to sneak in.

It doesn't work.

The few guests who spot me as I enter are quick to tell the people next to them and before I know it, everyone's eyes are on me standing in the back of the banquet hall.

I hate it.

As whispers circulate, I slip into the second to last row, hoping to hide. There are so many people, people who I don't know, people who are watching my every move. People who aren't Indy and don't bring me the calm she does. With my toes bouncing, I keep my head down, pretending to read over the wedding program in my hands and trying to block out the noise of the growing hushed tones.

The music shifts, and immediately the crowd settles, the focus returning to the real reason they're all here.

The groomsmen enter and he's the first one I spot. Blond-haired piece of shit who couldn't handle his girl being smarter than him. The guy who made her believe something was wrong with her, that she was too much.

The same guy who delivered the best thing to ever happen to me right to my doorstep.

He's wearing a smug smile and I can't figure out if he's naturally that annoying or if he arrogantly got someone back that never should've been his in the first place.

Then a different set of doors opens and there she is. Angel in lavender. Blonde hair curled and partially pinned back, white flowers in her hand and in her hair. She's taller too and I fucking love her in a pair of heels.

She walks down the aisle right past me, and I can't keep my eyes off her. She glides with a sense of confidence, her head held high, and that radiant smile on her lips.

She's breathtaking.

When she reaches the makeshift altar, she stands to the far left as the rest of the women wearing the same dress file in front of her.

Alex has his eyes glued to her and I can't exactly blame him. She's magnetic.

They're practically facing each other from opposite sides of the room, and I watch as her attention flickers to him, but I can't read her expression. I don't know what that look means.

She doesn't know I'm here, hiding in the last rows, but she's the only thing I can see. Even as the doors open and the music shifts for the bride to walk down the aisle. I stand with the rest of the guests, but the only person I'm looking at is the tall blonde who owns my heart in the front of the room.

Indy smiles, watching her friends' moment, but I notice her eyes bouncing around the audience as she does. It takes a while for her wandering gaze to coast through the entire crowd, but eventually those brown eyes lock on mine.

That polite grin of hers morphs into a full-on beaming smile and I have no idea where we stand or what the fuck that could mean, but I sure as shit know Alex didn't get that smile.

She keeps her focus on me, a slight flush crawling up her cheeks. "*Hi,*" she silently mouths while no one else pays us attention.

"*You're beautiful,*" I say right back.

She refocuses on the bride's walk and my attention falls back to the groomsmen. I shouldn't have assumed no one was paying us attention because Alex is glaring at me, and fuck do I love that kind of attention.

Giving him a wink, my eyes are right back on my girl.

In a room full of her previous life, she's all I see during the entire ceremony. Golden skin glowing from the ambient lighting, chin held high, and a kind smile as her friends say their vows.

As the words roll off their tongues, speaking of better or worse, sickness and health, and richer or poorer, Indy looks at me. Her attention is locked on *me*. I'd love to know what she's thinking because my formally unromantic heart is making up all sorts of scenarios in which she didn't entertain a second of that conversation with her ex and sees only me as the person she could say those words to.

The ceremony ends with the crowd cheering, but even as I stand and clap, my body boils when I realize her so-called friends paired Indy with Alex to walk back down the aisle. I'm not dense enough to misunderstand the dynamics here. Her friends want them back together.

Alex leans in and says something in her ear as her arm is politely wrapped around his, but she doesn't respond with words. She only wears a smile for the crowd to see. Her perfectly happy mask.

But I'm privileged enough to know what's underneath the polished girl, and I get one final glance from her before she exits the room.

The time between the ceremony and the reception is agonizing, knowing she's here somewhere, taking pictures and not with me. I want to speak with her, hold her, hide away from the rest of these people who haven't left me alone.

I've signed countless autographs and worn my professional smile, answering their probing questions diplomatically.

*I'll be back on the court soon.*

*My knee is feeling great.*

And *my roommate is in the wedding party* when asked how I know the bride and groom. Truthfully, I know we aren't just fucking roommates, but I have no idea what Indy wants me to introduce myself as.

These are her people, *were* her people, and I'm not sure what she wants them to believe.

She and I, we aren't as different as I once believed us to be. We both put on a facade for the rest of the world, knowing what people want to hear and see, but at home, we're ourselves, and I love that I have that piece of her.

After thirty minutes of being "on," I find a small hidden cove outside of the reception area to hide away in. It's hard to live up to fans' expectations of the real-life Ryan Shay when all I can focus on is finding out if Indy wants to be with me.

With my hands in my pockets and my head low, I take a few moments to center myself, knowing I need to be a professional when I go back out there. When I go *anywhere.*

There are so many strangers, it makes my skin crawl, knowing my every move is being watched, but I'd do it a hundred times over and be here today if Indy needed me to.

"You hiding, Shay?"

Looking up, Indy's neck is craned, peeking into the isolated cove, bouquet of white flowers dangling in her hand. Beautiful as ever. Happy too. And I can only hope I'm the reason for that.

"You know me too well, Ivers."

"Can I hide with you?"

Head leaning back on the wall, I take a deep breath thanks to her proximity. "You can hide with me forever, baby."

Ducking into the small cove, she tucks away with me for no one else to see. "You've been avoiding my calls."

"I know."

"I have something I need to tell you."

"Me first."

"Ryan—"

"I've got to say some things, Ind. I need you to know where I stand

and what I want, in case I haven't made it clear. I need to throw my hat in the ring."

"You don't have to say anything."

But I do. With a room full of her previous life, there are things she needs to know.

I take her hand, intertwining our fingers, memorizing the way we look molded together.

"I want you, Indy. I want us. I want our little life we've built even when we thought we were pretending. I want you in our house because you've made it a home. I want your mess and your chaos. I want your genuine smiles, the ones you wear when you're around my sister, the hockey team, and me. I want you happy, and I want to be the reason you are. I want you to choose me."

"Ry—"

"I understand what I'm competing against. I know I don't have your history, but I want your future."

"Ryan—"

"You deserve the grand gestures, the big moments. I'm not great at making a show. I don't like the attention, but if that's what you need to understand how much I want you in my life, I'll do it. Fuck, I should've done this in front of a crowd or standing in the rain or something romantic instead of hiding away and saying it. God…" I chuckle without humor. "I'm telling you you're the best thing to ever come into my life while hiding in a random room with terrible carpet and shitty wallpaper—"

"Ryan!"

I swallow. "Yeah?"

Her lips lift, a smile overtaking her face. "I never thought I'd say this, but you can stop talking now."

A small chuckle rumbles in my chest as she closes the space between us. Hand wrapping around my neck, she pulls my eyes to meet hers.

"You didn't have to say anything. I already know. And I'm the talker in this relationship, in case you forgot, but today, I only have three words I need to say."

She leans up on her tiptoes, her mouth level to mine as she whispers the loudest words I've ever heard.

"I love you."

Her brown eyes bounce between mine. "If you would've answered a single one of my calls this week, I could've told you exactly what I told Alex. My home, my heart, all of it, is with you. There was never a moment of doubt for me, Ryan. The only reason you heard me crying on the phone after that conversation is because I finally felt free, and more than that, I felt clarity. I don't want you to change. I don't need you to shout from rooftops or show me off. I just need your quiet love because those moments are the loudest declarations I've ever heard. I want you for exactly who you are. I'm in love with you, Ryan Shay, and I don't need the entire world to know that for it to be true."

A sharp exhale of relief shudders through me, but besides that, I'm stunned silent.

In all these weeks, I had convinced myself it would take Indy time to get on the same wavelength to feel about me as I do her. I never thought she'd be the one to admit it first. I had intended to stay quiet, continuing to love her through my actions until I was certain the admission wouldn't scare her off, but here she is, my romantic girl, sweeping *me* off my feet.

Nervousness washes over her from my silence as she leans back on her heels.

Her throat works a swallow. "I know I said I like your quietness, but now would be a good time to say something."

I chuckle. My confident girl, vulnerable and nervous.

Pushing her hair behind her ears, I cup her cheeks and ensure her focus is on me. "I'm glad you finally got on my page."

A smile slides across her mouth.

"I'm sorry someone let you believe you were hard to love, because, Blue, it's the easiest thing I've ever done." I shake my head. "God, I love you. I think in a way, I've loved you since our first breakfast together. You brought me back to life, Ind, and I will love you as long as you'll let me."

"Promise?"

Pulling her in, I take her lips with mine. "I'll even add it to the fridge."

Indy has tried to stay by my side during the reception, but almost anytime we're alone, the bride decides she needs her.

She and I start dancing, Maggie needs help with her dress.

She takes a seat on my lap for cake cutting, Maggie needs her help to reapply her makeup.

We also weren't seated together for dinner, but that didn't stop us from eye-fucking the hell out of each other from across the room even while she shared a table with her ex.

The drastic measures her friends have taken to get the two of them back together is laughable. It would've started a pit of jealousy in me before today. But today, Indy loves me.

She loves *me*.

I need this wedding to be over so I can take her home. Indy is over it, that much is clear. I can see the visible shift she's taken from separating who she is now from her previous life. I guess I should be thanking Alex for that. If he hadn't given her that closure, I'm not sure how long it would've taken my girl to fully move on.

Her friends are so busy keeping her occupied and away from me, as if we don't live together, that I have plenty of time to thank him in person.

"I'll have what he's having," I tell the bartender, leaning my elbows on the bar top.

"Oh, for fuck's sake," Alex whines next to me.

A couple of his buddies are on his other side, slack jaws.

Typically, I hate the stares, the attention. But I fucking love how much this guy hates that he's a fan of mine. Him and all his friends.

The bartender puts a glass of amber liquid in front of me with a single spherical ice cube. Taking a sip, the smokiness of it burns my tongue and throat in the most delicious way.

The guy has good taste, I'll give him that. If that wasn't already evident by his ex-girlfriend.

Leaning down to his level, I keep my words hushed but clear.

"Unfortunately, Indy's old friends are your friends. You'll be around, I get that. But if you ever, and I mean *ever* make her cry again, I will do everything in my power to make your life a living hell. My face will pop up everywhere you go. You will see me in your goddamn nightmares. I will make myself a daily reminder that you fumbled the best thing you'll ever have in your fucking life. Got it?"

He stays staring straight ahead, but I note the nervous flicker of his eyes.

"Got it?" I repeat.

He nods in confirmation, and I plan to leave him with that, but then he decides to open his fucking mouth.

"Aren't you supposed to be the good guy of the NBA? I doubt stalking me would be good for your golden boy image."

A condescending laugh escapes me. "Says the guy who camped outside of my place of work to talk to a girl who wants nothing to do with him. But let me make this clear, when it comes to her, I have no issue ruining my reputation. I will burn the world down to protect her and I'll proudly wave the match, so everyone knows I'm the one who did it."

I pop off the bar to go find Indy, but then I add one more thing. "You know that jersey you've got with my last name on it? When you see it hanging there in your closet, let it serve as a reminder to you, that soon enough, it'll be her last name too."

I clink my glass with his because sometimes I'm an asshole, and then I go find my girl.

She's off by herself because her friends have no reason to spend time with her if I'm not around to distract her from, so I sneak up behind her while she's wearing that forced smile and speaking to guests.

As soon as my palm slides around her waist, her hand is on mine, fingers linking together.

"Well, I'll be damned," the older gentleman she's speaking to cuts in. "Ryan Shay. I'm a huge fan of yours. I cannot wait until you're back on the court. The team needs you."

I wear my professional smile once again. "The guys are doing great without me."

"Well, that's because you're on the sidelines, still running every game." He chuckles a hearty laugh. "Don't let us down, son. We need to make it to the playoffs. It's been too damn long and I'm getting too damn old."

"Yes, sir. I'm going to do my best."

"Excuse us," Indy cuts in. "I'm going to steal my boyfriend for a bit."

*Boyfriend.*

She pulls me away and straight towards the exit.

"Boyfriend, huh?"

"Oh, you don't like that? Would you prefer something else? My honey? My boo? Or how about my lover? Everyone"—she turns around and pretends to announce to the crowd behind us—"I'm going to go get railed by my lover now!"

I shift her shoulders, ushering her towards the exit. "Okay, you're not allowed to give nicknames."

"So only you're allowed to hand out nicknames?"

"Well, yeah, mine are good."

*Blue.*

*Ind.*

*Baby* when we're in bed.

*Mrs. Shay* is another I'd like to add to the list in the future.

"What do you want me to call you then?" she asks, halting us in our tracks.

Cupping her cheeks, I kiss her for everyone who wants to see. "You can call me yours."

She smiles into me. "Can you take me home now?"

"You don't want to stay here?"

She has a room upstairs for the night and I have a bag in the car in case things went my way today.

"I want to go back to the city where it's just you and me in our home."

*Our home.*

"I like the way that sounds."

"Are you leaving?" Maggie cuts in before we've made it to the door.

The night is over, the majority of the guests have gone, and I haven't seen most of the other bridesmaids in well over an hour so I can only assume, they've left too.

"Mags, do you really want me here?"

"Of course, I do."

"I mean *me*. Do you want *me* here? Not as Alex's girlfriend and not as a part of the group."

Maggie stays silent for longer than I like.

"Look, I love you. We've been friends our entire lives, but I don't fit in anymore, and I'm okay with that. If you want to be my friend, truly be my friend without any hidden agendas, I'd love that, but if you don't see us spending time together because your husband is friends with my ex, I'll be okay with that too." She runs a hand down Maggie's arm. "You look so beautiful today and I'm so happy for you."

She really is. I can see it in her face. There's no hidden jealousy or sadness. Indy seems entirely content.

Indy leans in to hug her. "We can talk about it another time if you'd like, but I'm happy, Maggie, and I'd love if you were happy for me too. Go have fun, okay?"

Taking her hand, I lead her to the exit.

"Indy," Maggie calls out. "I am happy for you."

Indy offers her a small smile before we are finally out of that fucking wedding.

# 33

# Indy

**Me:** *Daily update—I'm in love with your brother.*
**Stevie:** *Best daily update I've ever received.*

As soon as we are back in my hotel room to gather my things so we can go home, Ryan's arms are around my waist, his lips ghosting the back of my neck.

For a man who I assumed was practically terrified of women, he has no issue touching me every chance he gets.

"Let's get you packed up so I can get you home and in my bed."

He grabs my things from the bathroom as I stuff my duffel bag with the clothes I wore yesterday.

"Ryan?" I call out.

"Yeah?"

"When did you start learning sign?"

He peeks out of the bathroom, half the door frame covering his tall body. "Your mom texted me to check in on you a couple of days after I met your parents. I asked for her advice on the best way to start learning since she was an adult when she learned too. We've been video chatting once a week ever since, and they've both been teaching me."

Tears prick the back of my eyes before pooling at the base of my lashes because this man turns me into an emotional wreck in the best way possible.

"Your mom also helped me enroll in an online class which I'm passing with flying colors, thank you very much." Ryan's lips tug into a beautifully soft smile as he watches me from across the room. "Don't cry, Blue."

"I can't help it." I suck in a sharp intake of air. "I adore you."

He chuckles, leisurely making his way to me, thumbing underneath my eyes.

"That's why you sounded so casual with my mom when you walked in on us talking the other day," I surmise.

"She's funny. I like her a lot."

"But not as funny as me, right?"

He laughs again. "Of course not."

The pads of his fingertips graze against my cheeks before running down the column of my neck.

"Why?"

"Why what, baby?"

"Why are you learning sign?"

I'm fairly certain I know the reason, but I want to hear him say it.

"Because they're your family and you're mine, and the fact you even have to ask is mind-blowing to me. Learning to communicate with your family is the bare minimum, Ind."

I guess it is, but I didn't know the bar was on the floor until Ryan Shay walked into my life and quietly raised it to the fucking moon.

"And because I love you and when I tell your dad that, I'll be the one to say it."

The pads of his fingers skate along my collarbone, dusting the skin at the top of my breasts. Ryan's eyes roam every inch of me, his pupils dilating and going dark. His hands are so commanding and controlling in his career, but he touches me with a soft delicacy as if he's savoring every inch of my skin.

His middle finger traces my sternum, dipping into the "V" of my strapless sweetheart neckline.

"Two hours is a long drive."

His deep voice alone has heat pooling between my legs.

"Too long," I agree, stepping into him, my palm flattening over the zipper of his pants where an impressive bulge is waiting. "This would be awfully uncomfortable to drive with."

"You going to take care of it, Blue?"

I unfasten his belt. "As long as you take care of me."

His warm lips meet the soft flesh under my ear. "I'll always take care of you."

And though we're speaking in sexual terms here, it's not lost on me that Ryan will always take care of and protect me, the same way I will him.

By nature, I'm a nurturer, and now that I can look back with clarity, that part of my personality has been exploited in the past, but not once has Ryan taken advantage of me. He's been alone for too long, and it's a privilege to take care of him.

Hands sliding under his button-down shirt, I untuck it from his pants, meeting his warm flesh with my palms. I'll never tire of touching this man. He's big and smooth, and I plan to memorize the way his stomach quivers when my nails skate over his abdomen.

His lips trail kisses over my throat and collarbone while he quickly unzips the back of my bridesmaid dress. Thanks to the built-in strapless bra, I'm bare when it pools at my hips.

Ryan exhales a gravelly hum in appreciation, looking down at my bare chest and peaked nipples. He runs a thumb over one.

"These fucking tits, Ind." He pinches me, drawing out a low moan from my throat. "And these goddamn nipples. So pretty between my fingers."

"Even prettier on your tongue."

He chuckles a silent laugh. "Needy tonight, Blue?" Pulling a single white flower from my hair, he toys with it, spinning it in between his fingers before brushing the petals over my chest. "Because there's nothing in this world I'd love more than hearing you beg, and trust me, baby, I won't stop until I hear it."

There's a different energy to Ryan tonight, and I'm quickly realizing that the night we had sex was simply a warm-up. As if he was dusting off the cobwebs after years of celibacy. The realization is equal parts thrilling as it is terrifying.

The silkiness of the petals lightly brush over my nipple, the delicate sensation almost too much on my heated skin.

I shudder, but don't speak.

He moves to the other. "I'll give you everything you want, but you're going to have to use that talented mouth of yours and ask for it. I liked how polite you were the other night, so make sure you use your manners to say 'please' while you do."

Taking a centering breath, I sling my arms over his shoulders as he continues to toy with the flower over my stiff flesh. "Will you have your way with me, Ryan? Will you to do all the things you've always wanted to do to me?"

A single brow lifts.

"Please," I add.

"That's an awful lot of things, Blue."

"Then I guess it's a good thing we live together and have all the time in the world, but Shay, if you don't replace that flower with your mouth, there will be no 'pleases' tonight, just a string of colorful curse words directed straight at you."

He huffs a laugh before swooping me up, my legs around his hips. "It's cute you think you'll be able to speak while I'm pounding into you."

Taking me across the room, my back slams against the wall as his mouth slams onto mine. Frantic kisses, clashing teeth. I love controlling Ryan, but *unhinged* Ryan makes me weak.

There's nothing calculated about the way he kisses and grinds his body into mine. It's messy and I fucking love it.

Finally, he takes my breast in his mouth, wet heat surrounding me. He gnashes with his teeth, pulling at my skin and biting me. My body will be decorated with colorful marks tomorrow, which is more than fine by me. Purple is my favorite color after all.

"If I touch your pussy right now, is it going to be wet for me?"

I quickly nod. "Touch me and find out."

"Was that in the form of a question?"

"Jesus," I breathe out. "What is this? Jeopardy?"

Ryan laughs. "I need you to hear yourself ask for it, Ind."

I give up the fight because more than anything, I need him to touch me. "Will you touch me and find out just how wet I am for you?"

Using his hips to pin me to the wall, he pulls my dress up, the chiffon fabric bunching around my waist. He adjusts, looking down at the space between us, pushing the material out of the way. To no surprise my nude-colored thong is soaked.

"Mmm," he hums in satisfaction. "Good girl. You're drenched."

My head falls back to the wall behind me as I watch him run the back of his finger up my slit. He uses that same finger to push my thong to the side, baring my throbbing center. He circles my clit before gathering my arousal and slipping it into his mouth.

"Dear God," I exhale, watching him taste me.

"Who are you praying to?"

"I'm not sure."

He moans at the taste of me. "Well, just be sure to use my real name when I make you scream."

Ryan takes me to the bed, tossing me on the mattress. I'm tall for a girl and I've never had the pleasure of being thrown around. I want to be bent into different positions. I want to be held and heaved. I want to feel dominated.

With the predatory way Ryan is stalking towards the bed, I have no doubt I will be.

He unbuttons his shirt as he stands over me, slowly revealing his cut chest and carved stomach. "Ask me for what you want."

"I want you to fuck me."

He doesn't react, only continues to undress for me.

"Will you please fuck me?" I correct without guidance.

His ocean eyes flicker to me with a wash of pride. "My smart girl is learning, I see."

"Do you like this, Ryan? Do you like me begging for every little thing?"

He tosses his shirt on the floor—surprisingly.

"Do you?"

A flush heats my cheeks. "Yes."

Unzipping himself, he steps out of his pants, once again reminding me of just how impressive he is. "That's because you know I'll give you every fucking thing you could ever ask for. You stopped worrying about your own needs a long time ago, Indy, but I want you to hear yourself ask and I want to watch you take."

Goddamn. I'm fairly certain this man could make me orgasm from his words alone.

But he's right. I never thought about it that way, but there's a vulnerability in asking for the things I want and expecting them in return. I spent a lot of years asking and hoping for the life I wanted. It's almost as if my words were never heard so I stopped asking at all.

Ryan wants me to ask and expect a return because he'll deliver, and I know he's not only referring to the bedroom, but our life outside of these walls.

"So, ask me for what you want, Indy."

"Will you explain, in detail, everything you're going to do to me?" Licking my lips, I find myself enjoying the taste of those words.

He grabs my dress bunched at my hips and yanks it, pulling me to the edge of the bed before slipping it down my legs. It meets his pants and shirt on the floor, and I want to praise him for being in the moment and not giving a shit about them.

A wicked grin lifts on his lips. "First"—he pulls me by my wrists to sit up—"you're going to take these off me." He places my fingertips on the waistband of his boxer briefs. "Then you're going to make some of your pretty noises that I love so much when you put my cock inside your pussy. I'm going to pull your hair. I'm going tell you how well you're taking it, how pretty you look stretched around me. I'm going to fuck you on your back then on your knees. And when you come, it'll be after I give you permission to."

My thighs rub together, but Ryan separates them, taking another step towards me.

"And the whole time, I'm going to give you everything you need because I love you."

Hands threaded into my hair, he does exactly what he promised, pulling my head back to kiss me. Languid strokes of his tongue run against mine as we take our time, savoring every lick and taste. There's nothing rushed about it, until I pull his briefs down and circle the base of his cock with my fist.

Tugging and stroking it in my hand, Ryan's kisses become deeper, more passionate, punctuated by grunts and moans. Even though he's in control, both of us are acutely aware of who is truly in charge. If I wanted to take over, he'd gladly let me, and I love that dynamic. I *choose* to let him use me however he wants.

Ryan pulls my underwear off, quickly discarding them, and my legs automatically circle his, pulling him into me. I lie back as Ryan's cock slides against me.

We both whimper.

He repeats the motion, staring as my arousal coats his dick. Skin to skin. Hard and soft. I want him bare and inside of me so much it hurts, but I'll never say it. Not yet anyway.

"*Fuck*," he exhales, running his length through me. "Look how good it looks with you all over me, Blue."

His cock is stiff and hot, angry veins running the length. A simple slip and he'd be inside of me, filling me. I can see him thinking, watching with admiration. He doesn't want to stop to grab a condom.

I stay as still as possible, letting him make the decision, but my arching back and heaving breaths make it hard to do so.

Pulling his hips back, he runs himself over me one more time before cursing under his breath, closing his eyes, and pulling away.

The condom is on him before I know it. I scoot back, hauling my head up to the pillows as Ryan crawls onto the mattress between my legs.

"Open these nice and wide for me, Ind." Sitting up on his knees with his hands hooked under my thighs, he spreads me open. "Good girl. So fucking pretty on your back. Now put it in."

"*You* don't have to ask?"

His laugh is dark. "There's not a world in which we exist that you want me to ask for permission once you've already given it. You act like I don't know you, but I've learned you, Blue. I see how wet you get when I tell you what to do. You want me to boss you around and you want the praise when you meet the challenge. You don't need me to beg for you out loud because you already know how fucking weak I am for you."

He's right. I don't want polite. I want him to demand then tell me how well I'm doing.

"Now put my cock inside your pussy. I want to watch myself sink into you."

I take him, rubbing him against me to coat the condom, and when I tap the head of his cock against my clit a couple of times, Ryan's head falls back.

"Will you to look at me, Ryan?"

Without hesitation, dilated pupils meet mine. His chest heaves with heavy breaths and he keeps his intense stare right on me as I guide him inside.

Our mouths mirror each other, falling open.

He meets some resistance from my body because after only one time together, there's no way I'm used to his size yet. Ryan thumbs my clit, relaxing me as he slowly pushes inside, letting my body adjust along the way.

"So fucking good," he breathes, staring at our connection. "You take me so well, Ind. So tight, but so perfect."

He feels amazing once I'm fully stretched around him. He threads his hands through mine, pushing them into the mattress. He takes my lips, and he doesn't move until I adjust my hips, asking for it.

Pulling back, he thrusts into me, the headboard hitting the hotel wall behind it.

"Oh, *fuck*, Ryan."

He moans and it's the hottest sound I've ever heard. "You feel so good, Blue."

Body rolling, he thrusts inside me again. The wall rattles with the movement, and part of me feels sorry for our neighbors, but most of me doesn't have the capacity to feel much sympathy with how full I am of him.

Eyes never straying, we watch the effect we have on one another.

His hands leave mine, instead lifting the back of my thighs and pushing my knees to my chest. The slight change in angle has him driving deeper, and my eyes roll back when I swear I can't take any more of him.

"You like that?" he asks with deep, punishing thrusts.

And Ryan wasn't wrong when he said I wouldn't be able to speak while he's pounding into me. The words are caught in my throat from the overwhelming fullness of him hitting just the right spot. I can't see straight. I can't think straight. All I can do is feel. There's so much of him.

Ryan eases back when I don't respond, keeping his thrusts consistent, but less severe.

"Harder," I beg, the heels of my feet digging into his shoulders. "Will you fuck me harder?"

He watches me for a moment, a slight gleam of sweat shining on his forehead. After a beat, a devilish grin spreads across his lips. "You have no idea what you just did."

He pulls out of me, instantly flipping me onto my stomach. "Get on your knees."

His palms wrap around my hips, pulling them up, and I find myself on all fours. Ryan doesn't want that though, evident by the way he pushes between my shoulder blades until my head is buried in the bed and only my ass is in the air.

He circles my clit. "So wet, Ind. You like being thrown around?"

Turning my face into the mattress, I watch him from over my shoulder and nod.

His dark eyes soften, running an appreciative palm over my ass and spine. "You should see yourself, baby. Goddamn breathtaking."

"Ryan?"

His eyes find mine.

"Will you fuck me now?"

He chuckles before the air shifts again and the untamed beast is back to play. Hand brushing over my hair he wraps it around his fist once. Twice.

Reaching underneath my legs, I take his cock and center him, guiding him inside.

His free hand grips my hip as he rams into me. He's so deep at this angle, his pelvis bone smacks against my ass.

The room fills with the squeak of the mattress and mixed moans from us both. Sweat beads on my forehead and though Ryan is dominant and controlling in this position, the desperate sounds that come from his throat reminds us both that he has absolutely no control when it comes to me.

He pulls my hair, lifting my back to his chest. One arm wraps around my waist as his lips meet my ear. "I'm gone for you, Ind. I love you so fucking much."

Our parted lips meet. "I love you too, baby."

He whimpers at the name, forehead falling to mine.

His soft vulnerability has me clenching around him.

"Not yet. Don't you dare come until I tell you to."

"Ryan," I cry when he changes his tempo.

He flips me over, keeping my legs wide as he fills me again. "Ask me, Blue. Ask me because I will give you everything you could ever want."

Holding himself over me, every muscle in his chest and stomach contracts, rippling under his skin. He's clearly on the verge of coming himself, but he's attempting to keep his promise of making me come only after I ask.

I wrap my arms around him to pull him down, needing his skin on mine, wanting him as close as possible.

"Ryan, will you please make me come?"

He drives into me over and over again, and though he doesn't say a word, when he circles my clit with the pad of his finger, I know that's his silent permission.

"That's my girl," he praises. "There you go."

Blinding euphoria flows through me, arching my back off the bed as he fucks me through it, and as soon as I can see straight again, he pulls out before he comes.

He switches us, him on his back and me on top. He takes both my hands in a single of his, holding them behind my back as he positions me to sit on his face.

"Ryan," I cry out when his tongue lashes my swollen and sensitive clit. "Oh God, it's too much."

He doesn't listen, doesn't stop, because though I'm complaining about another impending orgasm building directly after the last, I'm still rubbing my pussy over his mouth.

He sucks and licks, holding me restrained and at his complete control.

Falling forward, I whimper when his tongue dives into me. He growls a satisfied hum at that, vibrating my whole body.

"Come for me again, Blue. You can do it." Then he flicks my clit after giving me permission, and I'm coming on his tongue.

I'm still trembling from two orgasms in less than two minutes when he flips me onto my back and opens my legs. Slowly, he slides back in and my contracting walls have his eyes rolling back when I pulse around him.

Ryan falls on top of me, fingers threaded through mine. He leans in close to my ear as he evens his tempo, taking his time and we're no longer fucking. Our soaked skin slides against one another and the space around us is filled with promises and whispers of how much we love each other.

"Ind, I need one more from you."

"I can't."

My body is wrecked and overwhelmed, and even after two exploding orgasms, it betrays my words, ready for a third.

"Give me one more, and I'll come with you this time."

He kisses me, tongue sweeping in as his cock thrusts in and out, filling me and ruining me at the same time.

I fucking love this man and I love watching him unravel because of me.

"Will you make me come, Ryan?" I whisper against his lips.

His hands clench around mine, fingers locking before he rolls his body, his pelvis bone hitting my clit with a rhythmic tempo.

I'm coming again, and as soon as I do, his entire body is shaking, muscles tensing, stomach contracting. Burying his head in the crook of my neck, he releases, holding me through his orgasm while repeating breathless reminders of how much he loves me.

We're both sweaty messes and entirely lost in our own world where it's only him and me existing. Happy, unbothered, and completely in love with each other.

# 34

# Indy

**Me:** *Daily update—your brother almost split me in half last night when I got home from the airport. Holy hell, that man.*
**Stevie:** *Indy, put me out of my misery. I thought these would end now that you're together.*
**Me:** *No, babe. Not a chance.*
**Stevie:** *And here I was planning to ask you to be in my wedding when I see you tonight.*
**Me:** *WAIT!! Please ask me! I'll be the best bridesmaid ever. I'll throw you the most epic bachelorette party, and I'll even hold your dress while you pee. Please!*
**Stevie:** *You drive a hard bargain.*
**Me:** *Do I get to walk with your brother?*
**Stevie:** *Depends. Will you promise not to jump his bones halfway down the aisle?*
**Me:** *No guarantees.*
**Me:** *Wait. I'm seeing you tonight?*
**Stevie:** *Is Ryan home?*
**Me:** *Not yet…*

It's been a few weeks since Maggie's wedding, and Ryan's and my life hasn't changed too much from how it was before.

Only now, we openly tell each other how we feel, nothing is pretend, and we share his bed every night. My room has turned into one giant walk-in closet which works out real well for my extensive wardrobe.

We continue to have breakfast each morning that we're home together, but now, more often than not, we're nearly naked and I'm sitting in his lap while we eat.

And if all four of us are in town, we have dinner almost every night with Zanders and Stevie either at their place or at ours. It's the closest thing we have to dates outside of the apartment.

Determined to knock off his bucket list, which may as well be void seeing as he gives my fictional boyfriends a run for their money as is, Ryan had planned a dinner date for us. One in public. We were quickly bombarded with fans and media, and the stress it caused him to instantly be "on" took away a lot of the joy from our night.

It's not easy for Ryan to leave the apartment, but that's okay. I love our little life inside these four walls.

"Ind!" he calls as soon as he comes through the front door from his morning shootaround.

"In here!"

He ambles into his bedroom where I'm tucked under the covers, not yet ready to start my day. I didn't get home from my road trip until two this morning. Ryan was waiting up for me and let's just say, we were both still awake with the sun.

A soft smile slides across his lips as he leans against the doorframe, a fresh bouquet of flowers in his hand. "Well, don't you look cozy?"

"Are those for me?"

He pops his shoulder before placing them on the nightstand. "Maybe."

"Ryan, the romantic." Words I never thought I'd say. "I love peonies. Thank you."

Opening my arms, Ryan crawls onto the bed and nuzzles up to me. "And I love coming home to you."

Scratching his scalp, I place a couple of kisses on his cheek. "That's good because I'm not going anywhere."

"No?"

"Are you kidding? I've got a free ride here. I get flowers hand delivered every week and I'm getting laid on the regular. I'm living the dream."

His chest heaves against mine.

"And then there's the whole thing about me being in love with you."

"That little detail."

His smiling mouth meets mine.

"Are you coming to the game tonight?" he asks.

"Of course." I have yet to miss one if I'm in town. "I'm going to sit with Annie and the girls in their family box tonight."

"Okay, well I guess you wouldn't want the Morgans' courtside tickets then."

I pull away to get a better look at him, trying not to get too excited. "They gave you their tickets?"

"Yeah, they thought maybe you, Zanders, and my sister would want some good seats seeing as I'm back in the lineup tonight."

"Ryan!" I smack his chest. "Are you serious?"

He laughs at my reaction. "I got cleared this morning."

"Ryan Shay! This is huge! Are you excited? I'm so excited!" I slip out from underneath him, rushing to my old room across the hall. "I need to figure out what I'm going to wear!"

I can hear his easy laughter as he stays in his bed.

Turning around, I make my way back to the doorway of his room. "Are you happy, Ry?"

Hands folded under his head, he crosses his legs at the ankles, a soft smile on his lips. "I've got everything I could ever ask for. I've never been happier in my life, Blue. Now, I just got to get us to the playoffs."

*"The Devils must win four of the next five games to make the playoffs. How confident do you feel about that?"*

*"You have a lot of ground to make up now that you're back in the lineup. This entire city is counting on you getting them to the playoffs, and you're coming off a month-long injury. Do you feel the pressure to come back as if you never left and get some wins under your belt?"*

*"Ryan, you have no time to ease back into the game. You guys are in a must-win situation. How do you feel about that?"*

How do I feel about that? I feel fucking anxious and stressed. I don't need the constant reminder of how many people are counting on me. I put that pressure on myself every single day, but regardless, I'm constantly reminded during my first pre-game press conference back from my injury.

I wanted to fly under the radar tonight. Give myself time to feel the game and make sure I'm up to speed, that I haven't lost too much strength. But I'm coming back into the lineup under a must-win situation. I don't have time to ease my way in, and the pre-game press conference was a dose of reality.

The questions are on a constant loop, replaying in my mind as I bounce on my toes in the tunnel, ready to run out with my team.

Leon Carson did a hell of a job taking over for me the last four weeks. We split wins and losses, and that's all I could ask for from a rookie given the starting role when he wasn't fully ready for it.

But tonight? Tonight, I'm taking my spot back. Tonight, I'm going to spend the next two hours playing the game I love with the guys who have become my friends. Tonight, I'm going to try not to worry about the outside pressures even though I can feel them with every fiber of my being.

"Good to have you back, Cap." Ethan pats me on the back of the head. "Are you ready for this?"

Stretching my neck, I shake out my shoulders as the rest of the team huddles up for a quick pep talk before we run out of the tunnel for the game.

Nodding, I put a fist up. The rest of the team joins in, connecting our fisted hands in the center of a circle.

"All right, boys," I announce. "I'm back."

The team hollers with cheers.

"Thank you for holding us down, but we have some work to do. We're in a must-win situation here."

The team goes quiet with concentration. Focused nods and intense eye contact all around.

"But how about we go have some fun and play the way we know how, yeah?"

Confused stares come my way. These guys are used to me being extreme and unrelenting but being an ass to your teammates and throwing more pressure on their shoulders doesn't make them play any better, so for now, I'll carry that burden on my own.

"You heard the man!" Ethan adds, breaking up the awkward silence.

The energy shifts once again, fourteen guys bursting with adrenaline. "Devils on three!"

The tunnel echoes with the cheers and shouts as we run out for warm-ups.

The crowd is loud, but it turns deafening when I run out of the tunnel. It's been far too long since I've been on the court instead of sitting my ass on the bench. I missed the way the hardwood feels under my soles. I missed the way it feels to wear red, black, and white for Chicago.

It feels like coming home and that feeling is only amplified when I see my girl wearing my jersey as she stands and cheers just like the rest of the crowd, rowdy for my return. The only difference is that Indy is wild, like a woman gone mad.

Just the way I like her.

I'm fully dialed in for warm-ups, blocking out the fanfare, and focused on my pre-game ritual of running through ball-handling drills off to the side of the court. Only now, instead of being solo, Leon joins me as we run through them together.

The National Anthem is sung, warm-ups are complete, and the adrenaline is back for the starting lineup announcements.

I don't know why I'm nervous. I've been announced countless times, but the four weeks I've been without this game remind me of how special it is. How privileged I am to make a career out of something I love so much. How much I missed it, and now I want to savor every second I have of it.

And yes, I still want to win. More than anything.

The arena is dim, spotlights dance along the darkened hardwood as the rest of the starting lineup is announced. Ethan smacks my leg, leaving me as the last player on the bench before he jogs through the makeshift tunnel the rest of the team has made, meeting the other starters at the end.

"And last, but certainly not least, making his return to the lineup tonight," the announcer booms through the speakers. "Number five, ladies and gentlemen, your starting point guard, Ryan Shay!"

The fan's deafening cheers turn to a dull white noise in my ears as I stand from the bench. The arena shakes, vibrations bouncing off the hardwood from the sellout crowd standing to clap and yell for my return.

Running through the tunnel of my teammates, I make sure to hit each of their hands, and when I make it to the rest of the starters waiting at the other end, I jog right past them to the opposite sideline of the court.

When I'm in my uniform, I never lose focus. I don't look into the crowd. I don't pay attention to anyone outside of the game. But if the last four weeks taught me anything, it's that this game doesn't matter much without the three people sitting courtside for me.

Indy doesn't need the world to know I love her, she's said it herself, but that doesn't mean I don't want them to.

Holding my fist out, I connect it with Zanders'.

Leaning down, I pop a kiss on Stevie's cheek.

"Love you," she says.

"Love you, Vee."

Next to my sister sits her best friend, the brown-eyed beauty who owns my entire heart. With my knuckle, I tilt her chin up and lean down to kiss her lips. "And I love you."

She smiles into me. "Go give them hell, Five."

Jogging back to my team, Zanders shouts from behind me. "What about me? You don't love me?"

"Love you too, brother!"

It took half of the first quarter to get into a rhythm.

My knee is healed. It feels strong and stable, but I can't help but favor my left side in fear of another injury. I quickly remembered, thanks to too many turnovers, that I can't play scared at this level, and by the second quarter I felt like my old self again.

Up by ten deep into the fourth quarter. I'll average ten less minutes than my usual court time. My coach is clearly trying to ease me back into the game, but, thanks to the constant reminders, we don't have time to ease into anything. We have five games left and need to win at least four of them to make the playoffs.

As much as Leon can handle himself out here, I'm not ready to call it a night. I missed this rush too much.

The next two times on defense, Dom blocks a shot and Ethan gets a steal, putting us up by fourteen with four minutes left on the game clock. Without a doubt, the three of us will be subbed out at the next dead ball, but I want to feel like myself one more time before the night is over.

I tighten my defense, testing my speed, and I'm right there, just as I used to be. My opponent drives the lane, dishing the ball to another player out on the perimeter. They shoot, but miss, and Dom is there with the rebound.

We quickly transition. I take off towards our end, letting Dom outlet the ball to Ethan who is fast to throw it ahead to me.

I can feel my defender on my back and the scene playing out in my mind as I gather the ball on my way to the hoop is all too familiar. I don't want to leave my feet. I want to play it safe, come to a complete stop, ensuring he isn't flying underneath me before I safely put the ball away.

All those thoughts run through my mind in the half second I have to make a decision.

I can't play scared.

With one swift dribble, I'm in the air, grabbing the rim with a single hand and putting the ball through the net. An internal breath of relief flows through me when my feet safely return to the floor once again.

The guy defending me sure as shit fouls me on my way up, holding my other arm and pulling me down, but do I get the call? Nope, and that's nothing new for me.

Proud of myself for simply getting it done and not playing in fear, I get back on defense without saying a word. I've never been the player to complain to the refs even when they're doing a shitty job.

"Hey!" Indy jumps from her seat, yelling at the referees as I jog past her. "What the hell was that? Are you blind? That's an and-one! Why don't you start blowing that whistle instead of blowing this game?"

My girl is red-faced and angry, stomping around on her strappy red heels as she continues to berate the refs.

Waiting for the other team to bring the ball up, I stand with my hands on my hips, watching her. Ethan and Dom join, sandwiching me on either side.

"He's an MVP nod, for fuck's sake! Give the man some credit! What the hell are they paying you for?" she continues before adding a few more colorful curse words. "Goddamn. Are your knees sore from blowing that call?"

An amused smile is fighting to break free, but I just shake my head as I watch her.

"Your girl is kind of scary sometimes, Shay," Dom notes from one side.

Ethan laughs from the other.

"I know," I admit proudly. "And I fucking love it."

We win by seventeen.

# 36 Indy

Grabbing my keys, I head towards the front door. "Ry, I'm heading to Michael's."

Sitting on the couch with a book in his hands and his feet propped on the coffee table, Ryan stiffens before slowly lowering his book to his lap.

"Say that again for me."

"I'm heading to Michael's."

"And who the fuck is Michael?"

*Huh?*

As realization hits me, I try my hardest not to laugh. Jealous Ryan is hot, so I'll let this play out before admitting that Michael's is the craft store where I buy my embroidery thread to cross-stitch.

"Don't worry about it."

His brows rocket up towards his hairline. "Oh, don't worry about it? Okay then."

"You don't get to tell me what to do unless we're both naked."

He lifts his book again, refocusing his attention on the pages. "Have fun, but just know that you're responsible for whatever happens to *Michael* tonight. In fact…" He eases into the couch as if he's casually unaffected. "It'll give me something to do later."

It's then that I double over in laughter. "You're insane."

Ryan peeks an eye over his book.

"Michael's is a craft store, you psychopath."

He pops his shoulder, not denying the statement, and is entirely unapologetic that if there were a real man named Michael I was going to see tonight, he'd have no problem standing behind his promise.

Unable to contain my laughter, I take a seat across his lap. "Would you like to come with me so you can confront Michael while I pick up a new embroidery hoop and needles?"

He drops his book to the couch, slipping his arms around my waist. "I was about to body slam Michael through the floor."

My head falls to his shoulder, and finally, Ryan is able to laugh at himself. "Do you want me to go with you?"

I want him to go everywhere with me, but it's hard enough for him to leave the apartment as is, and now, coming to the end of his regular season, it's essentially impossible.

Not to mention, the attention is overwhelming for him, and the pressure from the media, fans, and upper management since his return has been taking its toll. He's been trying to play it cool, but I've noticed it eating away at him.

"That's okay. I'll go tomorrow after you head on your road trip instead."

Ryan's stunning smile sparkles. "Read with me?"

"*God*." My head falls back. "Talk dirty to me, why don't you."

Slinging a leg over his lap, I straddle him.

One hand splayed over the expanse of my back, Ryan leans forward to grab my most current book from the coffee table.

"What's this one about?" he asks, handing it off.

"A mafia boss cuts a deal with another mafia boss by using his daughter for payment. Marriage of convenience. Normal stuff."

Opening my book, I restart right where I left off.

"Why do you like reading fiction so much?" he asks without a hint of judgment.

"How else would you get to live a thousand lives in the span of only one? The beauty of fiction is that it makes you feel things on a visceral level. You can cry with those characters, laugh with them. It teaches you to look at another's perspective, to have empathy. In nonfiction, you simply learn about something instead of feeling it."

"You already feel more than most people I know." Ryan closes his book, cocks his head, and watches me with a softness I didn't know existed when I first moved in. "You haven't been reading much lately."

I pop my shoulders. "Well, that's because I don't feel the need to live in someone else's reality. I enjoy my own far too much these days."

That stunning smile is back, puckered dimples and all as Ryan runs his palms up the length of my thighs.

"Can I read some of your book?"

"Really?"

He nods excitedly.

"Okay, let me find something you might like—"

He stops me from flipping through the pages. "Let me read the page you're at."

*Well…this is going to be interesting.*

I hand it over, watching him with caution as Ryan leans into the couch behind him and begins to read my book. Blue-green eyes widen as soon as he starts because I left off at a detailed scene of the female main character getting eaten out on the mafia boss's desk right after he killed a man in cold blood.

"Shit," Ryan exhales, burying himself further into the couch as if he plans to stay there long enough to finish the entire book. "This is hot."

"That's what I'm saying!"

One hand holding my book, he uses the other to grab my waist, pulling me against him. My legs are opened around his and all it does is cause me to grind against him which I'm quickly realizing is what he wanted.

"This is practically a how-to manual on how to please a woman. How are more men not reading these?"

Falling forward, I use one arm against the back of the couch to keep myself hovering over him. Ryan's eyes stay glued to the pages until I roll my hips against his and earn his attention. Those studious ocean eyes turn dark when he looks up at me.

"This might be the hottest thing I've ever seen." I admit.

"Oh, yeah?" Ryan drops my book, his hands sliding into my hair to pull me down before he kisses me so deeply I can feel its intensity in every nerve of my body.

He moans into my mouth and the desperate sound has me moving against him. Ryan being vocal and unrestrained with the noises he makes, is part of what makes him so sexy to me. He's confident and unafraid to let me know the effect I have on him.

My hand slips under his shirt, but as soon as my palm touches the warmth of his skin, a knock sounds at our front door.

"No," I disagree against his lips. "Not happening. You're leaving for four days. Do not answer that door."

He laughs into me.

The knock sounds again.

Rolling my eyes, I climb off his lap and fall onto the couch beside him, letting him stand to answer the door.

"That's weird that David didn't call up," Ryan says as he looks through the peephole. "Oh, it's Kai."

And it's no wonder Dave didn't call. Kai lives in this building too.

"Hey, man."

"Hey." Kai waves to me. "Hey, Indy."

"Well, if it isn't baseball's very own Clark Kent. To what do we owe the honor?"

Standing in the doorway, a sly smile slides across his lips at the nickname. Kai Rhodes is a looker. Wildly tall, dark wavy hair, and black-rimmed glasses. Not to mention, the charming grin that would melt most women on the spot. Those things, and the fact he's one of the top names in baseball, have always had me confused on how the hell he's single.

And I haven't even mentioned the adorable baby he's got slung over his hip who is hands down my favorite visitor.

"I have a huge favor to ask of you two. We have a preseason dinner with some of the season ticket holders tonight and I fired my nanny."

"Again?"

"Yes, again." Kai avoids eye contact because this is the sixth nanny he's fired and that's just since I've known him.

Ryan, Kai's coaches and agent, including the rest of his team, have been on him to find a nanny he trusts enough with his son not to fire them after only a week. And now, with baseball season starting, it's even more imperative he finds the right fit. He needs someone willing to travel with the team for the MLB's insane schedule since Kai is a single dad, and to be honest, I've lost a bit of hope he's going to find the right person for the job.

"I'll be back in less than two hours. I'll make it quick. Max will be asleep most of the time," Kai continues.

Ryan looks back to me, awaiting my input. Even though our night was about to look a whole lot different, I jump at any chance to hold Max.

"Yes!" I say for us from the couch. "We'd love to watch him. Take all the time you need, Kai."

"You guys are the best." He slings the diaper bag off his shoulder, handing it to Ryan. "Everything he needs is in there. He's ready for a bottle in an hour, and after he eats, he will probably be asleep until I get home. Please call me for any reason. If he's not eating or sleeping, I'll come right home. There's a list of emergency contacts tucked in the diaper bag, but please call me if—"

"Kai." I stand from the couch. "He'll be fine. Go to work and don't worry about us."

I'd like to add that I was born to do this but saying anything to that extent would most likely freak Ryan out.

"I need my fix." Holding out my arms, Kai passes his sleepy son to me.

"Call me," Kai begs.

Ryan reassures. "We will. See you later."

Closing the door, Ryan sets the diaper bag on the kitchen island as I bounce on the balls of my feet, hoping to keep Max from getting fussy now that his dad is gone.

"Well, this isn't exactly how I pictured our night going."

I give Ryan an understanding smile because he's about to be gone for four days and the man fully expected he'd be getting laid tonight. Multiple times.

As I cradle Max's head and continue to bop around the apartment, Ryan pops a kiss on my temple. "I'll make us some dinner."

It isn't more than ten minutes into Ryan cooking, that Max begins to wail his high-pitched cry. I attempt to soothe him, quietly speaking in his ear, rubbing his back, but it's no use. He's upset.

Ryan looks over his shoulder while standing at the stove. "Want me to try?"

We've watched Max a few times since I moved in, and Ryan has never once held him.

"Really? I kind of thought you were afraid of him."

Ryan exhales a sharp laugh. "Please. The only reason I've never taken him from you is because I know how much you love having him, but I babysat Max on my own multiple times before you moved in. I'm not afraid, Blue."

I truly have no idea how many times this man will continue to surprise me, but it's just like Ryan to stay quiet until needing to say something.

Max wails once again, and as much as it pains me, I'm not who he wants right now.

Reaching out, Ryan takes him from me, situating Max's head on his shoulder. Effortlessly, he holds him up with a single forearm and continues to cook us dinner as if nothing has changed. The softest singing voice echoes throughout the kitchen as Ryan sings into Max's ear, and I swear to God my ovaries are on high alert because Ryan Shay holding a baby while cooking me dinner has got to be the sexiest thing I've ever seen.

He soothes him, placing soft kisses on his head between lyrics and within a minute or two Max is fully content snuggled into the crook of Ryan's neck.

My boyfriend shoots me a mischievous smile over his shoulder, infinitely proud of himself and I've got to admit, I'm right there with him.

Ryan continues to cook as I watch the two of them, and there's even a couple of times that he pulls a sweet giggle from Max. I offer to help, but Ryan refuses, saying he's got it handled and I don't need much convincing that he does. He's a natural with him, and the only thing that understanding does is cause a rush of realization that I want this life with him.

I've always wanted to be a mom. Clearly, the whole reason I moved in in the first place was to save enough money in order to make that dream a reality. But it's no longer this innate desire to parent. Instead, I want to parent with *him*.

This might be horrible to admit, but in a way, I was selfish in wanting kids. *I* wanted to be a mom. *I* wanted to have children, and for the first time in my life, there's someone else I picture right alongside me while I do it.

We take our food to the couch and when I offer to feed Max his bottle while Ryan eats first, he refuses. He feeds him and insists I eat while my food is still hot.

Max passes out asleep before his bottle is fully emptied, just the way his dad said he would and Ryan repositions himself back on the couch, allowing the sweet baby boy to sleep on his chest while he eats his now lukewarm dinner.

Taking a forkful of pasta, Ryan smiles at me with his mouth full and a sleeping baby on his chest.

I want to speak. I want to say something about how natural he looks or how sexy it is to see him so confident with a baby, but I keep my mouth shut. I'm so afraid to scare Ryan away, to give him any reason to question me. The man abstained from sex for years because he didn't want to give someone the chance to take advantage of him.

Because he was afraid.

But I'm equally terrified that he'll never want the things in life I ache for and seeing him like this tonight is nothing but a reminder that it wasn't long ago he vocalized just how differently he viewed his future from the one I want.

# 37

# Ryan

"You're aware that you lost last night."

"Clearly." I try my hardest not to roll my eyes at the reporter sitting in the third row of this morning's press conference, but if that wasn't the most obvious statement I've ever heard.

"Which means if you lose one of the next two, the Chicago Devils are out of the playoff run."

"Was there a question in there?"

A small chuckle washes over the room of reporters. This is by far the most attitude I've had towards the press in my career. I'm typically even-keeled and diplomatic, but we lost last night, flew a red-eye flight home afterward, and I was immediately whisked into a press conference this morning before I even made it home.

And the last thing I need while going on no sleep and stewing over my loss is some reporter throwing out obvious statements.

"How do you feel about that?" he amends.

"Not great. That loss is on me, I know that. Coming back from my injury, I know what's riding on my shoulders, and I didn't deliver."

We lost by two to Sacramento, and I was the one to miss the game winning three.

Hands shoot up around the room and the team's media coordinator chooses the next reporter to ask his question.

"There are rumors floating around the league about a possible trade if the team doesn't make the playoffs this season. What kind of pressure do you feel to deliver these next two wins?"

My eyes dart to Ron Morgan standing in the back of the room, arms crossed. There's no expression on his face whatsoever, and I couldn't tell you what he's thinking. Is he truly thinking of trading me? The rumor mill has been spinning with that one all week.

So yeah, not only do I feel the pressure from the city and the Devils organization to finally make the playoffs, but there's the added weight I've put on myself knowing my girlfriend, sister, and future brother-in-law are rooted in Chicago.

I've never felt more stressed about two games in my life.

"I don't feel the pressure," I lie. "I know what I have to do, what the team has to do in order to get the job done. And we will."

Looking back to Ron, he gives me a curt nod of his head.

"Next question," our coordinator continues as I sink into my seat, ready to be hounded with questions I don't want to answer.

Dragging my suitcase through the front door, I finally make it home.

I'm dead on my feet, not sleeping a wink on the airplane as last night's loss replayed in my mind on a constant loop. All I want to do is find Indy, pull her into my bed, and sleep the entire day away.

"Ind!" I call out, but she doesn't answer. "Blue, I'm home. Where are you?"

I check my room and her old one, the shower, and the kitchen. She's not home. Grabbing my phone to call her, I already have a text waiting.

**Blue:** *I have something to tell you when I get home and I've been so excited to see you that I couldn't sleep! Went to grab two coffees for us and one for Dave, just in case you're home before I'm back!*

With a smile on my face, I take a seat on the entryway bench and kick off my shoes. I'm far too fucking exhausted to stand while doing it, and I'm fairly certain I'll be sitting my happy ass right here until my girl is home and can take me to bed.

Reaching down, I tuck my shoes under the bench, but while bent over, I'm stopped in my tracks when I find a white plastic stick with a blue cap wedged underneath one of the wooden legs. As if it were dropped there and forgotten about.

I keep my house tidy as fuck, and even Indy has gotten better about it, so something so obviously out of place is easy to spot.

As soon as my hand reaches it, I know what it is, and my erratic heartbeat has a feeling it knows what it says. All the confirmation is right there in front of me as I hold it in front of my face in utter disbelief.

This can't be happening. *How* is this happening? I mean, I know *how*, but we're always safe. Always cautious. She told me it would take a miracle for it to happen naturally. How the fuck did this happen? And why the fuck is this down here? To hide it from me?

Clearly, she wasn't lying when she said she has something to tell me when she gets home because in my hands, I'm holding a pregnancy test that's practically screaming the word *positive* with its bold letters.

*Indy's* positive pregnancy test.

# 38

# Indy

I nearly sprint through the front door with a tray of coffees in my hand because I haven't seen Ryan in four days and I'm a needy bitch who wants his attention. Plus, I get to tell him that my parents booked a flight and are coming to visit soon. I can't wait for them to formally meet face-to-face.

But I don't have to make it far to find him sitting on the entryway bench, elbows to his knees and his head hanging low.

"Hi! I missed you!"

He draws his head back, but doesn't look at me, instead focusing on the ceiling, those ocean eyes filled with too many emotions I can't place.

"What's wrong?" Setting the tray on the kitchen island, I stand between his legs and run my hand over his hair. "Are you upset about the game last night?"

He chuckles a humorless laugh but there's no smile to accompany it. "No."

"Okay," I draw out. "What's bothering you?"

He shakes his head, unable to find the words to speak.

Attempting to shift the tone of this conversation, I take a deep breath. "Well, I have something exciting to tell you!"

Hand reaching up between our bodies, he holds a small plastic stick out for me to see. "I already know."

"What is that?"

He doesn't say anything.

"Is that a pregnancy test?"

"Clearly, Ind. How long have you known?"

*Wait. What?*

His eyes finally meet mine. It's evident now that he's not angry about last night's game. In fact, he's not angry at all. He's scared. As if every one of his insecurities is becoming a reality in this moment and I'm the face of them all.

I keep my tone soft. "There's nothing to tell, Ryan."

"Did you do this—" he begins before stopping himself, shaking his head.

Eyes widening, I take a step back and away from him, putting my hands up in defense.

"Fuck." He stretches for me, regret in his voice, but I keep myself out of reach. "No, Ind, I didn't mean it like that."

"Ask the question, Ryan."

He stands, shaking his head as he slowly steps towards me, but I mirror his actions, retracting at the same pace.

"No, baby, I didn't mean it like that."

Fear bubbles inside of me. "Ask the fucking question, Ryan!"

I refuse to cry when he refuses to speak. I'm too angry to cry. Too mad at myself for falling in love with a man who made it clear he didn't want the same things I did from the beginning.

"Ask me if I did it on purpose," I say for him. "That's what you're wondering, right?"

Ryan's eyes gloss over, regret pulling at every feature. "I'm not putting this on you, Indy. I'm just scared out of my goddamn mind and I'm fucking exhausted and I'm not thinking straight. I'm not reacting the right way."

For the first time in our relationship, I'm not the emotional one. He's on the verge of all out crying and I'm not sure if it's because he thinks I'm pregnant and that's the last thing he wants or if believes I betrayed him by getting knocked up.

He circles the kitchen island to meet me, but I maintain distance, my back to the front door.

"Blue, please."

He looks equally sad as he does hurt and part of me wants to hug him, but most of me is angry that he'd ever think I'd trap him, even for a second.

"You don't need to be scared, Ryan. I'm not pregnant. It'll be a miracle if that ever happens so thank you for reminding me of that and thank you for reminding me that the last thing you want in life is the thing I desire most." I exhale a humorless laugh. "We've never been on the same page, have we?"

With parted lips, Ryan's brows pinch together. "Indy." He squeezes the bridge of his nose. "I just need a moment to wrap my head around this. I…I didn't expect it."

Clearly, Ryan is ignoring the part where I told him I'm *not* pregnant. Maybe he's in shock. Maybe he can't grasp any of this. I'm trying to be understanding of his fears, but I refuse to spend my life convincing another man to want the same things I want.

"Sometimes I wish you had a normal job because then maybe you could trust there are no ulterior motives to loving you." Snagging my keys off the kitchen island, I quickly slip out into the hall. "Take all the time you need, Ryan."

"Indy!" I hear him shout through the door, but I don't turn around.

# 39

# Ryan

I should go after her, but I can't. All my feet are willing to do is pace the length of the living room as I freak the fuck out.

I completely blacked out. I can't recall half of what she said, but I know I fucked up.

I didn't mean to react that way, but my God, the look on her face. She wasn't even crying and that's the scariest part of all. My emotional girl wasn't emotional at all. She was hurt and I caused that.

This is what I've wanted. I just didn't expect it so soon. I'm a planner, a preparer. I would meet her parents, ask her to marry me, then do everything in my power to make her a mom. I'm not accustomed to my plan going out of order. I don't just dream and hope for the best.

At least, I didn't dream before her.

For only a split second, I saw Marissa standing in front of me. I relived that day she told me she was pregnant. I went through every emotion I felt for those nine months I thought I was going to be a dad. I was thrown back into that evening at the hospital when I found out her daughter wasn't mine. Every painful second of that day flashed in front of my eyes before the fog cleared and I saw Indy in front of me.

They're not the same. They've never been the same, and I treated Indy as if they were.

God, what the fuck is wrong with me? I'm equal parts ecstatic now that the realization is settling in, and terrified that I ruined what should be one of the best days of our lives.

She must be so upset. This is everything she's ever wanted, and I made her believe I didn't.

Just as I'm heading out the door to chase after her, it busts open. But instead of my girlfriend, it's my sister who is barreling into our home.

"Vee? What are you doing here?"

She doesn't look up or answer me, she simply rushes through my apartment, lifting pillows and pulling out drawers. She jogs into my bathroom, and I follow to watch her comb through every inch. I finally put a stop to her when she begins frantically sifting through the bathroom's trash can.

Bending down with her, I take the it from her grip. "Stevie, what the hell is going on?"

She stands with me, panic and worry covering her features. Her blue-greens gloss over as her chin begins to wobble.

"Ryan, I'm—" Her attention darts to my hand. "Where did you find that?"

Looking down, Indy's pregnancy test is sticking out of my closed fist.

Fuck. This isn't how she should find out. Indy should be here too, but I can't exactly lie to my sister in the moment I feel my most vulnerable.

Studying my face, her eyes narrow. "Have you been crying?"

"Vee, Indy is pregnant."

Stevie closes her eyes, exhaling a deep breath as tears stream down her freckled cheeks. "No, she's not, Ryan." Opening, her lashes brim with tears but at the same time, a smile pulls at her lips. "I am."

"What?"

"That's my test." Her smile widens but holds an apologetic edge. "Zee was home yesterday, and Indy was out running errands. I knew the apartment was empty, so I came here to take a test. Well, six tests." Chuckling, tears continue to stream down her face as she wipes them away with the sleeve of her shirt. "This morning I could only find five and I didn't want Indy to be the one to find the sixth."

An odd pit in my stomach forms as the realization settles in that this test isn't Indy's. Disappointment washes over me, but I shake it away, taking in the words that my sister just said.

"Stevie." My voice cracks as tears prick my own eyes. "You're pregnant?"

She nods with a laugh that quickly turns to a sobbing cry.

"Hey. Hey," I soothe, wrapping her in a hug, cupping her head to hide in my chest. "Why are you crying?"

"I don't know. Why are you?"

"Because my twin sister is going to be a mom, and you're going to make me an uncle."

"I'm scared."

"Why?"

"Because I didn't spend my entire life dreaming of this the way you did. I didn't think about kids until I met Zee."

"Stevie. You two are going to make the best parents. I mean, if they're anything like their dad we might be in trouble, but…"

Finally, Stevie laughs into my chest. "I hope they're just like him."

"Does he know?"

She shakes her head against me. "Not yet. I'm going to tell him today." Pulling away, she cleans up her face. "Do me a favor? Let me be the one to tell Indy. I'm… I don't know. I want her to hear it from me. I'm happy, so happy, but I don't want to rub it in her face. This is everything she's ever wanted."

A tsunami size wave of regret crashes over me as the blacked-out fog lifts, every single one of her words barreling back into my mind.

*I'm not pregnant.*

*It'll be a miracle if that ever happens.*

*Thank you for reminding me that the last thing you want in life is the thing I desire most.*

*We've never been on the same page, have we?*

"Stevie." Putting my hands on my head, I turn around and pace my bedroom, trying to take deep enough breaths to fill my lungs. "Stevie, I fucked up. Indy came home so excited to tell me something, and I thought it was hers. I didn't handle it well. She thought I was going to ask if she did it on purpose. I don't think I was going to ask that, but I'm not entirely sure I wasn't."

"No, Ryan."

"Everything with Marissa came flooding back and I got scared. I freaked out. And she was so hurt. She didn't even cry, Vee. She just looked at me as if I completely betrayed her. I did. I think I did betray her. This is everything she wants, and I made her feel like I didn't."

My sister's hands hide her face. "Ryan, Indy probably can't get pregnant on her own."

"I know that! God, I'm an idiot. I wasn't thinking."

She closes her eyes, pained. "She must be so upset."

"I made her feel like I don't want the same future she does. She probably thinks I've been stringing her along this entire time with no plans to give her the life she wants."

"Are you?" Stevie asks softly. "Ryan, I love you. You mean more to me than anyone in the world, but if there's even an ounce of you that doesn't want the same things she does, then you have to let her go. She's wasted too much time with someone who strung her along, and I can't let you do that to her again."

As much as Stevie is my other half, there are things not even she knows. Steps I've taken to give Indy the future she wants. The future *I* want too. I've always wanted a family but knowing I could do it at the same time as my sister, coupled with that quick but fleeting belief Indy was pregnant, I want it now more than ever.

"I would never let us get to this point if I wasn't on the same page. I saw what she went through, and I'd never do that to her."

Stevie nods.

"I need to go find her. Talk to her. Apologize. Do you think she went to your place?"

"I doubt it. You know how smart she is. I'm sure she put it together that it was my test right away. I think I know where she could be, but Ryan, I need to talk to her first."

Wrapping my sister up again, I kiss the top of her curly head of hair. "I really am so happy for you, Vee. You're going to be an incredible mom, and Zanders will be one hell of a dad."

"So will you, Ryan. When the time comes." She holds on tighter. "And in the meantime, you're going to be the greatest uncle. I know it."

# 40

# Indy

Rio's house reeks of boy.

There are piles of laundry and empty beer cans decorating his place, and the house was bursting with noise while he and three more guys from the hockey team played Xbox on the giant screen in his home theater.

I can't complain, though. As soon as he opened the front door and saw my bloodshot eyes, he kicked his teammates out and got me a fresh set of sheets for the guest bedroom.

"Ind, you've got a visitor," Rio says from the doorway.

Laying on the bed even though it's mid-morning, I keep my back to the door. "I don't want to talk to Ryan."

"How about me?"

Peeking over my shoulder at the sound of Stevie's voice, I find her leaning on the doorframe with Rio. Her bouncy curls are lively, but those eyes that match her twin only remind me of the fear I saw in his this morning.

I don't know if I'll ever be able to forget the absolute terror on Ryan's face, and I couldn't be more thankful that it wasn't my test. As much as I want a family, I'd rather be alone than have my partner feel trapped with me.

"You'll do."

A smile tugs at her lips as Rio leaves us alone.

Stevie climbs into the bed behind me, wrapping her arms around my shoulders.

"This is nice," I sigh. "Your brother always calls little spoon."

Stevie's chest vibrates behind my back. "You didn't send me a daily update today."

"Daily update, Vee—your brother doesn't want the same things I do, and I don't know where we go from here."

She runs a hand over my arm soothingly. "Did he say that?"

Tears fall down my face, hitting the pillowcase. "You should've seen him, Stevie. He was terrified." Sucking in a deep breath, I try to find enough oxygen to speak. "I've avoided bringing up the topic our entire relationship, hoping that when the time came to have it, he would be more open. But this morning, he made it evident that he never will be."

Stevie pauses, staying silent for a stretch of time.

"I love you, but I shouldn't be having this conversation with you," I continue. "Ryan needs you."

"Indy, you're still my best friend."

"And so is he. Will you make sure he's okay for me? Keep an eye on him? I can't do it right now."

She squeezes me tighter. "Of course, I will."

Turning around on the bed, I face her. "Are you really pregnant?"

Stevie's ocean eyes glass over. Unable to speak, she simply nods.

"Vee…" I wrap her up in a hug. "That's incredible. I'm so happy for you. That baby's genetics? Dear God, they're going to be stunning."

Both of us laugh and cry as we hold each other. Her because she's probably hormonal and me because well, I'm me.

She sniffles. "I was so afraid to tell you."

"Why?"

"Why do you think, Ind? And then Ryan goes and assumes. God, I feel terrible."

"Don't you dare." Pulling back to look at her, I move her curls behind her ear. "I'm so happy for you and Zanders."

"Yeah?"

"Of course, I am! I'm going to spoil the shit out of that babe. I hope they have a big enough closet because between me and their dad, they're going to have *the* most excessive wardrobe imaginable."

A smile breaks out along her lips, and though I would never say it because I refuse to make her feel bad, knowing my best friend—the love of my life's twin sister is about to start a family, has me longing to do it right along with her.

"Promise me that even if I'm not with Ryan, I'll still get to be Auntie Ind."

"You'll always be Auntie Ind." She offers me a sad smile. "Just talk to him, okay? When you're ready."

Nodding, I wipe at my wet cheeks as she does the same. "Well, aren't we pathetic," I laugh.

"The most pathetic." She pulls me into a hug again. "I love you."

"I love you too."

"Talk about a fantasy come to life! The two of you all wrapped up around each other in *my* bed? Lord, have mercy!"

I throw a pillow at the door. "Rio, get out!"

He lets the pillow smack him in his goofy face. "Someone else is here to see you."

Stevie wears an understanding smile. "You don't have to if you're not ready yet."

I look back to Rio. "I'm not. And he can't be here. He needs to get to practice."

Rio takes a deep breath as if he were about to tell his celebrity idol to leave, which is exactly what he's going to do. Gearing himself up, he leaves us alone once again.

"Do you need anything?" I ask. "Water. Food. How are you feeling?"

"I need to go tell Zee he's going to be a dad."

"What?" I sit up. "Stevie Renee Shay, are you kidding me? I know before him?!"

She sits up on the bed as well. "I had to make sure you were okay."

"Please go tell Zee Daddy Zanders that he's going to be an *actual* daddy."

"His name in my phone is about to take on a whole new meaning, huh?"

"Come on, man. Just let me talk to her. I already let you send me away once this morning."

I can hear Ryan's voice from Rio's guest room where I had myself a little cry before sleeping away the afternoon. I couldn't tell you what time it is, my phone has been turned off all day. Turns out that trying to come to terms with the idea of not spending your life with the person you love is exhausting.

"Ryan, you know I practically worship the ground you walk on, so telling you not to come into my house or resist asking you to autograph the poster I have of you hanging in my game room is testing my limits to the max. But she's not ready, and she's also one of my favorite people, so I'm going to take her side on this one."

"I know she's upset, but if I could just talk to her, everything would be okay—"

"She doesn't want to talk to you."

Ryan pauses. "She said that?"

"Verbatim." Another awkward silence. "Give her some time. I'm sure she will come to you when she's ready."

"Fuck," Ryan exhales and another stretch of silence lingers as if he were coming to terms and accepting the fact we won't be speaking tonight. "Will you keep an eye on her for me? Make sure she's okay?"

"Of course."

"Do you have food she can eat?" I can only imagine the horror on his face as his eyes roam the messy hockey frat house in front of him. "I'll have some groceries sent over. She's a vegetarian. And she likes her coffee over ice, so maybe put some in the fridge in the morning for her. Can you give this to her for me?"

The last thing I hear is the front door closing before my bedroom door opens.

Rio stands in the doorway with a duffel bag in his hand. "I know you're mad at him but let me make this moment about me. Indy, that was the hardest thing I've ever had to do. Ryan *freaking* Shay was standing on my front porch asking to come inside and I said no. Stevie should truly step aside because if that doesn't earn the title of best friend, I don't know what does."

"Thank you. I'm sorry I made you do that."

He drops the duffel bag on the bed. "He brought this for you." Rio turns to leave but stops once again in the doorway of his guest room. "He's devastated, Ind."

I nod, understanding that sentiment all too well. "I am too."

With a sympathetic smile, he leaves me alone for the night.

The harsh reality is that I don't love Ryan any less than I did this morning but recognizing that only hurts more to know we aren't on the same page. Just because our futures don't align doesn't mean the life-altering love I have for him has gone away.

Opening the bag, I find a pair of pajamas on top. The silky sleep set I wore the night we went camping and shared a bed for the first time. Underneath, there are more clothes, underwear, and socks. My toiletry bag I use to travel for work. He tucked my latest cross-stitch project and my current book in here as well.

And as I pull out each item, more tears fall from my face because I love him, and I love the way he loves me. So attentively. So quietly.

But today, it's the words that were the problem.

Words that were on the tip of his tongue, wondering if I tried to get pregnant on purpose. I can hardly wrap my head around the idea that he would compare me to someone who caused him the worst pain in his life.

He knows how badly I want that life, and it felt like a slap in the face to be accused of trying to steal it.

Needing an escape from my reality, I open my book and restart where I last left off. But what's holding my spot is not my usual bookmark, but a scrap of paper, torn and quickly scribbled on.

*Blue,*
*I'm not great with words, so I'll keep this short. I love you. I will love you as long as you'll allow me the privilege, and even longer after that. I have every intention to give you the life you want. I hope you'll let me.*
*You can even add this promise to the fridge when you get home.*
*-Ryan*

Sleep was almost nonexistent. In a bed that's not his. In a house that's not ours. Stacked pillows did nothing to trick my mind because every part of my body knew Ryan wasn't there.

Dragging myself out of the dark and lonely guest room, I find Rio in the kitchen with his signature boombox on full blast.

Seeing Rio in the kitchen making breakfast causes my chest to physically ache at the memories it induces.

It's been twenty-four hours and I miss Ryan more than I've ever longed for another person and one night apart has me questioning if the future I envisioned for myself is even worth it if Ryan isn't there.

Rio turns down the music before proudly sliding a cup to me. "Iced coffee."

Taking a sip, I almost choke on the bitterness of it, not to mention the texture of the grounds that found their way in. But I offer him a smile because the guy is trying.

"It's good."

"It's shit, isn't it?"

"Well, now that you say it…"

"I've never made the stuff. I don't drink coffee. Look at me." He motions down his body. "I'm wired enough as it is without the added help. The only reason I even have a coffee maker is for when the other guys from the team come over and want a cup."

As always, Rio makes me smile. It feels weird after an entire night of crying into my pillowcase for there to be a grin on my lips.

"You didn't have to make me some but thank you. I appreciate it more than you know. And thank you for letting me stay."

"Of course, Indigo. You're my girl. I've got your back."

He turns back to the stove where a few vegetarian sausages are sizzling over the flame, and without asking, I know Ryan took the liberty to have groceries sent over.

"You're wrong, by the way," he says.

"Wrong about what?"

"Me not having to make you coffee. I had Ryan Shay standing in my doorway telling me how his girlfriend likes her coffee and if you don't think the look he gave me while he said it screamed *'you better fucking make her coffee when she wakes up'* well then, babe, you're wrong."

An audible laugh bubbles out of my lips and I almost shock myself at the sound. Rio always knows how to put a smile on my face. The same way Stevie does and Zee. The same way I'm always wearing one around Ryan. This family I've created over the last year and a half is new in my life but holds a weight far more significant than the friends I kept for an entire lifetime.

Sometimes history really means nothing when the right people walk into your life.

"Speaking of Ryan Shay," Rio begins again. "There's a basketball player sleeping in my driveway who's worth more money than I'll ever see in my lifetime."

"He came back?"

"He never left. The guy slept in his car, and honestly, if I were into dudes that right there would have me folding."

I push his head away with a laugh. "He's already spoken for, so don't even think about it."

I still have no idea what to say to Ryan. These hours away from him have only confused me even more. Is any of it worth it without him?

Regardless, he can't be sleeping in his car. He's got two of the most important games in his career coming up, and I refuse to let something as trivial as lack of sleep be the reason he doesn't perform at his best.

Heading for the front door, I grab my coat.

"Please don't tell him how shitty my coffee was!" Rio shouts from the kitchen.

Ryan's Range Rover sits parked on the curb outside the front of the house, windows rolled up, but I can see him reclined in the driver's seat with a coat bundled around him.

Tapping on the glass, I stir him awake.

He startles, taking a moment to reacclimate himself to his surroundings until his attention falls to me, just outside the window. His brows pull in, but a breath of relief blows from his lips.

I assumed he'd roll down his window so we could talk, but instead, Ryan opens his door and instantly pulls me into his body. Standing and swaying, he keeps his chin on my head and holds on to me like he never plans on letting me go.

"Did you get some sleep?" he asks.

"Not really. Did you?"

"Not really."

"I would bring you a cup of coffee, but Rio's coffee sucks compared to yours."

His laugh rumbles in his chest, until finally, he pulls away enough to see me. "Please come home."

Tears prick the back of my eyes. "Ryan, I can't."

"Please, Ind."

"Do you remember what you said to me the first morning we had breakfast together? You told me that I should never have to beg someone to be ready for a future. And I won't. Not again. Those were your words, Ryan."

His eyes close as he runs his palm down his face. When they reopen, they're as glassy as mine.

"You don't have to beg, Ind. I'll give you everything you could want."

I'd love to believe him. Everything would feel better if I did, but I know deep down it would only fix the hurt on the surface. Ryan has never once shown any signs of wanting the family I do, and I blindly turned away as if I didn't notice. Anytime children came up in conversation, his desire for them was always used in past tense.

"But is it what *you* want? Or would you have children with me just because it's what *I* want? Ryan, I love you far too much to allow you to spend the rest of your life fulfilling my every wish if those dreams aren't yours also."

"They are," he begs me to understand. "I told you, I'm in it."

It might hurt, but I don't know how else to get him to comprehend my fear that the words he's saying could just be pretty words he knows I want to hear.

"Ryan, I spent six years hearing those exact words."

He jolts, his head falling back to his car. "I'm not him."

"I know you're not. I just want you to understand where I'm coming from. Yesterday scared me, Ry."

"I didn't mean to say that. To compare you to her. I didn't really even think that."

As if it were second nature to him, Ryan thumbs under my eyes, more concerned with my emotions than his own.

"You could tell me until you're blue in the face that you want to have kids with me, but what if that *was* my test? What if I really was pregnant? You were petrified, almost upset, thinking I was. Ryan, promised words don't mean much when that reaction was our reality."

His Adam's apple moves in a deep swallow. "I know. I fucked up and I'll own that."

"Let's think for a second, okay?"

"I don't need to think! I know what I want."

"But I do need to think," I say softly. "I love you, Ryan. So much, but I can't go back to that apartment right now when I know the second I walk through the door, I'll forget about everything simply because being there with you makes me happy. I owe myself a moment to think clearly. This is the rest of my life. Yours too."

He blows out a deep exhale, looking away from me as he tries to come to terms that I'm not going home with him today.

Ryan folds his arms around my shoulders, kissing my forehead before leaving his lips to linger there. "I love you." He threads his fingers through my hair, cupping my head to tilt my attention up. "Promise me you're not giving up on us."

"I'm not."

Bending down, he kisses me with warm, parted lips and I lean into him, deepening it. His fingers curl into my hair, holding me there and I give in, memorizing every pull of his lips, every satisfied sound from his throat.

Pulling away, he dots another kiss on my cheek then on my forehead before sending me on my way back to the house.

He watches as I walk inside, folded arms on the roof of his car. "Tell Rio if he's gonna fuck up the coffee then he needs to have some delivered for you!"

With a small smile on my face, I close the front door behind me, all while knowing I'll have a coffee delivered in less than thirty minutes from the man outside.

# 41 Indy

The fertility clinic's waiting room doesn't look much different than that of a hospital. White sterile walls, terribly upholstered seats, outdated oak furniture, and magazines that came out six months ago.

I sit, holding my paperwork with bouncing knees as I wait for my name to be called. The timing of this appointment couldn't be worse, but with the regular season of hockey winding down, I need to be ready as soon as the playoffs end, whether that's next week or after another Stanley Cup Final.

Today's appointment is simply a pre-check to make sure I'm healthy and all my lady parts are cooperating. As soon as the hockey season ends, I'll begin right away with the injections. Honestly, it's a bunch of doctor talk that I don't fully understand, but I do know the process causes my eggs to mature so they can go in, get them out, and put those suckers on ice.

There are three other families in the waiting room. One with a newborn baby, another with a toddler, and the other is a couple who looks hopeful for their first. I'm the only person here alone.

I didn't tell Ryan that my appointment was today, because in all honesty, I don't know that I should even be here.

If Ryan isn't involved, what's the point? Yes, I've always wanted kids, but not without him. That realization hit me like a truck this morning as I was getting in my car to come here, and now, as I sit here alone, I'm still asking myself the same thing.

If he doesn't want this, do *I* want it still?

I was already worried this would be a waste of money before I found out it was covered by insurance because who knows if it'll even work. But now I'm wondering if it's also a waste of time. I can't see myself doing this without him.

"Indigo Ivers," the older woman at the front desk calls out.

"That's me." I hold up my paperwork before making my way to her.

She types in some of my info as I stay standing and waiting on the other side.

"How's your day going?" I ask, attempting to drown out my own thoughts.

"It's going great, baby, how's yours?"

"I'm not really sure how it's going."

She laughs. "Are you nervous, honey?"

"I think I am."

"Are you by yourself today?"

A knot forms in my throat. "Yes."

"Good for you," she says, impressed as she continues to type, her long nails clicking against the keyboard. "It's smart to plan ahead for yourself. You never know when you'll meet the right person."

"I already have."

Her eyes lift above the monitor and a sly smile curves on one side of her lips. Just as quickly, her attention falls back to her computer where she *tap, tap, taps* away, adding all my personal information into their system.

"I should have a copay due today."

She looks over her screen with detail, shaking her head. "Nope."

"Really? That's weird. I always have a copay when using my insurance."

"Oh, you're not using your insurance."

"I should be. Could you please check?"

*Tap. Tap. Tap.*

"No, baby, your insurance policy doesn't cover any of it."

Are you freaking kidding me? There's no way in hell I can pay for this out of pocket. I stopped saving months ago, back in January when I was told my insurance benefits changed with the start of the year.

Exhaling, my entire body slumps. "Are you sure?"

"Positive. I can show you if you'd like."

"No, that's okay."

Fuck. I'm on the verge of calling my parents for a loan, even though I promised myself I never would. Something about needing my parents' help to start my own family feels off, but I'm desperate now. The time to save money has run out.

And once again I'm asking myself if any of this is even worth it.

Nervously, I fidget with my debit card in my hands. "How much is due today?"

*Tap. Tap. Tap.*

"Nothing. It's fully covered."

"But you said—"

"Not by insurance. Personal credit card paid for the whole thing months ago."

*He didn't.*

Closing my eyes, I repeat her words over and over again until they sink in. She doesn't have to tell me the name on the card on file, I already know.

With my elbows on the counter, I bury my face in my hands. "Can you tell me when it was paid?"

"Looks like it was back in mid-December."

Right after we went camping, when I first told him why I was saving money. Right before there was ever an "insurance benefit change."

"Honey, are you crying?"

With my hands covering my face, I nod. "It's kind of my thing."

She chuckles, deep and hearty. "Sounds like you were right when you said you had already met the right person."

"Indy." Rio reaches over his couch from behind me and closes the book in my hands. "Look, I love you, you know this, but you can't stay here forever."

"I've only been here for a few days, and you said I could stay however long I'd like."

"I changed my mind."

Turning back, my head over my shoulder, I look at him with confusion.

"I have my broker coming by to take you to go look at some apartments today."

"What? No, I don't want to look at apartments." I stand from the couch to face him. "I don't know that I'm even planning to move out from Ryan's. I just needed a few days."

"It's been a few days."

Jolting back, I eye him. "Do you have a girl coming over? Are you just trying to get me out of the house? Is that what this is about? I can go hide in the guest room if you'd like."

He scoffs. "I wish I had a girl coming over. Now go take a shower and put on something that isn't that three-day old sweatshirt with spaghetti sauce on it." He cringes. "You need to look good for... my broker."

Taking slow steps towards the guest room, I keep my narrowed eyes on him over my shoulder. "You're being so weird right now."

"I love this part of town," Rio's broker, Cindy, says as she continues to drive us thirty minutes outside of the city. "Real quiet. Good place to raise kids. Great school district."

"I'm only looking for myself."

*Actually, I'm not looking at all.*

"This part of town has a wonderful safety score. Walkable. Quaint grocery stores and a lot of land. Plenty of hiking spots. Give it a couple of months and this whole town will be covered in greenery and flowers. It's beautiful."

"That does sound nice."

*If I were looking.*

She continues to drive us around and she was right. It does seem like a quiet town, thirty minutes away from the hustle and bustle of downtown Chicago. Ryan would like it here. He'd probably be able to go to the grocery store on his own without being bombarded or take a long walk outside without the media on his ass.

"Here we are."

She pulls into the long driveway of a stunning house. White exterior with black trim. Elm trees line the driveway and their color is beginning to come back after a harsh winter. A cozy porch wraps around the entire house where a swing hangs by the front door. There isn't another home in viewing distance, and I can tell, just from the front, that the property in the back is vast and seemingly endless.

"I think this is the wrong address," I tell her. "It's only me. I'm not looking for anything this big and even if I were, I couldn't afford it." An awkward laugh bubbles out of me and I keep my seat belt in place, ready for her to drive off to the *correct* location.

"Well, let's go in and take a look, shall we? Stunning home. Would hate to just drive away."

Cindy is already out of the car before I have another moment to protest. Unfastening the seat belt, I cautiously follow her up the large set of stairs leading to the front porch.

The area surrounding the house is silent minus the distant chirp of birds. It's a complete and utter change from the apartment on the twenty-second floor in downtown Chicago. I can't help but wonder how many stars you'd be able to see out here without the glaring lights of the city.

The fresh garden beds lining the staircase with small buds sit ready for dirt and rain to create something beautiful.

Cindy doesn't use a key to unlock the double doors that lead into the house. She simply turns the knob and opens them. Staying on the front porch, she ushers me in.

The waft of fresh coffee overwhelms me along with that distinctly sweet smell of French toast.

A large double staircase frames the foyer. There are rooms to both my left and right. The house seems mid-renovation, but one is definitely a family room and the other is for dining.

But straight ahead, the kitchen stove crackles, and I can see puffs of steam even from here.

Cindy closes the door, and when I look back, she's nowhere to be found. She left me inside alone.

I follow my nose to the giant kitchen in the back of the house. White cabinets, stainless steel appliances, and an island large enough for a family of six to eat breakfast at.

But the most beautiful part of the house is the man with his back to me, working at the stove. Backwards hat, hoodie, and joggers. He seems as relaxed and comfortable as he does at home, and I couldn't be more thankful to Rio that he made me get off my ass and brush my hair.

And it's quickly becoming evident that there were no apartments to look at with his broker. He just needed to get me out here.

"Ryan?" I look around. "What's going on?"

Turning to face me, that stunning smile spreads, showcasing his puckered dimples. "Take a seat." He motions to the kitchen island.

In a daze, I pull out a stool and sit, my eyes wandering to the colorful bouquet in the center of the island.

"I'll have you know I've kept those alive for three whole days now."

The ease of his voice causes a grin to fall across my lips.

Ryan puts a plate in front of me. French toast, eggs, and a side of fruit, but he doesn't have more food to plate for himself. He slides an iced coffee to me before setting down a new creamer to try—mint chocolate chip.

"What's going on? Where are we?"

He doesn't answer my question.

"I said the wrong words the other day," he says instead. "And there are some others you need to hear."

Swallowing, I give him my full attention.

"I didn't realize how lonely I was until you. All this time, you were existing outside of those four walls of my apartment. Everything I've ever needed existed outside of that apartment. Then you came inside and brought me back to life and I refuse to go back to my world before you. I won't go back to life before you, Ind."

"I don't want a life without you either, Ryan, but sometimes it's not as simple as that. Life isn't black and white."

"You don't think I know that? I haven't seen black and white since the second you walked into my apartment. Now it's pink-painted toes, purple clothes, green plants, and those goddamn yellow curtains." He shakes his head. "And so much fucking Blue. All I see is Blue."

Translation: All I see is *you*.

Tears prick my eyes and I'm shocked I have more to shed.

"I love that you read romance novels to feel something. I love that you love flowers and plants because nurturing and allowing something to grow is second nature to you. I love that you experience every emotion so hard it takes over your entire body. But baby, I want to be the one to make you feel how your favorite books do. I want to be the one to give you children to nurture and grow. When you think of me, the only emotion I want you to feel is unconditional, earth-shattering love. Because when I look at you, I see my entire future and I can't stand to live in a world where you look at me and don't see the same thing."

Wiping, I dry my cheeks. "I do, Ryan, you know that. I'm just so afraid of pulling you into a life that you don't want. Or *didn't* want until the other day. This wasn't part of your plan."

"What if I had changed my plans for you?"

A rebuttal sticks in my throat.

"I heard you, Blue. The other morning when you said words were just words, you were right. We've both been told a lot of things that didn't hold weight, and because of that, I've loved you through my actions. I let them speak for me."

His quiet love. It's always the loudest.

Quickly, my eyes dart to the fridge where our lease agreement and bucket lists hang, accompanied by another stack of papers.

"I know what I signed up for when I fell in love with you. From the beginning, you made it perfectly clear what you wanted your life to look like, and I've been taking steps to make that happen even when you weren't aware. So no, Ind, you don't have to beg me for a future because this is what I've wanted all along."

He takes the new papers I've never seen off the fridge and places them next to my breakfast. "I bought us this house back in January." Flipping to the last page of what I realize now is the deed, he points to the final line. "And if you don't believe me, your name is right there."

It is. He put my name right along his on the title of the house with a date in January. Only days after his knee injury.

"I've always known, Ind. I've wanted everything you want ever since you walked into my world and reminded me of who I am. You made me hopeful for those things, a real partner, a family, children. Parts of life I had convinced myself I would never have because no one would ever truly love me for the man I am and not just the name I carry.

"I want this place to be where everyone gathers. I want team dinners here. I want our friends over. I want our kids to have their friends over.

We can breathe out here, Ind. There are no fans or media waiting outside of the building. You should see the stars at night. It's incredible, and there's so much room outside. You can have a whole garden or a greenhouse. And I can't wait to watch you turn this house into a home just like you did with the apartment."

He's so light out here, a stunning smile beaming on his handsome face. The heaviness of the city, the burden of the game is too far away, and I love seeing him so free.

"I think part of me will always want to hide away, but I want to hide here, with you." Rounding the island, he wipes at my tears. "Baby, you can't get makeup and tears on the deed to the house."

Chuckling, the tension breaks.

Pulling me in, he kisses my temple. "I've been having the house worked on since I bought it. It's not quite done. Some rooms still need paint and obviously we need more furniture, but it's livable. Your bed is in the primary bedroom and some of your clothes too. I'll have your car brought out today, but will you stay here while you think? This place has five bedrooms and when I bought it, I had every intention of filling them all. I want you to see this house when you're asking yourself if you're trapping me into a life I don't want, okay?"

Through shaky breaths, I nod. "Words of affirmation."

"What?"

"You said you weren't good with words, but I think words of affirmation might be your love language. Or acts of service. Or gift-giving. God, I don't even know anymore."

He chuckles.

"I love you."

"I love you, Blue. So fucking much and I'll fight for you forever, but I need you to fight for us too. Now eat your breakfast, it's getting cold."

He adds one final kiss on my forehead before heading towards the front door.

"Ryan."

He turns to face me.

"Why did you pay for my fertility treatments? I didn't want anyone paying for that."

"No, you didn't want your *parents* paying for that. You said you felt uncomfortable for someone else paying for you to start a family. Well, it's going to be my family too, so I don't count."

"But that was back in December. Even then?"

*He knew even then?*

"Even then."

With that, he leaves me with my breakfast and a giant house that he wants to fill with our family.

# 42

# Indy

I can only eat half of the French toast Ryan made me. I wish he stayed and finished the rest.

I'm overwhelmingly full from his words, from the knowledge that he bought this house months ago. That he paid for my fertility treatments months ago. It has absolutely nothing to do with the money. I might joke that I'm an expensive girlfriend, but I couldn't care less about how much money he makes. I'd be happy to live in a cardboard box with that guy.

But the meaning behind the gesture, that's what's so overwhelming. That he's known all this time he wanted to have a family with me. I just wanted us to be on the same page, but this? This is more than my romantic heart could dream of.

Finally leaving the kitchen after a solid hour of sitting in pure shock, I take myself on a self-guided tour. The first level flows from one room to another, separated only by walls when necessary. It's open and airy. The perfect space for guests to mingle while I host. I can picture Ryan's team dinners here, and nights of having our friends over. Stevie's baby shower, and hopefully, one day, my own.

The walls still smell of fresh paint, and the floor looks newly replaced. The first floor boasts both a family and living room, a dining room, and a casual breakfast nook. Even if I picked my dream home out of a magazine, it still wouldn't be as perfect as this one.

Taking one set of stairs, I find the second floor. Four bedrooms are connected by two jack and jill bathrooms. This floor also includes a large loft and all I can picture is the potential for it to be a playroom.

Up one more flight of stairs, I'm greeted with the primary bedroom which makes up the entirety of the third floor. Tall windows face the backyard, letting in so much warmth and light. There's a bench seat under one of them and I can't help but dream of reading here or watching my family play together outside. My bed is in this room as are my books and clothes, all set up and put away.

The room is huge, this house is huge, and I can feel this space bursting with energy, needing to be filled with family and friends.

And as I step outside onto the back porch, filling my lungs with fresh spring air, I can imagine it all. But being here feels wrong without him, which I'm sure was his intention when he asked me to stay and think.

I don't need to think. The second his actions backed up the words, I didn't need to ponder anything else. Ryan is it for me. It didn't take six years for me to know. It didn't even take six months. My heart has been his even when I thought I didn't have any left of it to give.

He healed it when someone else broke it, and now it's his forever.

I never liked being alone. The silence would allow the insecurities to creep in. That I'm not enough or that I'm far too much. That I'm not deserving of the life I want. I'd wear that perfect mask in public, ensuring others were comfortable around me. Not too happy. Not too sad. Not too talkative, but not too quiet either. It was exhausting.

But here, sitting on the back porch of the house Ryan bought for us, I'm content. I'm at peace.

I'm home.

I've gained a new appreciation for the quiet since I met Ryan. The silence allows for a moment of introspection. Now, that silence screams with reminders that I'm worthy. That I'm deserving of the love I read about. I'm deserving of the family I desire, and I know this because I fell in love with a man while I was being completely and utterly myself and he fell right alongside me.

As I sit on the top step of the back porch, the front door creaks open behind me. Over my shoulder, I find my curly-haired best friend headed straight towards me, two bottles in her hands.

She takes a seat right next to me as we both keep our attention on the never-ending acres of land in front of us.

"I brought your car," Stevie finally says before handing me a bottle of beer.

"Thanks, Vee."

She clinks hers with mine.

"I'm more of a gin and tonic kind of gal." Stating the obvious, as if she didn't already know, I take a swig.

"Even at ten in the morning?"

"There's no time limit on a good cocktail."

"Well now that your best friend is preggo, you're a non-alcoholic beer type of gal." Her blue-greens make their way to me as a smile creeps across her lips.

"Did that feel funny to say?" I laugh.

"So weird."

Redirecting my attention to the greenery in front of me, we both stay silent for a few minutes, taking in the crisp air, the fresh smells. The freedom this place provides.

"What are you thinking about, Ind?"

I'm thinking about raising kids with the woman next to me. About getting to call my best friend my sister-in-law. About being an aunt to that sweet baby she's growing. About spending our days together at the United Center watching Ryan or Zanders play then spending our evenings out here.

I bring my bottle to my lips. "I'm thinking about how hot I'm going to be as an NBA wife."

Stevie laughs, her head leaning on my shoulder. "How lucky am I that my best friend and my brother love each other so much?"

I lean my head on hers. "Are we doing this forever or what? The four of us. Raising babies, and growing old together?"

"You tell me, Indy. Are we doing this forever?"

All I can see in this backyard is the rest of our lives. Every birthday. Every holiday. Every warm summer evening and chilly winter morning. And every image centers around the man my heart, mind, and soul loves.

For the first time in my life, I don't have to romanticize any of it. Ryan has made my dream a reality.

I dreamt for him.

"Daily update, Vee—we're doing this forever, but first I need your help with something."

"You let me know when you're ready," David, my doorman says.

"Harold should be pulling up any minute."

Standing in the lobby, the two of us eye the horde of fans outside the building. After last night's win, we're only one away from securing a playoff spot for the first time in six years. It's not the equivalent of winning a championship by any means, but it's still big for this city.

"I haven't seen Miss Ivers in almost a week, and I heard there were movers taking her stuff away the other day."

David is a discreet man, but we've known each other far too long for him to pretend to be discreet with me.

"I bought a house about thirty minutes away from the city. Indy is staying there."

His white brows shoot up. "You're moving?"

"I don't know about that. I bought it for her, and I won't live there without her."

He nods, lips pressed together as if he's thinking better of speaking, but decides to anyway.

"Mr. Shay, in my almost four decades of doing this job, you have been my favorite tenant. You're kind, generous, and more down-to-earth than any twenty-seven-year-old who makes the kind of money you make should be. But son, in the almost five years you've lived here, the only time you've been able to step outside is to rush into a car or rush into the building across the street to see your sister. You're not *living* here. You're being watched." He motions towards the crowd of fans waiting for me out front. "I will miss the heck out of you, but I hope you and Miss Ivers get out of here and find a place where you can have a moment of peace."

That's exactly what that house means to me. I sensed it the second I walked in. It had the potential to be a home, and I could picture Indy in every room. I could see her in the garden or the kitchen. I could see her lounging in the living room or in our bedroom.

It's the perfect place to hide, and I hope she decides to hide with me.

I pat him on the shoulder. "Dave." Pausing, the two of us exhale a small laugh at my accidental use of Indy's nickname for him. "*David*, if I do move, you and the family will have to come over to visit, yeah?"

"We'd love to."

Harold parks right in front of my building and David opens the lobby door for me.

Keeping my head down, I sign a handful of autographs all while quickly continuing to the car. As soon as I'm safely inside, Harold takes off towards the practice facility where I'll be rushed into yet another press conference before I'm even allowed to step foot on the court.

Resting my head back, I watch the city zoom by.

I haven't slept much this week thanks to an overwhelming combination of missing Indy and regretting how I handled that morning a few days ago. I'm proud of her though. If I were an outsider looking in and saw the way I reacted to thinking she was pregnant, I'd want her to leave me too. She deserves to have everything she wants out of life, and a year ago, I'm not sure she would've been strong enough to walk away the way she did.

The last thing I want is for her to leave me, but I do love seeing her brave enough to stand up and demand what she wants.

But I *am* what she wants. I know without a shadow of a doubt that I am.

Now, if she could fucking call me and ask me to move in to the house with her, that'd be great.

She's lived there for three days now and, yes, I've bombarded my sister with texts and calls. She doesn't tell me much other than that my girlfriend is fine, so I try to leave it at that.

In our press conference, Ethan sits to one side of me and my coach to the other. It's a nice reprieve to not be the only person behind the mic, but it doesn't much matter, most every question is still being directed at me.

"Shay." A reporter in the first row stands and speaks into the microphone. "How are you holding up under the pressure?"

"I don't feel the pressure."

*Lie.* Ethan watching me out of the corner of his eyes confirms that he knows I'm lying too.

"First potential playoff berth in six years if you can pull off the win tonight. You don't feel any pressure?"

As always, I put on the mask. *Calm. Cool. Collected.*

"Nope."

Another reporter stands. "What do you think it will say about your future in this game if you don't make the playoffs this year? You've been in the league for five years now, and you've yet to lead your team into the postseason.

"I haven't thought about it, seeing as I fully intend on us making the playoffs."

The questions continue, and I couldn't tell you my response to half of them.

"Since college, you've been referred to as the next Michael Jordan. At what point will fans stop making that comparison?"

"Do you think you're adequately producing to justify the salary you're bringing in?"

"Do you want a trade? There are stronger teams out there who would snatch you up in heartbeat if you became available. Do you think it may be best for Chicago to start fresh with younger talent?"

"Speaking of trades, do you think this is your last night in a Devils jersey if you can't pull off the win?"

"No," Ethan says into the microphone even though the question was directed at me. "He's signed here for three more seasons. He's not going anywhere. Anyone got a question for me? I'm here too, you know."

A small chuckle settles among the crowd, taking some of the weight off my chest, but it doesn't last long.

"Shay, do you feel the burden to be on at all times? To constantly be perfect?"

Ethan eyes me again before leaning forward to take over this press conference.

"Yes," I say before he can stop me. "I feel the burden every day."

Those words echo off the mic as the reporters go eerily quiet at my candor. I've never been so honest with the media in my life.

"I love this team and even more, I love this game. But for the past four seasons, part of me despised it. There's been a constant pressure to not show any weaknesses, to not let you all know how scared I am to fail or to let this city down."

The last reporter who asked a question takes a seat alongside his peers. Cameras continue to roll, and heads are buried in notepads as they jot down my statements.

Clearing my throat, I sit up and closer to the mic. "There's this insane pressure in professional sports to be perfect at all times. To be a machine. I have thousands of people watching my every move to see if I'm worth my salary, and I can't complain. I have the best job in the entire world, and I love our fans, but I am human. As much as I tried to convince myself I wasn't, I am. I make mistakes. I have bad games. I miss important shots and I beat myself up over those failures more than any fan, coach, or GM would."

Ethan adds an encouraging squeeze to my shoulder just as I catch Ron Morgan's attention, standing in the back of the room.

"I've done some outrageous things to convince others I'm the right man for the job." I take my eyes off Ron, returning them to the media. "And even more so, I convinced myself of things in order to believe I could be this machine who doesn't lose his cool, who isn't scared to fail. I've cut out friendships and relationships. I've isolated myself, and all it's done is taken this game I love and turned it into something I resent."

I clear my throat again when the room remains silent.

"My first two years in the league were some of the hardest of my life. Ticket sales were through the roof and my jersey was selling like crazy, so what's there to complain about, right?" I chuckle a humorless laugh. "Fuck, those years sucked. I was in a dark place. Being new in the league was a wakeup call that I was no longer a man, simply an asset, and I didn't handle the realization well at all. I've been lying to y'all for years.

I feel the pressure every fucking day, but this season, for the first time in a long time, the game has been fun again.

"So, yes, I hope we win tonight, but the sun will still rise if we don't. I'll still have my family and friends and teammates if we don't. And I hope I don't get traded because I fucking love this team and I love this city, but that's out of my control. So I'm going to go out there tonight and try my best while I have some fun with my guys."

I stand from my seat, with a wave. "Thanks."

There's a blanket of noise behind me, reporters calling out my name, cameras flashing, but I don't stop and turn around. I take off down the private hall blocked by security.

Ron enters into the hall through a side door. His back is to me, unknowing I'm behind him as he starts down the walkway.

"Mr. Morgan," I call out, jogging to meet up with him. "Sir."

He stops, turning on his dress shoes, his pressed suit perfectly in place.

"I apologize if what I said in there causes the organization any grief."

He shakes his head, confused.

"I know that's not really on brand for me to admit those things, but—"

"Thank God you finally did." He laughs. "That's the Ryan Shay I've been wanting people to see all these years. That's the Ryan Shay I scouted out of college. It's good to see him again."

He smacks my shoulder, turning down the hall again.

"Are you trading me if we lose tonight?" I call out.

He laughs so loudly it echoes off the empty hallway walls.

"Hell no. I've got the best point guard in the league. Hell, maybe the best point guard the game has ever seen and he's on *my* payroll. You think I'm giving that up? Not to mention, you're kind of growing on me, kid."

As I stay silent, Ron eyes me curiously before continuing.

"This probably isn't what any profitable General Manager would say, but I'm not worried about the scoreboard. I want guys that want to be here. That enjoy their teammates. I want the rest of the league to look at the Chicago Devils organization and wonder how they could get traded here because the guys who play for me love their jobs. *That* is what's going to win us a championship. *That* is what's going to make us successful, and Shay, for the first time in five years, I think you might love your job."

"I do, sir."

"Good."

He lingers as if I have something else to say and maybe I do. Maybe there's something about this utter honesty thing.

"Can I tell you something that might make you change your mind and trade me?"

He chuckles. "Shoot."

"Indy wasn't my girlfriend when I first told you about her. We pretended to be a couple to convince you that I had softened up enough to be the kind of captain you wanted me to be. I completely lied to your face."

Ron's expression turns cold and stoic.

"She was just my sister's best friend who moved in because I had an extra room."

Ron's serious face melts into a smile which morphs into uncontrollable belly laughs.

"No way!" He holds a hand to his chest. "Caroline was right all along! God, I'm going to hear so many 'I told you so's' tonight when I get home."

"Sir?"

"My wife, she knew you two were full of shit as soon as she saw you at the fall banquet together. On the other hand, you had me convinced. The only reason I had any doubts was because she was chirping in my ear."

"She knew?"

"Of course, she knew! Who the hell goes camping in the middle of winter in Chicago?" He laughs again. "She assumed if we kept getting you two together, maybe it'd happen for real, and it did. Shay, you may have been lying to convince me you were someone else, but you became that man regardless."

"So, you're not mad?"

"No." His chest rumbles. "I think the whole thing is hilarious."

I smile, feeling much lighter now that all this fake shit is off my chest. "I really do love her though. Now."

"Yeah, no shit, Shay. You don't make the kinds of changes you've made for any reason other than love."

He puts his hand out to shake mine and as I do, he pulls me into a hug.

"So, to be clear," I ask again. "You're not trading me?"

"I'm fairly certain Caroline would trade *me* for a new husband if I did. She really loves having Indy around and I couldn't think of a better captain for this team."

Lips pressed together, I dip my chin. "Thank you, sir."

He takes off down the hall again. "Dinners don't end when the season does!" he calls out. "I expect to see you, Indy, Ethan, and Annie at least once a month all summer long."

A smile slides across my mouth. "We'll host."

*Hopefully.*

# 44

# Ryan

I caught a flash of blonde hair in the middle of the third quarter when I allowed myself a moment to look into the stands.

Indy is here with Zanders and Stevie, and that alone feels like a win. The second win is coming in about fifteen seconds as the clock runs down on the final regular game of the season, ending with the Devils up by fourteen.

Our first playoff berth in six years.

It's about time. For me. For this team. For this city.

For the first time since I've been in the league, my future with this organization feels hopeful. Like we could make a real championship run in the coming years. Our attention no longer lies on how to avoid being the last in the league, but instead, it's figuring out how to be the best.

For now, we'll take our eight seed and see what comes of this playoff run in the coming weeks when we go against the number one seed in the Eastern conference. Realistically, this season might not last too much longer, but we accomplished the one thing we set out to do, and that right there feels like our own version of a championship.

As the buzzer sounds, I stand from the bench where I enjoyed the majority of the fourth quarter and Ethan is the first man I see. He puts his hand in mine, swinging his other over my shoulder in a hug.

"Hell of a job," he says into my ear, patting the back of my head.

"You too, man. Thank you."

I'm not about to get all sappy on the spot, but he knows what I mean.

*Thank you for mentoring me. For having my back and supporting me as we transition from his captaincy to mine. For being my friend when I thought I didn't need any.*

There are no confetti, no banners, or parades for this win. This isn't a championship by any means. On the big stage of the NBA, this is just another victory, but here in Chicago, it's everything.

Leon jumps onto another rookie like a couple of kids on Christmas morning. Our coaching staff hugs and congratulates each other, and Dom rushes to his mom sitting in row three.

We still have a long road ahead of us, but this is a milestone I've yet to meet in my career, and I'll take it.

My shower is quick, as is our postgame meeting, and I practically sprint to the family waiting room once released. Stevie and Zanders are the only two waiting for me, and as much I love them, the disappointment is obvious.

"Nice game!" my sister exclaims.

I wrap my arms around her, before doing the same to my future brother-in-law.

"You weren't complete shit," he says.

"Can't say the same for you. What the hell was with you in that game I watched last night?"

"I was distracted! I just found out I'm going to be a daddy. Sorry that hockey wasn't the first thing on my mind."

I playfully clap my palm against his cheek. "Well, at least somebody will call you that so you can stop asking my sister to."

Zanders' hazel eyes swing to Stevie. "I'll never stop begging, sweetheart."

She slides her bottom lip between her teeth. "I do love when you beg."

"Okay," I cut in. "Can a man not get one night of peace? And at my place of work?"

"It's my place of work, too, buddy."

Turning to my sister, I get straight to the point. "Where is she?"

She shrugs. "She had to go do something."

"What the hell could be so important that she had to leave as soon as my game ended?"

"She might come by our place later. You'll come over tonight, right? After you go home."

"Yeah," I sigh, defeated. "Let me go home and change and I'll come by after."

Leaving the arena without a real celebration felt off and my drive to the apartment was lonely. Just as it's been lonely every time I've had to walk into the empty space over the past few days. Not seeing her mess when I walk through the door, not finding her reading on the couch. Having all my lights off because I was the last one to leave.

I hated this apartment almost immediately after I purchased it, but over the past few months, the shift in energy made me excited to be home, to be with her. Now, I despise it more than I ever had before.

But when I open the front door, it's not the lack of her books or clothes or flowers that stop me in my tracks. It's the lack of everything else that does. My apartment is entirely bare and if it weren't for the high level of security around this place, you'd think I was robbed.

My couch and television are gone. My bookshelf is gone. My goddamn coffee maker is gone.

The smell of fresh paint lingers in the air, and I follow the scent to Indy's old room. It's empty as well, but that's because I had all her things sent to the new house days ago. The only difference is the yellow walls that once haunted me are now covered in a fresh coat of white paint.

My eyes are burning with realization as I quickly jog across the bare living room to find my bedroom just as empty.

There's nothing here. Not a single article of clothing or dish left in the sink. It's completely unlivable and I think that's the point. I think last night was the last time I had to sleep in this apartment that felt like a prison more times than it felt like a home.

I didn't expect to feel lighter, but my chest deflates from the lifted weight, no longer having to see the physical representation of my trust issues every single day.

Instead of crossing the street to see my sister, I get in my car and head thirty minutes outside of the city. I remember the first time I drove up to this house. The overwhelming knowledge that this was where I wanted us to spend our lives hit me like a freight train, and making the drive tonight, it feels the same.

The front porch is fully lit as is the entire house and when I step inside, it's almost unrecognizable from the place I drove away from three days ago. There are rugs, and curtains, and so many fucking throw pillows on the living room couch I'm not sure how you're supposed to sit on it. A brand-new dining table takes up another room and is long enough to seat twelve. There are framed photos of us and our friends. There's artwork on the walls, bright and colorful just like the girl who put it there.

This place is bursting with love and attention. I don't know how else to explain it other than it feels like the textbook definition of a home.

I head straight through the foyer and under the stairs, not wasting a second to look at anything else while I look for her. In my gut, I know where she is. I'm drawn to her as always, finding her in the kitchen where we tend to have all our important conversations.

The flowers I left her are thriving in a vase in the center of the island, and my coffee machine is plugged into the wall with my mug resting below it and her pink cup beside it.

And there she is, blonde hair, lavender sundress, and embroidered Converse. Beautiful as always with that sunshine smile I'll never tire of seeing. My best friend and the person who owns every part of me.

"Hi."

I want to go to her, hold her, kiss her, but I'm also stunned into place seeing her in this home. The daydream I've replayed in my mind for months is now tangible and in front of me.

"Congrats on your game," she continues. "I'm so proud of you."

"Thank you, baby." Cautiously, I look around the room, noting the changes she's made. The dish towels that hang from the handle of the stove. The colorful rug she's standing on. The curtain draped over the window behind the kitchen sink. "What's going on?"

She motions for me to sit across the island from her, exactly where she sat a few days ago as I spoke. But this time, it's her turn.

"Should we talk about the lease?"

I laugh. "The what?"

"The lease."

You can hardly see the fridge through the papers littering the front thanks to all the promises we've made to each other. The deed to the house, our bucket lists, our original lease I made when she first moved into the apartment, which I knew from the morning I wrote it was a load of shit. That girl didn't need to follow a single rule, didn't need to pay a penny, because deep down there was that lonely part of me, desperate for her to stay.

Indy removes the newest add-on.

"First line item," she says, grabbing a pen and hovering it over the paper. "Rent."

"Blue, we own the house outright."

She ignores me. "I'm going to need at least two 'I love yous' every morning and another before bed. I'm a bit needy, you know. Words of affirmation and all that. And we should really build an in-home library, and maybe a greenhouse in the back for winter."

A laugh heaves in my chest. "I think I can handle that form of payment."

"Well, that was easy. Let's move on. Rules." She writes the word down, identically matching the lease I made for her.

"What are your rules, Ind?"

Her soft brown eyes meet mine, melting in front of me. "We live our happiest lives out here. You and me. Even if it's always just you and me. Even if children aren't in our future, we remember how grateful we are to have found each other."

I couldn't agree more. "Deal."

"But at the same time." She holds up a single finger. "We try our hardest to fill every room in this house. I'm talking morning, afternoon, and evening. You think you practice a lot for basketball?" She laughs condescendingly. "That's nothing, Shay."

I can't help it anymore as I stand from my stool and round the island to meet her. Gripping her hips, I kiss the top of her shoulder. "Deal."

She turns to face me. "Ryan, I need you to know, when I was staying at Rio's I didn't have to think about whether you were the right person for me. There's no question of how badly I want you or how much I love you. You know that, right?"

Shockingly enough, that was never my concern. Indy has always made me feel wanted, and I'm sure it only made things worse for her, wanting me while believing our futures were headed in different directions.

"I know."

"And I didn't call over the last few days because I wanted to surprise you with a finished house, but as soon as you left, there was nothing for me to think about."

"It looks incredible."

"Well." She shoots me a guilty smile. "I only had three days so I might be hiding a little mess in the bedrooms on the second floor."

Leaning down, I rest my forehead on hers. "I love you."

"God, I love you so much," she says, snaking her hands around my neck, intertwining her fingers. "I missed you. Thank you for understanding my fears and treating them with patience. You make me feel deserving of all the things I want in life. I don't know where you came from or how I got so lucky to be loved by you, but Ryan, I adore you."

"You are. You deserve every little thing you manage to dream for yourself. I hated being away from you, Ind, but I loved seeing you stand up for the things you want. Don't stop doing that. Even if it's me you're facing off with, don't settle for less."

Reaching up on her toes, she kisses me. Softly, quickly. "I don't think there's a way for me to even begin thanking you. For this home, for planning for our future."

"You could start by asking me to move in."

She tilts her head in contemplation. "I don't know. We haven't been dating all that long. You don't think it's too soon to be living together?"

As I lift my brow, Indy is unable to contain her mischievous smile.

"Oh, you think you're funny, huh?"

She giggles, finding herself hilarious as I pick her up and seat her on the island. Stepping between her legs, I keep my lips only inches from hers. "Ask me."

She drapes her arms over my shoulders. "What do you say, Shay? Want to be my roomie? Hide away with me in this big, beautiful house?"

"I think that sounds like the right move."

Fingers threaded through her hair, I pull her into me, foreheads and noses touching.

"I will love you for the rest of my life," she whispers against my lips.

It's a promise, coming from the most loyal woman I know.

"Forever, Blue."

I'm lost when her mouth meets mine. Soft pulls of her lips, sweeps of her tongue. She's warm and tastes like fucking heaven. Her coconut soap lingers on her skin, and I inhale as much as I can, reminding my body that she's here. That we're okay.

I've gone far longer than three days without kissing Indy, when I'm on the road for work or when she is, but this intentional distance was torture. Kissing her now, in our kitchen, feels like it's the first time all over again, with a reassurance that there will never be an end.

Her legs wrap around my waist, pulling me against her body. Her pretty sundress bunches around her hips as the ridge of my erection rubs against her pussy and though Indy's first plan for this house is to decorate every room, my plan is to christen every flat surface I can find. This house is ten times the size of the apartment, so it might take a couple days, but I'm up to the challenge.

Gliding my palm up her thigh, I squeeze and knead her flesh until my fingers dip under the hem of her dress. I'm looking for silk or lace, something I need to tear off, but there's nothing but soft skin over her hip bone.

"No panties tonight?"

She scoots off the side of the counter, bringing her center to rub against my erection, and now that I know she's got nothing on, I lift her dress, watching her soft, needy pussy writhe against me.

"Easier access for you," she breathes out.

Her lips work against my neck and jaw, kissing and biting as she fiddles with my belt. I hold her to me, tilting my head back and letting her work. She frees me from the zipper and quickly dips her hand in my briefs, grabbing me.

"*Fuck,*" I exhale.

"You got your team to the playoffs tonight."

"Is this my reward?"

"One of them." She kisses my throat. "You're going to have lots of rewards, Shay. I figured it is only fair that since you bought me a house, I should blow you in every room of it."

"Well, you are pretty on your knees, baby."

"Mmm, thank you."

Wrapping a fist around me, she strokes and twists, but before she can free me from my briefs, I pick her up off the counter and carry her to the stairs. As much as I want to fuck her on the kitchen island, the floor, the couch, the goddamn back porch, the first time we do this, I don't want it to be frantic or hurried. I want to savor every moment of it.

While holding her, I climb onto the mattress in our new bedroom. *In our new house.*

Fuck, that feels good to say.

Twisting, I pull her on top of me as I lay back on the bed.

"What the hell?"

She pauses, hands on my chest. "What's wrong?"

"Why is this bed so fucking comfortable? Has it always been this comfortable?"

She laughs. "Yes, it's always been that comfortable. I'll have to ask my roommate where he bought it and let you know."

Finding the hem of her dress, I lift it over her head. "I can't believe I bought you a bed that was a hundred times better than mine and never slept in it."

Indy's tits give a little bounce when she reaches behind her and unclasps her bra, and instantly my hands are on them. I roll her nipples with my thumbs before giving them a little pinch. She bites her lip at that, circling her hips over my cock.

"Get these pants off me, Ind."

She does, pulling my boxer briefs right along with them. I take off my own shirt and in one movement, have her on her back with my face between her legs. With long, languid strokes of my tongue, I taste her and lick her. Kiss her pussy. Suck her clit.

She pulls at my forearms as her back arches off the bed, her hips rocking into my face. She's soaked and needy. Her clit is swollen and begging, but before I can make her come, she stops me, tightening her fingers through my hair.

Her breaths are ragged. "I want to come with you."

Indy's brown eyes are pleading with me, flushed cheeks and chest. I climb right on top of her, kissing the pathway up her belly, her tits, her throat. My dick slides against her core, coating in her arousal.

We both watch.

"I love you, Ryan," she says, seemingly out of nowhere.

But it's not random. She knows we're about to do something that I spent years telling myself I would never do. I would never have a woman I trust enough. I would never have a family. It's not as easy as flipping a switch, but as soon as I slide my bare skin against hers once again, any old lingering fears that don't apply to her are out the window.

"Put it in, Blue. Let me watch you."

But before she does, she reaches up and kisses me. Slowly, deeply. Then she takes my cock, centers it, and I push inside her with no barrier between us.

She gasps and I almost lose it right there, with only my tip inside her.

She's fucking tight and warm and wet, and the sensation is almost too much. Her slick skin on mine.

"Fuck, Ind. You feel so fucking good."

"More," she begs, unknowing I'm about to come right here on the spot.

She wraps her legs around my hips, and I have no other choice but to drive into her. She lets out the prettiest scream when I do, and I want to hear it again. Louder this time. There's no one within miles to hear her taking my cock.

Rolling my hips, I pull out and thrust in again, making sure to rub her clit with my pelvis each and every time I do. Her head pushes back into the pillow, giving me an opportunity to suck and nibble on the column of her throat.

"You're going to ruin me," she whimpers.

"I already have. This is mine." I push into her.

She moans.

"Tell me."

I thrust again.

"Tell me that every part of you is mine."

"*Yes*. I'm yours. I'll always be yours."

Evening out my tempo, I press my chest to hers, kissing her lips and whispering all the things I adore about her in her ear. She wraps her arms around me, and I do the same, wedging my hands between her body and the mattress to hold her as tightly to me as possible while I allow my body to show her just how much I love her.

And then she comes.

So prettily. So quietly, like it was just for me to experience with her.

She keeps her eyes on me as she does, and I watch her through it. Her dropped mouth, her contracting muscles. And then those muscles tighten around me, clenching my cock and pulling out my own orgasm.

I push inside of her one more time and come.

It's overwhelming. Her skin on mine. How much I love this

woman. I'm almost dizzy with blurred vision as her body pulls every last drop I have to give. It's euphoric and calming at the same time. This woman ruined me the day she walked into that apartment, then she brought me back to life soon after, and I'm hers. I've always been hers.

Falling on top of her, she holds me, our chests rising and falling together.

"I love you," I murmur into her neck.

"I love you."

Slowly, I pull out and watch as my cum drips out and down her body. With a single finger, I collect it, pushing it back in, and loving the way it looks to have me inside of her.

I'm fairly certain I growl or some shit. I don't know. Some possessive caveman noise comes out of my throat at the sight in front of me.

"Did you just develop a breeding kink, Shay?"

Quickly nodding, I keep my eyes locked on her open legs. "I think so. Give me ten and let's do that again."

She laughs, such a lovely sound tickling my ears.

I'm going to stay here all night, naked with the love of my life in our home. Or at least that's what I was planning before the doorbell rings.

My eyes snap up to hers. "Who's that?"

Indy's head jerks to the clock on the nightstand. "Oh shit! I should've told them an hour later than I did!"

Frantically, she jumps off the bed, grabbing her bra and dress to throw on.

I'm not sure why, but I follow her lead, redressing as quickly as possible. "Told who?"

Guiltily, she looks back at me over her shoulder. "Everyone."

"Everyone?"

"Well, everyone in our circle. You bought this house to get away from the chaos of the city, but also because you wanted a place to spend time with your friends and family without feeling like you're constantly being watched. I just figured"—she hesitates—"there's no better way to break in this house than celebrating Chicago making the playoffs for the first time in six years."

The doorbell rings again and I follow her down the stairs. As she opens the front door, Indy adjusts her bra and I focus on rezipping my pants only to find Zanders and my sister waiting on the front step.

"Well don't you two look freshly fucked." Zanders pats my cheek before barging into my house.

"I'd give you both a hug"—my sister holds her hands up in surrender—"but I'm going to pass this time."

The two of them take off to the kitchen, leaving Indy and me alone in the foyer.

"Can we celebrate?" she asks with an excited sparkle in her eye.

I bought this house for her to host. For her to have as many people over as she likes. I'm sure I'll continue to be a bit of a lone wolf, to want my time alone as long as that time alone includes her. But Indy, as much as she's learned to be content in the quiet, will always be a social butterfly.

I didn't buy this place to hide her away from the entire world, I bought it so she could bring our world to us.

"Please?"

I won't lie and say tonight felt complete when I left the arena. Though this is simply another win to the rest of the league, to my teammates, to me, it's everything and we've yet to celebrate our accomplishment.

Bracketing her jaw, I kiss her one more time, smiling into her mouth. "Yeah, Blue, let's celebrate."

The house is filled with my teammates. Drinks are flowing and food is on a constant loop as Indy glides through the house with trays of appetizers to pass out.

Dom and his mom are here as well as Leon and the rest of the guys. Even the Morgans made an appearance. Ethan and Annie brought their three girls who are running around in the backyard with never-ending energy. Ethan's mother-in-law has been in the kitchen teaching Indy her secret recipe for *kimchi jjigae* which she would make in batches for me and the boys to take home after team dinners when Ethan hosted. It's my favorite comfort meal, and Indy should be careful learning Mrs. Jeong's recipes because if they end up tasting half as good as the original, she will be the one cooking our meals for the rest of our lives.

The doorbell rings again, but I'm not sure who else could be joining us. Everyone who is important to us from Chicago is here, but as I go to open the door, Indy chases after me so we can do it together.

"Mom!" she exclaims as soon as it's partially open, throwing herself into Abigale's arms.

"Oh, I missed you, Ind!"

Turning towards her dad, I immediately concentrate, trying to remember everything I've learned. Flat open hands, one on top of the other, I slide the palm of my dominant hand over my non-dominant hand, perpendicular to each other. Then I sign "meet" before pointing at Tim.

*Nice to meet you.*

I continue and speak aloud in case Indy needs to correct me if I sign incorrectly. *"Welcome to our home."*

Tim smiles with pride before slowly signing back to me. *"Has my daughter been a handful?"*

*"The best handful."*

He chuckles. *"Thank you for taking care of her."*

This time I don't use my voice as I sign, wanting this conversation to be strictly between Indy's dad and me. *"I love her. She's my whole world. My best friend."*

Tim nods thoughtfully before wrapping me up in a hug.

"Ryan," Abigale beams when Tim moves on to giving his daughter some attention. "About time."

I hug the woman who I've spent every Tuesday afternoon Facetiming for months. "I didn't know you two were flying in tonight."

"We were supposed to come in a few weeks, but then Indy told us about the house and the party, so we changed our trip. The house is lovely, Ryan. Nice work."

She signs her words for her husband as she speaks before patting my chest like we're old friends, and honestly, I feel like we are. The Ivers all do a hell of a job at making those around them feel comfortable and welcome.

Indy's hand slides into mine as we show her parents around our new home.

Tim has kept his signs slow and clear for me as we chat. I'm still so new that Indy and her mom translate for me when needed, but there are multiple times I'm able to communicate with him entirely on my own.

There's a burst of pride and achievement that rattles through me when our conversation flows without help, and I look forward to the day when I'm fluent.

He signs again, but I'm not able to catch his entire question. I recognize the signs for *win* and *game*. But there's one sign that Tim makes that I've never seen before.

It looks similar to the sign for *protect*, but on his dominant hand, his index and middle fingers are crossed like the letter "R".

"Oh," Indy squeaks out. She swallows thickly. "Yes, Ryan won his game."

She signs back to her dad while speaking and again I see that same unknown sign, but recognize it used in place of the fingerspelling of my name.

Tim turns to me, points, then signs the word *protect* again with his fingers creating the letter "R" at the same time. He points at me again.

*"I'm Ryan?"* I ask, using his sign for my name.

He nods, smiling.

Abigale leans her head on Tim's shoulder as she looks at me.

*"Is that my sign name?"* I ask him to the best of my ability.

*"Yes."*

Words stick in my throat, so I simply nod, sign, and mouth, *"Thank you."*

*"No. Thank you."*

He doesn't have to say anything else. I know what it means. Thank you for protecting my daughter, for loving my daughter. But later tonight, I'll hopefully be the one saying thank you right after I ask for his blessing to *marry* his daughter.

It was the first question I learned to sign, so you could say I've been practicing it for a while.

Grabbing a Sharpie from my gym bag, I find Rio sitting on the back porch with my sister, Zanders, Kai, and his son Max.

"Okay, what am I signing?"

His head snaps to mine, green eyes sparkling with excitement. "For real?"

"You let my girl crash at your place, you took care of her, and got her out here. It's the least I can do."

Rio shrugs casually, attempting to play it cool as if he hasn't been thinking about this moment since I first met him. "I don't really have anything on me to sign."

"No? All right, well, I tried."

"Wait! I have two jerseys and a poster in the car. I also have an old Wheaties cereal box that you were on." He quickly stands from his seat. "Do not put that pen away!"

The rest of us can't help but laugh, watching his dark curls bounce with him as he sprints through the house, dodging my teammates to make it to the front door.

"That's my teammate," Zanders says with a weird sense of pride.

Stealing his chair, I take a seat in the circle of Kai, Zanders, and my sister, completely and utterly at peace.

"You're happy." Stevie smiles softly. "It looks good on you, Ry."

I rest my head back, letting the sounds of Ethan's kids playing in the backyard and my teammates having a good time fill my ears. "I am. This is everything I didn't know I could have."

Looking through the back door, I find Indy refilling more drinks and that girl could not look more excited to be hosting a get together in her very own home.

"Indy is happy too, yeah?" I don't know why I feel the need to ask, I guess I just like to hear the confirmation.

"She's been so excited, planning tonight for you. You should've seen her the last three days, Ryan."

"And if we happen to have lost?"

"She was having a party regardless. There probably would've been a bit more booze involved though."

Ethan and Annie join our group.

"The house looks incredible, Ryan," Annie says.

"It was all Indy."

"The girls love it out here." Ethan nods towards the backyard where his three daughters haven't stopped chasing each other since they got here.

"You guys should make the move out here. Get out of the city. This town has a great school district."

Annie's brow raises. "A great school district? Why have you looked at that, huh?"

I shrug.

"Ryan Shay, is Indy pregnant?"

"Not yet."

Ethan stills. "Not yet?!"

I pop my shoulders. "We're trying."

I catch Stevie's eye at that, and across the way, her lips lift in a soft smile. I don't have to say it. Our twin brains can communicate with a simple look that I don't want to miss out on raising a family right alongside her.

"I'm moving out of the condos too," Kai announces. "I just bought a house."

All eyes shoot to him as Max sleeps soundly on his chest.

"You did?"

"Max is getting bigger. He's going to be walking soon, and with baseball season starting, I'm going to need way more help. We were outgrowing the condo."

"Ann, we should move out here," Ethan says. "The girls would love it."

"How about you retire and then we can move?"

Ethan looks to me. "This one is on you, Ryan. I'm going to need you to get me that championship ring so I can hang it up for good."

I cheers his bottle with my own. "Let's do it."

As the conversation continues to flow around me, I watch Indy chat with my teammates and the Morgans. She does another loop around the house. My confident girlfriend has no issue barging into the small circles of basketball players hanging out in her house to see if they need anything else.

"Ind!" I call out as she passes by the open back doors. "Come sit with me."

She drops what she's doing to come outside and take a seat across my lap. Bringing her knees up to her chest, I wrap her up, hoping to keep her warm in that little dress.

"Can I help you with anything?" I whisper.

She shakes her head before dropping it to my shoulder. "I'm having so much fun."

"Me too."

She looks up at me. "Yeah?"

I nod. "Thank you for planning this for me."

"I'm happy that you're happy."

"I'm happy that *we're* happy."

Indy and I might be opposites, but we're more alike than I initially thought. We care about those we love. She's nurturing and I'm protective, but it all comes down to a common denominator— we love hard.

She swings her arms over my shoulders as we get back to the conversation between our family and friends.

"Kai, when do you leave for spring training?" she asks.

"We're headed to Arizona next week."

"And what about Max?"

This is Kai's first baseball season since finding out that the baby boy dropped off on his doorstep is his son, and though he's one of the biggest names in the MLB, his first priority is Max. I'd imagine balancing his hectic baseball schedule while raising his son all on his own is going to be tricky.

"I'm still looking for a nanny that'll stick."

"Well, stop firing them all," I laugh.

"I can't help it." He drops a kiss to Max's head. "I don't trust anyone with him." He looks to Indy. "Hey, Ind…"

"Don't even think about asking," I cut in before she could agree.

"But he's really cute," Kai adds innocently.

Indy sighs. "The cutest."

He waves us off. "I need someone willing to travel with the team and put up with our insane game schedule, anyway. And I highly doubt your boyfriend would let me steal you for an entire summer."

I wrap her up tighter. "Yeah, not a chance in hell."

The group continues to talk among themselves when Indy leans her head on mine, speaking quietly. "I'm excited to be home with you all summer, neither of us traveling for work."

"I'm excited to be home with you forever, Blue."

She smiles, soft brown eyes filled with so much love. "Forever sounds perfect."

Forever does sound perfect.

I could not be more content, with my people, with my girl, and with my team on the way to the playoffs. This life, this home, this relationship is everything I never let myself want, and it's more than I knew I was allowed to dream for.

# EPILOGUE

## Indy

FOUR YEARS LATER

Iverson lifts his sweaty little head from my shoulder. An imprint of my shirt creases his cheek as he stirs awake from his afternoon nap. His sister, Navy, has been up for over an hour, running around our family box at the United Center.

It doesn't happen too often, but at least once a season, both Ryan and Zanders will play at home on the same day. I intended to spend the afternoon at home while they transformed the arena from a hockey rink into a basketball court, but the kids fell asleep after their uncle's game, and I wouldn't dare mess with nap time.

"How's my favorite niece?" Zanders asks, barging into the room as he carries *my* favorite niece.

Taylor Shay Zanders is my *only* niece, the same way Navy is his.

"She's a little fussy." My little girl's hair is a mess from her nap and her eyes are still swollen from crying. "Navy, we'll go see Daddy before his game starts, I promise."

My daddy's girl hates when Ryan has to go to work. Even though he's only in the locker room downstairs and spent the entire morning with her watching her uncle's game, it's never enough time for her.

It's not enough time for him either.

Iverson is my laid-back guy and Navy is my emotional girl. They're both just over two years old with completely defined yet opposite personalities.

Zanders hands his daughter, Taylor, off to me so he can console mine.

"Hi, Tay Tay."

"Goldfish?" she asks, holding her hand out to Iverson.

He smiles and takes one from her palm.

"Baby Iverson sleeping?" she asks me.

"He was. He just woke up."

Tay pets his head as if she were putting him back to sleep. The girl absolutely adores both her cousins.

She calls him baby Iverson, but he's only the baby of the family by three months. Ryan and I began trying to conceive as soon as we moved into the house, but not so surprisingly, it didn't work. When I did my first egg retrieval, we came away from the entire process with only one embryo, so I did a second egg retrieval later that year. Again, after all was said and done, we only got one more viable embryo.

We transferred one immediately, and unfortunately, our first attempt was unsuccessful.

I took it hard. Those months were rough. I felt like I was letting myself down, letting Ryan down, but he couldn't have been more supportive. He didn't even bat an eye as he began looking into foster and adoption options. We wanted nothing more than to provide a safe and loving home to someone who needed it. Even if we were simply a stop for them until their biological parents were back on their feet. We never saw a difference between biological or un-biological. We'd love them with everything we had.

The entire process was lengthy and time-consuming, and while we were going through it, I came to a point where I finally felt mentally prepared to attempt transferring our last embryo.

It worked. I was finally pregnant with our son, and I had never felt the kind of joy and excitement as I had that day when we were told we were going to be parents.

That is, until about two weeks later when we got the call that an expecting mother wanted to meet us. After endless conversations and exploring every option, making sure we were not only the best choice for the baby but for the mother as well, that same unexplainable love overwhelmed me once again.

Navy Renee came into the world just three months before her brother. The new Shay siblings might not be biological twins, but they'll be raised as if they are. They'll share the same class in school and hopefully the same friend group. And if we're lucky, they'll stay as close as Ryan and Stevie have.

Just then, as I'm thinking of my best friend, she and Rio join us in our box.

All season long, this is the Zanders and Shay family box at the United Center. It doesn't matter which of Chicago's teams is playing that night, it's ours.

On her way in, Stevie pops a kiss on my daughter's cheek who is now giggling and happy with her uncle as they dance around the room.

"One win down. One to go." She takes a seat next to me. "Tay Tay, how many is Uncle Ry going to score tonight?"

She throws her hands up. "A hundred!"

"A hundred? So confident."

Understatement of the year. Taylor Zanders is as confident as they come, but also sweet in equal measure.

"Yeah, and they win like Daddy win."

"And like how Uncle Rio won," Rio cuts in, taking the chair on the other side of me. "Don't forget about me, Tay."

"Uncle Rio didn't score."

The family's newest comedian does a great job at keeping us all humble, and I can't help but laugh at my friend's expense. Rio rarely scores. He shares the blue line with Zanders. It's not typical for a defenseman to be a high scorer on the team, but Taylor rarely reminds her dad he didn't score after a game the way she does Rio.

"Yeah, well, Tay, Uncle Rio hasn't scored in quite a while."

He shoots me a look to remind me that he's not only referring to the ice.

Rio DeLuca is one of my very best friends. Our bond has only gotten stronger since we met five years ago, but the guy is a giant kid. He's twenty-seven years old, playing in his sixth year in the NHL, and his place is *still* the team's party house.

He's got a heart of gold and absolutely no idea how to talk to women.

Hopefully, someday, someone will see past the goofy exterior to realize his potential, but at the same time, he might need to grow up a bit for that to happen.

"How's this year's flight crew?" I ask.

He pops his shoulders. "They're not you two."

"Honey, we quit years ago. You're going to have to move on."

His green eyes concentrate on the court in front of him. "I refuse to accept that you both quit."

"Three years ago," I add for him.

"Yeah. Yeah."

As much as I miss seeing the team on every road trip, I'm glad I left when I did. I flew for one more hockey season before calling it quits. Ryan and I were trying to get pregnant, and by the end of that year, we were. Plus, The Ryan Shay Foundation was taking off, and I was running the business end of it all.

By the time Navy and Iverson were here, my job was a full-time gig that needed my attention. I've loved every second of working for Ryan's foundation. What used to be a summer camp, turned into a year-round passion project. We've been able to keep Chicago's outdoor courts clean and usable, Ryan's sneaker donation has tripled since we started, and what was once a provided lunch during the summer, has turned into daily after-school meals to those who need it.

Our latest project was one of my favorites. We've been able to upgrade thirty percent of Chicago's public school libraries with new textbooks and tools for research. There's also plenty of new books for those kids who want to read for fun, and we're hoping to reach at least the next thirty percent this year.

Reading is something that Ryan and I first bonded over, and though we don't have the same taste in books, being able to step into someone else's shoes and read a story from their perspective, not only helps with learning and literacy, but also cultivates empathy.

The kids lose their shit when Ryan Shay, NBA champion and two-time league MVP shows up at their school or playground and shoots hoops, reads a book with them, or makes sure they have shoes to play in. He does a fantastic job not only being the face of The Ryan Shay Foundation, but also pouring everything he's got into giving back to the city that loves him.

"Daily update, Vee."

"Absolutely not."

"This morning in the shower—"

"Make it stop."

I cover the kids' ears. "Your brother had me pressed so hard against the glass that I'm pretty sure there's a permanent outline of my tits etched into our shower wall."

"It's been over four years, Ind. Put me out of my misery."

"I made you a promise all those years ago," I remind her. "I'm nothing if not loyal to my word."

Stevie takes Iverson from me, and Tay makes herself even more comfortable in my lap, leaning her head back to lay on my chest.

"How's my favorite guy?" Stevie asks her nephew.

"I'm good, sweetheart!" Zanders calls out from the back of the room.

Navy's giggle fills my ears as she plays with her uncle.

"Is Uncle Zee full of himself?" Stevie pitches her voice higher, and Iverson loves it. He smiles at her, all deep-set dimples and baby teeth. "Yes, he is! He's a cocky guy, isn't he?"

She peppers her nephew's cheeks with kisses, and I will never get over how much my kids love their family. How much *I* love my family. How lucky I've been to surround myself with my favorite people, for them to love on my kids the same way I love on theirs.

They've got grandparents that adore them, aunts and uncles that treat them as their own, and a dad who spends every free moment he has making sure they know how adored they are.

Taylor laughs in my lap at Stevie's voice.

"Tay, is your mom talking like a baby?"

"Yeah!" She covers her mouth to contain her laughter. "Iverson is a baby, but I'm not a baby anymore."

"You're not?" Stevie sighs. "You're still *my* baby, though."

"No!" Taylor laughs. "I'm three." She holds up her fingers to make sure her mom knows. "Iverson and Navy are two. They're babies."

"Ah. Then I guess you don't want to go see Danny the Devil at half-time. I think only babies are into team mascots."

She sits up on my lap, her curly hair bouncing with the movement. "No! I want to go!"

"Oh, okay. I must have been mistaken when you said you weren't a baby."

She brings her cheek to her shoulder, showing off that cheeky smile her dad passed on to her. "I'm *your* baby."

Stevie laughs before leaning over and popping a kiss on her cheek. "Yes, you are."

Stevie and Zanders were one and done. Taylor was born and that was it, their family was complete. Rosie was obsessed with her from the moment she was born. They've recently moved into a house close to ours and adopted a few more pups, but Taylor is the center of their universe, and it works perfectly for them. She's witty, charming, sweet, and sharp as a whip. It's a dangerous combination and they're going to have their hands full as she gets older. She's also stunning, with hazel eyes and curly hair. Zee will be getting a taste of his own medicine when she grows up and has everyone in school chasing after her.

"Navy girl!" I call out. "Do you want to go see your dad before his game starts?"

She hops her bare feet off Zanders, stopping their dance for now. "Yes!"

"Daddy?" Iverson quietly asks. "Basketball." He makes the American Sign Language sign for basketball with his hands.

It's his new favorite word to speak and sign. He doesn't have quite all the syllables down, but knows it starts with the "B" sound and ends with 'ball', but he caught on to the sign no problem. Both my kids are learning ASL as they learn to speak English, and Ryan is essentially fluent now as well. I love that my dad gets to experience his grandkids learning new words in the same way we do.

"Yeah, baby, he's playing basketball, and you can see Dom."

"Dom!"

He loves that word too.

With Navy's hand in one of mine and Iverson's hand in my other, we slowly make our way down to the court with their tiny steps, using the back tunnels to navigate our way through the arena. We take our time because just about every staff member here knows the kids by name and Navy needs to show off her bedazzled Converse while Iverson wants to throw them the stuffed basketball toy he carries everywhere he goes.

They give high fives and waves until finally, we make it to the court while the Devils are still shooting around before formal warm-ups begin.

"Daddy!" Navy bounces on her toes as soon as she sees him.

There he is, number five, all sweaty and all mine. Ryan Shay has only gotten sexier with age. He's still the same confident and controlled basketball player out there on the court and I love watching him run every game he plays. But when he's at home, he's relaxed and knows how to let loose. Moving into that house has been amazing for many reasons, but it's truly given Ryan enough distance from the city to leave the basketball superstar with two MVP titles at the door.

When he's home, he's Dad and Husband, and he excels at both.

"Dad!" Iverson catches on, wearing a little Shay jersey of his own with Ryan's number on it.

Ryan is entirely focused as he always is on the court, running through ball-handling drills with Leon off to the side. Leon sees us first and while continuing to dribble, he gains Ryan's attention, nodding our way.

Ryan looks up and that serious and stoic expression melts, my favorite beaming smile stretching across his lips. He drops both balls he's working with and jogs over to us without a second thought. I let go of the kids' hands and they charge at him full speed, which granted, isn't very fast on their little legs. Bending down, Ryan scoops them up, one in each arm, covering them both in kisses.

It's my favorite view, the three of them together. I could sit and watch them all day and never tire of the sight. Ryan Shay as a dad is not only sweet and fun, but he's also hot as hell while doing it. Have you ever seen a 6'3" basketball player laying shirtless with his newborns or in a nursery building cribs with his hands? Because I have and let me tell you, it's a vision that will forever be branded into my memory.

"Are you checking me out, Shay?" Ryan asks, wearing a cocky little smirk and breaking me out of my daydream.

No use denying it. "Yes."

His smile only grows as his eyes rake every inch of me, all the way from my head to the Converse of my feet. As much I still love my heels, I've got a couple of toddlers to chase after these days, so they only really see the light of day when Ryan and I attend events or have date nights.

"Daddy play basketball now?" Iverson cuts in, interrupting his dad's blatant perusal over my body.

"Yeah, buddy, just like you."

Iverson waves his stuffed basketball around. The kid is an athletic freak for a two-year-old, already making the majority of his shots on his mini hoop at home and learning new tricks on his tiny scooter every day. His balance and coordination are out of this world, and he's in the ninety-ninth percentile for height in his age group. I have a sneaking suspicion that Ryan's mini me will be following in his dad's footsteps one day.

Dom comes up behind them, holding his arms out in front of him, creating a circle like a giant rim.

"Can you show me how to score, little man?"

Iverson throws his stuffed basketball through Dom's open arms.

"Nice shot, my guy!" Ryan cheers with so much pride on his face.

Iverson claps for himself then points to Ryan's teammate. "Dom! Dom!"

Ryan passes our son off to him, and Dom instantly takes him to the real hoop, helping him throw a ball though the net before putting his little hands around the rim to hang all while Dom holds on to his legs.

Navy takes the rare opportunity of being her dad's only kid and wraps her arms around his neck, burying her head in his shoulder.

"Are you my needy girl today?" Ryan quietly asks her. "Did you learn this from your mama?"

Ryan's teasing ocean eyes find mine.

"Yeah."

"I love you, Navy girl."

I watch her little lips tilt slightly as she closes her eyes.

Navy is my sweet baby. Emotional but fierce. She loves hard and she's a good friend to her brother. We love our girly dresses and bows, and our favorite morning activity is picking out our outfits together. But when it comes to bedtime, the only way she'll fall asleep is if her dad reads her a story. It doesn't matter if he's on the other side of the country for work, she has to see Ryan's face before falling asleep. I couldn't count how many times he's read to her over Facetime from the locker room before a game.

Ryan loves it. He cherishes the nights when he's home and makes an even bigger effort when he's on the road. I truly couldn't ask for a better father to our kids.

Navy catches Ethan's girls running by. She pops her head up from Ryan's shoulder before wiggling her body to get to her feet, wanting to play with them. Our daughter can't keep up with the older girls whatsoever, but they're good about slowing down and making sure she's included.

I find Ethan chatting away with Ron Morgan, but Annie shoots me a wave as she watches over her girls and mine.

Ethan stuck true to his word and retired after the Devils got their first championship last season. They came close the year before, losing in game six of the finals, but Ethan held on for one more year and ended his career on a high note.

Ryan misses him on the court and in the locker room, but Ethan still comes to most of their home games and swings by our house on nights we host team dinner. Not to mention all the weekends our families spend together now that they moved out of the city and closer to us.

Ryan slides his palm around me, grazing my lower back until his fingertips rest on my ass. "Did the kids sleep for you?"

"Iverson a bit longer than Navy, but yes. She was crying and wanting you."

"She sounds like her mama."

I wrap my arms around his neck. "Yeah, yeah."

Peacefully and fully content, he smiles. "I love days at the arena, having all of you here."

"We wouldn't be anywhere else. Give them hell tonight."

"I'll do my best." He pops a kiss on my lips. "I love you, Blue. I better hear you screaming for me from the box upstairs."

"You will. And later, you'll hear me screaming for you in a different way."

"Jesus, baby. I'm wearing basketball shorts. Can you try to not give me a hard-on on national television?"

"No guarantees." I give him one final kiss. "I love you. Good luck out there."

I turn around to gather our kids and head upstairs so we can watch him play the game he loves.

"Oh, and by the way," I call out. "Tay told everyone you're scoring a hundred points tonight, so it might be kind of embarrassing if you don't follow through on that."

He laughs. "I'll do what I can." His eyes rake over his jersey I'm wearing. "You look good wearing our last name, Mrs. Shay!"

Over my shoulder, I watch him check me out as he slowly walks backward to the court.

I take him in just the same. Glistening skin, freckled cheeks, and silicone wedding ring on his finger that he's allowed to wear during games. "Right back at you, Five."

He shoots me a playful wink before jogging back to the court and refocusing on his game.

The kids and I rejoin the rest of our family upstairs, and I can't help but count my blessings. The man I love gave me the life I always dreamed of, but it's so much more than I ever could've pictured for myself.

He swept my romantic heart right off her feet, and little did I know the day I moved into his apartment, that my new roommate would be the center of my happily ever after.

**THE END**

# Thank you!

If you enjoyed *The Right Move,* please consider leaving a review! Your support means the world to me and helps spread the word to other readers!

Join my newsletter for bonus scenes and sneak peeks of what's next!

Scan the code to join my newsletter

**www.liztomforde.com**

# Acknowledgments

Let's start off with the most important thank you of all— You, the reader! Thank you for giving my words a chance.

Thank you to BookTok, Bookstagram, and to every reader who has shared my work. It's because of you I've been able to continue to do something I love, and I hope that in return, I've given you something *you* love. The encouragement and kindness you have poured into me will never cease to amaze me, and I am so grateful that you've taken time to read, rate, review, and share. This career has been such a blessing in my life and it's all thanks to you.

Allyson- You put up with months of constant texts and emails, me being needy with feedback, and constantly picking your brain. So, I'm not sure if a 'thank you' is sufficient, but as the first person to see this book while it was still a giant mess that needed to be sorted, I can't thank you enough for the encouragement you gave me to keep going. I'm very lucky to call you one of my best friends.

Megan- You helped bring this novel to life. I was feeling lost in my first draft and needed another set of eyes on it. I couldn't ask for a better alpha reader. Having another person validate the direction of this story gave me that push and excitement to keep going. I hope you expect to alpha read forever because you don't really have a choice in the matter.

Samantha- I am so lucky to not only have you as my PA, but also my friend. Thank you for being in my corner and taking care of things that sometimes I just don't have the mental capacity to handle. You've really been a rock for me, whether you're checking in on my word count, helping me with my socials, or simply telling me to go have a drink.

You've been a game changer in my career, having someone to bounce ideas off of or just to vent. This release has been so much more fun because I've had you by my side, so thank you for all that you do!

Kristie- My number one hype woman. You truly have changed the direction of my career and I could not be more thankful for you! Thank you for beta reading for me and giving me that validation I needed before release. Whether you like it or not, you're stuck with me.

Marc- Thank you for the music and for the effort and detail you put into finding songs for the playlist. We're gonna need every artist out there to release some bangers in 2023, or we're moving onto country for Windy City Series #3.

Erica- Thank you for editing and understanding what this story needed. I'm looking forward to working on many more books together!

Cat- Thank you for being my bridge to the Deaf community. You were so helpful and kind and informative. I loved getting to learn about your stories and experiences. Thank you for being an essential part to bringing this story to life!

And now… it's time for Windy City Series Book Three!

# Also by Liz Tomforde

**Windy City Series**

MILE HIGH- A Chicago Hockey Romance- *Zanders and Stevie's Story*

THE RIGHT MOVE- A Chicago Basketball Romance- *Ryan and Indy's Story*

CAUGHT UP- A Chicago Baseball Romance- *Kai and Miller's Story*

Scan the code to read more books

# About the Author

Born and raised in Northern California, Liz Tomforde is the youngest of five children. She grew up watching and playing sports. She loves all things romance, traveling, dogs, and hockey & basketball.

She herself is a flight attendant, but when she's not traveling or writing, Liz can be found reading a good book or taking her Golden Retriever, Luke, on a hike in her hometown.

www.liztomforde.com

instagram.com/liztomforde.author
pinterest.com/liztomforde
tiktok.com/@liztomforde.author
facebook.com/LizTomforde.author